GRAND CENTRAL
PUBLISHING

LARGE
PRINT

ALSO BY LEILA MEACHAM

Roses

TUMBLEWEEDS

A Novel

Leila Meacham

GRAND CENTRAL
PUBLISHING

LARGE PRINT

Copyright © 2012 by Leila Meacham

Grand Central Publishing
Hachette Book Group
237 Park Avenue
New York, NY 10017
www.HachetteBookGroup.com

Printed in the United States of America

RRD-C

First Large Print Edition: June 2012

10 9 8 7 6 5 4 3 2 1

Grand Central Publishing is a division of Hachette Book Group, Inc. The Grand Central Publishing name and logo is a trademark of Hachette Book Group, Inc.

The Hachette Speakers Bureau provides a wide range of authors for speaking events. To find out more, go to www.hachettespeakersbureau.com or call (866) 376-6591.

The publisher is not responsible for websites (or their content) that are not owned by the publisher.

Library of Congress Cataloging-in-Publication Data

Meacham, Leila, 1938–
  Tumbleweeds / Leila Meacham. — 1st ed.
    p. cm.
  ISBN 978-1-4555-0924-9 (regular edition)—
  ISBN 978-1-4555-1348-2 (large print edition)
  1. Football stories.   2. Texas—Fiction.   I. Title.
PS3563.E163T86 2012
813'.54—dc23
                              2011034197

*For you, Ann Ferguson Zeigler,
with appreciation for the pleasure of
your company on the journey*

*Our sins, like our shadows when day is in its
  glory, scarce appear.
Toward evening, how great and monstrous
  they appear.*

—Sir John Suckling

TUMBLEWEEDS

Prologue

The call he'd been expecting for twenty-two years came at midnight when he was working late at his desk. He had a second's start, the kind of stab he'd experienced often in the first years when the telephone rang in the early hours, but with the passage of time the duties of his office had accustomed him to its ring in the middle of the night.

The name of the caller appeared in the identification screen, and his heart did a flip-flop. He plucked the receiver from its holder before a second ring could disturb the household. "Hello?"

"John Caldwell?"

"Trey?"

1

A chuckle, dry and mocking. "The same. You up?"

"I am now. Where are you calling from?"

"I'll get to that in a minute. How are you, Tiger?"

"Surprised. It's been a long time."

"Not so long that you didn't recognize my voice. I find that kind of comforting. I'm coming home, John."

John drew up in his chair. "You are? After all this time? What for?"

"I have a few loose ends to tidy up."

"Don't you think it's a little late for that?"

Another chuckle, devoid of mirth. "Still the same old John—guardian of my conscience."

"I seem to have failed miserably."

"Oh, I wouldn't say that."

John waited, refusing to rise to the lure the loaded tone invited. After a probing pause, Trey added, "The Tysons are interested in buying my aunt's house. I told Deke I'd come to Kersey and we could talk about it. I've got to do something about Aunt Mabel's things anyway, arrange for their disposal."

"The Tysons? I thought they'd moved to Amarillo and Deke had bought a home security business there."

"They did, but Deke's retiring and wants to come back to Kersey to live. His wife's always had an eye on my aunt's house. A surprising turn of events, wouldn't you say?"

"Not as surprising as some I've known. Where are you?"

"In Dallas. A connecting flight would have gotten me into Amarillo too late for my indigestion. I'll fly in there in the morning, pick up a car, and meet the Tysons at Aunt Mabel's around eleven o'clock."

"Staying long?"

"As long as my business takes. A couple of days is my guess."

John asked after a guarded silence, "Where are you staying?"

"Why, I was hoping you would put me up."

Shocked, John asked, "Here? You want to stay here at Harbison House?"

Another dry laugh. "Why not? I don't mind a bunch of runny-nosed kids. The Harbisons still with you?"

John answered warily, repulsed at the thought of Trey Don Hall sleeping under the Harbisons' roof. "Yes...Lou and Betty are still here. They help me run the place."

"That must be nice for you," Trey said. "I'll drive out after I've met with the Tysons. That should be in time for lunch. We'll break a little bread together,

3

and maybe I'll have the good padre hear my confession."

"I didn't think you were planning on staying that long."

Another chuckle, this one familiar. "Spoken like my man. It will be good to see you, John."

"Same here," John said, realizing with an ambush of feeling that he meant it.

"Don't bet on it, Tiger."

The line went dead, Trey's last words raising a tickling sensation along John's nape. Slowly he replaced the receiver and rose from his desk, aware that he'd broken into a mild sweat. He went to stand before a framed picture on the wall. It was an official shot of Kersey High School's 1985 uniformed football team. Below was the caption DISTRICT CHAMPS. John had been a wide receiver on the team that had made it all the way to win the state championship, and in the picture he stood beside the tall, grinning quarterback and his onetime best friend, Trey Don Hall. Even then, Trey had been called "TD" Hall, a sports announcer's moniker that had stuck all through his dazzling college playing days and his subsequent career as a quarterback in the National Football League. There were three other group photos of the team lined along the wall, each representing the Kersey

Bobcats' victories in the following play-off games, but the district contest against Delton High School was the one John remembered the most clearly. It was to that group picture that he most often turned his gaze.

What could be bringing Trey back home after twenty-two years? John didn't believe for a minute that it had to do with selling his aunt's house. The place had stood locked up and vacant for the two years since Mabel Church had died and left her nephew the home where he'd grown up, everything still in it but the food perishables and pet parakeet. Trey had no sentimental attachment to his aunt's things or the handsome brick house where the three of them—he and Trey and Cathy—had hung out all the years of their childhood. He had people who could sell it and dispose of its belongings long-distance. What then? Was he seeking reconciliation and forgiveness? Absolution? Atonement? John might have considered those possibilities had Trey's tone suggested them, but on the contrary, it had sounded mocking and mysterious. He knew his former friend and football teammate well. TD Hall was coming home for some other purpose, one that most likely would not bode well for anyone. He must warn Cathy.

PART ONE

1979–1986

Chapter One

On the night of January first, 1979, two hours into the New Year, Emma Benson saw a cross on the moon. Wrapped in her old flannel robe, awakened by a strange disquiet, she stepped outside her clapboard house in the town where she'd lived all her life, deep in the Texas Panhandle, and stared up at the unearthly sight, disturbed by a sense the cross was an omen meant personally for her.

The next day, she was informed that her last surviving child and his wife had been killed in a car accident coming home from a New Year's Eve party. The caller identified himself as Dr. Rhinelander, a neighbor and close friend of Sonny and her daughter-in-law. He and his wife would keep the couple's eleven-year-old daughter, Cathy, with them, he said, until the courts or whoever was in charge decided what to do with her.

"What do you mean—the courts?" Emma asked.

She heard a painful sigh. "I'm speaking of foster care, Mrs. Benson."

Foster care. Her granddaughter, blood of her blood, growing up under the roof of strangers?

But who else was there to take her? Where else could she go? There were no family members left. Emma's daughter-in-law had been an only child, adopted by a couple long past childbearing years and now deceased. Her other son, Buddy, had been killed in Vietnam. She was the only surviving blood connection to the child, but she was someone the little girl had met only once and had probably forgotten, since Emma suspected her name and family place were rarely, if ever, mentioned in her son's household.

But she heard herself say, "If you'll allow Catherine Ann to stay with you until I arrive, Dr. Rhinelander, I will bring her home with me."

Emma, who had never flown in an airplane and had ridden the train only twice in her youth, booked a flight from Amarillo to Santa Cruz, California, and in the confining six hours in the middle seat of her row—cotton inserted into her ears to block the petulant whining and fractious misbehavior of the four-year-old boy behind her—worried to what extent her second son's genes had infected his daughter. Her observation had been that, nine times out of ten, first daughters took after their fathers, not only in physiological structure and temperament but also in character, whereas firstborn sons echoed their mothers'. Her first son, Buddy, had proved no exception.

But Sonny, coming along later, hadn't a drip of sap from the family tree running in him. Vain, materialistic, self-entitled, with a capacity for empathy no bigger than the eye of a needle, he had felt designed for a more exalted plane than the one on which he'd been born. "I was cut out for something better than this," Emma could remember him stating, wounding her profoundly, and at the first opportunity he had taken off to correct the mistake that nature had made. He had rarely come home again, and after his marriage to a woman who shared his temporal values, only once. He said he'd come to introduce Emma to his wife and daughter, but he had come to borrow his brother's life insurance money paid to her when he was killed. She'd refused. Sonny's disaffection for her continued, abetted by his stylish wife who had barely been able to conceal a sniff at the surroundings in which her husband had grown up. Emma had read her disdain to mean that hell would freeze before she exposed her daughter to the place of her father's birth and the stern, no-nonsense woman who had raised him. And as Emma had correctly interpreted, they'd never come again, nor invited her to their home in California. But she remembered well the delicate, feminine, startlingly pretty little four-year-old who almost from Emma's hello had crawled into the safety of her daddy's lap and refused to have anything to do with her.

Emma had thought her lamentably spoiled. You had only to look at the expensive clothes and toys, to hear the cooing and baby talk, to observe how her parents stood at the ready to grant her every wish and desire, to know that when she grew up she'd have the substance of a cube of sugar. Still, she was an enchanting little thing with her father's curly blond hair and big blue eyes, gazing—shyly or coyly, Emma couldn't tell—from beneath long lashes that in sleep lay like downy feathers on the sweet, creamy curve of her cheeks. Emma had a picture of her from that time displayed on her bedside table.

Catherine Ann was now eleven years old, perhaps a legatee of the chemical unit that carried hereditary characteristics from parent to child, her attitudes already formed by her upbringing and the ways and lifestyle of her native state. How did you transplant such a child from palm trees and ocean and permissive parenting to prairie and scrub brush and the care of a grandmother who still maintained that children should be raised to understand they were precious but not the center of the universe? That little boy in the seat behind her was a good example of the new child rearing. Heaven forbid that, despite his confinement, he should be expected to respect the eardrums of those around him.

There were bound to be fundamental conflicts, perhaps never overcome, but Emma understood her duty and, at sixty-two, was prepared to put her heart at risk for the loss of yet another child.

Chapter Two

Here we are, Catherine Ann," Emma Benson said, striking a light tone as she drew into the garage of her house in Kersey, Texas. "It won't take long to get the house warm, but we'll hurry it along with a cup of hot chocolate. Would you like that?"

As had been the case since their meeting in Santa Cruz, her granddaughter's answer was an inscrutable stare, but Emma could guess what was going on behind those blue eyes now that Catherine Ann had gotten her first glimpse of her new home. "I'll take that as a yes," Emma said, and hurried to unlock the kitchen door before the child was too long exposed to the freezing temperature in a coat too thin for Panhandle winters. "Oh blast!" Emma said. The key would not turn—another blow to first impressions—and now she'd have to go out into the wind and sleet to the front door to let them in.

Her granddaughter stood shivering beside her, silent, stoic, expressionless as she'd been all week. *Selective mutism*, Dr. Rhinelander had termed her condition, claiming to be only a pediatrician and no child psychiatrist, but Catherine Ann demonstrated every one of its symptoms. "It's usually a temporary disorder associated with anxiety or trauma and is characterized by an inability to speak in certain settings," he'd explained. "Right now Cathy is mute to all but those she knows and trusts." He'd given Emma's six-foot, unadorned, rawboned figure a quick, clinical glance. "I mean no offense, Mrs. Benson, but you look a formidable woman, and Cathy has gone mute in your presence because she doesn't feel safe with you. You are a stranger to her. She chooses to remain silent because, considering everything that's happened, she finds safety in silence. She'll speak when she trusts you."

Emma gave the key another try. "The darn key won't work. I don't know when I last locked this door. Not in years, I reckon. In this town, we don't lock doors." She gave up the effort and turned to Cathy. "Tell you what. You get back in the car to stay warm until I go through the front of the house to open the door from inside. Okay?"

Resolutely the little girl stepped to a shelf in front of the garage and stood on tiptoe to take down a can of motor oil. She brought it to Emma. *Try that,* she said with her eyes, her tool of communication in the last seven days. Emma took the can, heartened at even this small exchange. "Aren't you the clever one!" she said. "Why didn't I think of this?"

A little dab on the key and they were inside the kitchen within seconds. Emma bustled about to turn on the stove and a wall panel heater while the little girl stood motionless, rigid from the cold, the knot of her balled hands visible in her coat pockets. *She probably thinks she's been dropped into a rabbit hole like Alice in Wonderland,* Emma thought, feeling the child's bewildered gaze inspect her outdated kitchen. The Santa Cruz kitchen, like the rest of the house, had been large and sunny and as state-of-the-art as the latest layout in *Better Homes and Gardens.*

"Would you like to go into the den and sit while I make us that cocoa?" she asked. "You'll be more comfortable in there once the room warms up."

The child replied with a brief nod and Emma led her into a comfortably shabby room where she watched television, read, and did her needlework. The child flinched at the sudden *whoosh* and flash of fire behind the grill when Emma turned on the wall heater. Cathy's home in California boasted central heating, of course.

"Would you like to watch TV?" Emma asked.

A head shake, also barely perceptible. The child, still in her coat, sat in a chair close to the heater and turned around to inspect Emma's book collection that occupied an entire wall. A librarian by profession, she had organized the books according to interest rather than by author. Catherine Ann removed *The Little Prince* from the shelf of young people's books. Her gaze returned to Emma. *May I?*

"Of course. You've never read that book before?"

Her granddaughter held up two fingers. *Twice.*

"Oh, you've read the book two times? *The Little Prince* is certainly worth reading more than once. It's always good to return to familiar things. They can remind us of happy times."

It was the wrong thing to say. Emma saw a flicker deep in the blue eyes as if a memory had surfaced, and a veil of sadness fell over the child's delicate face. She returned the book to the shelf. "Well, then," Emma said, swallowing quickly, "I'll just get that cocoa."

In the kitchen, she slumped against the counter, giving in to a feeling of overwhelming helplessness. She'd thought she was adequate for the task at hand, but how was it possible, considering all that her granddaughter had lost and what little Emma had to give, to fill the gap left in that little girl's life? How could she ever be a substitute for her parents? How could the schools in Kersey, with their emphasis on football and other sports, provide her the quality of education and cultural advantages she'd known? How would this little girl with her air of refinement fit in with the countrified ways of her classmates? And how in the world could she be happy here in Emma's modest house when she'd been growing up in a luxuriously furnished home with her own TV set and stereo record player—and, shining in one corner of the living room, a baby grand piano!—and a backyard outfitted with swimming pool and playhouse and every conceivable object on which to slide and jump and climb?

How could Emma rescue what was left of her childhood?

"Give her time," Dr. Rhinelander had told Emma. "Children are so resilient, Cathy more than most. She'll come around."

Was the man insane? In the course of a week, Catherine Ann's parents had been killed and her home gone on sale. She'd been parted from her best friend, her piano, the progressive private school she'd attended since kindergarten, the pretty town she'd lived in all her life—from everyone and everything dear and familiar to her—to go live in the Texas Panhandle with a grandmother she did not know.

And today the region had never looked bleaker. When Emma had turned onto Highway 40 out of Amarillo toward Kersey, the child's eyes had dilated, speaking louder than words her panic that she'd been carted to the end of the earth. Emma could hardly disagree with her impression. The prairie in winter offered nothing to crow about. It stretched dead and brown into a vast, endless nothingness, broken now and then only by a distant farmhouse or a knot of cows huddled miserably against the wind-driven sleet. The little towns they passed through off the interstate looked especially dismal this gray Sunday afternoon with their main streets deserted and store windows dark and forlorn Christmas decorations still strung from lampposts, beaten about by the wind.

To coax the child from her despondency, Emma had described the prairie in spring, how it looked like a never-ending carpet of wildflowers—"the most beautiful, transformed sight you'd ever want to see," she declared, when her enthusiasm was interrupted by the awestruck pointing of the child's finger.

"Oh, my God," Emma said.

A mass of gray tumbleweeds barreled toward them

off the prairie, dozens of dried uprooted Russian thistles propelled by the wind and looking like a band of malevolent ghosts set on attacking the car. Emma could not pull to a stop before the horde was upon them, clawing at Catherine Ann's side of the Ford. Her granddaughter squealed, tucked her elbows close to her sides, and covered her head with her hands.

"It's okay, Catherine Ann," Emma said, stopping the car to enfold her granddaughter's tightly compressed body into her arms. The tumbleweeds had scattered and scuttled off, those that had not broken apart from the assault on the Ford. "They're only dried plants, a weed," she explained gently. "You'll find them throughout the Southwest. In winter when they've matured, the parts aboveground break off from the root and tumble away in the wind. That's why they're called tumbleweeds. Sometimes a whole colony takes off together and forms the phenomenon we just saw. They're scary as all get out, but they're not harmful."

She could feel the terrified pounding of the child's heart through the fabric of her coat. Most children, seeing such a spectacle, would have flown to safety in the arms of the nearest adult, but Catherine Ann had not. She'd looked to herself for protection. The observation had left Emma with a well-remembered feeling of rejection.

"Cathy is very self-sufficient, despite the doting of her parents," Beth, the wife of Dr. Rhinelander, had told Emma.

Self-sufficient. Emma pried the lid off a box of Nestlé's Quik. Was that another word for indifference to parental love and instruction she'd endured from the child's father?

At their reintroduction, Catherine Ann's cool, blue-eyed gaze had reminded Emma so much of Sonny's that a chill had gripped her, and she'd instantly felt the conflict of love and revulsion that had plagued her feelings for him. In the hectic week of arranging for the funeral, getting the house ready for sale, packing boxes to be shipped to Kersey and luggage for the plane—all without hearing a word leave the child's lips—Emma had looked for genetic indicators that pegged Catherine Ann as Sonny's daughter. Other than the fine features and coloring of her handsome father, Emma had found none, but they were hard to spot behind a wall of silence.

Most of the information she'd learned of Catherine Ann had come from Beth. "She's very bright, curious, often treated younger than she is because she's small for her age. But you learn fast enough who you're dealing with. She's been so good for our shy daughter, Laura. She's given her confidence she wouldn't have otherwise."

When Emma had gone to collect Catherine Ann's school records from Winchester Academy, an institution founded exclusively for gifted children, the principal had confirmed Beth's impression of her granddaughter's intelligence. "You do know what Cathy aspires to be when she grows up?" he'd asked.

Emma had to say she'd no idea.

"A doctor. Most children toss that notion about with no more strength behind it than crepe paper in the rain, but I wouldn't put the goal past Cathy."

Emma peeked into the TV room to find her granddaughter sitting where she'd left her, hands folded on her lap, feet crossed, body still, the look of an abandoned child on her face but the self-containment of her father evident in every line of her posture. A wave of despair washed over Emma. She'd shouldered a lot of sadness in her life—her husband's railroad accident early in their marriage that had left her a widow and her sons father-less, her firstborn's death in Vietnam, his brother's years-long alienation from her, and now his eternal loss without hope of their reconciliation—but how could she bear Catherine Ann's refusal to accept the love she was heartsick to offer? How could she withstand the extension of her son's indifference in his little automaton of a daughter?

Emma brought in the cups of cocoa. "Here we

go—," she started to say, but her voice broke, and she could not go on. Grief blocked her throat, grief for her boys she would never see again, for the son lost to her in war and the other from his birth, the one she'd loved the best. Tears began to slide down her cheeks, and then, to her astonishment, the little automaton rose and stood stiffly in front of her, her smooth brow puckered—*what's wrong?*—and an empathetic cast in her eyes. *Don't be sad.*

Inside her, the little seed of hope sprouted that now Emma realized Beth Rhinelander had meant to implant as they'd said their good-byes. "Cathy is her own person," she'd whispered into her ear. Emma was still holding the hot cups, and as her granddaughter came between them she bent down to receive the child's arms around her neck and the tender pat of a small hand on her back.

Chapter Three

Through the kitchen window overlooking her backyard, Mabel Church watched her eleven-year-old nephew, Trey Don Hall, and John Caldwell, his best friend, toss a football to each other in the last light of the winter afternoon. Trey's face still held a trace of petulance in contrast to John's good-humored expression, and Mabel heard him say, "Oh, come on, TD. We just have to look after her for a week or so, and then our *indenture* will be over!"

Indenture. One of the words on the boy's sixth-grade vocabulary list. Trey insisted on using double negatives as a way of sounding macho, but both of them enjoyed flinging about new words in their conversations with each other, a practice

Mabel hoped would impress Catherine Ann Benson. Regrettably, Emma's granddaughter sounded too smart for her own good—certainly for Kersey Elementary School, one of the reasons Emma had requested Mabel to ask the boys to look after her for a couple of weeks after she enrolled. The other was even more off-putting in a primary school setting. Emma's granddaughter suffered from "selective mutism," but only temporarily, Mabel's old friend had explained, "until Catherine Ann can adjust to her new surroundings."

Emma had the idea that Catherine Ann's transition into Kersey Elementary School would be made easier if Trey and John, the undisputed leaders of the sixth grade, were to set the example of how she should be treated—with courtesy and respect. "Appeal to their male vanity," she'd suggested. "Tell them that since they're the kingpins of their class, the others will take their cue from them, follow their lead." Emma was convinced that no one would dare make fun of Catherine Ann if the boys took her under their protective wing.

Mabel had broached the subject that afternoon as the boys were doing their homework around her kitchen table. As she'd expected, her nephew's face had screwed up as if he were eating turnips when she explained what looking after Catherine Ann entailed.

"Forget it, Aunt Mabel. We're not babysitting a mute, sitting with her in the cafeteria, sticking with her on the playground. How would that make John and me look? We sit at the jock table at lunch and play football during recess."

"She's not a mute," Mabel had attempted to explain. "She's simply lost the will to speak for a while. It's a condition brought on from the shock of her parents' sudden deaths and her whole world being turned upside down in a matter of days. She's been hauled away from everything and everyone she knows to an unfamiliar place of strangers. She's been totally orphaned. No wonder she's lost her voice. You can understand that, can't you, Trey Don?"

John had spoken up. "Of course he understands it. We both do." He looked at Trey. "Think about it, TD. The girl's parents just died. She's an orphan. We know what that's like. Miss Emma's right. The other kids will make fun of her if we don't protect her. You know how mean Cissie Jane and her group can be."

Mabel's heart had warmed toward him. She loved that he called her aunt. John Caldwell was not her nephew, but she felt as much akin to him as she did to her sister's child. It was times like these that Mabel saw the clear results of family heredity, a subject she and Emma often discussed and on which they agreed. The generous blood of John's mother, God rest her soul, flowed in John, while Trey Don's veins ran with her selfish baby sister's. But John's reference to *orphan* had grazed a nerve in her nephew. His parents were alive. They just didn't know where. Trey's father had disappeared before he was born, and his mother had taken off with who knew what sort of trash after she'd deposited her four-year-old son with Mabel and her husband "for only a few days."

They never saw her again.

Trey had asked reluctantly, "What does she look like?" his dark eyes hopeful that Catherine Ann did not favor Miss Emma.

"Well, I'm glad you asked that," Mabel said, brightening. "Emma says she's very pretty. A blue-eyed blonde. She's small in size, but independent and gutsy, not clingy at all."

"It doesn't matter what she looks like," John said. "We'll do it, Aunt Mabel. Count us in. When do we meet her?"

"Not until next Monday. I suggested that you children meet beforehand, but Emma doesn't think that's a good idea because of the speech problem."

Trey had fumed and argued, but John's reference to *orphan* had taken the wind out of his objections. He'd gotten in the last word by saying, "Don't expect us to carry her books!"

It was too cold for them to be outside, but Mabel observed them for a few more minutes before attempting to call them in. It was easy to see why they were the princes of the sixth grade. Already, at eleven, burgeoning athletes, they were tall and well formed and handsome—heartbreakers in the making. They were intelligent, too, and interested in their studies and making good grades. No slouches, either one, but what would Emma's cultured granddaughter think of them—and they of her? The child could read and speak French, had studied art, had taken ballet since she was six, and excelled at the piano—"and here I am with no piano to offer her," Emma had called to lament.

Mabel recalled Sonny Benson well. He had broken Emma's heart. God help her oldest and dearest friend if daughter was like father, and God help Catherine Ann if she took his snobbish ways into Kersey Elementary School.

SIX DAYS LATER, on a late Sunday afternoon, Trey left John's house and made a detour. Usually when leaving John's, he went straight on down the block to Aunt Mabel's home on the corner, but on this particular afternoon Trey decided to walk over to the next street where Miss Emma lived, despite his hatred of the cold and wind and snow.

He'd never dreaded anything more than the adjustment in his life coming tomorrow morning when he and John had to act as Catherine Ann Benson's bodyguards. He'd made John promise they'd be enslaved for only a week. There had been daily bulletins of the new girl's progress in adjusting to her "culture shock" (his aunt's term), telephoned in by Miss Emma, but he still had no idea what he and John were in for.

The girl was finally starting to speak a little, and Miss Emma had taken her to Penney's in Amarillo to buy her a warmer coat and shoes and jeans and flannel shirts, the type of clothes the sixth-grade girls wore in Kersey Elementary School. He'd been relieved to hear that. How embarrassing if she'd shown up in the kinds of things they wore in her private school back in California—uniforms and knee socks, so Miss Emma had told Aunt Mabel. Imagine, *knee socks*!

Miss Emma had tried to keep Catherine Ann occupied with things like baking cookies to take to the nursing home, looking at photo albums of her father as a boy, and searching for soil breaks in the flower beds that meant the daffodils would soon be up. How those activities could fill anybody's time Trey didn't know, but he guessed they were the kinds of things girls liked. He and John had wondered how Miss Emma's granddaughter would react to Sampson, the old turtle that lived in her backyard and looked like a prehistoric monster. Trey had bet she'd faint right on the spot when Sampson crawled out of his hole on his powerful, reptilian legs and made a beeline for the treat in Miss Emma's pocket like a military tank on the attack. To Trey's surprise, the two had cottoned to each other right away, and the new girl took over the job of feeding him. The day before, after the night's big snowfall, Miss Emma had helped her to build a snowman or, rather, a snow *queen*. Miss Emma had gone on and on telling his aunt how creative Catherine Ann was in choosing a fluted fruit bowl for a crown, a barbeque fork for a scepter, and a portion of red oilcloth for a sash. It was the first time the new girl had ever seen snow.

A big panel truck with ACE PLUMBING written on the door was parked on his side of the street across from Miss Emma's house. He stopped beside it, his feet beginning to tingle inside his boots from the cold. The snow queen was in the front yard. It had black bottle caps for eyes, a funnel for a nose, and red buttons arched into a smiling mouth. The look was actually pretty neat.

The front door opened and Catherine Ann Benson ran out. Hatless, mittenless, her coat unbuttoned, she rushed to the snow queen, her cheeks flushing red almost immediately, her hair dancing in the wind, her small white hands like butterflies fluttering with the sash, the funnel, an awry button. Then she flew back up the steps and closed the door behind her.

Trey stood stock-still on the sidewalk. As he was hidden by the truck, she had not seen him. A feeling he'd never known before took command of him. He felt unable to move, as if he'd been captured in the beam of a spaceship. He could not feel the cold and wind. His hands and feet did not exist. He felt only the shock of having glimpsed an angel drop to earth, then disappear, the most beautiful creature he'd ever seen. Slowly, when he could get his feet to obey, he turned homeward, the snow like magic dust beneath his boots. He would keep his brief glance of Catherine Ann Benson to himself, a secret he would not share even with John, until tomorrow morning when he would introduce himself to her and become her protector for the rest of her life.

Chapter Four

Bowing into icy wind that felt like splinters hammered into her face, Cathy Benson ran with her grandmother from the Ford to the entrance of Kersey Elementary School. Butterflies batted about madly in her stomach, increasing her queasiness, and she wanted to cry, *Don't leave me here! Let me go back with you!*

Cathy was certain they'd turn around and head for the car the instant she said it, but the trouble was, she couldn't say it. It had taken her almost a week to unthaw her tongue to speak to the woman who called herself her grandmother, but now it had frozen again, and she'd gone back into that silent place where her parents lived and all was warm and safe and familiar.

"Now, Catherine Ann, you know the number to call if you want to come home," her grandmother told her for the tenth time once they were inside the door. "There's no shame in calling me to come get you."

But there would be shame. The woman didn't want her to suffer, but Cathy sensed Emma would want her to stick it out—be a big girl. She suddenly recalled a memory of her father saying angrily, "That damn woman and her spine of steel!"

That damn woman, Cathy realized, had been his mother, this tall woman who was her grandmother. She'd want her to have a spine of steel.

She pressed the woman's hand. *I'll be all right*, and her grandmother rewarded her with a proud beam in her eye.

A heavyset man in a business suit and tie hurried toward them, a fold of flesh resting on the neck of his too-tight collar. The hard shine of the hall floor stretched cold and unwelcoming behind him, and Cathy could hear student chatter behind the closed doors. Homeroom—the first class of the day, she'd been told—had begun. Everyone would have already been seated when she walked in. Against her struggle to be brave, her ears plugged like they did in an airplane when it descended.

"Weldon, this is my granddaughter whom I've

told you about," she heard through the blockage in her ears. "Catherine Ann, this is Mr. Favor, the principal."

No, no, my name is Cathy, Cathy wished to correct her. It was all right for her to call her Catherine Ann in her house, but in school she wished to be called Cathy.

"Hello there, Catherine Ann," the principal said, shaking her hand. His hearty manner reminded Cathy of the men who worked for her father at the Jaguar dealership he managed. "Welcome to Kersey Elementary School. My goodness, what a pretty girl you are, and plenty smart, so I hear." He turned his wide smile to her grandmother. "Now, don't you worry one bit, Miss Emma. We'll take good care of her."

"See that you do," her grandmother said in a tone crisp as lettuce—proper for the president of the school board, Cathy supposed. The woman turned to her. "There's a lunch inside your satchel, Catherine Ann. You have a nice day, and I'll be waiting for you right here by the door when school lets out. Okay?"

Cathy swallowed and nodded. *Okay.*

The woman bent down and peered into her face. "Have you gone silent again, sweetheart?"

Cathy shook her head emphatically. *No!*

"Oh, dear." Her grandmother lifted a concerned glance to the principal and elevated her brows.

Mr. Favor threw up large palms. "Now, like I said, Miss Emma. Not to worry. The boys will take care of her. They'll see that nobody teases her."

Alarmed, Cathy tugged at the woman's sleeve. *What boys?*

Her grandmother sighed and explained. "Mabel Church, my best friend, has a nephew who lives with her like you live with me. His name is Trey Don Hall. I thought I would ask him and his best friend, John Caldwell, to look after you this first week to help with your orientation. Mr. Favor here thought it a good idea, too. You'll be glad to have them by your side. They're the leaders of the sixth-grade class. Isn't that so, Mr. Favor?"

The principal said with an aggrieved roll of his eyes, "I'm afraid that's so."

Cathy didn't want any boy by her side. All the boys she knew at Winchester wore glasses and were either scrawny or fat and ran around in little groups. She and her friends called them the Nerd Herd. Why couldn't her grandmother have recruited girls?

"Okay, young lady, let's go take a look at your locker," the principal said, and offered his hand, but Cathy gripped the handle of her satchel with both of hers—*why did people insist on treating her like a kindergartner!*—and walked beside him without a backward look at her grandmother, but her heart clutched when she heard the push of the handlebar and the door slammed shut by the wind.

"Your books are already in your locker," the principal said. "Your grandmother returned them so you wouldn't have to lug a heavy load around the first part of the day."

For the last two days Cathy had memorized her schedule and thumbed through her textbooks, thinking the material awfully simple. She was especially disappointed to learn that science was not taught in the sixth grade but rather geography, and she would have to wait until her sophomore year to take biology. At Winchester, her class was already studying anatomy and the digestive system. Next year the students would begin dissecting frogs. Her grandmother, knowing Cathy wanted to become a doctor and seeing her disappointment, had told her not to worry. She would send away for home-schooling materials dealing with subjects in the medical field and Cathy could learn from those.

Principal Favor explained that her first period was homeroom, a class where roll was taken and announcements made and students did their homework. Cathy thought the last part strange. At Winchester, homework was done at home. He stopped in the middle of a row of metal storage compartments lined along a wall, quite different from the polished wood cabinets in her former school. "Miss Emma requested a top locker located between Trey Don Hall and John Caldwell," he said, his grin spreading wide. "Most of the little girls in your class would kill to have it."

There were those names again. Why would any girl kill to have a locker between two boys? Cathy watched the principal demonstrate how to open the locker by turning the dial of a combination lock. She learned the numbers immediately, but he repeated them several times and insisted she write them down on her schedule and practice dialing her combination. Then she followed him to the closed door of a classroom through which could be heard loud laughing and talking.

Mr. Favor's face turned an explosive pink. "Miss Whitby needs to take her homeroom in hand," he said as if he owed Cathy an explanation. "I don't know how many times I've told her." He mustered a smile. "Well, young lady, are you ready?"

Dumbly Cathy nodded, and the principal opened the door.

Instantly all chatter ceased. Everyone's attention swiveled to their entrance. Several students who were out of their seats lowered themselves back into them, mesmerized with curiosity. The teacher who must be Miss Whitby froze in the act of writing on the board, a flash of panic in her startled stare.

The butterflies swarmed up to Cathy's throat and choked off her breath. The arrested faces dimmed like stars behind clouds. Only one shone through, glowing like the moon. It belonged to a handsome boy in the back row whose head and shoulders rose above everyone else's except for the blurred figure of another boy two seats over.

Miss Whitby recovered and came forward with a strained smile. She was very pretty and looked too young to teach. "You must be Catherine Ann Benson. I wasn't expecting you until tomorrow. Thank you, Mr. Favor. I'll take over from here."

Mr. Favor spoke in an undertone from behind his hand, "As I hope you will your students, Miss Whitby, and I told you she'd be here *today*." He dropped his hand and addressed the class. "Boys and girls, this is Catherine Ann Benson, Miss Emma's granddaughter. She's from California. I don't want to hear of anybody not being nice to her, understand?" He ran a stern eye around the room. "You know what'll happen if you do." To Cathy he said, "Don't hesitate to call me if you need me, Catherine Ann."

Cathy. My name is Cathy! she wanted to cry,

feeling her insides dissolve in embarrassment at her introduction. The principal had *threatened* the students and now, on top of everything else different about her, they would hate her for that reason alone.

She dropped her eyes to escape their stares and heard a voice call from the back of the room, "Let her sit here, Miss Whitby." Cathy sneaked a peek from under her lashes and saw that the command had come from the handsome boy in the last row. He was pointing to a desk between him and the other tall boy. There were giggles and girls covered their mouths with their hands, but the speaker did not laugh. Perfectly serious, he dragged his book satchel out of the aisle as if expecting to be obeyed.

"All right, Trey Don," Miss Whitby said after a pause. "We'll try it for a little while. Catherine Ann, you may take your seat."

In the complete silence, Cathy walked down the aisle and slipped into the desk seat, conscious of every eye following her, curiosity mixed with surprise and excitement. Rigidly she focused her gaze on unzipping a compartment of her satchel to withdraw paper and pen to write down the material from the board. Her movements held the fascinated attention of the class, as if they were expecting her to perform tricks.

The boy named Trey Don Hall—now revealed as the nephew of her grandmother's best friend—leaned over. "Hi. I'm Trey Hall. I'm supposed to look after you. Me and John. That's John Caldwell over there."

She turned to the other boy and blinked shyly. *Hello.*

"Hi," he said, and smiled at her.

They were different from any other boys she'd ever known. There was nothing nerdy about them. She thought they may have been held back a year, they were so tall for the sixth grade. It would be hard to say who was handsomer. Both had brown eyes and dark hair, though John's was a little curlier. They were big and strong compared to her, and she felt even smaller sitting between them.

The boy named John said, "You can put your pen and paper away. There's nothing to write down in here. This is a goof-off period." He noticed the staring students and irritably waved at them with the backs of his hands as if he were shooing chickens. Immediately, in one movement, every set of shoulders rotated to the front.

Indeed she was sitting between the definite leaders of the sixth grade. Trey Hall leaned over again. "You can call me TD. Everybody does."

She glanced at him, wanting to speak but held silent by the familiar powerlessness of her tongue.

The boy on the other side of her whispered to him across her desk, "She's mute, TD. Remember?"

Cathy turned to stare at him in shock. *Mute? She wasn't mute!*

"Oh, sorry. I forgot," Trey said. He smiled at her. "*TD* stands for 'touchdown.'"

She must make them understand that she could speak. She faced the other boy, but he misunderstood the anguish in her eyes and explained, "Like in football. Trey is our team's quarterback."

"Do you like football?" Trey asked.

She swung her gaze back to him blankly. *Football?* Her father thought football games were for monkeys.

Trey grinned. "Well, that's okay. And it's okay to be like you are. We understand, don't we, John?" He touched her arm. "John and me, we don't have no parents, either. My old man split before I was born, and my mom left me with my aunt when I was four, and I never saw her again, and John's mother died when he was seven. His dad—if you can call him that—is around, but we don't see much of him. So..."—Trey's grin widened—"we got being orphans in common."

Orphans... The word pierced through her like an arrow shot from a bow and shattered her secret place. Pain flooded where her parents had been alive and well, blinding her, forcing her to see.

"Catherine Ann, are you okay?" John asked.

Tears welled in her eyes. Her mouth trembled. "Cathy," she said. "My name is Cathy."

Chapter Five

What did I say to make her cry, John?"

"I think it was the word *orphan*, TD. Maybe up until you said it, she hadn't realized her parents were dead. It took a while for me to feel my mother gone, and then one morning, I woke up and it hit me that she was dead and I'd never see her again."

"I remember that morning," Trey said. "You ran around like hornets were after you."

"It's the most terrible feeling in the world."

"Ah, jeez, John, I didn't mean to make her feel like that."

"Of course you didn't. She knows it, too."

"I want to do something nice to make it up to her."

"Like what? Pick her some flowers?"

"For Pete's sake, John, where am I going to find flowers to pick in the dead of winter?"

"You could *buy* them."

"With what? I've already spent my allowance."

"*John! Trey!* Stop talking and pay attention!" The order came from Coach Mayer, head coach of the ninth-grade football team. He stood at the blackboard, tapping at diagrams of game plays with a yardstick. John's and Trey's school schedules had been arranged for them to attend the physical-education class made up of the players of the junior high football teams, seventh through ninth grade. It was really a bull session designed to give the coaches extra time to tutor their players. In the long history of the school's successful athletic program, John and Trey were the youngest students and only sixth graders ever assigned to the class. Big things were expected of their respective talents as they got older and moved into the higher ranks—Trey as quarterback and John as a wide receiver.

The boys drew apart and focused their attention on the blackboard, but Trey's fingers, already long and sinewy, beat out a rapid tap on the surface of his desk, a signal to John that he was in his thinking mode. That could be good, and that could be bad. One thing John knew, Trey had it bad for Catherine Ann—Cathy—Benson. Well, who wouldn't?

She looked like a little angel, all blond curls and blue eyes and sweet dimples when she smiled. Which wasn't going to happen too often now. After that morning when John realized his mother was gone for good, his world had gone black for a long, long time. It would be a while before he and Trey saw those dimples again.

Trey snapped his fingers. "I know! We can get her a puppy," he whispered. "Gil Baker told me that Wolf Man's collie had a litter last week."

John caught Coach Mayer's frown in their direction and wrote on his notebook for Trey to read: *You think he'll give us one?*

Trey mouthed, *Why not?*

To their consternation, the coaches did not dismiss the class, the last period of the day, until after the bell rang and Cathy had gone by the time they reached the home economics room to escort her to her locker. Except for athletics, she was in all their classes and shared the same lunch period, and they'd been able to watch her every move for most of the day. She'd looked lonely and lost and kept to herself, speaking to no one and barely to them, but everyone knew of the new girl in school and that he and Trey were looking out for her. When they were finally released, they flew down the hall to waylay her before she could leave, only to catch a glimpse of her blond curls bouncing under her cap as she went out the front door with Miss Emma.

"Catherine Ann!" Trey called, his voice stricken, swallowed up in the end-of-school-day noise.

John felt a pang of sympathy for him. He'd never seen Trey moony-eyed over anybody, and in the cafeteria at noon today John had been embarrassed for Cathy at the attention he gave her. "Is this seat okay, Catherine Ann?" "What do you want to drink? I'll get it for you." "You can have my Jell-O, if you want. My cookie, too."

And to John he'd said afterwards, "Did you see how nicely she ate, John? And did you notice how clean her fingernails were—like little white half-moons."

Actually, Cathy had eaten very little of the big sandwich Miss Emma had prepared and nothing else she'd packed in her sack, but he agreed she chewed daintily, and her hands were pretty and delicate and didn't look as if they belonged at the sleeve ends of the flannel shirt she was wearing. Her shirt collar was too big for her little neck, too, and he figured Miss Emma had bought a larger size in case the shirt shrank or maybe she expected Cathy's body to catch up to it. Miss Emma wasn't rich like Aunt Mabel and probably couldn't afford to replace the clothes Cathy grew out of.

Cathy had looked at Trey as if he'd skittered in

from a different solar system and for most of the time ignored him. They'd selected a place away from the jock table situated next to the one where Cissie Jane queened it over her silly bunch. Lots of giggles had come from that direction, and John had been pretty sure the cause of the laughs was Cathy.

Trey's interest was probably temporary, but right now she'd become the moon and stars in his sky. His, too, actually.

"Relax, TD. We'll see her tomorrow," he said, placing a consoling hand on Trey's shoulder.

Trey shrugged it off in an unwillingness to be comforted. "Dadgummit! We could have ridden home in Miss Emma's car with Catherine Ann if Coach Mayer hadn't been so long-winded. Okay, let's go talk to Wolf Man about that pup."

"Well, now, wait a minute, TD. Maybe she'd like a kitten," John said, as they made for their lockers. "They're less trouble than dogs, and I'll bet Cissie Jane would give us one of hers. Her mama cat had a litter about three weeks ago, and she's trying to find homes for them."

Trey whooped. "A kitten! No way! Cats got no soul, man. Dogs do, and it'll protect Catherine Ann when it grows up."

"Cathy," John corrected. "She likes to be called Cathy, TD."

"I really like the sound of 'Catherine Ann.'"

"Well, her name is Cathy."

Trey shrugged the point aside. "Here's a news flash, Tiger. Cissie Jane's not going to give us no—any—kitten for Catherine Ann."

"How do you know?"

"Didn't you see the way Cissie looked at her when we sat with her at lunch? Them green eyes of hers shot fire—I mean *those* green eyes."

"Why do you keep correcting yourself? It's annoying," John said.

"I've got to watch how I talk from now on. It's not cool to butcher the English language, like my aunt keeps telling me."

John returned to the discussion. "Cissie Jane's jealous of her, TD. She's not the prettiest girl in class anymore."

"No kidding, and Catherine Ann's a whole lot smarter and nicer than she is, too. You can tell. I just know she'd really love a puppy. Collies are so warm and cuddly. I bet she'd really like one to hold right now."

John agreed. A dog would be better than hugging a pillow. He should know, but what if Miss Emma didn't want a dog in the house? "Don't you think we ought to ask Miss Emma first if it's okay to give Cathy a puppy? Collies shed."

"For goodness' sakes, John, why do you always have to think that way? If we ask Miss Emma, she's liable to say no out of hand. If we spring it on her, and Catherine Ann likes it, she has to keep it."

Trey had a point, but as usual, it was a little shady. "Tell you what," John said. "Let's run this idea by your aunt. She knows Miss Emma better than anybody. If she thinks a dog's okay to give Cathy, we'll go ask Odell Wolfe for one from his litter."

Trey's countenance brightened. He threw up his hand, and they high-fived. "Way to go, Tiger!"

Trey called him Tiger mainly when he agreed with his way of doing things. Trey had given John the nickname when they were playing pee wee football and he'd made good on Trey's pass and carried two tacklers with him across the goal line, Trey yelling, *"Thataway to go, Tiger!"* John knew that Trey had in mind to *sell* his aunt on the idea, rather than simply run it by her. He always got his way with her, but maybe this time it was okay. Aunt Mabel had told them that Miss Emma was already insane about her granddaughter and that her heart felt "like a rusty old trunk with its lid pried open." She might agree to just about anything to make Cathy happy.

Chapter Six

No, boys! Absolutely not." Mabel Church shook her head vigorously to add emphasis to her rare assertion of authority over her nephew. "I cannot permit you to go to Odell Wolfe for a puppy. We don't know a thing about him, and who knows what would happen to you once you set foot in his house?"

"We won't set foot," Trey argued. "He wouldn't keep his dog in his *house*, Aunt Mabel. She's probably laid up in one of his mangy old sheds."

"*Property.* I should have said 'set foot on his *property*,'" Mabel corrected herself. "You'll have to think of something else to give Catherine Ann." She shuddered at the thought of two eleven-year-old boys doing business with the recluse who lived at the end of a neglected road in the least desirable section of her neighborhood. Wolf Man, everybody called him, and the moniker fit the man in the most uncharitable light of the species. Dirty and unkempt, red hair and beard a matted mess, he had come from nowhere at least ten years ago and taken up residence in a falling-down house that had lain vacant since its owners had abandoned it in the fifties. Few ever saw him. No one knew anything of his history, how old he was, or how he made his living. It was rumored he wandered about at night, carried a whip, and raised fighting chickens in the ramshackle pens in the backyard. It was Mabel's policy to have no truck with folks you didn't know anything about.

"I don't want to think of something else," Trey wailed. "Catherine Ann *needs* a puppy, doesn't she, John?"

"A puppy would probably be a comfort to her, Aunt Mabel," John said. "I don't think Miss Emma will say no to the idea. She'll want Cathy to be happy."

Mabel could feel her resistance soften. John's insights always melted something inside her. *Out of the mouths of babes.* "It's not the puppy I'm opposed to, John," she explained. "It's the fact that you'll be dealing with Odell Wolfe. And what makes you think he'd give you one for free anyway?"

LEILA MEACHAM

"Why wouldn't he?" Trey said. "He's just going to kill them anyway. He'd probably be happy for us to take one off his hands."

"We'll compromise," Mabel said. "This weekend, I'll drive you boys to the pound in Amarillo, and you can get one there for the little girl. We could even take her with us to make the selection, if she'll go. Meanwhile, we'll broach the idea to Miss Emma."

"Aw, Aunty, this weekend will be too late. She needs one tonight, and we want to *surprise* her with a puppy ourselves!"

"And by taking one of Wolf Man's, we'd be saving at least one from the litter," John put in.

As usual in these debates, Mabel had begun to feel helpless. She agreed that a pet might be just the right stroke to help the child work through the trauma of everything that had happened to her. When Mabel had called to find out how Catherine Ann's first day at school had gone, Emma had said, "Not good. She's in her bedroom now, curled up in the fetal position, and she won't speak to me. Something must have gone terribly wrong at school today."

Yes, Mabel thought, *a warm puppy might be the exact thing for Catherine Ann right now, but not at the expense of the boys' lives or limbs.* "I'm sorry," she told them, "but you'll just have to wait until Saturday when you're out of school. Now, I want you both to give me your word that you won't approach Mr. Wolfe for one of his pups. You're forbidden to have any contact with him, is that clear?"

Her nephew's word was of dubious value, she'd learned by now. He got his peculiar brand of dishonesty honestly—from his mother—but if his word was coupled with John's, he wouldn't go back on it. John kept him ethical. Their friendship was the darndest thing. The two were like a tandem bike, always together but seats apart, one driving, one pedaling, one in front, the other behind, exchanging positions often. What bound them together was beyond her ken, but ever since she and John's mother had introduced them at four years old they had been joined—if not by the soul (Lord knew where Trey's would eventually end up, while John's was sure to fly to heaven), at least by the heart, for there was no accounting for the attractions of the heart. There were wrangles from time to time, but they didn't last long. Trey couldn't go a day without making up. John was the only person in his life he couldn't seem to live without, the only relationship he minded carefully.

"I give my word," John said.

"Trey?"

"Me, too." He looked defeated or had suddenly

lost interest in the matter, not unusual for him. One minute he was all for something, and then as rapidly as a summer rain shower his enthusiasm could disappear.

Satisfied, Mabel said, "Okay then. Now what are you boys going to do before supper and you get down to your homework?"

Trey spoke up promptly. "Go to John's. I left my baseball glove at his house."

"Very well, then," Mabel said, "but be back by six o'clock. "You know you're to come, too, John. We're having beef stew."

"That sounds mighty good, Aunt Mabel," John said.

They hurried out without taking time for a snack, and it wasn't until Mabel entered her nephew's room to place his freshly washed underwear and pajamas in his bureau that she saw his baseball glove on top.

CATHY LAY WITH HER KNEES drawn up to her chin, a blanket covering her head, her face buried in the pillow. The realization had now sunk in, down to the fatty substance in the cavities of her bones, that her parents were gone from this world and she would never see them again. She would never hear their voices or her mother call her by her nickname, Honey Bun, or her father say each morning, "Rise and shine, sun of my world." They would not be coming to take her home, back to her pretty room with its bay window lined up next to Laura's that provided a secret channel of communication. Cathy would never again walk into a classroom at Winchester Academy and sit down with her classmates, be instructed by her wonderful teachers. Everyone and everything she loved had all disappeared the second she'd heard that awful word *orphan* and now she had to live forever with the old woman who was her grandmother in this worn-out house in a brown, cold place where the sun never shone, and her only friends were two boys she did not know who wore cowboy boots and one talked in double negatives.

There was nothing now inside her but empty space where once her parents had lived.

She heard her grandmother outside her door and knew she listened for sounds that she was awake. Cathy remained quiet as a stick until she heard the sad shuffle of her footsteps move back down the hall to the warmer part of the house, and then she pulled the covers tighter and buried her head deeper into the pillow.

Chapter Seven

Okay, in case Aunt Mabel's watching, let's take off toward your place, John," Trey said.

John glanced at him sharply. "That is where we're going."

"No it isn't. We're going to circle back to Wolf Man's place."

John stopped. "What? You gave your aunt your word that you wouldn't go there."

"Now, Tiger, listen to me," Trey said. "Remember what she said, and what we said okay *to*. She asked us to give our word that we wouldn't *approach* Mr. Wolfe about one of his pups. Those were her exact words, John. I was listening."

"So?" John said.

"So we're not going to approach him. We're

going to snatch one of them—those—pups without ever seeing him."

John closed his mouth to avoid his teeth freezing. It was fiery cold this time of the afternoon when the sun disappeared and the wind blew out of the north. He longed to be out of it, even if it was to his house that smelled like sour beans. He walked on. "You're crazy, TD. How are we going to get a pup without Wolf Man catching us?"

Trey hurried after him. "How's he going to see us? We'll use the alley and go in the back way. That poor old mama is probably freezing her tits off under one of them—those—outbuildings. We'll hear her pups, and we'll just grab one and run." He pulled at John's arm and made him stop. "John, if we don't do it now, tomorrow might be too late. He'll take an ax to those pups' heads, sure as shooting."

"They're not even weaned yet," John said. "If a pup's taken too soon from its mother it could die."

"John, why do you have to be so stupidly practical? So what? It's not going to live long enough to be weaned if we don't rescue it. And we can be its mama, feed it milk from a bottle. Catherine Ann would probably love holding the little thing, feeding it like a baby. It'd give her something to put her feelings on rather than her sadness."

"That's so," John said. Trey had a way of working

him with words, which most of the time he didn't listen to, but this time he made sense. He wished he'd had something to hold and love when his mother had died, but he couldn't risk his father taking his foot to a dog or cat in the house. This time Trey was right. Seems like, when it came to Trey, he was always torn between what was right and what was almost right. He wanted Cathy to have the puppy more than anything in the world. On the other hand, they had sworn to Aunt Mabel they'd have no dealings with Odell Wolfe and, no matter how Trey worded it, they'd be going back on their promise. "You know how Gil Baker exaggerates," he said. "How does he know Wolf Man's collie had pups?"

"Because Gil's always sneaking around the place trying to find out something to sic the law on him. His mama wants Wolf Man run off, but even though he's a squatter, Sheriff Tyson won't do anything unless there's proof he's done something wrong."

"Why can't we wait until your aunt takes us to the pound?" John asked, gritting his teeth to keep them from chattering.

"Because I want to make up for what I said to Catherine Ann *now*—tonight! I want to see her face when I hand her the pup."

That was another Trey thing: Once he thought of a plan, he couldn't wait to put it into action. He had to have it—or do it—*right now.* "We'll need something to wrap it in," John said.

Trey slapped his shoulder. "You're my man, John. I'll put it under my jacket."

They almost had to hold their noses when they approached the Cyclone fence of Odell Wolfe's backyard. "Godamighty," Trey said. "Have you ever smelled such stink?"

"The gate's padlocked, TD," John observed. There was also a huge NO TRESPASSING sign attached to the fence.

"We'll go over it."

"Only one of us can. The other one has to stay outside and give a leg up."

The boys' eyes locked. They could hear the soft, clucking sounds of chickens bedding down for the night. Dusk had fallen, gray and cold as frozen steel, and the wind had died, as if it had been chased away by night, which was fast creeping in. A single light shone in the coop, none in the ramshackle house, though smoke spiraled from the chimney.

"Then I'll go," Trey said. "You be ready to catch the pup when I drop it to you."

John studied the stretch of ground between the alley and a series of lean-to shelters. It was a no-man's-land of trash and garbage and rusting metal parts of indecipherable origin. In the semi-darkness, heading helter-skelter to the sheds, Trey would never see a broken bottle or the lid of a tinned can just inviting him to step on it. Trey would take no mind to that sort of danger, and probably make a racket to boot, and what if the mama didn't want to give up her pup?

"I got an idea," John said. "Let's do rock, paper, scissors. Whoever wins goes over." It was a game he nearly always won when he played it with Trey.

"Why not whoever wins stays behind?" Trey suggested.

"I'm going over, TD. I'm quieter than you, and dogs like me."

"Not on your life, Tiger. I'm going after the pup so I can tell Catherine Ann I got it for her. You helped me, of course, but I got it for her."

"You'll just mess it up, and if Wolf Man gets after you, you're cooked."

"Don't worry about me, John," Trey said quietly. "You're always worrying about me."

"You need worrying about," John said, and made a stirrup of his hands. "Watch where you step, for Pete's sake."

"You're my man, John."

Trey was over the fence in seconds and landed

with a soft thud on the ground. He gave John a thumbs-up and, bending low, headed for the lean-tos. John hooked his fingers through the wire openings of the fence and hoped with held breath that Trey had chosen the right shed as he faded into the shadows. The chickens must have heard him. John listened, horrified, as they started up a disturbed squawking. In less than a second, a light went on in the house that he could see dimly through the dingy kitchen window. John's heart lurched. *Oh, my God.*

He called in a loud whisper, "*Trey!*"

But it was too late. A figure with a bushy beard emerged quietly from the back door, closing it softly. *Wolf Man!* He carried something in his hand. *A gun?* Darkness was falling fast, but the man spotted John and ordered, "Just stay right there!" and lifted the object in his hand.

A high-powered beam of light struck John dead in the eyes, blinding him, almost knocking him over. "You just stay right there," the voice called again.

"Y-y-yessir," John said.

He heard cautious footsteps approach. "What you doin' here, boy?"

John put up his hands to shield his eyes from the light. "I—I—"

"Put your hands down so I can see your face."

"I can't see."

"Makes no matter mind to me. I can see you. Why're you spyin' through my fence?"

"I wasn't spying, sir." John kept his fingers splayed before his eyes, praying that Trey would see what was going on and take off toward the street. He heard a jangle of keys but figured he could escape down the alley before the man could unlock the gate and come after him.

"What have you done to upset my chickens?"

"Nothing," John said.

"Well, somethin' must have—" He swung the flashlight around. John, still blinded, had heard nothing, but the man had the ears of a wolf. "Well, well, what have we here?" he said, and John knew Trey had been caught. When John could clear the dazzle from his eyes, he saw, horrified, that Trey stood snared in the beam of light, a bulge under his jacket, and something else: The man held a whip coiled at his side.

"Why're you in my yard, boy?" Odell Wolfe demanded of Trey. "What kind of mischief did you come in here to do?"

John wanted to shout, *Run, Trey!* but suspected that Wolf Man could uncoil that whip faster than a rattlesnake could strike and snap Trey's neck off his shoulders before he could sprint two steps.

"Nothing," Trey answered. "I didn't come in here to do mischief."

"Then why are you in here?"

"We came in here to get one of your puppies," John answered through the wire. "We heard your collie had a litter and thought that...you wouldn't miss just one."

The flashlight swung around to John again, and once more he shielded his eyes from the sudden assault. "And just why did you figure that?" Wolf Man asked.

"It doesn't matter why," Trey said. "Take off, John—now!"

"Well...as long as I got one of you for my pot, it don't matter about the other," the man drawled, and John, his fingers gripping the wire, felt his bowels churn to butter.

"What do you want with one of my pups?" Wolf Man asked Trey, directing the beam back to his face.

"We want it for Miss Emma's—Mrs. Benson's— granddaughter. Both her parents just got killed, and she's an orphan now. We thought it would cheer her up."

Trey spoke without moving his jaws. He was shaking visibly from the cold, and John could feel its grip through his shorts. Wolf Man wore a flimsy jacket with the tail ends of his shirt hanging out

63

and moccasins with no socks, like he was part of the night and freezing temperature.

"We'd have gone to the pound in Amarillo to get one," John volunteered through the Cyclone fence, "but we'd have to wait until Saturday, and Cathy needs one now."

"Emma Benson," the man mused, lowering the light. "That pup's for her granddaughter?"

"Yeah," Trey said.

"Then why didn't you just ask instead a stealin' in here and takin' one? I don't reckon Miz Benson would cotton to that."

"Because my aunt told me to have no dealings with you, that's why," Trey said.

"She did, did she? Who's your aunt?"

"None of your business."

John's heart pumped faster as Wolf Man nailed Trey again with the high-powered beam. He rubbed his thigh with the whip, and John could make out his hard grip on the handle. "Hey, I know you," the man said. "You're that flashy little quarterback everybody's setting their hopes on for Kersey in a few years and you"—the light arced back to John—"you're John Caldwell, his receiver. Well, well."

"How do you know about us?" Trey demanded.

"I've watched you play." He chuckled. "Mabel

Church—that's who your aunt is. She was plenty right to warn you to stay out of my yard." He unhooked a ring of keys from his pants and threw the set over the fence to John, who automatically whipped out his hand and caught it. "Good catch," Wolf Man pronounced. "Now unlock that gate."

"You mean—you're going to let Trey out?" John said.

"He'll hurt the pup if he climbs over." The man laughed quietly again and shook his head. "You boys must think an awful lot of that girl to risk comin' around my place on her behalf. Is she pretty?"

"Yeah. Very," Trey said.

"Is she nice?"

"Yes!" both boys chorused together.

"I'm not surprised, her being Miss Emma's granddaughter an' all." Wolf Man's lips slid into a sly smile. "Two boys and a pretty girl. Nothing good ever came from that equation. Lob those keys back to me, John Caldwell, and you boys get on home to your suppers. Mind you, feed that critter 'fore you sit down to a bite. Soak the end of a towel in warm milk and let it suck on it. And next time you want something of mine, you better ask."

John had finally managed to unlock the gate, his hands numb beyond feeling. "We will, sir," he said, and tossed him the keys, his nerves still at fever pitch that Wolf Man might change his mind and wrap his whip around Trey to keep him penned in.

But Wolf Man allowed Trey to escape, and once outside the gate the boys ran to the end of the alley, Trey's arms wrapped protectively around the small lump under his jacket. There they stopped to catch their breaths and savor the miracle of their triumph. Panting, John said, "Wolf Man wasn't so bad. Imagine him seeing us play, and he sounded like he knows Miss Emma."

"Yeah," Trey agreed. "He had rigged up an electric heater in the shed for the dogs and left them lots of blankets. What do you suppose he meant by that *equation* crack?"

"Beats me," John said.

Chapter Eight

Mabel Church eyed them with stern disapproval when they stormed through the back door, the heat of the kitchen striking them like a hot shield. "Now, Aunt Mabel, don't say a word," Trey said, unzipping his jacket. "I know I'm in trouble, but we got to take care of this puppy first. He has to be fed and kept warm."

Guiltily John said, "We have to soak the end of a towel into hot milk and let him suck on it, Aunt Mabel."

"Is that so?" she said, her tone surprisingly mild. She took the shivering, closed-eyed little ball of fur from Trey and wrapped it in a thick bath towel she had ready. She then removed a container of warmed milk from the microwave, filled an eyedropper lying on the counter, and inserted it into the tiny mouth. The boys looked at each other, their surprised gazes asking, *How did she know?*

"So you *did* have dealings with Odell Wolfe, which I expressly forbade. John, you're not my responsibility, but Trey Don, you'll have to be punished."

"Yes, ma'am," Trey said as if she'd threatened no more than withholding dessert if he didn't finish his milk. He tossed a careless explanation to John. "She found my baseball mitt and figured out what we were up to."

"So, you will stay here while John and I deliver this little fellow," Mabel said, "and you'll be happy to know that Miss Emma highly approves of the idea of a puppy for Cathy."

Trey's mouth opened so wide John could see his bottom filling. Horrified disbelief filled his eyes. "What?" he cried. "Aunt Mabel, you can't mean it! I risked my life for that puppy."

"Exactly. Thank you for admitting it. Now you go to your room without any supper and don't come out until I get you up in the morning."

"Aunt Mabel, please...You can punish me some other way." Heartsickness filled Trey's eyes, shredded his voice. "Please, Aunt Mabel. You can't do this to me."

The bottle finished, Mabel laid the swaddled

puppy in a box of bedding she'd prepared. "I'm afraid I have to, Trey. You need to learn that there are consequences for breaking your word. I'm going to give you one more chance to prove that you can keep it. I want you to promise me that you won't poke your head out or even open that door until breakfast time. I imagine you'll be pretty hungry by then."

"Aunt Mabel..." Trey's plea thinned to a plaintive cry.

"Promise me—right now!"

"Oh, all right. I promise."

"State your promise before God, John, and me."

Trey, hanging his head, said, "I won't open my bedroom door and come out until you call me in the morning."

John, stiff faced and silent as a totem pole, dared not look at Trey. His glance would have given away what they both knew. Trey would be out his bedroom window and on his way to Miss Emma's before his aunt turned the ignition key to her Cadillac—and all done without breaking a word of his promise. She was the sweetest woman in town, but how could she be so...well, dumb?

Aunt Mabel slipped on her coat and anchored her handbag over her shoulder. "John," she said, "I'm guessing you'll be eating your supper with Miss

Emma and her granddaughter tonight. They're having stew, too." John still didn't look at Trey as she picked up the box and deposited it in his unwilling arms. She turned to her nephew. "Trey, go right now to your room and do your homework."

"Yes, ma'am," Trey said.

"And don't you dare slam your door."

"No, ma'am."

John said, "I'll be sure and tell Cathy you got the pup for her, Trey."

"Tell her I hope she likes it," he said, and shuffled off down the hall. They heard his bedroom door close softly.

John said, straight-faced, "I thought he took that pretty well."

"Didn't he though?" Mabel said.

John held the box on his lap while Mabel drove the few blocks to Emma Benson's house. It would be just a matter of time before Trey showed up and horned in—after his aunt had left Miss Emma's, of course—but he, John, would be the first to see Cathy's face when she saw the collie puppy. Next to her, he was the cutest thing John had ever seen. The puppy was asleep now and dreaming, and John could picture the dog's little pink nose nuzzled against Cathy's soft cheek and her eyes closed in bliss from the velvety feel of him, like girls do. He felt a pang of betrayal for being glad that Trey wouldn't have first crack at Cathy's gratitude and sorrow for Aunt Mabel's disappointment if she checked on Trey when she got home and found him missing. Maybe she wouldn't. Maybe her trust in him would protect her.

Emma opened the front door before they could knock. "I told Cathy about the puppy," she announced, standing back so they could hurry inside. "That got her on her feet fast. I can't thank you enough, John."

"It was Trey's idea to get her a puppy, Miss Emma."

"He'll be thanked properly when the time comes. How did he take his punishment, Mabel?"

"Very well, actually. He realized he'd over-stepped the line this time. I punished him as you advised—denied him the opportunity to present the puppy in person—and now he's in his room, where he will remain until the morning."

"Uh-huh," Emma said. She patted her friend's shoulder. "Well, I'm proud of you for standing your ground, Mabel. Now, let's have you come meet my granddaughter and Cathy her new companion. She's in the kitchen, stirring the stew. John, you'll stay for supper, of course." She whisked off his ski cap and hung it on a hall tree in the foyer. Neither saw Mabel's lips curve in a small, private smile.

John was sure his hair was standing straight up. Because of the box, he couldn't comb it back in place with his fingers and hoped by some miracle Cathy wouldn't notice. She didn't. She appeared not to see him at all when she turned from the stove, her tender face flushed from heat and the anticipation of what he had brought. She went directly to peer into the box, and John took advantage of the moment to check his reflection in the darkened kitchen window over the sink, nearly choking on his breath when he saw Trey's face staring in. It dropped from view the second his aunt turned to thump his back.

"You okay, John?"

"Fine, just fine, Aunt Mabel. My windpipe got blocked there for a second."

"Ohhhh...,"Cathy cooed, lifting the little ball of fur from his bedding and cuddling him under her chin, every detail of her delight perfectly matching the picture John's imagination had drawn.

Emma looked approvingly at John. "A good move, mister. Pass on my compliments to your sidekick."

"He's so soft and warm," Cathy purred, and kissed the tiny head. "Is he really mine, Grandmother? Mine to keep?"

"Yours to keep," Emma said.

"I've never had a pet before. He's just . . . he's just beautiful."

"Is it all right that he's a boy?" John asked, watching her worriedly. "We didn't know . . ."

"It's perfect that he's a boy." Her gaze swept up to John curiously, and his heart pinched at the definite impression she'd noticed him for the first time. "Where *is* your sidekick?"

"He's doing his homework," Mabel said, "but I know he'll be delighted that you like the puppy. I'm Mabel Church, by the way, Trey's aunt."

"I've heard so many nice things about you," Cathy said, extending her small hand from beneath the blanket, and John thought how polite and grown-up she was as Aunt Mabel shook it. "It's lovely to meet you at last. Thank Trey for me, will you? And John—" She turned to him, and he had trouble with his breath again when she looked into his eyes. "Thank you, too, so much. I just love him."

"Well, on that perfect note, I'll be on my way," Mabel said.

Emma followed her to the door, and John stood awkwardly, his glance going from Cathy's blond head bent over the puppy swaddled in her arms to the kitchen window. John was still holding the box and didn't know where to set it. Three bowls and spoons had been arranged on the table for supper, along with an extra place mat across from where he supposed he was to sit.

He knew who the place mat was laid for when Emma returned to the kitchen and said, "John, poke your head out and tell Trey Don to come in. We don't want him to freeze to death out there."

Chapter Nine

She was sure once her newness wore off, the boys would forget about her. After all, she was a girl and boys did not play with girls. "How long are Trey and John to look after me?" she asked her grand-mother. It was the end of February. The daffodils were up. All their delicate golden heads had broken through the soil, and Rufus had been taught to stay away from them. The boys had helped her train him most afternoons.

"No, no, Rufus!" they would say when they saw him heading for the beds, clapping their hands softly so as not to scare him. "Over here, boy. Over here," and they would pat a tree or coax him to another spot.

"Why? Are you getting tired of them?" her grandmother asked.

"Oh no. I just wondered when they didn't have to be with me anymore."

"If anything was said about a set time, it's passed, sweetheart. The boys like being with you. They enjoy being your friend."

She found it odd having two big boys as her friends, but it was also nice. Without Trey and John, she would have missed Laura and her home even more. Her classmates at Kersey Elementary School were friendly enough, but they were shy of her. It didn't take long for them to notice she was smart. She finished tests before everyone else and read library books when she wasn't working, and the teachers called on her for answers when nobody else knew them and read her themes before the class as an example of how they should be written. The teachers praised the neatness of her papers and her penmanship while she burned with embarrassment under her classmates' sidelong gazes, but not enough to make herself one of them by doing sloppy work.

Trey and John were perfectly comfortable with her and didn't mind that she was "gifted and talented" and wanted to be a doctor and could speak French. They did not think it strange that she sat with her back straight in class and her feet crossed at the ankles. Good posture, she'd been taught, could improve your height.

It was not yet time for baseball season, when the boys would attend practice after school, so they had time on their hands to spend with her. They popped up everywhere, wearing silly grins, trying to make her think they were just passing by and in the neighborhood. It was not unusual to see them stroll into the county library, where her grandmother worked, if the bus dropped Cathy there after school, or in the park where she'd taken Rufus, or at the First Baptist Church, where her grandmother had arranged for her to practice on the piano in the sanctuary. They seemed to manufacture every excuse and invitation to be with her.

"Trey and I need help with math, Cathy. Is it okay if we come to your house after school?"

"Of course, John."

"My aunt has an attic full of old hunting trophies. Want to see them, Catherine Ann?"

"I'd love to, Trey."

"Let's play Frisbees with Rufus after school today. What do you say?"

"Fine with me, boys."

"Aunt Mabel has a sack of old lettuce for Sampson. Mind if we feed it to him?"

"What a splendid idea."

She expected they'd be gone by the time the daffodils died, but they were not.

One afternoon they found her morose. "What's the matter?" John asked, sitting down beside her on the front porch swing of her grandmother's house. Trey took the other side, next to Rufus.

"My daddy did not leave any money for my care, and now I'm a financial burden on my grandmother," she said.

"Ah, how do you know?" Trey asked.

Cathy related her grandmother's conversation with Miss Mabel she'd overheard. "As I suspected, Sonny was completely broke when he died," Emma had confided when she'd thought Cathy was out of the house. "They lived entirely beyond their means, and their lifestyle was supported on credit. He let his life insurance premiums lapse, and everything was mortgaged to the hilt. The money from the sale of the house and possessions will go to his creditors. There's nothing left."

She had gone on to say that now she'd really have to watch her pennies to provide properly for Cathy, but she would manage. She still had Buddy's insurance money put away and that would help toward college expenses. She'd ask the county to waive the retirement age for her job, and so what if she didn't take the trip to England she'd planned?

Cathy had already realized her grandmother did not have much money. She never failed to check the prices of things and served leftovers and turned off lights when they weren't needed—things Cathy's family never had bothered to do. It hurt her dreadfully to know her grandmother would have to give up things because of her.

"She loves you, Catherine Ann," John said. "That will make her sacrifices easier."

"Yeah," Trey said. "You're better to spend money on than a dumb ol' trip to England."

A warmth spread through her, easing her hurt. Sometimes she felt like a valley sitting between the boys. They blocked the wind and storms like friendly mountains. "You really think so?"

"*Yes!*" the boys said together.

They were as different from each other as bacon and eggs, but they went together as nicely. John was quiet and calm, patient and steady. He blended in. Trey was someone who stood out. You knew he was there—in the classroom, hallways, cafeteria, school bus. You couldn't miss him. "Tempestuous," she'd heard his aunt describe him, and Cathy agreed. Her grandmother had explained that Trey's brash attitude was a shield against the hurt and humiliation of his parents not wanting him. If his uncle had lived, Trey might have grown up a different boy. Harvey Church had been a man's man, a big-game hunter and fisherman who would have taken him in hand, and Trey was of the nature who would have adored him for doing it. But four months after Trey had come to live with them, his hale and hearty uncle had died unexpectedly of a heart attack and Trey had been left in the sole care of a retiring aunt ill-equipped to handle a precocious, willful nephew.

And poor John's mother had died when he was seven, leaving him to the mercy of his hard-drinking father.

So Trey's remark had been right that day in Miss Whitby's class. They were all orphans one way or the other, and that created a special bond among them. Without Trey and John, she couldn't have endured attending Kersey Elementary School.

The winter thawed to spring, and the trio turned twelve. For two weeks in March, Trey was older than John. Trey looked upon the fourteen-day age difference as a cause for celebration at least in his own mind, for it gave him some sort of edge over his friend.

The boys were shooting up in height, and—just as Cathy was losing her little-girl shape—so maturity was slowly chiseling the boyishness from their features. To mark their last year of innocence, Mabel decided to honor Trey's and John's birthdays by throwing a party in her backyard. It was the first time Cathy had ever seen John's father, Bert Caldwell. She knew he worked in the oil fields and was gone much of the time. John never spoke of him and spent the days he was at home at Miss Mabel's. He drank heavily when he was "between rigs." He arrived at the party sober and clean-shaven, wearing starched jeans and a crisp long-sleeved white shirt, party attire for Kersey's "menfolks," as Cathy's grandmother referred to them. He was shorter and stockier than John, burlier of features, and John was wary in his presence, as Mr. Caldwell appeared uneasy in his. Cathy felt sorry for both of them. Didn't Mr. Caldwell know how lucky he was to have a son like John, and couldn't John realize how fortunate he was to have a father?

To celebrate her birthday in April, her grandmother invited Laura to come for a visit over spring break, a time that corresponded with the promised arrival of the prairie's wildflowers. "What in the world—?" her best friend, fashionably dressed in a suit and matching tam, exclaimed the second she saw Cathy in the waiting room of the Amarillo airport.

Cathy aborted the hug she'd intended to give her and drew her jean jacket tighter. "This is what they wear here."

Only Trey and John softened Laura's appalled impression of her new home and environment.

"They're gorgeous," she said. "I could endure cactus and cockleburs for *them*."

Laura was the kindliest girl Cathy knew. She did not mean her pity for Cathy's reduced circumstances to hurt her feelings or awaken longings for her parents and Winchester and her old classmates and the pretty house and neighborhood where she grew up.

John sensed her blue mood immediately once Laura had gone. "You miss her, don't you?" he said. It was her first time to witness John and Trey almost come to blows.

"Yes," she said, "and the way it used to be."

"Listen to me, Catherine Ann," Trey ordered, stepping in front of her as if his height and size, like a barrier before the sun, might block all thoughts of her former life. "We're your friends now. You like it here. Tell us you don't want to go back where you came from."

"Let her be, TD," John said, pulling at Trey's jacket sleeve.

"*No!*" Trey jerked at his arm, jealousy and panic tightening his face, Cathy recognized. "You don't want to leave us, do you, Catherine Ann?"

"I—" Tears welled, spilled down her cheeks. Her throat constricted from an agony of memories—visits to the beach with her parents, piano recitals, trips to museums and concerts in days filled with warm sunshine and cool sea breezes—and she could not give him the answer he wanted to hear.

"Now see what you've gone and done?" John confronted Trey angrily. "You've made her lose her voice. It's okay, Cathy. You can miss Laura and how it used to be all you want."

"Shut up, John!" Trey shoved at his friend. "It's definitely not okay. You're going to talk her into leaving us."

John shoved back, fixing Trey with a furious, dark-eyed look that made Cathy step between them before punches could fly. She had never seen John angry before. "Boys! Boys! I'm not going anywhere," she said, startled out of her despondency. "How could I go off and leave my grandmother and you and Rufus?"

Trey cut his angry gaze away from John back to her. "Promise?" he said, and she could see the fires slowly banking in his eyes.

"I promise."

"It's still okay to be sad, Cathy," John said with another look at Trey that dared him to dispute it.

The near fracas had brought home to Cathy the surprising importance she had assumed in their lives, and she decided to keep to herself the plans that she and Laura had made to reunite at the University of Southern California, where they would pursue their dreams of becoming doctors.

Chapter Ten

The children entered their teens, and Emma and Mabel often discussed and kept an eye out for changes in the trio's relationship. It was just a matter of time before the boys discovered Cathy's developing breasts, and how could Cathy miss their burgeoning biceps? For the moment, they were simply friends. When Trey and John weren't playing sports, they came home with Cathy after school and roughhoused with Rufus. Most evenings, they did their homework together and sometimes the boys even sat in on Cathy's home-schooled lessons. Often they stayed for supper, which both loved. John had to get his own meals at his house, and Trey much preferred Emma's delicious cooking to Mabel's notoriously tasteless fare. They even continued to show up at the First Baptist Church to hear Cathy play the piano.

They never seemed to tire of her and were proud that she knew things that she could teach them, like how to set a splint and speak French. Both women loved to hear them practice the few phrases they'd learned at their supper tables and which, of course, they flaunted to their friends in the school cafeteria.

"Passe-moi le sel, s'il te plaît, Trey." *(Pass the salt, if you please, Trey.)*

"Avec plaisir, mon amie. Et le poivre aussi?" *(It is my pleasure, my friend. Pepper also?)*

"Oui, s'il te plaît." *(Yes, if you please.)*

"Il me plaît." *(I please.)*

Would their unit dissolve of its own accord as the boys responded to the natural temptations of other girls who were now beginning to throw themselves at them? Emma wondered. Where would that leave Cathy? Her granddaughter had still not made close friends among the girls in her class. She had acquaintances among those of her gender in Sunday School and the junior high band, but none had become a bosom pal to spend time with after school.

Or would their friendship take a predictable turn that would leave John in the cold, for it was clear to everyone that Trey was sweet on Cathy, except perhaps to Cathy. And, of course, what everyone but

Trey could see was that John was keen on Cathy, too. Would a possible triangle develop that would lead to its own set of hurts and concerns?

The women watched and waited as the children's birthdays came and went, and the three remained inseparable, their union unsullied.

"What *is* it about Cathy that has Trey so enraptured with her, especially given the way she feels about football?" Emma demanded of Mabel. "John I can understand. In Cathy, he recognizes a fellow pilgrim...mind of his mind, heart of his heart, but Trey Don? Do you suppose it's the orphan thing they share in common?"

"Without a doubt, but I believe Trey sees in Cathy as well as in John what he lacks in himself. He's too young to realize it, of course, but he's like a sapling in the forest that instinctively reaches for the sun to survive."

"What are you talking about, Mabel Church?"

"I'm talking about integrity," Mabel answered. "The plain, old-fashioned kind inherent to Cathy and John, whereas it isn't to Trey. He has to be led by example. It took me a long time to recognize it, but I'm proud of Trey for desiring the sun when he more naturally could seek the shade."

Emma pondered Mabel's remarks and decided that, despite the fanciful wording, she had hit the nail on the head. Of course, John and Trey had enough in common to be twins and what red-blooded American boy wouldn't be enamored with Cathy, but Emma agreed with Mabel that those reasons alone did not account for Trey's special need of them. It all boiled down to his admiration of their trustworthiness (though where Cathy got hers Emma had yet to determine). Trey recognized he operated better—and was safer—in the light of their influence. Emma thought Mabel had every right to be proud of her nephew, since with his increasing good looks and athletic talent, intelligence and charm, he could get away with, and be forgiven for, just about anything with anybody. She worried only that Trey's unswerving trust in Cathy and John made him vulnerable to disappointment—and her granddaughter and John open to its consequences. All human beings were subject to falling below others' expectations, and Trey was of the particular bent that, once betrayed, there would be no rescuing of the ties that once bound. Still, despite awakening hormones and developing figures, their union continued unmarred and unbroken.

And then the spring of their sixteenth year arrived.

Chapter Eleven

He was sick. There was no doubt about it. He was running a fever, and his jaws had swollen. Trey couldn't imagine what was wrong with him, but he mustn't tell Coach Turner. Coach would send him home. It was the first day of spring football practice, and he might miss the scrimmage Friday night when he could give his coach something to look forward to over the coming summer: a starting quarterback with a wide receiver who just might over the next two years lead the team to state. Coach needed something to lighten up his life, with a sick wife at home and a daughter who gave him fits. Besides, a recruiter from the University of Miami in Florida would be in the stands Friday to watch him and John strut their stuff, and without sufficient practice he might flub their chances of a scholarship offer to play for the Miami Hurricanes.

He could beat this; he knew he could. Drink lots of water and other fluids, get rest. It was a virus or something that had settled in his teeth. His gums were red and irritated. Or it could be an abscessed wisdom tooth like Cathy had extracted last year. He'd take aspirin and swish his teeth with mouthwash to give him some relief, and at the end of the week he'd go to the dentist.

This was one period on the calendar he'd never forget. For starters, it was one of the few times in his life he'd been sick. He'd missed most of the childhood diseases and wasn't prone to catching colds or flu or getting upset stomachs, and Friday, last day before spring break, he'd asked Catherine Ann to be his girl. He'd always felt something different toward her from just friendship, ever since his first sight of her that freezing January day when she ran out of her house to check on her snow queen, but never anything like the moment that particular feeling became something else—when he wanted her to be more than a special best friend. It had happened one day in early spring when she walked into English class. She was wearing a new sweater in "azure blue," so he was told, a color that set off her hair and skin and the irises of her eyes, and his heart had stalled in mid-beat. The smile she'd flashed him had faded in concern, and she asked as she took her seat, "What's wrong?" He had no breath to answer. The way he'd always thought of her had vanished as suddenly and completely as the boy's make-believe playmate in the song "Puff, the Magic Dragon." His once-upon-a-time feeling for her was simply over. The Catherine Ann he knew had disappeared. *A dragon lives forever, but not so little boys*...or little girls.

He hadn't known what to do with his new way of thinking about her. It saddened him really. If he did anything about it, he believed he'd be giving up something that would not come to him again. The special world he and John and Cathy had created just for the three of them would never be the same.

He'd thought it over for some time, weighing what he would lose and what he would gain, but she grew prettier by the day, and the upper-class boys were sniffing around her—guys he had no sway over—and he knew he must act.

"I want to ask Catherine Ann to go steady with me," he told John.

"You already are going steady with her, TD."

"No-no. That's not how I mean."

"You mean you want Cathy all to yourself—without me in the equation."

The word *equation*, spoken in John's quiet, serious way, leaped out from memory. *Wolf Man's word!* Trey had forgotten it, but John had remembered. Now he understood the man's meaning. But... John not in the equation? Hell no, that wasn't what he meant at all! John was his buddy. He was like the stake his aunt tied her tomato plants to—not that he felt he couldn't stand on his own, but John was his support system, even when half the time they were at odds over something.

"That came out wrong," he'd protested. "I mean that I want her to go steady with me in a different way. You know, wear my letter jacket. We'll hang out like we always have—you and me and Catherine Ann—but she'll be my girl and your friend. That is okay with you, isn't it? You love her like a brother, but I love her like...a girl. You do think of her like a sister, don't you?"

"Sure I do," John had said. "Cathy's...the sunshine in my day." He'd punched his shoulder in a brotherly way. "You're the dark cloud."

He'd grinned back. "I knew it'd be all right with you, but I wanted to make sure. Catherine Ann loves you, too, you know—just in a different way."

"I know, TD."

He'd asked her Saturday night in front of Miss Emma's after they'd dropped John off at his house.

They were sitting in Trey's new Mustang that Aunt Mabel had bought him for his birthday. "Catherine Ann, I want to ask you something," he'd said.

She'd turned her blue eyes on him. "Okay."

"Uh…" He'd had to swallow, hoping she wouldn't notice. "I don't know exactly how to say this."

"Say what?"

"Say how I feel about you."

"I know how you feel about me."

"No, no, I don't mean like—like you're thinking." Hot with embarrassment under her steady blue gaze, he wished he hadn't brought up the subject until he was sure she felt the same way about him. They'd never even held hands, let alone kissed! She liked him, he was sure of that, but did she *need* him like he needed her? She was so…so *independent*!

"That is," he said, "I want…you to go with me and…only me, like in…go steady, but only if you want to, Catherine Ann. I don't want to…ruin anything between us."

She'd smiled and shocked the bejesus out of him by scooting closer to him and wrapping her arms around his neck. They were soft and fragrant as flower petals, and her face was like an angel's, framed by hair so blond and silky, he could have melted in it. She'd stared straight into his eyes. "I already am going steady with you," she said softly. "Didn't you notice?" She had the look she sometimes got when she pointed out the answer to a calculus problem staring him and John in the face.

His reply had stuck at the back of his throat, but he found his arms going around her, and, small as she was, her body filled them as if it had been made for them. "I'm...afraid I didn't," he said, sounding as if he had a bad case of laryngitis.

"Now that you have, don't you think you ought to kiss me?"

"I...would really like that," he said, and when he pressed her lips it was like dissolving into the deliciousness of a chocolate cake.

And that was that. As easily as his boat's sails catching the wind, they were under way, and he felt no sadness at all.

He pulled on his helmet behind the players grouped around Coach Turner in the locker room. Usually he sat with John at the front to hear Coach's last instructions before heading for the field and he never put on his headgear until he trotted out to the huddle, but he couldn't risk one of the coaching staff noticing his jaws. Only Cathy knew he wasn't quite up to par, but he'd made her swear she wouldn't tell his aunt or John. He'd ride this out on his own until spring practice was over.

*　　*　　*

FROM WHERE SHE SAT WITH Rufus near the top row of the bleachers, Cathy looked down in concern on the field where Trey and John were practicing their pass and catch routine. "You never throw directly at a quarterback in practice," the boys had enlightened her in one of the many sessions in which they'd tried to explain the game of football to her. "You could injure or break his thumb. You pass it to somebody *beside* him who then hands it *to* the quarterback."

"Oh." That explained why they no longer played throw and catch in the center aisle of the First Baptist Church while she practiced the piano.

Today she was worried about more than Trey's thumb. He should not be down there. He should be in a dentist's chair. The pain in his jaw must be killing him in that tight, hot helmet, but not for the world would he have disappointed Coach Turner, who was depending on Trey taking the starting quarterback's position next season. If she'd been with Trey Saturday, when his tooth flared up, she would have insisted he see his dentist, but after their watershed date Friday night she'd taken off early the next morning to a Baptist retreat for girls in Amarillo for the weekend.

"Don't you forget about me while you're there,"

he'd said, disappointed that he wouldn't be seeing her the next day.

"As if I could," she said.

Sunday night, as promised when she returned, she'd telephoned him and heard a difference in his voice that worried her. Had he regretted asking her to go steady? But he explained that he was down with a toothache and wouldn't be good company if he came over. He'd see her the next night, he said, and made her promise she wouldn't say anything about his tooth problem to anybody, including her grandmother, who would then mention it to his aunt. "Promise me, Catherine Ann."

"I'll promise if you promise that you'll go to the dentist if it gets worse."

"I promise."

But he obviously hadn't, and from the skill and perfect timing of his surefire passes to John's hands, you'd never guess he had a problem.

Nods of approval came from the western hats and ball caps lined along the wire fence behind the sidelines, reinforced by admiring murmurs from the crowd in the stands. The fence dwellers were fathers of the players and local businessmen, ranchers, and farmers who'd taken off from work on this first day of spring practice to get an idea of what to expect from the Bobcats next fall, and the bleacher sitters were students and teachers and townspeople. Among them was Father Richard, pastor of St. Matthew's Catholic Church, who had driven in from his parish in Delton, the other town in the county and Kersey High's rival—to see his former altar boy perform. John would be pleased when she told him. After his mother died, John had stopped going to mass regularly, but he thought of Father Richard like Trey regarded Coach Turner.

Also down on the sidelines, dressed in their sequined uniforms and shaking their pompoms, were the cheerleaders, led by Cissie Jane Fielding, who was sweet to Cathy's face while she had a dagger at her back. Behind their row, sitting in specially set up bleachers, the Bobettes waved their white and gray streamers. Her two friends Bebe Baldwin, Cissie Jane's best friend, and Melissa Tyson, the county sheriff's daughter, were members, and Cathy waved back when they spotted her in the stands.

Bebe and Melissa had encouraged Cathy to try out for cheerleader—"you'd be a shoo-in"—or at least to join the Bobettes, but she preferred to play flute in the band. She had no interest in leading cheers at sports events or being a member of an organization that catered exclusively to athletes, some so dumb it was a wonder they could tie their shoelaces. Each Bobette was "assigned" an athlete, and it was her responsibility during a sports season—especially football—to make sure her player wanted for nothing. She baked him cookies, decorated his locker, made posters to celebrate his status, helped him with his homework—anything to keep his spirits high. Cathy thought such servility disgusting.

"You're such a feminist!" her friends accused her. "What's your objection? You'd be assigned to Trey!"

"I will be *assigned* to nobody!" Cathy had announced, appalled at the idea.

Coach Turner's daughter, Tara, had been assigned to Trey. She was well developed and had acquired a reputation for being easy, and Trey was embarrassed at her lavish attention and did everything he could to discourage it. Bebe looked after John.

For as many years as Cathy had lived in Texas, she'd never understood the state's delirious enthusiasm for high school football or the importance given to its program over other school activities or achievements. She didn't make a point of it to Trey and John, but they knew she didn't buy into the game. "No problem," John said one night when she confessed she'd never really gotten the hang of a sport whose violent objective was to get a ball over a goal line.

"No problem is right," Trey had said with a grin, and given her a soft cuff on the chin. "That means you love us for who we are, not because we play football."

She gazed down at the pair on the field with a sense of pride and ownership, Rufus beside her, quivering to join them, his attention riveted on their every move. As Laura had commented on photographs of them Cathy had sent in her last letter, they were "beyond cool." Both had shot up to over six feet during the winter and carried 185 pounds of hard, teenage muscle. They'd escaped acne and braces and prescription glasses. They were smart and witty and funny. They made excellent grades, almost tying her for valedictorian last year at the graduation of the ninth-grade class to high school.

But it was their skill on the football field that made them the darlings of the school and heroes of the town. As early as last season, at only fifteen, they'd been looked over by college recruiters, men whose job it was to fill the rosters of their football programs, and Trey and John were counting on being offered football scholarships at the university of their choice by the end of their junior year. Both wanted to attend college where summer never ended, and they dreamed of going to the University of Miami, which had won its first national championship in 1983.

Trey had had it all worked out since eighth grade when he knew she had her heart set on becoming a doctor and attending the University of Southern California with Laura.

"Forget California," he said. "You're coming to Miami with John and me. Miami has a great medical school, and what's the difference between sand and surf in California and the beaches in Florida?" He was obsessed with the idea of the three staying a unit, and as time went on, to her surprise, her grandmother supported his notion. "What does USC's medical school have that the Miller School of Medicine at Miami does not?" she asked. "You'd have a ride to school and home for holidays and summer break, and I'd feel easier knowing the boys were looking out for you."

Cathy had known that last Friday night was coming for some time and had speculated how it would alter the nature of their threesome relationship, since John was always with her and Trey. Other kids she knew were already experimenting with sex, and Cissie Jane, it was rumored, had lost her virginity to last season's captain of the football team. Until last Friday, she and Trey had never even kissed.

Yet, almost since that first day in Miss Whitby's homeroom, she'd felt *linked* to Trey. Not *tethered*, but *connected*. It was as if, no matter where she went, with whom, or what she did, she was the shore and he was the ocean lying at low tide, but always in sight. Why Trey and not John she didn't know. John was a dream, and if she were pressed, she'd have to say she admired and respected him more than Trey. John loved her, too, and in the same way as Trey. Not by word or gesture had John expressed it—he never would—but she knew. Her heart ached for him, but there was an undeniable chemistry between her and Trey that had always been there, quiet and untapped, and lately when she'd catch him watching her from under hooded lids her skin would tingle and she'd feel as if the air had been sucked from her lungs. In those moments, she sensed the ocean stir, move closer to land, and that feeling, too, made her go warm all over. Someday, the tide would surge in and take the beach. It was only a matter of time.

Rufus's ears shot up. There was a disturbance on the field. Somebody was down. Players were gathering around their fallen teammate, and coaches and student trainers ran from the sidelines to elbow their way through the huddle. Murmurs of concern rose from the stands and along the fence. Cathy searched for Trey and John but could spot neither one. Rufus whimpered and would have bounded down the bleachers if she had not grabbed his collar. Suddenly she caught sight of John standing and glancing toward the stands as if looking for her. She waved her hand, and he pointed toward the parking lot where they had left their vehicles. He'd removed his helmet and his expression was bleak. *Oh, my God!* It was Trey who was hurt. He was being helped to his feet. His helmet was off, and even from where she stood, she could see the red and swollen distortion of his face.

Bebe and Melissa turned to look at her in dismay as she snapped Rufus's leash onto his collar. *It's only a toothache,* Cathy told herself. Antibiotics and a strong inflammation-fighting drug would fix him up once the tooth was pulled. Still, she waited beside her grandmother's car with her knuckles to her mouth until the boys finally appeared from the field house—John still in his football gear and Trey in school clothes, escorted by the head coach himself. Apparently, she was to drive Trey home while John returned to practice. There was applause from a large group of concerned adults and students who had gathered to hear firsthand what had happened to their quarterback.

"It's okay, folks!" Coach Turner called to the

group. "Trey's just got a problem with a bad tooth. He'll be back with us in a few days. Let's let Cathy get him home so he can go to the dentist."

Trey gave her a weak smile, all he looked capable of, and Cathy held tight to Rufus's leash to keep him from jumping on him. "I'm sorry to let you down, Coach," Trey mumbled.

Coach Turner laid a hand on the back of Trey's neck and gave it an affectionate squeeze. "You didn't let me down, son. Don't worry. It's not like you've lost your place in line. You'll be back, but not until you're well, okay?"

"Okay," Trey said. He turned to John. "If I don't get back by Friday night, Tiger, you don't need me to show that Miami scout what you got."

"You'll be back, TD."

Cathy was busy loading Rufus into the backseat of the Ford while John helped Trey into the car. Her heart in her throat, she started the motor. "All in?" she managed to ask.

Trey laid his head back and closed his eyes. "All in for sure. Take me home, Catherine Ann."

One of the coaches had already contacted Mabel, and her Cadillac was out of the garage and she was waiting on the front porch when they drove up. "I have Dr. Wilson standing by," she announced. "He'll take care of that tooth in a hurry. Good lord,

Trey, look at you! How did I miss seeing how sick you were?"

"Because I didn't let you see, Aunt Mabel. I thought it would go away." He touched the tip of Cathy's nose, his eyes swimming in pain. "We'll talk tonight, Catherine Ann," he said.

Cathy nodded, and Mabel said, "We'd better go, dear."

"I need a glass of water first, Aunt Mabel."

Inside the house, Mabel said, "Sit down, Trey, and I'll get you that water."

"I don't need water, Aunt Mabel."

"What? But you said—"

"And I don't need a dentist. I need a doctor."

"*What?*"

"It's not my teeth. I've got something going on..."—he dropped his eyes to his groin—"down there."

"MUMPS?" MABEL SAID in surprise when Dr. Thomas delivered his diagnosis.

"That's it. The poor kid thought at first the swelling was due to a problem with his teeth."

Mabel clapped her cheeks. "My baby sister must not have had him immunized when he was an infant. Merciful heavens, I feel terrible that I didn't take more notice, but lately Trey has kept so much to himself, hasn't even taken his meals with me. I just thought he was being a typical teenager. If he'd just said something..."

"Now, don't go blaming yourself, Mabel. What kid getting ready to suit up for spring football practice is going to tell his aunt he's not feeling well—especially the quarterback of the team? He'll have to be quarantined and the school notified, but fortunately, mumps is the least contagious of children's diseases, and it's rare for a youngster to contract mumps at Trey's age." He wrote on a pad. "These prescriptions will ease his pain and get his fever down, and I'm going to give you a sheet of instructions on how to make him more comfortable. Then, in about a year, we'll need to run some tests."

"Tests? What kind of tests?"

The doctor held her eye. "I think you know, Mabel."

Mabel felt the blood leave her head. "Oh, Doctor, you don't think—"

"Let's just make sure, shall we?"

Chapter Twelve

Here, Son, let me do that," Bert Caldwell said to John.

John reluctantly turned from the mirror to allow his father to line up his tuxedo tie, keeping his mouth closed to prevent inhaling Bert's whiskey breath. To John's surprise, the familiar smell was absent, but then occasionally his father stayed sober a few days between jobs. Tonight was one of them. For some reason, he thought the night of his son's high school junior prom reason enough to lay off the bottle, at least until John had left the house.

Bert stepped back to admire his handiwork. "That'll do it," he said. "You need help with the cummerbund?"

"No thanks. I got it," John said, fastening the

pleated sash of maroon silk around his waist. Feeling uncomfortable under his father's gaze, wishing he'd leave, John removed the satin-lapelled jacket from its hanger and slipped it on, turning to adjust the French cuffs of his shirtsleeves in the mirror.

"Not bad for a rented outfit," Bert pronounced. "But I would've bought you one. You'll probably need a tux for certain occasions at Miami."

"That's still over a year away," John said, and granted his father a slight smile. "I may grow another inch or two by then."

Bert nodded and shoved his hands into his pockets. "I suppose so. You look…dashing, Son. I wish your mother were here to see you."

"Me, too," John said.

There was an awkward silence. "Are you sure you don't want to take my car? You're too gussied up to ride in a pickup."

"No thanks. I washed and polished Old Red to a high shine, vacuumed the seats. It'll be good enough."

"Well then—" Bert removed a number of bills from his wallet. "Take these. You'll want to have enough on a night like tonight. It comes only once in your life."

John slipped his own wallet into the coat of the

tuxedo. "That's okay. I don't need it. Everything's already prepaid."

"Take it anyway." Bert thrust the bills at him. "I'd feel better knowing you had some extra cash."

John took the offering. "Thank you," he said simply.

The two men's gazes intersected for a fraction of a second, Bert having to lift his a couple of inches. "This girl you're taking to the prom...what's her name again?" he asked.

John had never told him her name, but he said, "Bebe Baldwin."

"Her dad owns the filling station off Main."

"That's right."

"She's one of them Bobettes."

"Right again."

"Well, she's a lucky girl. I imagine a couple of football studs like you and Trey could have your pick of the litter."

"I'm lucky. Bebe is a nice girl."

Bert's nod conceded that the claim was probably so. "I'm sure," he said. "Well, you kids enjoy yourselves. Drive carefully." He flicked two fingers from his forehead in a Panhandle salute and left the room.

John noted the shuffle and slumped shoulders

and felt a pinch of pity for him. There were some things you could never make right again, no matter how much you'd like to begin anew. That day of nine years ago John might have made go away if his father had mended his ways, if his moments of sad regret didn't come between floozies and drinking bouts that turned him into a monster capable of whipping an eight-year-old boy into a welt.

He threw the money on the bureau and swept a comb through his hair again, annoyed at his father for jimmying loose the memory of that afternoon nine years ago. John's mother had been gone a year when he'd come home from school and found a strange woman in bed with his father. "Why didn't you knock, you goddamned little bastard!" Bert had roared, throwing back the covers, and John was not able to make it to safety before Bert had yanked a belt from his pants tossed on a chair.

Trey heard the commotion. He and John always walked home together, and thank God Trey had gotten only to the gate and guessed what was going on. He flew to the next-door neighbor's home to call Sheriff Tyson and then ran back to tear through the house screaming, "Stop it! Stop it!" He threw his body between John and the belt and took a few licks himself before the floozy blonde warned his father that a squad car had pulled up. The next thing John knew, the sheriff and his deputy had slammed into the house and Deke Tyson was ordering his father to put down the belt.

"The hell I will. This is my house, Deke. I can do anything I damn well please in it."

"Maybe so, but not to your son."

"*My son!* Hell, he ain't my son. He's some bastard's who screwed my wife when I was out on a rig!"

Silence fell like a stone. Sheriff Tyson and the deputy looked curiously from Bert to John and saw what John had suddenly realized. He looked nothing like his black-haired, blue-eyed father. Trey, wide-eyed, let out a delighted yelp. "Hey, that's cool, John! He's not your old man. You got no parents, either."

John had gotten to his feet unsteadily, all four feet of him. He stared up at his father, who was biting his lip, averting his eyes. "You're not my dad?"

Bert Caldwell threw down the belt. "Forget I said that. You got my name, ain't you?"

"You're not my father?"

Bert spat on the floor. "I shouldn't have said that."

"But you did."

"Don't sass me! I didn't say that. I said it's hard to believe you're my kid sometimes. That's what I said."

"*Liar!*" Trey yelled, going for Bert's knees.

109

Sheriff Tyson had intervened, taking Trey gently by the shoulders and passing him to his deputy. Deke Tyson was a tall, powerfully built man, a former Green Beret, and John saw that even in Bert's drunken stupor, he knew better than to tangle with him. "We're taking John with us tonight, Bert," Deke said. "You sober up, and we'll talk in the morning."

John had an idea what they'd talked about. In the Texas Panhandle, a county sheriff had pretty much a free hand to do what he had to do to protect the citizens of his jurisdiction, a license Deke Tyson wouldn't have hesitated to take to safeguard a child. John's father never laid another hand on him again.

But he carried the faint scars still...both on his back and in his heart, and he never felt the same about the man who had raised him.

John pocketed the comb, made sure of his keys, and settled the florist box containing a carnation corsage under his arm. He shouldn't be recalling bad memories on a night like tonight. He had other unpleasant thoughts to occupy his mind. Tonight Trey planned to make a move on Cathy.

"What do you think, John? Don't you think it's time?" Trey had asked John earlier in the week after telling him that he'd reserved a motel room in Delton.

John had bent down to tie his shoe. They were

in the field house, just showered and dressed after running laps around the track.

The muscles of his jaws tensed when he finally said, "There's only one way to find out, TD, and the sooner the better considering that we're all planning on going to Miami together next year. But why after the prom? Cathy will be in her finery, her hair done up in a fancy do. And if you two don't go to the breakfast afterwards, everybody will know where you are, what you're doing. They'll talk. You have to think of Cathy's reputation."

"What's there to think about? Everybody knows she's my girl and always will be. I'm going to *marry* her once we're out of college."

"That's a long way away, Trey. A lot can happen between now and then."

"*Nothing* is going to happen to us. Nothing can. I won't let it." Frustration darkened his face. "I can't keep myself from her much longer, John. I'll have to have her or stop going with her, and I'd rather die than give her up."

"Have you discussed this with Cathy?"

"Which part?"

"Both, TD, for God's sake. Does she know that you're hurting for her and the consequences if she doesn't play ball?"

"You make it sound like I'm *threatening* her!"

"Well, aren't you?"

"No, dammit! Jesus, John, I thought you'd understand. If you were in love with somebody as much as I am with Catherine Ann, you'd know the hell I'm going through."

John said nothing for a few minutes. He opened his locker door to take out his latest varsity letter jacket, the sleeves covered in sewn-on badges of sports in which he'd qualified and excelled. Trey had one like it, but it hung in Cathy's closet, far too big for her, and he wore last year's version. John hoped his cheeks weren't burning. He knew exactly the hell that Trey was going through.

"Have you thought of Miss Emma?" John asked. "She'll wait up for Cathy and know the minute she lays eyes on her what you guys have been up to."

"That's why we're going to a motel. She can fix herself up afterwards, and her grandmother will never know the difference."

Don't bet on it, John had thought. "Why haven't you told Cathy how you feel?" he asked.

"Because I don't want to scare her."

"Cathy doesn't scare easily."

"I know, and I guess that's what scares *me*—explains why I've waited so long. We're close, but would she want to become...intimate? What if she...doesn't want me like I want her?"

"Just because she doesn't want to have sex now doesn't mean she doesn't love you or will not want it later. We're only seventeen. Cathy might be afraid of becoming pregnant."

Trey twirled the knob of the combination lock to secure his locker, a muscle jumping along his jawline. "I'm not going to let that happen."

"How can you prevent it? Condoms aren't all that guaranteed—not with the workout you probably give 'em." Trey had been initiated into gymnastic sex by a popular senior cheerleader when he was a sophomore, their secret carried safely away with her when she left for Texas Christian University in the fall. John knew of two other girls Trey had known sexually—high school students from Delton. News of his sorties had never drifted back to Cathy. John wondered what would have happened if it had. Would she have been jealous, hurt, outraged? Would she have dumped Trey and turned to him? Or would she have looked upon Trey's canters off the range not as a breach of trust or faithlessness but as his way of protecting her from him until she was ready? It was hard to tell. Beyond being an open book when it came to certain things—like attitudes and principles and her strong self-image, for instance—Cathy wasn't easy to read, or anticipate. Of the three of them, she was the most mature.

She may look small and defenseless, but physical size didn't matter when you had the strength of a healthy self-esteem, and Trey had yet to test that in Cathy.

"Those girls mean nothing to me, John," Trey had assured him. "The only girl who means anything to me or ever will is Catherine Ann. She's my world, my life, my heart. I couldn't breathe without her. I've tried to. I've thought of what it would be like to…cool it with her for a while, sample the field, but then I think of what it would be like to lose her…." His voice had trailed off and he'd stared into space like a shell-shocked war veteran.

John had a pretty good idea of what it would be like to lose Cathy, worse than loving her from afar, but she'd gravitated toward Trey from the start, the reason he'd never given away by so much as the twitch of an eyebrow how he felt about her.

He tried one last argument. "Don't you think you ought to tell Cathy your plans beforehand—give her a chance to say, 'Some other time'?"

Trey made a fist and struck the locker door. "That's so *like* you, John—to give people an *opportunity* to reject what in your gut you know is best for them."

There was no point in trying to make Trey see that what he perceived as best for someone else was really best for him, especially when most of the time his gut was right.

Which was why John hoped with all his heart that whatever went on between Trey and Cathy after the prom tonight, they were both ready for it.

Chapter Thirteen

Trey checked his reflection for one last time in the floor mirror in his aunt's bedroom. Too tall to get a full view, he bent down to make sure his black tie was aligned with his matching cummerbund. He hadn't particularly looked forward to wearing a monkey suit to the prom—too much to get out of—but he did look pretty sharp in it, and the girls would go wild over him. He hoped Cathy was one of them.

He took another handkerchief from his drawer, not from the box of crisp new linen ones that his aunt had insisted on buying when they went to select his tuxedo—"you simply can't carry along an everyday handkerchief in the pocket of your tuxedo, Trey, dear"—but from the stack of his old ones. His forehead was damp, an outward manifestation of his nerves. The tension in his gut annoyed him, since his looks told him that not a girl alive would be able to resist him tonight.

But his looks might have no effect on Cathy. She simply didn't fall for the things that grabbed other girls. She wasn't like any other girl he knew, period. Other girls were good-looking. They were fun-loving and loose with their favors. They bounced and jounced and flirted and flipped their hair and batted their lashes and he smiled back, but none had a lock on his heart like Cathy. The first time he heard the song "My Funny Valentine" sung was by Frank Sinatra crooning forth from one of Aunt Mabel's old long-playing records. The lyrics had made him think of Cathy. She played in the band, a flute, and wore a uniform a size too big for her small build and a hat that forced her to tilt her head back in order to see under the brim when she marched in the halftime activities. But like everything else she did, she stayed in step and never missed a beat of the maneuvers. She hated that she wasn't tall and regarded her less-than-medium height as a physical imperfection, but to him, she was just right. She was his funny valentine, and he wouldn't have wanted her any other way.

But now he wished he'd tested the waters more

for some indication of her willingness to go along with his hopes for tonight. It wasn't that they didn't make out, but it was done on a...well, *spiritual* level—a special plane reserved only for them, and that was very satisfying, too. He'd been content with those times when they studied or watched television or Rufus's antics together, their thighs touching, his arm around her, now and then kissing but never making it something heavier. There was just nothing like those delicious, goose-bump moments when their eyes caught in a crowd, or in passing she brushed her hand over his shoulder, the back of his neck, straightened his collar, carelessly, like you do something that is yours, and he felt more intimately connected to her—more physically fulfilled—than when he made out with another girl in the backseat of his Mustang.

There had been something exciting about waiting—like a cake you want to bite into but don't want to spoil its frosting.

So he hadn't pushed it. The time would come, he'd thought. And now it had. He loved her. He loved her until it hurt, and he'd come to a point in their relationship where he needed to express that love and feel hers for him. Wasn't that the whole point of sex? But if her feeling for him wasn't the same...The fear that it wasn't almost nauseated him, but he had to know, and he intended to find out tonight.

He wiped his forehead and shoved the handkerchief into another pocket. He'd use that one and save the linen one for Cathy if she should need it.

"Trey Don? Are you ready for your close-up?" his aunt asked, coming into the room. "I've got the camera ready."

"Ready as I'll ever be," he said, certain his aunt would miss the irony. He turned from the mirror. "How do I look?"

"Simply too smashing," Mabel said. "When did my little nephew grow up to be such a tall, dark, and impossibly handsome man?"

It wasn't her fault, but "my little nephew" added further play on his nerves. It should have been "my little son." Lately, he'd been thinking of his parents a lot, wondering where they were, if he'd ever see them again, if they'd be proud to learn he was among the top "blue-chip" high school quarterbacks in the state and that he had earned almost a four-point grade average. Aunt Mabel was close-mouthed on the subject of his parentage, but he figured his father had gotten his mother pregnant out of wedlock and wanted no part of her or her kid. He gathered his mother was the flighty sort who didn't have a maternal bone in her body, so she'd given him as a gift to Aunt Mabel and his uncle, who couldn't have children. That possibility made Trey feel better than believing his mother hadn't wanted him.

He felt guilty mooning for his deadbeat parents when Aunt Mabel had been so good to him. As an orphan, he'd had a better go of it than John, even better than Cathy, though Miss Emma loved her dearly. John's father—or whatever you wanted to call him—wasn't worth the cost of an ounce of cat meat as a dad, and Miss Emma struggled financially to provide for Cathy. Aunt Mabel had been left well off by Trey's uncle, who'd owned a farm equipment business, the reason she could buy Trey a tuxedo while John, who allowed Bert Caldwell to pay only for the essentials, had to rent his suit with money he'd earned as a bag boy at Affiliated Foods over Christmas vacation.

Scholarships would be a godsend to all of them, the only way Cathy could go to premed school and John earn a business degree and he get out from under his aunt's financial generosity. And they would all do it together. They'd get their college diplomas, he and Cathy would marry, he'd shoot for the NFL, and if that didn't work, he'd fall back on his own business degree, and they'd all live happily ever after.

But first, there was tonight. "Shoot away, Aunt Mabel," he said. "This will be one evening I'll want to remember."

"You're not double-dating with John and Bebe?" Emma asked Cathy. "Why not?"

Behind the towel she'd used to screen her face from the cloud of hair spray Emma was applying to her party do, Cathy said, "I'm assuming because John wants to be alone with Bebe."

"Since when?" demanded Emma. "You've always double-dated."

"Well, I guess since they've...become tighter," Cathy answered. "We'll see them at the dance and sit with them at breakfast afterwards."

"And after that, you're coming straight home, right?"

Cathy dropped the towel from her face, and Emma's breath caught. Her granddaughter was ravishing. She was wearing makeup for the first time, and her mass of luxuriant curls was clipped away from her face by a set of rhinestone barrettes that matched the floor-length gown of blue chiffon they'd selected from Lillie Rubin's Evening Wear in Amarillo. The barrettes had been the saleswoman's suggestion and cost the earth, but seeing how perfectly they set off the dress and Cathy's blond hair, Emma was glad they'd been added to the bill.

"Of course I'm coming straight home," Cathy said. "Where else would I go?"

"You and Trey...you don't..." Emma gestured helplessly. "Well, you know..."

"Yes, I believe I do know," Cathy said with an amused smile, "and no-o-o-o, Grandmother, Trey and I are not doing it. We have a tacit understanding to wait until we're older and more ready for that sort of thing."

More ready? Emma set down the can of hair spray. Trey had been ready for a long time and he'd done something about it, but she was certain it hadn't been with Cathy. A boy got a look about him when he'd lost his virginity. Emma had raised two sons, so she knew. She was surprised that Cathy hadn't seen it, but then maybe she had and chose to ignore it. A lot went on in that smart head of hers that Emma wasn't privy to, but her granddaughter was so focused on getting into medical school—her chemistry teacher already called her Dr. Benson— that she appeared blind to about everything that other girls her age would have spotted in an instant.

"Sweetheart," Emma said, clearing her throat, "if you and Trey ever decide you're...ready, you know what to do, don't you?"

"You mean like in preventing myself from getting pregnant?"

"That's exactly what I mean."

"Sure I do. I'd simply take the pill."

"Ah, well now," Emma said, taken aback, "that's mature thinking."

Cathy smiled at her. "Don't worry, Grandmother. I've known about the birds and bees for a long time."

The doorbell rang. "There's Trey," she announced, flashing a wide, delighted smile that made her eyes sparkle. "I can't wait to see him in his tuxedo!"

"I'll let him in," Emma said hurriedly. "You take a final twirl before the mirror."

Emma opened her front door. *Good lord!* The boy was enough to make her drop her own knickers, perish the indecency of the thought. Momentarily speechless, she stepped aside to allow Trey to enter her small living room. "Good evening, Trey. You look...nice."

Trey grinned. "'Nice'? Is that the best I can muster from you, Miss Emma?"

"Your head is big enough," she said, and heard the soft swish of chiffon behind her. She saw Trey's eyes grow large, his mouth slowly open.

Heaven help us, Emma thought.

"Catherine Ann..." Her name foundered in his awe of her. "You're...you're so beautiful...."

"Yes, she is, and she is to be *returned* that way, if you get my meaning, Trey Don Hall," Emma articulated crisply.

"Now, Grandmother...," Cathy scolded with a laugh, and gave Trey a look of mock suffering.

"I get it, Miss Emma," Trey said, his eyes on Cathy. "Trust me, I'll return her to you more beautiful than ever."

Chapter Fourteen

Are you sure, Catherine Ann? We can wait," Trey said, his brows drawn in concern and doubt deepening his dark eyes. "Maybe I should have warned you—"

"I'm glad you didn't," she said. Her heartbeat sounded like tennis shoes thumping in the dryer.

"Would you have...said no?" he asked, the question suspended between hope and despair.

They stood before the door of the room he had reserved, she within the wide space of his shoulders, her head barely reaching the level of his tuxedo tie. He held the room key in his hand, a passport to a moment in their lives from which she knew there would be no going back to the way they were. She swallowed hard and turned to allay her

anxiety by stroking his jaw. "Do you ever give anyone a chance to say no?" she said, smiling softly.
"But no, I wouldn't have said no. I'd have brought
some things along, that's all."

He looked distressed. "Oh, I didn't think of that.
I...brought along a new toothbrush and paste."

"I'm sure that's all I'll need."

He had arranged for the room beforehand and
had even picked up the key so that she would not
have to wait in the car under the harsh lights of
the motel entrance for him to collect it from the
night clerk. There were flowers on the bedside
table and a couple of his aunt's throw pillows on
the bed, the ones Cathy used to support textbooks
when she studied at his house or when Trey laid his
head in her lap. "Won't your aunt miss those?" she
asked.

"I'll think of something to tell her. I thought
they'd make you feel...more at home."

"That was sweet of you, Trey."

"Catherine Ann, I—" He stepped close to her,
and she could see the tension in his throat muscles
as he tried to form his words.

"What, Trey?"

"I love you. I love you with all my heart. I've
loved you since the first second I laid eyes on you
running out of your grandmother's house to see

about your snow queen. I just need to show you how much I do."

"Well, then," she said, slipping her arms up around his neck, "suppose you get started."

"I DON'T WANT TO LET you go," Trey said, taking her face between his hands at Emma's front door hours later. The passionate intensity of the last hours still showed in the deep flush of his face, the fever in his eyes.

"I know," Cathy said softly, "but I have to go in. I'm sure my grandmother is not asleep."

"You think she'll kill me when she sees you? I did promise I'd bring you back more beautiful than before, but I meant—"

"I know what you meant, and I *feel* more beautiful than before."

"You are, if that's possible. You're not sorry?"

"No, Trey. I'm not sorry."

"Will you ever be?"

"Not ever. Good night, *mon amour.*"

She pulled his hands from her face after he kissed her, and they exchanged lingering looks of regret when she stepped inside before he could kiss her again under the porch light for anyone to see who might be up and about at three o'clock in the morning. A small decorative pane was set into the door. After she closed it, he pressed his open hand to the glass and she answered with her own splayed against it. After a while, they broke contact, but Cathy kept the porch light on until she heard his Mustang drive away.

Rufus had come out to greet her in the living room, wagging his tail, his eyes large and questioning, asking, she was sure, *Did it go okay?* She laughed quietly and knelt down in a puff of chiffon to hug his neck. "Yes, yes, it went okay," she said in a whisper bubbling out of her on a tide of happiness. The house was quiet. A light shone in the kitchen, and she went in to find a teapot, cup, saucer, and spoon in the sink, her grandmother's clear message that she had waited up until she was forced to call it a night. Cathy was glad. Her hairdo was wrecked, her makeup gone. There would be enough to answer to in the morning, but for the rest of the night she wanted to be alone to cherish her memories.

In her room, she undressed slowly, touching where Trey's hands had been, feeling him still warm and alive inside her. She'd had a sense that tonight would happen sooner than later, but not after the prom and not in a motel room. That move had come as a complete surprise. Not even when he'd whispered huskily in her ear, "Let's skip breakfast. I have a place reserved just for us," did she suspect what he had in mind. Naïvely, she'd thought that in order to be alone with her he'd planned to take her to Denny's in Delton for pancakes and sausages.

It had all been as natural as a bee finding its rose. There had been nothing self-conscious or awkward about undressing in front of each other. It was as if they'd been hanging up their clothes together all their lives. Their eyes had never left each other's until every piece of clothing was removed, and then he had drawn her to the bed, his eyes devouring her, but in the most reverent and caring way. "Catherine Ann...," he murmured, over and over like a prayer as he held and caressed her, and his body had felt so *right*, so *perfect*, next to hers that she'd hardly noticed the prick of pain in the moment the ocean had surged to the shore and sand and sea became one. It had been so wonderful that afterwards she'd been astonished—horrified—to feel wetness on her cheek and had turned in his arms to see tears on his face. "Trey!" she'd exclaimed, her heart seizing. "What's the matter?"

"Nothing," he said, clutching her fiercely to him. "Nothing is the matter. It's just that I...don't feel like an orphan anymore."

EMMA HEARD CATHY COME IN and tiptoe down the hall to her room, Rufus following behind, his nails clicking on the hardwood floor, making stealth impossible. Emma had been awake all night, the blinds of a window open to allow her to see the stars. A night sky of stars was comforting, for some reason. She had a habit of looking at them when she was troubled as she was now. Maybe *sad* better described her feelings. It had happened. She was sure of it. Her granddaughter had been deflowered. A grandmother sensed these things. Cathy and Trey had not gone to the breakfast hosted by the Kiwanis Club after the prom. One of the sponsors had called, concerned when the belle and beau of the ball had not shown up. If what Emma feared had happened, Monday morning, first thing, she'd make an appointment with Dr. Thomas for Catherine Ann to get a prescription for birth control pills.

MABEL CHECKED HER ALARM CLOCK. Three fifteen in the morning. Trey was home. Her bedroom was next to the garage, and she'd heard him drive in. She felt depressed. Often when he was gone from the house, she checked his room for contraband—things like drugs, girly magazines, alcohol, lurid diaries—all for the responsible purpose of knowing what was going on in her nephew's life. She'd found the box of condoms long ago, tucked into a desk drawer, and drawn a sigh of relief. Trey had refused her pleas to go back for the tests Dr. Thomas had recommended, and Mabel had never felt her lack of influence over her nephew more. "When I'm ready," he told her, but at least he was taking precautions against a favorable prognosis. From time to time, the number of condoms had decreased, but never when he had a date with Cathy. Tonight there were several missing.

She hoped Trey had been gentle with Cathy and that he would continue to love her as he always had, but her nephew was of such a mercurial nature. However, Cathy had a hold on him that no other girl was likely ever to have. Cathy was one of a kind, the kind he required to make him whole.

JOHN LET HIMSELF INTO HIS HOUSE, struck by the smell of greasy cooking that always greeted him when his father was home. He had left the light burning under the stove hood for him, and it shone on the pan of bacon fat and splatters remaining from his supper. John looked at the stove top, the sink of dirty dishes, the grimy dish towel hanging from the oven door, his father's holey socks and scuffed boots under the table where he'd removed and left them, and felt the sickness spread through him that he'd fought all night. He pulled at his tie and passed through the kitchen without stopping for a drink of water to ease his dry throat. In his bedroom he lay down fully clothed, linked his hands behind his head, and stared at the ceiling.

In the morning he was going to mass, he decided. It had been a while since he'd attended. When his mother had been alive, he'd never skipped a Sunday going with her to St. Matthew's, but now he went only when he missed her and needed the peace it gave him. Tomorrow he would go to seek another kind of peace.

Chapter Fifteen

Spring gave way to summer. In former years during the three-month break from school, Cathy and Trey and John took advantage of every opportunity to be together in the sun. Slathered in suntan oil, they "laid out" in Mabel's lush backyard with a swimming pool, hiked and picnicked in Palo Duro Canyon, plied the waters of Lake Meridian in Trey's prized sailboat, and rented horses to explore the attractions of Caprock Canyons State Park. Trey's and John's skin would turn the color of chestnuts, Cathy's the deep tone of unrefined honey. The boys' dark hair lightened a shade, and Cathy's took on the hue of her favorite palomino's mane.

But this last bridge to their final year in high

school was different. All three had secured summer jobs. Trey and John worked as bag boys at Affiliated Foods, one of the Panhandle's grocery store chains, easily edging out the competition for the few jobs available for teenagers since the manager believed their celebrity status would be good for business. Neither gave him reason to regret his hiring choice. Both boys were hard and reliable workers—Trey unexpectedly, since John had already proved himself during Christmas vacation. Customers would wait in line at their checkout stations for the opportunity to exchange chitchat with the local superstars who, as seniors next fall, were expected to lead the Kersey Bobcats to their first state championship football title in ten years.

Cathy had landed a job as a general helpmate for Dr. Graves, the local veterinarian. Dr. Thomas, the town's family practitioner, had also offered her a position, but Trey had talked her out of accepting it. "You'll just be filing papers for Dr. Thomas, but you may learn a lot about medicine from Dr. Graves, even if it's to do with animals," he'd told her, and he'd been right. Cathy had worked for her employer only a couple of weeks before Dr. Graves, impressed by her quick intelligence and way with his patients, smocked her up to assist him in performing some of his minor medical procedures.

For John and Cathy, the jobs were essential to meet college expenses not covered by the scholarships they hoped to be awarded. For Trey, employment was necessary to keep him from missing his friends in the long hours he'd have to spend by himself in the sun.

The summer evenings were different, too. In school vacations past, they'd all gathered at Emma's or Mabel's as a trio. Now, unless John was invited, Trey alone showed up at Cathy's at the end of the day. "I feel guilty excluding him," he said. "We've always done everything together, but Cathy, I can't finish the day without having you to myself."

"Having you to myself" often meant simply driving to a place to talk about their dreams and experiences of the day under the stars while music played on the radio, Cathy's head nestled on Trey's shoulder. Other times they "chilled out" in Mabel's parlor or Emma's den to watch television, not minding the presence of either of their guardians. Piling into cars and pickups with other couples to cruise Main or to drive to Amarillo to the movies or to raise a ruckus at beer parties did not appeal to them.

"You'd think they were a couple of old married folks," Emma would say to Mabel, referring to the times their charges seemed content merely to be in each other's presence. But both women knew full well what they were doing when they did not return home until much later than the usual time. Mabel thought of the condoms that had disappeared from Trey's desk drawer days after the junior prom and Emma of the prescription for the wheel of yellow pills she insisted Cathy drive to Amarillo to have refilled, and each would be thankful for the children's brains prevailing over their glands.

Trey and John and Cathy were the town's star-studded trio. In their junior year, Cathy had made the top score in Kersey High School's history on the PSAT (Preliminary Scholastic Aptitude Test), which qualified her to ascend to the next rung in her quest for a National Merit Scholarship, and was voted "Most Beautiful" (the vote carried by the boys versus the majority of girls, who pulled for Cissie Jane). Trey and John tied for "Class Favorite" and "Most Popular," and as seniors the trio were expected to compete for the title "Most Likely to Succeed," since after graduation they would be going to the University of Miami in Florida and then on to fame and glory—Cathy as a doctor and the boys in the NFL.

"Catherine Ann, do you know why you're the only girl for me?" Trey asked one night. They lay side by side on the quilt that Trey always carried in his Mustang. He'd heard of "security blankets" and knew for a fact that John possessed one. His mother had made it for him when he was only a toddler, and once Trey had seen it folded and tucked away high on John's closet shelf.

"What's that?" Trey had asked.

"What's what?"

"That blue blanket."

"That's the blanket my mother knitted for me when I was a baby."

"Did you suck on it?"

"Well...yes, sometimes."

"When?"

"When I was afraid."

"Carry it around with you?"

"Yes, TD. Why're you asking? What's the big deal?"

"Because I never had one."

But he had one now. He'd never admit it to anybody in the world, but this was his security blanket, the quilt on which he felt like the king of the world each time he and Cathy lay on it. It was sacred to him. It carried her scent and their body secretions. No other girl had ever lain on it. He washed it from time to time, in the local Laundromat so Aunt Mabel wouldn't see, but that didn't remove the memories from it.

"Why am I the only girl for you?" Cathy asked. She knew that every girl in school was hot for him and that they came into the grocery store in their short shorts and tank tops and flirted outrageously with him and John. She wondered—surprised that she felt no jealousy—if Trey was ever tempted to accept their offerings.

Trey traced his finger down her throat to the nipple of her breast that he thought as sweet as a tiny plum. He took her into his arms, filled with the music and thunder she roused in him. "Because you love me like I need to be loved."

Different as well, or more intensely felt than in recent summers, was the sense of the town marking time until the dry, baking heat yielded to milder days and cooler nights and set the tone for the grid-iron mania that would grip Kersey until December, when everyone expected to head out for the state play-off game. No one doubted that the state championship trophy for Class 3A would be won by the Kersey Bobcats. They would be led by the best quarterback and wide receiver in their division, indeed "the whole damn state," so the booster club declared—TD Hall and John Caldwell.

A threat to their confidence to win the district title, though, was the challenge rising from the other town in the county and home of Kersey's chief rival, the Delton Rams. To be a contender for the state crown, the Bobcats had to get past the Rams, and scouting reports indicated that for the first time in years Delton would be a strong competitor for the district trophy and possibly knock Kersey out of the play-offs before it even got a foot in the door. The prospect of such a fluke added to the stream of anxious discussion in every gathering place in town—the post office, drugstore, pool hall, church meetings, the Masonic Lodge, Bennie's Burgers, and on front yards where neighbors congregated in lawn chairs after supper to enjoy the cooling-down period of the day.

To the townspeople, John and Trey appeared unbothered by the scuttlebutt, but Cathy, disgusted with the pressure put on them, noticed a change in Trey as August drew to a close and the first game of the season was a week away. "What's wrong?" she asked one Saturday afternoon, believing she knew. "You're unusually quiet today."

The booster club's football kickoff barbeque was to be held that night on the rodeo grounds, a time-honored event where the team, wearing ball caps and their number jerseys in the gray and white of the school's colors, would parade down a red carpet as their names were called. The starting lineup would be presented last, Trey and John—the main attractions—the finale of those. The town's expectations were a heavy weight on their shoulders.

"I'm worried," Trey said.

"About what?"

"That clause in Miami's offer letter."

Cathy's brow puckered. She was familiar with the contents of the letter from the University of Miami that had offered Trey a full scholarship to play football for the Hurricanes. It had included two important conditions: Trey's grades and college entrance exam scores must meet the qualifications for admission into the university and his level of play must not slip below the coaches' expectations.

"What's worrying about it?"

"What if we don't win district? Coach Mueller could change his mind about taking me on Signing Day."

Cathy was equally familiar with the name Sammy Mueller since it was often on Trey's tongue. Mueller was the powerful head coach of the Miami Hurricanes. She had also been thoroughly versed in the importance of Signing Day. It was a media-publicized event traditionally held on the first Wednesday in February, when high school seniors signed binding letters of commitment to their choice of colleges offering them scholarships. It was a date constantly on Trey's mind and circled in red on Mabel's calendar. Coach Mueller's letter had made it clear that he would take only a certain number of players at a position, and once the spots were filled the offer of the scholarship would be rescinded. Such wording obviously gave Miami another out clause so that Coach Mueller and his staff wouldn't get stuck with a player they no longer wanted come Signing Day. In Trey's case, he was the only blue-chip quarterback Miami was considering.

She slipped her hand up Trey's hard, browned arm. He was wearing a sleeveless T-shirt for the dirty task of helping Cathy clean out animal cages in the back of the veterinary clinic. The office closed at noon on Saturdays, and they were by themselves. "I'll tell you what John would say. 'Take it one game at a time and give it your best. That's all you can do.'"

"Well, that's fine for John," Trey said, his tone irritable. "But I can't be so laissez-faire! I have *responsibilities*."

Trey loved tossing about French words, a conceit that secretly amused her, but she wasn't smiling now. He was genuinely distressed, and she did not know how to "make it all better," as he would tenderly ask her to do on his blue days. "Responsibilities?" she repeated.

"Yes, Catherine Ann." The frustration in his voice implied she'd overlooked the obvious. "Because of me, you and John are putting your oars in the water for Miami. If I hadn't influenced you, you'd have indicated USC as your first choice on that form you sent to the National Merit Scholarship Committee and John would be playing football for Texas. I'm worried that if we get shut out at district, Coach Mueller will forget about John and me come Signing Day, and then where will we be? Other teams' positions will already be filled, and the big academic scholarships gobbled up. John can't go to college on his own nickel, and he'll have to take what's left. Even Aunt Mabel can't afford Miami tuition. It's one of the highest in the country. We'll all be split up, and you'd have to go to Miami alone."

His despair was so palpable, he might have already suffered the calamity. And now that he'd put it into words, she had to admit that Trey wasn't imagining the impossible. It could happen. She had never considered the consequences if he had to forgo his dream. She'd worried only that he could be hurt. For a second, a chill clutched her spine.

He wiped a towel over his face as if to rub the image from his mind. "I couldn't bear that, Catherine Ann. I couldn't bear being without you and John."

She reached up and pulled his head down to her eye level. "Listen to me, Trey Don Hall," she said. "Did you know that fewer than ninety percent of people's worries come true? Use your mental energy to make happen what you *want* to happen. You've got to focus on the future as a mountain you're aiming for and don't even consider phantom detours that may never occur. If they happen, they happen, but the mountain will still be there, and we'll get to it—all of us, together."

His worry lines softened. "You're so good for me, Catherine Ann. What would I do without you?"

She patted his cheek. "*That's* one concern you can take off your worry list. Now stop all this negative thinking and go get showered and dressed for your big night. I'll meet you at the barbeque."

"I will, but before I do..." He slung the towel around her waist and moored her to him. "Come here, you," and after he'd kissed her long and hard, he asked, as he always did, his gaze sultry with desire, "You won't forget about me while I'm gone?"

She pushed him away with a laugh and the usual, "As if I could."

"The pony show starts at five thirty. Don't be late. I want to see my girl there, looking proud as Punch for me." He kissed her quickly again. "You'll be okay here by yourself?"

"I'll be fine. There's not a warm body stirring out there. Everybody's getting ready to go to the rodeo grounds."

At the front door, he hollered back to the kennel section where she was removing a puppy from its cage, the last pen to be cleaned, "Don't forget to lock the door, Catherine Ann!"

"Okay!" she called back, cuddling the little male beagle in her arm while she removed the paper lining. She continued to hold the wriggling puppy, even after she'd replaced the lining and filled the bowls with water and food, enjoying the lick of the small tongue on her chin, but after a while she had to put him back into his pen. "Sorry, little guy, but I have to get home to dress for the barbeque."

Immediately the beagle began to howl, setting off the other boarders kenneled for the weekend, the noise almost drowning the tinkle of the front door bell. Her neck hair rose. Someone had entered in spite of the CLOSED sign.

She fastened the cage and quietly made her way in the clamor to the door leading to the reception area. Cracking it open, she drew back with a little gasp when she saw who was standing at the counter. *Wolf Man!* She had never seen him, but from the matted red hair and vagrant appearance of him, he could be none other but the scary recluse she'd heard about who lived in the shack at the far end of Miss Mabel's neighborhood. He held a bleeding black and white collie with a gray muzzle in his arms. Rufus's mother? Trey loved to tell how he and John rescued Rufus from Wolf Man's backyard on a bitterly cold January night as a surprise for Catherine Ann.

It took only a few seconds for Cathy to decide what to do. Dr. Graves would have her stay quiet and lock the door until Wolf Man was gone, but the poor dog needed help badly—and immediately. It was her duty to save the dog, even if she got fired. The man gave the counter bell an impatient tap as she pushed open the door. "May I help you?" Cathy said, drawing to her full height to give an impression of authority.

He turned to stare at her from under brows as bushy and reddish as his hair and beard. "Yes, miss, you can," he said. "My bitch here is hurt. Got herself mauled in a coyote fight."

The man was obviously deeply concerned for his dog and showed no interest in a pretty girl in shorts and T-shirt alone in an office with money in the cash register drawer. "I'm afraid Dr. Graves is not here at the moment," Cathy said. "I'm only his summer help, but I'll be happy to see what I can do."

"How long will he be gone?"

"Until Monday morning. There's an emergency number I can call, if you like." Dr. Graves wouldn't come if the patient were Secretariat. He was president of the Bobcat Booster Club and in charge of introducing the team tonight, a duty he'd looked forward to all week with a sappy pride. He was already at the rodeo grounds.

"He'll blow me off if you give him my name," the man said, "and my dog needs help now."

"I'm sure he'll ask," Cathy said. "Would you like me to take a look at her?"

The dog was whimpering pitiably. When she heaved, fresh blood seeped from the deep gashes on her side.

"I'd really appreciate that, miss."

"Follow me to the surgery," Cathy said.

She could get in big trouble for what she was about to do. "Lay your dog on the table and stay with her until I can get her sedated," she instructed.

"Thank you, miss." The man bent to the dog's ear, and Cathy caught a whiff of a barnyard odor. "Now just take it easy, Molly. This nice girl is going to fix you up."

Well, she hoped, but what if she couldn't fix Molly up? What then? The man was so fierce looking and the silence so profound from the lack of town traffic that he could scare the fight out of a pit bull, but she wasn't afraid. She was in her element. In the surgery she was always calm and detached no matter the dire seriousness of the animal's condition or the temperament of its owner. Quickly Cathy filled a syringe and inserted the needle gently into the quivering flesh. "There. That will take her out of her pain for a while until I can clean and suture her wounds."

"How bad, Miss?"

"She's sustained deep lacerations. She'll live, but she won't be as feisty as before." Cathy slipped into latex gloves, tied on a surgical mask, and set to work. The sedative had taken immediate effect, but the man remained stolidly by the table, stroking the dog's head. Cathy did not enforce the clinic's rule that patients' owners were to wait in the reception room. That would be pushing her luck, and the man's love for his dog was evident. "How old is Molly?" she asked. She noticed the collie had been spayed.

"Going on ten years. You're Cathy Benson, aren't you?"

Cathy cast him a surprised glance over the mask. "I am."

"Emma Benson's granddaughter, the girl them boys risked their lives for gettin' her a puppy."

Cathy shaved the hair away from the deep wounds. "So the story goes."

"That would be from me," Wolf Man said proudly, and peered at her closely—to see if the information alarmed her, Cathy guessed.

"So I was told," she said.

"Then you know who I am?"

Cleaning the serrated tooth marks, Cathy said, "Yes, I do."

"From my description, I suppose?"

Cathy was torn between kindness and truth. After a short pause, working quickly before the sedative wore off, she said, "Yes, sir, from your description."

Wolf Man emitted a short laugh of approval. "Well, that's telling it like it is. You're Miss Emma's granddaughter, all right." He caressed the dog's ears. "Your puppy is this here's son. Your boyfriends got him from the only litter I let ol' Molly have, because nobody would want a puppy from a dog of Wolf Man's. I ain't irresponsible like some folks would have you believe."

"I can see that."

Wolf Man said nothing more as Cathy continued her work on the sedated dog—swabbing, suturing, bandaging. When she had finished, she pulled down the mask and stripped off her gloves. "That should do it, Mr. Wolfe. I'm sending you home with some antibiotics and painkillers, and something for Molly's nausea when she wakes up.

Give the drugs to her when and only as long as prescribed. You'll have to keep her safe and comfortable for at least three weeks to give her injuries time
to heal."

"You're going to make a fine doctor someday,
miss."

Surprised, she said, "How do you know I plan to
become a doctor?"

He grinned, revealing the dark hole of his
mouth, his lips lost in the mat of brick-red hair.
"There's hardly anything that goes on in this town
that I don't know about, miss. Now, what do I owe
you?"

Most likely, he couldn't pay, even if she told
him, but she couldn't risk writing out a bill for the
charges. She had just performed minor surgery
and administered and dispensed drugs without a
license. "No charge," she said. "Let's keep this visit
our secret if that's all right with you, and if Molly
requires further assistance, you'd best contact me at
my grandmother's, and I'll see what I can do."

He smoothed his beard, a spark of conspirato-
rial understanding in his shrewd eyes. "Well, that's
awfully kind of you. I owe you, miss, and don't
think I won't remember. I never forget a kindness
any more'n I do an injury. Molly and I thank you."

He gathered up his dog, and Cathy opened the

door for him. On his way out, he paused. "One other thing, miss, if I may be so bold."

"What is it, Mr. Wolfe?"

"The boy you chose...I was sorry he was the one. Mind your heart with him."

Cathy was still standing with the door open and her lips parted in surprise when the phone rang. She glanced at the clock on the wall. *Oh, my gosh!* It was way past five thirty!

Chapter Sixteen

John had known the minute Trey telephoned to tell him he was coming to his place that he had something up his sleeve. Why would he want to hang out at John's house, without Cathy, on a cold, gray Sunday afternoon when he could be warm and cozy at Aunt Mabel's or Miss Emma's—and when *he*, John, could be there as well? He couldn't remember when he hadn't spent Sunday afternoon at either place and stayed for a good supper.

He'd never seen Trey so worked up over a game as he was over the one coming up against Delton. Trey was convinced that his whole future—all their futures, his, Cathy's, and John's—rested on beating Delton Friday night, knocking the one obstacle to the district championship out of the way so that

Kersey would have a clear shot to state. How could anybody be as cool and sharp as a knife under ice water on the football field and off it as jumpy as a worm over a fire? Everything was going fine. In early October, they'd been visited by Coach Sammy Mueller in person. Looking like a million bucks, he'd flown in to Amarillo, rented a car, made the hour drive to Kersey, and stayed in a motel overnight just to introduce himself to John's father and Aunt Mabel and to assure them how much he and the other coaches and the Hurricanes were looking forward to having John and Trey suit up in the orange, green, and white. So far the Bobcats were 9 and 0, having defeated their opponents handily. Trey's big and only worry was Delton, also undefeated, but in John's opinion the Rams were overrated. They had a good defensive line and a scrappy little quarterback, but the kid wasn't much of a field general. He couldn't touch Trey when it came to assessing the other team's defense, changing the game play in seconds when he saw something he didn't like. Trey called the shots right every time, and both he and John were on their way to being selected All-District in their respective positions and, if their luck held, possibly All-State.

Now Trey had just presented a cockamamie scheme to John that could put an end to all that.

"Jeez, TD, what's the matter with you? Have you gone crazy?"

"Far from it, Tiger. Look—this razor could shave a baby's butt without waking him from his nap." Trey demonstrated by running the battery-powered instrument down his forearm. "See?" He held up the razor to show John the hair caught in the blade that had left a swath of hairless skin. "I didn't feel a thing."

"Where did you get that? Did you steal it from Dr. Graves' office?"

"I didn't steal it. I borrowed it. I'll put it back once we're through with it."

"*We?*" John stared at him aghast. "Not this time, TD. I don't want to have any part in what you've got in mind. You do it alone, or you don't do it at all. You're our quarterback, for heaven's sakes. Quarterbacks don't pull the kind of stunt you're suggesting."

"That's why they'll never know we did it. Come on, John! Can't you just see the look on those goons' faces when they see their mascot?"

"I can see the look on Coach Turner's face when we get caught."

Trey had proposed shaving stripes on Delton's ram mascot to resemble bobcat claw marks. He'd discovered the ram was looked after by Donny

Harbison, a boy their age, when Aunt Mabel had sent him to pick up eggs and vegetables from Donny's mother. The Harbisons lived in a big farmhouse on the outskirts of Delton. John had a slight acquaintance with the family, who were Catholics, from St. Matthew's. Trey was absolutely positive that those shaved stripes would demoralize the Rams, and he wanted to do it tomorrow afternoon.

"We won't get caught," he insisted. "That's what I'm telling you. Mrs. Harbison told Aunt Mabel they're going to be out of town until Thursday. Their twerp of a son will be at band practice after school on Monday. We can cut English and be back in plenty of time for practice."

"I don't want to cut English."

"We'll say that by the time the last period rolled around, we were so sick from what we ate at Bennie's that we had to miss English. We went to the home economics room to lie down. Hell, John, we're four pointers and team captains to boot. Who's not going to believe us?"

"All we'll accomplish is to make the ram look sheared, not clawed, and that will just make the Rams more determined to win, not scared."

Trey got up angrily from the bed. There wasn't much room for him to pace in John's room. Twin beds and a bureau, desk, and chair took up most of the space, and two boys their size almost filled the rest of it. "Let's go outside," John suggested. "You need air."

"I need your help with this, Tiger. That's what I need." Trey's fuming expression and tone slipped into their appeal mode. "Why can't you realize what's at stake? Trust me, we'll be *roadkill* to Coach Mueller if we don't get a few more games under our belt after district. Do you want to see us go our separate ways if we aren't offered scholarships to Miami? To see Cathy go off alone—without me? *Do you?*" Trey's look was desperate.

"Your grades would get you into Miami, TD. Don't be so melodramatic. You don't have to go on scholarship."

"Without you?"

He made the idea sound unthinkable, and John admitted it was like a punch to his gut. Sometimes he thought it was almost unhealthy how tight the three of them were, but the truth was he couldn't imagine his life without Trey and Cathy. They were his family. They were the only ones in the world who loved him or that he loved. They were one for all and all for one, and they had looked forward to going to the University of Miami so long—and together—they'd put all other schools out of their minds.

"Besides," Trey said, "without a scholarship, I couldn't ask Aunt Mabel to pay the high out-of-state tuition when I could go to as fine a school anywhere in Texas. The only reason we're going to Miami is the prestige of their football program that will give us a leg up to the NFL."

John willed his expression inscrutable as a rock, but Trey could tell when he was getting to him. Trey sat down next to him on the bed. "We're going to need all the help we can get out there Friday night, Tiger, and I believe we should consider any idea that might give us an edge. Can't you just imagine what their players will be thinking when they see their mascot on the sidelines Friday night? Those stripes will scare them shitless."

"Oh, Trey..."

"If you don't help me, I'll get Gil Baker to go with me. I can't do this by myself."

Gil Baker? Gil Baker, one of their defensive linemen, couldn't keep his mouth closed if it were sewn shut. He'd spout the secret of their escapade—brag about it—and news of what they'd done would be all over town by the start of school Tuesday morning. Coach Turner wouldn't hesitate to kick both of them off the team—he was that kind of coach—and what would *that* do to Trey's record in the eyes of Sammy Mueller! Their prank might even be against the law and get Trey in trouble with Sheriff Tyson.

But John knew Trey. Once he made up his mind to do something, no logic in the world could persuade him to change it.

"I promise, Tiger, that if you do this for me, I won't ever ask you to do another thing that goes against your grain."

"I won't hold my breath. Okay, but this is the last damn fool shenanigan I'm ever going to let you talk me into, TD, and the only reason I'm going along with it is to make sure you don't hurt that ram."

Trey put up his hand for a high five. "You're my man, John."

On Monday, Trey initiated the plan from the moment he and Cathy, John and Bebe climbed into the Mustang after a lunch of hamburgers at Bennie's—the local grease hole, it was called—to return to school for afternoon classes.

"I don't feel so good," Trey said.

"What's wrong with you?" Cathy asked.

Trey bent over the steering wheel, holding his stomach. "I think...I think I may have picked up a food virus."

"Oh, my gosh. I hope it's not ptomaine."

"It might be."

John rolled his eyes and looked out the window.

By the time they were at their lockers, Trey had convinced a worried Cathy that something he'd eaten at Bennie's had made him sick. "Don't you feel queasy, too, Tiger?"

"Yeah, but not from something I ate at Bennie's."

The rest of the day worked according to Trey's calculations, and he and John arrived at the Harbisons' farmhouse about the time their English class was discussing the third chapter of *Wuthering Heights.*

"A piece of cake," Trey pronounced, and indeed the place looked theirs for the taking. It was a still autumn afternoon, blue and golden, only a whisper of wind blowing. All they could hear was the crunch of leaves under their feet as they walked around to the back of the house.

They spotted the pen at once and the small ram eating from his trough. He looked up with trusting eyes and bleated—a cute little guy, John thought. "Now be gentle, TD," he said.

"I will." Trey took the hoop off the gate, the battery-operated razor in his hand. "You hold him real tight, John."

Then two things happened simultaneously that John registered in a blur of confusion. First Trey dropped the razor and took some kind of large cat's paw from his jacket pocket, and next John heard the slam of the screened back door. They whirled in surprise to see Donny Harbison, a skinny kid three-fourths their size, running toward them brandishing a rolling pin.

"Get away from that gate, Trey Hall!" the boy yelled.

John looked at Trey, shocked. He recognized the foreleg as belonging to a stuffed bobcat stored in Aunt Mabel's attic. "I thought you said nobody would be home."

"Well, I was wrong."

It was over before they knew what had happened. Enraged, Donny Harbison brought the rolling pin down hard on Trey's shoulder, and he dropped the cat's paw, which John snatched up and threw away before Trey could use it against Donny. Then everything went crazy with Trey trying to dodge the blows of the rolling pin.

"Get the pin before he busts my arm, John!" Trey yelled, finally grabbing Donny's throat and digging in while the boy fought to free himself, the two of them going round and round in a mad, furious dance.

"Trey, let go!" John cried, pulling at his arms, terrified by the sound of Donny's strangled gasps, finally driving his shoulder into Trey's knee. Trey grunted and released his hold, and all three went down. There was a crack as somebody's head hit the picnic table.

John got up first, then Trey. John shook his head to clear his vision; Trey rubbed his shoulder. "Damn, he could have put me out of commission, John."

"You'd have deserved it, TD." He reached a hand down to Donny. "Here, I'll help you up," he said, and then his breath caught. "Oh, God..."

"What's wrong, John?"

"He's not moving."

The two of them dropped down beside the motionless body of Donny Harbison. "Hey, man," Trey said, patting the boy's cheek. "Stop fooling around. We're sorry, but come on now, say something!"

Donny stared up out of perfectly still eyes.

In a stupor of dread, John felt the boy's neck for a pulse and put an ear to his mouth. Nothing. In horror, John drew up and gaped into the boy's dead eyes. A coldness like a plunge into ice water swept over him. "He—he's not breathing, TD."

Trey's face turned caliche white. "But he has to be. He's only unconscious. Please, please wake up," he pleaded, pulling the boy up by his shirt collar.

John grabbed Trey's hands, a roll of cold sweat running down his back. "Don't do that, TD. It's not going to help. I—I think he's dead."

"He's just passed out. I don't see any blood. Nothing looks broken—"

"Well, it is. Inside, where you can't see it."

"He can't be dead. He's just... he's just knocked out." Trey began to cry, smoothing the boy's shirt as if the gesture might restore him to life. "How can he be dead?"

"He hit his head on the picnic table."

Trey cast an accusing look at the concrete offender. "Oh, God, John. I didn't mean this to happen. He wasn't supposed to be home. What are we going to do?"

John mumbled between stiff lips, "I don't know. Call an ambulance, I guess." Chills were sweeping his body.

Trey moaned and covered his face with his hands. "Oh no. Oh no..."

"Or maybe Sheriff Tyson."

Trey took his hands away. "He'll arrest me, won't he, put me in jail?"

"No, no. This was an accident."

"How'll we explain why we were here?"

John could not answer. His jaws had locked.

Trey lowered his catatonic gaze to the body. "Look at him, John. My finger marks are beginning to show around his throat. How will we explain those? Look at his shirt. There's a button off, and the ground's scuffed. Sheriff Tyson will know there was a fight. I'll be charged with—with murder."

"No, Trey, not if you tell him the truth. You were defending yourself. I'll testify to it."

"What if they don't believe us? Oh, God, John—"

Trey, charged with murder? John pressed the heels of his hands to his forehead. He couldn't think. His head felt as if a block of wood had been wedged into his brain, but some part of it told him that Trey could be right. The police might not believe them, but they couldn't go off and leave Donny Harbison like this. Somebody else could be blamed for his death.

"Could we—could we make it look like something else happened?" Trey said. "Like . . . maybe he hanged himself?"

John's brain cleared as suddenly as if wax had been flushed from his ears. "No, TD. No way! *No way!* Donny's a Catholic. Catholics believe you go straight to hell if you take your own life. We can't have his parents believe that's where Donny is spending eternity."

"What else can we do, John?" Trey sounded as if he had a crushed larynx. "They might not call it murder, but they could see it as manslaughter—'the crime of killing a human being without malice.' Remember that definition from civics class? We were trespassing. We came to do mischief. That's the way they'll look at it, Mrs. Harbison especially. She doesn't like me, and she'll try to get 'em to throw the book at me. Not you. You're off the hook. This was my idea, so it's all on me, but I could go to jail."

"You don't know that."

"Can you tell me for sure it wouldn't happen?"

John couldn't. Trey's panic was justified. There were likely to be charges brought against him. He was seventeen. In Texas, they held seventeen-year-olds accountable for their criminal acts.

John couldn't see his best friend—like a brother to him—hauled off to jail. The image of Trey behind bars, his future wrecked, his life ruined, brought up a taste of something so vile John had to spit before he gagged. It would kill Cathy. Besides, if he hadn't tried to break up the fight, Donny might not have fallen and hit his head. Trey hadn't reminded him of that. He wouldn't. John squeezed his eyes shut, remembering an incident from the summer they were nine years old. A bull had charged after him as he and Trey were crossing a pasture. Trey had yelled and screamed and thrown rocks to divert the bull, and he had changed course to storm after him. Trey had made the fence just as the bull's horns grazed the seat of his jeans. It had always been that way with Trey.... He would have attacked a cave of bears for John.

The little ram bleated mournfully. He had braved the threat in the yard to come out to investigate and was peering at his keeper lying on the ground. John's stomach turned over. Donny was dead.... There was no bringing him back, but Trey was alive. *God forgive me for what I'm about to suggest.* He gazed dully at Trey. "What about... what about that—that kinky method of masturbation Gil Baker was showing us in that magazine, the one where you get off by choking yourself?"

"Auto... erotic... asphyxia?" Trey stumbled over the word. John was referring to the magazine Gil had waved about in the locker room demonstrating the technique. It featured pictures of people in the act of hanging themselves to cut off oxygen to the brain in order to intensify an orgasm. John and Trey had thought the pictures and the whole idea obscene and disgusting. John hadn't touched the magazine, but locker checks were being conducted at school, and Gil had pushed it and several others of the same sexually explicit contents onto Trey to keep in his car until Gil could find a new place to hide them from his mother. They were in his Mustang right now, hidden under the seat.

"That's it," John said, sick with repugnance at

the thought of the boy's parents finding him in such a condition. "That way it looks like their son didn't intend to die. He just wanted a sexual high."

Trey got to his feet, brushing at his wet eyes. "That would cover up the bruises.... Oh, God, John, you're a genius."

Solemnly but quickly, fighting to keep their lunch down, they carried the lifeless form into the barn. Trey took the boy's shirt with him when he ran to his Mustang to get the illicit magazines, and, following instructions, they made a ligature from an extension cord, removed Donny's clothes, and hoisted the body to a position that simulated death by autoerotic asphyxia. Trey spread the magazines around the suspended feet of the body, leaving one open to the instruction page, while John arranged the boy's boots, underwear, jeans, and belt on a chair.

When they were through, John said, "Trey, we have to take a minute," and indicated the symbol of his and the boy's faith looking down upon them, a crucifix nailed to a rafter.

Trey nodded, and they clasped cold, clammy hands and bowed their heads. John made the sign of the cross. "In the name of the Father, the Son, and the Holy Ghost, we commend the body of Donny Harbison to You, Father, and may You forgive us for what we have done."

"Amen," Trey said. John turned quickly to go, Trey still clutching his hand. "One other thing, John." Trey tugged him to a stop. In the filtered light of the barn Trey's eyes looked like dark fragments of broken glass. "We can't ever tell anybody—for sure not Cathy—what happened here today. Agreed? We have to keep it our secret always—forever and ever—or we will be in big trouble."

John hesitated. Forever meant…forever. The boy's parents would live the rest of their lives never knowing how their son really died, but he was bound to Trey. He would never tell. "Agreed," he said.

Trey gave his hand a hard squeeze. "You're my man, John."

The sunlight had waned, and they knew football practice had begun. At the last hurried moment they thought of raking the ground, deciding to leave the hoop where it fell to allow the ram to get out and eat grass from the yard. They retrieved the razor and button and took the rolling pin with them, not having a better idea what to do with it, and remembered only when they were halfway home that they'd left the bobcat's leg behind.

Chapter Seventeen

Four days later, Deke Tyson, sheriff of Kersey County, had just sat down to a late supper when the telephone rang. His wife answered, motioning him to continue eating when he heard the call was for him. Her husband was off duty, she explained pleasantly, and suggested the caller telephone the sheriff's department for assistance. After a few bites, Deke could tell from his wife's tone that whoever was on the other end was not to be put off and held out his hand for the receiver.

Irritated, Paula handed it to him. "The voice is familiar, but he won't say who he is. The idea, bothering you at home after you've had such a long day." She pitched her complaint loud enough for the person on the other end to hear. "You haven't even had a chance to change out of your uniform."

Deke gave her a placating pat on the cheek and spoke into the mouthpiece. "Sheriff Tyson. How may I help you?"

The nature of the call must have shown on his face, for when he hung up, Paula's hands were on her hips. "No, don't tell me. You have to go out again."

"Could you cut a piece of that pot roast and put it between a couple slices of bread for me, honey? It's going to be a long night."

"Deke..."

"Please, just do it, Paula."

The call had come from Lou Harbison. He'd asked that Deke come alone to his house without a deputy and that he not tell anyone the nature of their brief conversation. Lou and his wife, Betty, had returned from a few days' visit to Amarillo and found their seventeen-year-old son's body in the barn. He had hanged himself. Lou had not called the sheriff's department because he wanted no law officer but Deke to view the body first. There was something Lou and Betty wanted to keep private from the public and the rest of their family if at all possible. Deke would see when he got there.

Hitting the highway, the sheriff kept hearing Lou's anguished voice and could think only of his own children—a nineteen-year-old son off at Texas Tech and a daughter, a high school senior, now at band rehearsal for the halftime show of Friday's big game—and how such a tragedy would affect him and his wife. Paula loved their daughter, but the sun rose and set on their son. Paula would never get over a loss like Betty's. Deke suspected Betty wouldn't, either.

Biting into his sandwich, he recalled what little he knew of the family, since they were from the other town in the county. He knew they lived in a rambling farmhouse on a good-sized piece of property just outside the city limits. The house and land had come to them by way of Betty's father when he died. Lou Harbison worked as an engineer for City Public Service, and Betty was a housewife who sold eggs and vegetables on the side. They'd both lived in the county all their lives. They had two children, one a daughter, Cindy, now living in Amarillo and married to somebody from Oklahoma City. Their son, Donny, had come along a bit unexpectedly, about six or seven years after Cindy. Deke's daughter, Melissa, had mentioned meeting him at band camp last summer. She'd thought he was cute but held out no hope they'd ever get together since he was from Kersey High's chief school rival.

The only time the county sheriff had an occasion

to make an official call on the Harbisons had come a couple of winters ago when he'd been summoned to handle the situation of a pet dog gone rabid. Lou had not been able to shoot her. Deke had obliged, sending the family back into their house with the soothing promise that Dot would not feel a thing. He recalled a pleasant home and hospitable people. Betty had sent him a note of appreciation later along with an assortment of her delicious jams.

But most of all, Deke remembered that the Harbisons were devout Roman Catholics, Donny included. Suicide was expressly forbidden in the Catholic Church, the penalty being the loss of the victim's immortal soul. Deke wondered what in the world had possessed Donny to take his own life and leave his parents to deal with the emotional turmoil of believing their son was spending eternity in hell.

By the time Deke drew in front of the house, the sun had completely set, leaving only a trace of grayish red in the endless Panhandle sky like blood seeping from a septic wound. Lou would probably prefer that Deke not show up in his official car with SHERIFF written on the door, but he was on the job and he'd leave it to Lou to explain what it was doing parked before his house. Not that he'd have to worry what the neighbors might think. Deke estimated that the closest lived a mile away in any direction.

Before Deke had unbuckled, Lou stepped out on the front porch, a haggard look dragging down the muscles of his face. He pulled the door shut behind him and met Deke on the walk. "Come on around to the barn, Sheriff, and I'm grateful to you for coming alone."

"Sorry it has to be for this reason, Lou. My condolences."

Without another word, Lou led the way to a barn set far back from the house. It had been partially converted to house Betty's chickens in the winter, and the smell of the coop was strong. At the entrance, Lou stepped aside and morosely motioned the sheriff to go first.

Deke entered and felt a jab to his rib cage. Hanging limply by the neck from a low beam used for drying flowers and herbs was a boy who looked his daughter's age. He'd been covered with a light-blue blanket from the chin down to the toes of his white athletic socks. Deke noticed that his feet were a little more than an inch from the floor, close enough to have supported himself with his toes if he'd been so inclined. Scattered around were several magazines featuring sexually graphic covers, one folded open to scenes like the one above. On a nearby chair, next to a scuffed set of precisely placed boots, was a pair of neatly folded jeans and white jockey shorts.

"Good God, Lou," Deke said, his nose wrinkling at the smell of decomposition. "What happened here?"

"We thought you'd know," Lou said. "Betty and I sure don't. Take the blanket off, Sheriff. It's all right."

Averse to what he would find, Deke stepped carefully forward, treating the area like a crime scene, and with the tips of his fingers pulled the blanket away.

"Ah, Jesus, Lou—"

The boy was naked except for his socks, his abdomen bloated and beginning to show the greenish tinge of decomposition. A thick industrial extension cord was knotted around his neck.

"His mother found him like this," Lou said. "What do you call this kind of...sexual perversion, Sheriff?"

"Autoerotic asphyxia," Deke answered, arranging the blanket back over the boy's exposed body. "I don't know much about it other than it's the latest crazy sex fad." He pointed to the open page of one of the magazines. "Looks like it's explained there. Basically, it's the act of hanging yourself in order to cut off oxygen and blood to the brain while masturbating. Apparently the lack of blood and oxygen contributes to the sexual experience."

Lou looked sick enough to faint. Deke took his arm and led him out of the barn into the backyard. At the kitchen window, Betty Harbison's ashen face appeared, looking like a corpse underwater. "How is your wife taking this?" Deke asked, rebuking himself instantly for the absurd question.

"'Bout as you'd expect. She's inconsolable. None of this makes any sense. There's so much about it not like him."

"Like what in particular?"

"Betty trained the boy well. He's like her in a lot of ways. Likes to keep things neat and tidy. He left the kitchen table a mess...."

"What do you mean?"

"I don't know anything about this...this autoerotic—whatever you call it. I guess the urge came on him while he was eating a snack at the kitchen table. He got up and left a half-eaten sandwich and some biscuits spread with peanut butter. There were crumbs everywhere, the lid off the peanut butter jar, the top off a bottle of mustard. He's never done that before. Always cleans up after himself."

"Will you show me what you're talking about?"

"Sure."

They went through the back door into a kitchen

spacious enough to accommodate a rooming house of boarders. Betty sat at the large, round table, mute and shockingly pale. Deke forced himself to meet the shattered look she lifted to him.

"Honey," Lou said gently, taking her lifeless hand, "the sheriff's here to conduct an investigation."

"What's there to investigate?" Betty asked, staring at him vacantly.

"Well, I told him that Donny would never go off and leave the kitchen table like this."

Deke saw what he was referring to. Orange peelings, a partially eaten sandwich, biscuits split open, the knife that had been used to slather them in peanut butter stuck to the table. But then, the boy's parents had been out of town for several days. Plenty of time to clean up after himself before they got back.

"Uh, Lou, when did you folks leave for Amarillo?"

"Monday morning after breakfast. Cindy's baby was due in the afternoon. We left today to come back for the football game tomorrow night."

"Monday morning," Deke repeated quietly. This was Thursday. The boy looked to have been dead since Monday or the day after. "Anything else that looks amiss?"

"Well, yes. Ramsey. He was half-starved when we got in."

"Ramsey?"

"Ramsey, our football team's ram mascot that Donny looks after. When we got home, the hoop was off the gate of his pen. We found it buried in the straw. Donny's never left it off before. The little fellow is so used to staying penned, he never thought about trying the gate. He could have gotten out and eaten the grass in the yard. As it was, he stayed in his pen and nearly died of starvation. The only thing I can think of…"—Lou stepped away so that his wife wouldn't hear him—"is that Donny thought that he…was taking a chance with his life and took off the hoop, figuring Ramsey would wander out when he ran out of feed."

"Stay with Betty while I look around," Deke ordered. "And can you throw some light into the backyard?"

"Sure," Lou said, and flipped on a switch.

The backyard flooded with light. Still, Deke took a minute to go to his unit for a flashlight. He returned and cast its beam around on the ground, looking for…signs of a struggle, maybe? He saw no indication of any, but the hard-packed ground with its sparse covering of dry grass around the ram's pen had been raked recently. He searched the enclosure with the flashlight, caught a pair of bright, wary eyes watching him, and heard an anxious snuffle, but the ram stayed in his bedding and did not come out to investigate. The hoop was back on the gatepost. Fresh feed was in the trough.

Deke directed the light under the concrete picnic table and saw something in the shadowy darkness. He got down on his hands and knees to draw it out in his handkerchief. It was the limb of a gray cat sawed from a taxidermist specimen, judging from the lack of bones or cartilage. The size of it looked too big to belong to the house variety. Its claws were hooked and wickedly sharp, and Deke thought it had to have come from something like a mountain lion or bobcat.

"Lou!" he called.

Lou, who had been watching from the open kitchen window, ran out at once. Deke held up the severed limb. "Ever seen this?"

Lou reached to take it, but Deke held it from him. "Better not touch it. Could be evidence."

"Evidence?" Lou echoed thinly.

"Just in case this wasn't an accident. Now, does this belong to you?"

Lou inspected it out of doleful eyes. "No. I've never seen it before."

"I found it under the picnic table. What was it doing there?"

"I don't know. We had a drifter in here last week, a hobo we found had slept in the barn. We locked it, but he was back the next night. Stayed in the ram's pen. This could've belonged to him. It'd be something his kind might carry for luck or a weapon."

"The ground looks raked around here. Why is that?" Deke asked.

Lou glanced at the area and shrugged. "Donny must have raked it while we were gone. He was a good one for keeping things tidy."

"So you said," Deke mused. "I'm just going to the car to bag this; then I'll be back."

"Sheriff..." Lou pushed his hands into his pockets and set his feet firmly. "We don't want no investigation. That's why I had you come out by yourself. This was an accident, pure and simple. Well..."—his mouth twisted—"not so pure and not so simple. Donny did this to himself. Why, God only knows. I never thought the boy was interested in pornography, sex fantasies—" He hunched forward, bowed by what was an obvious attack of fresh grief.

Deke put his hand on his shoulder. "Let's talk a little bit about those magazines," he urged quietly. "Did you ever see them before? Where would he have hidden them?"

"In his room, most likely, and no, I never saw them before."

"Wouldn't Betty have discovered them when she put away his laundry? Mothers have an uncanny nose for sniffing out illicit stuff like that." Deke remembered when Paula had come across racy magazines stuffed in their son's camping bag when she aired it out.

"Sons have ways of keeping such things from their mothers," Lou said.

Privately Deke disagreed, but he said, "How about from you? You had no hint whatsoever he was into this kind of thing?"

Lou shook his head. "None, and that's what's so shocking. Donny liked girls, but he had a healthy attitude toward them and toward sex, too, for that matter. I mean, I just never, ever heard him say or do anything lewd—"

"That's why we have to investigate, Lou, have the coroner determine the exact cause of death. There could be more to this than meets the eye."

"*No!*" Lou shook off Deke's hand. "You can't investigate, have the deputies out here, do an autopsy, have this get into the newspaper. I won't have it. The shame of it would kill Betty. We could never hold our heads up in this county again. I wish now I'd dressed the boy, but I wanted you to see that he...didn't commit suicide. That's what it would have looked like if I'd put a shirt and pants on him, gotten rid of those magazines."

"Where *is* his shirt?" Deke asked.

"What?" Lou said.

"His shirt. Where is it? I'm assuming he was wearing one when he went out to the barn. This is November, Lou."

"Why...I don't know," Lou said, frowning. "We didn't think about his shirt. We just left things as we found them. He didn't leave it in the kitchen."

"Look, while I go bag this, would you see if you can locate the shirt he may have been wearing? You don't have to say anything to Betty. I don't think Donny would have gone into his room and hung it on a hanger when the urge hit—not and leave the kitchen table as he did."

Lou turned reluctantly toward the house while Deke made for his squad car to slip the cat's limb into a paper bag. Little tattoos of doubt drummed in his head. He was the county's chief law officer. As much as he wanted to respect the feelings and privacy of the Harbisons, he wasn't convinced Donny's death was an accident. There was the discrepancy of the mess he'd left on the kitchen table and the neatness of his folded clothes. But what other explanation could there be? Suicide? No, Deke believed he could rule that out. The boy wouldn't have let himself be found in that condition, and he'd have left a note.

Also...a little thing, but would a student from Delton High want to miss the biggest game of the season against its archrival Friday night? Delton and Kersey were in a neck-and-neck race for the district championship. That left murder, but who would want to murder Donny Harbison and for what reason?

Deke made a mental list of things to investigate as he drew on rubber gloves to bag the magazines and extension cord. He'd learn more about AA, find out whether Donny's life was insured, search Donny's pickup for other porno magazines, ask the neighbors if they saw the vagrant, and interview Donny's friends and teachers at Delton High. He'd take the magazines and cord to the crime lab in Amarillo to dust for prints.

Lou was waiting for him in the backyard when he returned. "No shirt, Sheriff."

"Don't you find that a little odd, Lou?"

"Maybe, but it doesn't matter. Betty and I have discussed this, and we want the details of Donny's death squelched. Please, Sheriff. I'm begging you. Think if it were your son. How would you and your wife feel?"

Deke did not reply. Paula would plead to hush it up, but he would want to know what had happened to his son.

"I can't answer that, Lou."

Betty Harbison came out the back door, new tears flowing from her swollen eyes. "Please, Sheriff…" She went down on her knees before him and clutched his arm in appeal. "I'm begging you. Please don't let this get out. Our priest would deny him the Mass of the Resurrection if he knew. He wouldn't let him be buried in consecrated ground. He'd call Donny's death a suicide because what he did was willful and dangerous. We don't want our daughter to know how her little brother died. Please, Sheriff…" She released his arm and buried her face in her hands.

"Betty…Betty…," Lou soothed, dropping beside her to put his arms around her quaking shoulders.

Embarrassed by their naked grief, stricken to his father's soul, Deke found himself saying, "All right, Betty, all right. I'll call the JP to come out alone. He'll have to sign the death certificate, but he can be trusted. He won't say anything. The death will be ruled as accidental and that will be the end of it. Nobody but the four of us ever needs to know how it happened. You and Lou go back inside now and call the funeral home. I'll wait for Walter in the barn. We'll cut Donny down and take good care of the body until somebody from the funeral home gets here."

Betty, sobbing, collapsed into her husband's arms, and Deke walked away to call the JP from his unit, unable to bear the sight of Lou's tears falling on his wife's head.

Chapter Eighteen

The Kersey Bobcats won the game against the Delton Rams 41 to 6, the score so one-sided that Coach Turner pulled Trey and John to the bench for the last part of the final quarter to preserve them for the coming play-offs. Newspapers statewide described the Bobcats' victory over the Rams as steel ripping through papier-mâché. Members of the team lifted their quarterback and top pass receiver onto their shoulders at the end of the game, but no camera from either the fans and/or news media caught a triumphant smile on the faces of the two gridiron heroes.

Within the days leading up to the historic night, Trey and John waited to see Sheriff Tyson's squad car pull up to their houses, expected to hear his official knock on their doors, but neither came. There was nothing of Donny's death in the county newspaper except an obituary and one article briefly explaining that the boy's parents had returned from out of town to find their son dead from an accident in their barn. The flags of both schools in the county were lowered to half-staff. A funeral and burial were held privately, open only to members of the family.

"Why so glum?" an elated but worried Ron Turner demanded of his star quarterback and wide receiver in the locker room after the game. Trey and John were the last to depart. The rest of the team had already boisterously departed to enjoy the victory celebration hosted by the booster club on the blocked-off street of Main. Coach Turner had stayed behind to allay a growing concern. "You boys ought to be bustin' out of your T-shirts instead of looking like you lost the district championship."

"We're okay," Trey said. "Aren't we, John?"

John concentrated on snapping closed his letter jacket. "Yeah, sure."

Coach Turner placed a hand on each of his players' shoulders. "What's the matter, boys? You two have been distant from each other all week. You haven't had a falling-out, have you?"

"No, sir," Trey said. Coach Turner was one of

the few men Trey ever addressed as *sir*. "Me and John—we're tighter than ever. Aren't we, John?" His gaze at John pleaded with him to agree.

John nodded. "That's right," he said.

Ron Turner narrowed an eye at them. "You're not still battling that stomach virus you got from Bennie's, are you?"

"Sort of," Trey said, with a quick glance at John.

Coach Turner darted a skeptical glance at each boy. "Why don't I believe you? Something's got the wind up you fellows, but I won't try to pry it out of you tonight. I want you to talk it out with each other right here, right now. The party will wait. I'll tell Cathy and Bebe where you are. We've got a Bi-District game to play next week, and I want you to be ready for it, but more important, I want you to repair whatever is affecting your friendship. You boys share a rare and special bond that comes once in a lifetime and few ever know. Don't let something come between you that could be put to rights by a heart-to-heart talk. Okay?"

Coach Turner observed that his words did not put a spark in their plugs, but both boys nodded and Trey said, "Okay, Coach."

When he had gone, hunched in their letter jackets, avoiding eye contact, the longtime friends stood uneasily in each other's presence. They wore

185

the booster club's preordered ball caps with 1985 DISTRICT CHAMPS stitched across the crown that had been distributed to the players in the jubilant postgame frenzy. Since Monday, except for appearing together in their classes and at football practice, Trey and John had agreed by some sort of telepathy to avoid each other so that they might come to grips with what had happened privately. After practice each day, John had gone to St. Matthew's; Trey had spent every free hour with Cathy.

Shamefaced, shooting an uncomfortable glance at John, Trey cleared his throat. "I'm sorry, Tiger. I swear before God, I'm sorry."

"You ought to be, TD."

"I thought they'd be tougher."

"You were wrong. Why'd you bring the bobcat's foot?"

Trey's face bloomed deep rose. He sat down on one of the benches and removed his cap. He closed his eyes and pressed his fingers to his lids as if to relieve a migraine. "Because all season I've been afraid of...losing everything, John—all we've worked for. It's made me crazy. I thought...a few scrapes of a real bobcat's paw would make a bigger statement, give us more of an edge."

Trey looked up with remorse-ridden eyes, the high ridges of his cheeks showing the pale imprints of his fingers. "I swear the idea didn't even come to me until Sunday night when I was lying in bed and remembered Uncle Harvey's stuffed bobcat in the attic. You can ask Aunt Mabel. She heard me rummaging around up there around midnight and climbed the stairs to ask what I was doing. I...just thought I'd bring the paw along to see if I could go through with it."

"Would you have?"

"No. When I saw the ram, I chickened out. Besides, I knew what you'd think of me. When Donny came tearing out, I was going to ask what we could do with the thing to leave the Rams a message...."

Exasperated, John asked, "Why can't you ever play anything straight, TD?"

"It's not in me, Tiger. That's why I need you. That's why you're my man. You keep me on the straight and narrow."

John shoved his hands into his letter jacket and dropped his chin to his chest in resignation. He believed the cat's paw story. It was typical of the direction Trey's mind sometimes took. He'd choose to play a wild card—a joker—when he held an ace.

"I'll never get over it, TD, not ever."

"I know you won't, John. That's the difference between you and me. Look, you...you're not going to pull out on me, are you?" The note of disbelief in Trey's voice implied he'd been thinking about the possibility and found it intolerable. "John, you and Cathy are my family, the only people I have in the world except Aunt Mabel, and she's old." Tears flashed in his eyes. "I need you, man. I've been miserable this week. It's been like trying to sit on a three-legged stool with one of them missing. Tell me I didn't blow it this time, that we're still as tight as we've always been. I'll believe whatever you say."

John handed him a towel from a bin and joined him on the bench. "I'm not pulling out on you, TD. I'd never do that. I'm sick over what happened... leaving the body like that... for the parents to find... and all for nothing."

"I know, I know." Trey put an arm around his shoulders and joggled them. "Don't think about it. We'll get through this together. Someday it'll all fade, be nothing but a dim memory. You'll see. And when I make lots of money playing for the NFL, I'll start a scholarship fund in Donny Harbison's memory. You just wait. I'll do it."

"It won't make up for anything—not to the Harbisons. Without their son, they'll go through life feeling what we do without our parents." John shook off his arm. "Jeez, TD, somebody might come in and think we're a couple of queers. Has Cathy suspected anything?"

"She knows I've been...on edge. I could never have gotten through this past week if it hadn't been for her. You've been going to St. Matthew's, haven't you? What do you do there? Pray?"

"Sometimes, and sometimes I just sit in the pew. It's helped." He hadn't gone to confession. Father Richard would have him do the only thing possible to unburden himself—go to Sheriff Tyson—but he couldn't do that to Trey. He simply couldn't. He would have to live without absolution for the rest of his life.

Trey drove a playful fist into his shoulder. "So, we're still going to Miami and kick butt together, right? We're still best buds, joined at the hip, right?"

"I'm afraid so."

"And I'm forgiven?"

"Don't push your luck, TD."

Trey slapped his cap back on his head. "You're my man, John."

In the steady march to the deciding game for the state championship, the duo led the Kersey Bobcats from victory to victory in stadiums packed to capacity. John's star status made Bert Caldwell something of a celebrity to the point that he stopped drinking in order to be, he said, "in working order," at the games. The same standing was given to Mabel Church, who preened with pride over praise of her nephew, despite her secret hope that the Bobcats would lose to relieve her persistent worry that he would be injured.

The constant stream of telephone calls, telegrams, requests from college head coaches to meet with them personally, and the number of "offer" letters and invitations from prestigious university athletic departments to visit their campuses, all expenses paid, made John and Trey among the most hotly recruited high school football players in the country. In December, Mabel and Emma took their phones off the hook so the trio could do their homework undisturbed around their kitchen tables. Offer letters and telegrams piled up in drawers, unopened. No matter what the special allure of other schools, Trey Don Hall and John Caldwell let it be known they stood fast in their decision to attend the University of Miami in Coral Gables, Florida, and that was that. Come Signing Day in February 1986, they'd be writing their names on the dotted line to play for Coach Mueller and his Miami Hurricanes.

Trey's only peace from the stress and pressure of leading the team to the final game came when he and Cathy were alone together, John's when he was at St. Matthew's. He and Father Richard had become philosophical friends, the priest often inviting him to supper when John wasn't at Miss Emma's or Aunt Mabel's. They mainly discussed the history of the Catholic Church, which John found fascinating, especially the background of the Society of Jesus, from which the Jesuit Order evolved. Father Richard, an aesthetic, kindly man, was a Jesuit.

It was on one such visit that John encountered Lou and Betty Harbison face-to-face on the sidewalk leading to Father Richard's office. Before then, numerous times, John had visited their son's grave, sometimes bringing flowers from Emma's and Mabel's flower beds to place before the headstone.

"You're John Caldwell, aren't you?" Betty said. She and her husband had just come from the cemetery behind the church.

"Yes, ma'am."

"We've been keeping up with you Bobcats since you whupped us," Lou said, his brief grin overshadowed by his visible memory that the game was played the week his son died.

"And we hope you go all the way to state and make the county proud," Betty said.

"Thank you," John said. He paused, adopting a teenage boy's awkward stance. He looked down at his feet, pushed his hands into his pockets. "We'll try our best," he added.

"You're the one who sometimes leaves flowers on our son's grave, aren't you?" Betty said, bending down to peer up into his face.

John felt his chest compress. "Yes, ma'am... sometimes."

"Why? Did you know Donny?"

"Only slightly—from St. Matthew's. I...was sorry about his death."

"Yes...," Betty mused, her gaze thoughtful. "I can see that. Thank you for caring."

"No problem," John said, and stepped aside for them to pass.

Shortly afterwards, a college admissions book arrived in the Caldwells' mailbox from Loyola University in New Orleans, a renowned Jesuit university.

Chapter Nineteen

Finally it was upon them, the last game of the play-off season. The journey to Texas Stadium in Irving where the 3A State Championship game was to be played had been long and hard, but Kersey's defeated opponents had been left with no doubt who was the better team. Against the Houston White Tigers, however, the Kersey Bobcats were going in as underdogs.

The Houston team reputedly was made up of a group of street toughs—thugs, some called them, a few already having had brushes with the law—and was noted for its brutal tackling and blocking. Their linemen outweighed Kersey's by an average of fifteen pounds a man and had established a reputation for sacking quarterbacks and making short work of their favorite receivers. Everybody knew the Tigers would be gunning for Trey and John.

Throughout the entire season, Trey had escaped the fray virtually untouched—at least by game standards—because of Coach Turner's edict to the offense that their first and most important assignment was to protect their quarterback. The linemen were ready to do so. The instinctive skill that made Trey an outstanding team leader as well as field general was responsible for his blockers giving it their all to ensure the defense didn't lay a hand on him or his receivers. Trey was quick to praise and slow to condemn and, somehow, such graciousness, coming from Trey, meant even more and had greater effect than had it come from John. Charity was natural to John, not necessarily to Trey. Because the team trusted their pilot to lead them successfully through the storm, regardless of the largest share of media attention going to him and his wingman, they would have done anything for him.

But would it be enough?

Every night the week of the game, Cathy went to bed with fear clutching her heart. What if Trey and John, too, of course, were hurt? All bets would be off then. Why couldn't the boys have been tennis players or golfers? As the play-off season had progressed, her dislike grew for the sport of football and her disgust with a town that put such strain and pressure on its players. But as much as she hated to admit it, she owed the sport for her and Trey having become even closer. Ever since the days leading to the district game, he seemed unable to be away from her and could not get to her house fast enough after practice. "I need you," he'd say. "You make all the bad things go away."

What bad things? The school and town had thrown themselves at his feet, adoring him even more because he did not stick out his chest and strut and posture like some of the other players but accepted the adulation with John's quiet reserve and distance, which had deepened since the week of the district game. "A coach's dream—true team leaders," Coach Turner described him and John. They were offered free meals at Bennie's Burgers and Monica's Café, movie tickets, new jackets from a sporting-goods store, none of which they accepted.

"Please, God," Cathy prayed. "I do not ask for Kersey to win the game, only that you spare Trey and John injuries so that we can all go to the University of Miami together."

Sportswriters descended upon the small prairie town, hanging out in Bennie's Burgers and Monica's Café across the courthouse square to report on the excitement gripping the community the eve of the biggest football game in its high school's history. One reporter described the atmosphere as so electrically charged that "a lighted match could blast the whole place off the map of Texas." They searched out and limelighted anyone connected to the Bobcat team who could provide a human-interest story. One of them was its head coach, featured in an article that appeared in major Texas newspapers and began Trey's lifelong aversion to members of the news media.

"You'd have to live in Kersey to understand the influence of the man," the reporter wrote, stating that the town took its marching orders from Coach Ron Turner. He had strict rules that his coaches, players, water boy, and student assistant—anybody associated with the Kersey Bobcats—were to follow. There was to be no talking to the news media or fraternizing with the townspeople, including members of the booster club, two days before a game. After practice, every member of the team was to be off the streets and at home, where they were expected to concentrate on the task at hand in peace and quiet. They were to minimize TV viewing and telephone conversations and avoid distractions. He left it to the mothers to see that their sons ate right, got to bed at a decent hour, and avoided stress.

The "two-day blackout period," the reporter went on, was adhered to by everyone in town and had to be experienced to be believed. On late Wednesday and Thursday afternoons when dusk was gathering, you could hear a leaf drop on the streets. As if not to disturb the Bobcats at their rest, merchants and customers spoke in hushed voices, chatter was quiet in places like Bennie's Burgers, horn toots to summon waitresses for car service at the drive-in were short, and no teenager with loud mufflers dared drag Main.

Ron Turner was definitely not a man to be bucked. He ruled with the iron hand of deserved respect after six successful seasons as head coach of Kersey High School (though none had included winning the state championship). He took no guff from fathers, armchair quarterbacks, or booster club members who held the keys to the city and the ears of the school board. He lived by the rules he set for his players and eschewed alcohol, tobacco, and profanity. "Mouth filth," he informed his players, "is the language of the ignorant and insecure. Smoking and drinking are the crutches of the weak."

The article stated that he was made to order for a cocky, highly intelligent, fatherless quarterback like Trey Don Hall.

His face afire with humiliation and embarrassment, Trey read—in addition to being described as "recalcitrant"—of his parents' early abandonment and how Coach Ron Turner had filled the void of his missing father. Aware of Trey's sensitivity to his orphan status, Coach Turner apologized for the slant the reporter gave his interview, saying he'd praised Trey as the son he would like to have had. Trey had believed him and was thrilled Coach Turner thought of him that way, but he cringed that now the whole world knew his parents hadn't wanted him. That night, he held Cathy tighter than ever before.

Except for residents of the nursing home and a couple of sheriff's deputies who'd called the wrong side of the coin to determine who would have to stay behind, the town of ten thousand was practically deserted the day of the game. A caravan of assorted vehicles with gray and white window flags flapping and painted with exhortations to DECLAW HOUSTON WHITE had set off at dawn to carry the Bobcats' supporters to Dallas. On this Saturday in the middle of December, only one man walked the quiet, holiday-decorated streets, his dog limping beside him. He held a transistor radio to his ear and a coiled whip by his side. Far away and long ago had the star of this show stood shivering in his backyard, he recalled, listening to a pregame broadcast. Was the measure he took of the boy that night true for the man to come? Time would eventually tell. For today, the kid had what it took to make the town proud. Tomorrow was another day.

TEAM CAPTAINS TREY AND JOHN AND GIL BAKER lined up to meet the referees and the captains of the Tigers for the coin toss in the center of the field. Their appearance and bearing during these tense, dramatic moments had already become the stuff of legend. Other teams fooled around at their end of the field in a hodgepodge of footgear as long as their shoes met turf regulations. Since no particular standard dictated uniform socks of high school players, they could wear long, short, or none at all. Length and cut of hair were also the players' choice. Not so with members of Coach Turner's team. At his instruction, every aspect of the Bobcats' game regalia was uniform. Players must wear their jersey sleeves rolled down, knee-high socks tucked under the elastic band of their pants, shoes of the same make and style, hair cut short and neatly trimmed.

Thus presenting a united front, the three captains stood abreast in respectful silence, their expressions schooled to appear calm and impassive as they waited for the officials to walk out onto the field, the signal for the team leaders to join them for the coin toss. It was quite a moment when Trey and John, topping six-three, with a shorter, stockier, but no less impressive Gil Baker between them, set off in step at an unhurried pace, gazes steady, left arms cradling their helmets, right arms held straight at their sides.

One sportswriter would write of this contest: "The Bobcats' captains approached their challengers with the dignity of knights dispatched to confront a company of knaves."

Such descriptions set well with Coach Turner. "You wouldn't shake hands wearing gloves," he explained to his captains, "and you don't greet your opponents in your helmets. You show 'em the courtesy of your face. But when the toss is over, you put your helmets on in their presence to let 'em know you mean business."

Among a sellout crowd, Cathy watched these proceedings wedged between her grandmother and Mabel Church, her eyes glued on Trey. A sober Bert Caldwell stood on the other side of Emma, binoculars focused on the field. Cathy and Mabel held hands, both in the throes of the common fear that had weighed like rocks in their stomachs all football season. The band director had granted Cathy special dispensation to sit in the stands after she'd gone to him with the unorthodox request that she be excused from participation in this final game. Had he not done so, for the first time in her life she was prepared to abandon her part of the whole, inconsequential though it was. In other words, she would resign from the band. She reasoned that the contribution of her flute to the fight song and her marching position during the band's halftime performance would not be missed. Meanwhile, she'd be sitting with Mabel and her grandmother where she could keep an eye on Trey and never miss a moment of the game or a movement of him on the field.

This is what it's going to be like when he's playing football at Miami and after we're married and he's in the NFL, she thought, the tightness in her chest hardly allowing her to breathe. She would live in a daze of anxiety for his safety—a limbo of suspended peace until the season was over. She hated that he played football, but, dear God, he loved the sport and had played at the heart of it since he was old enough to hold a pigskin. People changed when they lost what they had always loved, so what was she to do but support him and nurse his wounds and soothe his bruises until the next week while she prayed that he would survive another game?

A cheer went up around her. The Kersey Bobcats had won the toss.

Helmets back on, Trey and John, looking like a double exposure, trotted with Gil to the sidelines. For a brief instant, Trey glanced toward the band section where she was supposed to be sitting. Her heart held. *He doesn't know where to look for me*, she thought, gripped by the foolish notion her disappearance might affect his concentration. *Don't be stupid. Nothing can prevent him from keeping his mind on his business out there.*

In the brightly lit locker room before the game, the Kersey Bobcats had gathered around their coach, some kneeling, each supporting himself with a hand on his helmet. The coach's voice was calm when he delivered his final pep talk to the finest group of boys he'd told reporters he'd ever coached. "They're bigger than you, we've already given them that," he said, "but you're smarter, quicker, better coached, and better disciplined. You've got integrity and courage, and the biggest hearts in the business. You know what to expect. Be ready for it. To win, they'll resort to what they are, all they know, but you let them draw the penalties, not you. And boys"—his voice wavered, trembled in his throat, "if you resort to what *you* are, all *you* know, you'll be bringing home the trophy tonight. John, how 'bout leading us in a little prayer?"

Coach Turner's prophecy was realized in the

final minutes of the game when the Bobcats trailed 21 to 24. Bloodied, exhausted, the offensive line held the Tigers away from Trey to allow him time to fire one of his bullet passes into the magical grip of John Caldwell, who, on his last legs, zigzagged his way around the defense's desperate grapples to run the final five yards for a touchdown.

In less than the minute left to play, the ball sailed over the crossbar of the goalpost for the extra point, and the sound of the final whistle was never heard in the ecstatic roar that exploded from the Kersey side of Texas Stadium. Cathy and Mabel sat stunned, their hands entwined, tears of relief rolling down their faces as the townspeople around them thumped their backs in joyous celebration. "It's over, Miss Mabel, it's over," Cathy kept repeating.

She had no way of knowing how prophetic those words would prove to be.

Chapter Twenty

At the beginning of February 1986, Cathy was notified by mail at her home that she had been selected as a finalist for a National Merit Scholarship, guaranteeing her a spot on the University of Miami's Miller School of Medicine's premed track. In a school ceremony, she was presented with a Certificate of Merit in recognition of her outstanding performance in the competition as well as awarded a full scholarship bestowed through a charitable foundation administered by the First Baptist Church of Kersey, Texas. Both were contingent upon her entering an accredited university in the fall after graduation for four years of uninterrupted study. She wrote Laura Rhinelander, with whom she'd stayed in touch and to whom the news came as no surprise, that she would not be joining her at USC in September.

And on the first Wednesday of February known as Signing Day, amid fanfare from reporters, TV crews, fans, and classmates, Trey and John signed letters of intent to play football for the University of Miami at Coral Gables, Florida. It was official: Trey had a shot at playing quarterback and John Caldwell wide receiver for the Miami Hurricanes. Sammy Mueller—as he had telephoned to congratulate Trey and John after the state play-off game—called to welcome them to the team.

"What is this?" Bert Caldwell asked John a few days after the signing. Frowning, he held up the college admissions book of Loyola University for explanation. "What's it doing in our house?"

John retrieved it from his hand. "I don't know who had it sent to me. It showed up in the mailbox one day."

"You've been reading it. There are some pages dog-eared."

"I was interested. Father Richard is a graduate of Loyola."

Bert Caldwell's frown deepened. He had not touched a sip of liquor since the district game. His job still called him away for periods at a time, but he came home without his blowsy blondes or temper or the smell of alcohol on his breath. He'd had the house cleaned from stem to stern and, following Mabel's decorating advice, bought new spreads for John's twin beds and draperies and slipcovers for the living room and replaced the carpet.

"You guys can start coming over here and spending a few evenings with your old pop," he told John, his tone jocular but his gaze like that of a dog hoping to be let in from the cold.

John and Trey and Cathy parceled out a few forced evenings where they sat around watching television and rehashing play-off games, Cathy praising the snacks Bert had provided. John found himself preferring the old Bert Caldwell before his star stature had given his father a new community standing.

"That priest better mind his own business," Bert said. "You're not going to some namby-pamby Catholic college. You're going to the University of Miami, and you and Trey Don are going to be the standouts when their quarterback graduates and goes to the pros. You're going to make yourself somebody."

Make you *somebody*, John thought, but did not say it. He ought to be grateful that the man who referred to him as "my son" had cleaned up his act, no matter for what deluded reason or his mistaken notion that his say would have the least influence on the decisions John made for his future.

"Father Richard says he didn't send the book," John said.

The next day it disappeared.

In May, the day after their high school graduation, Trey and John accepted Coach Mueller's invitation to visit the University of Miami campus, deferred from December of the previous year because of the play-offs. A visit had not been required to convince them that Miami was the place they wanted to go. Cathy had to remain behind. Trey's and John's expenses were paid for, but Cathy would have had to bear the cost of hers and Emma had refused Mabel's offer of financial help.

"I'd cramp your style anyway," Cathy told Trey. "This is supposed to be an all-boys adventure, and I'd be bored to death taking a tour of the athletic facilities. I'll wait my turn until I register for classes in the fall."

Two weeks before their departure, Trey submitted to the test Dr. Thomas had recommended he take the year before but which he'd refused. He'd read extensively about the complications that might result from boys' having mumps at sixteen. "I'm ready to find out, Doc," he'd told him. "I don't want to go any longer not knowing."

"The procedure is fairly simple," Dr. Thomas said, and handed him a small plastic cup.

Dr. Thomas made his pronouncement the day before the boys were to leave. Mabel was not present. Dr. Thomas had thought of calling her in, but Trey was eighteen, well into the age of consent, and the boy had expressed a desire to come alone. Later, with his permission, Dr. Thomas would share his findings with Trey's aunt.

"There is semi-bad news and semi-good news, Trey," he began, showing him a chart of the male genitalia. "Let's begin with the first." With his pen, he pointed out the areas of Trey's testes severely damaged by inflammation from the mumps virus as a result of the delayed treatment of the disease. "You suffered a condition known as orchitis," he said. "From your biology class, you know that a sperm cell looks like a tadpole that waves its tail. Nonmotile sperm cells lack flagella and cannot swim."

"What are you trying to say, Doc?"

"Your semen analysis shows that your sperm cells are abnormally shaped and cannot swim."

"And that means?"

"It means that you are presently sterile. In other words, your sperm cells cannot move forward from the vagina to the uterus after ejaculation, but your current condition may not be a lifetime sentence. Thirty-six percent of adolescents can still have abnormal sperm up to three years after recovery from the mumps." Dr. Thomas set the drawings aside and clasped his hands, his look sympathetic. "If you'd come to me at the first symptoms of the mumps..."

Trey had come expecting the worst, but he was Trey Don Hall, charmed boy wonder. He eluded the consequences of his actions. "You sound like I fall in the sixty-four percent range," he said.

"I won't lie to you, Trey. Your testicular tissue was severely compromised. You're two years into this and...improvement appears highly unlikely."

"What's the semi-good news?"

"You have no testicular atrophy, but..."—he spread his hands apologetically—"that's not to say there won't be down the line."

"What are the odds of that happening?"

"One-third of the boys who get orchitis caused by mumps after puberty will have a shrinking of one, perhaps two, of the testicles. You're young and strong. You live a healthy lifestyle. You've been well looked after. It could be you'll at least have escaped that bullet."

One out of three. Every morning for the rest of his life, he'd be checking his balls. The cold shock of reality hit him, numbing him. He'd never have a son...a daughter. He'd never be a father. Catherine Ann would never be a mother—not by him. She was the kind of girl—of orphan—who would want children. She'd want to have a family.

"How many people need to know about this?" Trey asked.

"Nobody, unless you give permission. It's a matter of doctor-patient confidentiality."

"Good. I want no one else to know." Trey rose on numb legs, reading the question in Dr. Thomas's regretful gaze if that included Cathy.

They had new clothes for the trip. Mabel had insisted on buying Trey a linen sport coat and trousers to wear on the plane, and Bert had surprised John with an expensive Hickey-Freeman navy-blue blazer and slacks to "let those Florida folks know my boy is no hick." Looking at them in the airport—so tall and strapping and handsome in their fine new clothes—Cathy marveled at how nature had favored them. No blessing had passed them by. Yet a strange apprehension played beneath the surface of her excitement for them. Something had come over Trey in the last twenty-four hours, beyond the moods that could sometimes strike him. He'd begged off seeing her last night, saying he had packing to do. Mabel usually did his packing. Noticing the admiring looks they drew from other passengers, she caught herself thinking—the thought like an ice-cold bullet to her brain—*Come back to me, Trey.*

They drew aside for a private parting before he and John boarded. She waited expectantly for Trey to recite their usual farewell, but he did not. "I'll miss you," he said instead, and kissed her between the eyes—a first when they were parting.

It was she who said, "Don't forget me while you're gone."

"How could I?" he said, and added, "I leave you my heart."

That spring, the season had hardly sprung before it succumbed to the hottest temperatures on record. The wildflowers died before they bloomed, and the tender green of the prairie grasses bleached in the dry, hot winds that parched the ground. The heat, like the below-freezing days of winter, drove the adults inside. It was an interim in which only the young could find pleasure.

"Do you feel something different in the quality of the atmosphere this spring, Emma?" Mabel asked.

"Yes, Mabel. Triple-digit temperatures."

"No, it's more than the unprecedented heat. There's something else."

"Sadness. Our children will be leaving us."

"Yes, there's that…but there's something else, too.…"

Mabel was having one of her fey moments, but Emma shared her sense that something, not yet seen, had entered their universe. Perhaps it was loneliness that perched like a big black bird waiting to swoop upon them when Cathy and Trey and John were gone. Even Rufus felt it. He whimpered without cause and followed closely at Cathy's heels wherever she went. He'd prop his head on first Trey's knee, then John's, when they dropped by, his expressive eyes sad as if some instinct had warned him of their ultimate departure.

Trey and John were gone five days. Mabel had surprised them with the money to rent a car and see something of Miami when their two-day introduction to the campus was over. They planned to book a motel room and play tourist. They ended their stay by having seen little of the city. There was too much to see and do on the university campus.

At the Miami airport, waiting for their flight to be called for the return home, Trey sat slumped forward with his head between his hands like a man who's just heard the worst news of his life. John sat beside him, coldly unsympathetic to his pain. Trey spoke between the clamp of his hands.

"I know what you're thinking, Tiger."

"How could you do it, TD?"

"I guess I'm just a sorry piece of shit."

John's silence confirmed his opinion.

"There are things you don't know," Trey said.

John combed his fingers through his hair. "Then tell me, Trey. What in hell got into you? You get off the reservation and you go wild. Did you ever once think of Cathy back home?"

Trey unclasped his head and turned to him, his eyes rived with anguish. "Of course I did! Otherwise, I wouldn't be so miserable. I'm...I'm ashamed of myself, but I...didn't know what else to do—"

"What do you mean you didn't know what else to do?"

"John, these last few days have got me to thinking...."

"Don't exaggerate."

"That...that maybe Cathy and I ought to cool it for a while—until I'm sure enough about myself to know I can stay faithful to her. Distance makes the heart grow fonder...isn't that what they say? I've got to give myself *time—space*—to understand how I could...go off the reservation, as you say, after only five days of being away from her."

John listened, sickened. But he shouldn't be surprised at what he was hearing. From the moment they'd stepped on campus, they'd been in the tow of the unbelievably gorgeous Hurricane Honeys, the school's official hosts to show recruits the school and facilities, sort of like the Bobettes, but skyboxes above them. He'd caught Trey's wandering eye, heard his admiration of the girls with legs "up to here," listened to him say that it was nice for a change to be around girls who were interested in football. There were other coeds, too, who'd thrown themselves at him—at both of them—sexy, stylish, sophisticated beauties, dozens of them, like roses ready to pick, worlds different from the pretty but, with the exception of Cathy, yokel girls back home. Assaulted by all that beauty and willingness on the Miami campus, Trey had gamboled about like a stallion released into a field of clover.

"I've got to find out if I'm the jerk I think I am, John—for Catherine Ann's sake. She deserves the best, and what if I'm not it? How do I find out without...freedom to do so? I'm not so much a bastard that I could fool around while I'm still going with Cathy."

Flabbergasted, John said, "How can you have a change of heart about the girl you've loved since you were eleven years old, the girl you've declared was your heart and soul—your whole life—after only five days away from her?"

214

Trey turned the shade of a Louisiana yam. "It's been a shock to me, too, Tiger—believe me. But I haven't had a change of heart. I *love* Cathy. That's what this is all about. I want to marry her, but is it fair to her when... Well, I'm not like you, John. I yield to temptation." His struggle for a grin collapsed, and his face fell. "I'm going to tell her I was unfaithful to her."

John felt as if a concrete block had landed on his chest. Trey's confession would kill Cathy.

"I'll... tell her how it is with me, how it's got to be with me until I'm sure that I can be the person she deserves," Trey said. "I hope like hell she'll understand and give me this break. We'll both be at Miami—apart but together. In sight of each other, but... distant enough to put some ground between us."

John's lip twisted. "So that when you feel an itch for her, she'll be accessible. Is that the idea?"

"No, that is *not* the idea! If you think Cathy would pull off her panties for me just because I came around, you don't know her. I'm saying that when I *know* I can trust myself, she'll be reachable. For chrissakes, John. We're only eighteen. There's a whole lifetime for the kind of commitment Cathy wants. Look at the high school sweethearts we know who married and are now divorced. They committed themselves too early, before they'd had a chance to look around and see what else was out there."

"There's nobody out there more wonderful than Cathy, TD, and you *know* that. When do you plan to tell her?"

"As soon as we get home. It wouldn't be fair not to let her know right away. You and I will be leaving for fall practice first of August. The summer will give her a few months to get used to the idea that we won't be seeing each other until we're ... ready."

Until you're *ready, you mean*, John thought, revolted. He couldn't believe he was having this conversation with Trey. "Telling her right away wouldn't have anything to do with those phone numbers in your pocket, would it?" he asked.

Trey flushed again. "Maybe."

"What if during this *hiatus* you're proposing, Cathy falls in love with someone else? What if she learns she can live without you?"

For a second, despair—soul deep—glimmered in Trey's eyes. "That's a chance I'm willing to take."

You're taking no chance at all because you're confident Cathy will wait for you, you arrogant sonofabitch, John thought. "You'll break her heart," he said.

Trey slumped again. "I know. God forgive me— I know."

"I hope He does, because Cathy may not. She could have gone to USC, you know."

"I know."

They barely spoke on the plane ride home.

CATHY THOUGHT FOR A MOMENT she was mired in a bad dream. This couldn't be Trey telling her that he thought it would be best if they gave each other "some breathing space" when they got to Miami. The list of logical arguments he'd compiled for their "chilling-out period" could not be coming out of his mouth.

"We've never given ourselves the opportunity to know other people, Cathy, and—and I believe we should so that we'll be certain we were meant to be together....And—and I got to thinking: What if—what if your feelings about football interfere with...with our happiness? What if we can't weave your career—a doctor!—with mine, a dumb old football player? Those are concerns to think about, Cathy. I—I wish I'd thought of them earlier, but I've been so crazy about you....We'll still see each other. We'll be on the same campus...within arm's reach. Not really apart..."

Several things she noted: Not once had he called her Catherine Ann, and he'd spoken in the past tense. She could not speak. Disbelief had frozen her tongue, and her throat stung as if she'd swallowed a hive of bees.

"Say something...please," Trey said. "Or...or have you gone mute again?"

She stood. They were sitting in the front porch swing on her grandmother's porch, Rufus lying at their feet. Reluctantly he clambered up on his legs and gazed at her with an uncertain wag of his tail. Trey wore the same tentative expression. "Come, Rufus," she said, and opened the door and held it for the dog to enter. Then she followed and closed it softly behind her.

Chapter Twenty-One

She put her wheel of yellow pills away. She'd taken the last one on the twenty-first day of her cycle and did not resume them as prescribed. Why should she? Listless, apathetic, she reported for work at Dr. Graves's clinic, this summer hired only for half a day because the economy had taken a tumble. Her free afternoons gave her time to organize her wardrobe for college. There was little money for additions. The money she'd planned to spend on a few new things was now reserved for her plane fare to Miami, since she'd no longer be driving with Trey and John to the campus. The arrangement would have been ideal. Her new roommate lived in Miami, and she'd invited Cathy to be her guest for a week before classes began, the same week as

Trey and John had been instructed to report. She could have ridden with John in his pickup, but he and Trey were caravanning, and sharing meals and stops and an overnight stay in a motel would have been awkward.

The little money she could spare afforded her a decent selection of college wear from a thrift shop in Amarillo, and she welcomed the drive through the brown, empty prairie on the deserted highway. Trey had been out of her life a whole week when one afternoon she left the clinic and turned her grandmother's car toward John's house.

LYING ON HIS BED in his room, John thumbed restlessly through the admissions catalog of Loyola University he'd rescued from the trash where his father had thrown it after Signing Day. If he had read it, John could understand what had incensed him. The college had abandoned its football program in 1972. It now excelled in intercollegiate sports. John had a good idea who had arranged for the catalog to be mailed to him and felt the reoccurrence of a buried sickness every time he looked at it.

The phone had rung every thirty minutes, but John had ignored it, forcing the caller to leave an impatient message on the answering machine.

"John, come on!" Trey pleaded. "I know you're there. Pick up, dammit!"

His room was at the front of the house, and he heard before he saw Miss Emma's Ford drive up. It had a peculiar twang under the hood that he and Trey could never find the source of, a protestation of age, probably. What would Cathy do without a car on campus at Miami? She'd planned to have access to Trey's Mustang when transportation was needed, and of course she could always borrow John's truck.

He hadn't seen Trey since their return from Miami and had talked to him only once after he'd laid the ax to Cathy. Trey had not confessed his infidelity. "I couldn't," he'd said. "I just couldn't. It was hard enough to get out the idea that we should split up for a while and see other people. I know I can trust you not to tell her about the girls, John."

"Only because I don't want her hurt more deeply, TD."

"There's that, but I know you'd never betray me, Tiger. You might slug me, but you'd never betray me."

News of their breakup was all over town, and a glimpse of Cathy's stoic face betrayed who had dumped whom. She was now the object of snide gossip—most of it from Cissie Jane and her pea-brained followers—so for John to hang out with Trey somehow condoned what he had done.

"How did she take it?" he'd asked Trey.

"Like...Cathy. She simply listened without a word, and when I finished she got up and called Rufus and went inside the house. She didn't even look back. She closed the door and that was that."

"What did you expect her to say?"

"Well, how she felt, at least."

"You didn't know how she felt?"

"God, yes, I knew, but I expected her to express it—cry some, try to talk me out of my decision. She didn't even shed a tear."

Trey was so dense sometimes. Cathy would never demean herself by trying to talk Trey out of his decision to dump her.

"I thought for a minute that I'd made her go mute—that her old condition had kicked in," Trey said, and John heard worry and regret in his voice, "but then I realized she'd simply gone silent, like she does when..."

"...she has nothing to say," John said.

"Oh, God, John."

"Yeah," he'd said, and hung up.

He and Cathy had talked every night. He'd made a point to be home, knowing she'd call. "You're my bedtime cup of cocoa, John," she'd said. "I can't go to sleep without hearing your voice."

Not that she'd sleep anyway, he'd thought, or

eat. He'd gone by the clinic twice to check on her and each time found her a little thinner.

He laid the book down on his bed and went to the door, his heart beating a little faster. "Hi," he said, shocked at her wan complexion.

"I hope I'm not disturbing you," she said.

"You could never disturb me, Cathy. It's good to see you. Come on in."

The instant he closed the door, she put her hands to her face and began to cry, loud, body-racking sobs, and John felt a kind of relief. The dam had broken. Without a word, he folded her into his arms and held her while she gave way to her first hysterical outpouring of grief.

"How could he do this?" She sobbed. "What did he discover in Miami that he couldn't find here?"

"Fool's gold—that's what he discovered, Cathy. He was blinded by it, mistook it for the real thing, and bought it. It won't take him long to realize he was duped."

She stepped out of his arms, and they felt suddenly empty, as if something he was used to holding had been snatched away. He smiled to hide the stab of an almost intolerable pain and asked, "What can I get you? I think we've got some Cokes in the fridge."

She blew her nose on a tissue, leaving the delicate

rims of her nostrils pink. "Your father—does he still have any liquor around?"

"Uh, well, yes, I think there's some whiskey...."

"I'd like some of that."

Their eyes held, hers ruined with loss. "Cathy... are you sure? You don't drink enough to say you do."

"I feel like it, John; I really do."

It was the one credit he could give the man under whose roof he lived: Bert had kept the whiskey to prove to himself he could stay away from it—or, more likely, to be available when he fell off the wagon. There was nearly a full bottle offering temptation or salvation. John poured a jigger for Cathy and one for himself. It was only one o'clock in the afternoon.

John wondered if they should move to another part of the house, but his bedroom was the only picked-up spot in the house. He turned on his radio and dialed to a station for music to fill the silence between their desultory talk. Each took a corner of the twin beds, and John watched the whiskey work its sorcery on the girl he'd loved since his first sight of her in Miss Whitby's class. There was not a single thing about Cathy's person, personality, or character he did not admire. The alcohol went to work right away in his own brain and bloodstream, and he was thinking how intimate and cozy it was to have Cathy all to himself in his bedroom when the one song came on the air that shattered the moment and destroyed any fantasy of the two of them. It was Sarah Brightman and Cliff Richard's rendition of "All I Ask of You," whose lyrics of promise and everlasting love Cathy and Trey had believed were written just for them.

Hurriedly John got up from the bed. "I'll change the station," he said.

"No, no!" she slurred, reaching for his hand. "It's all right. I have to learn...to live...with the reminders...."

He sat back down while Cathy added her own voice to Sarah Brightman and Cliff Richard's profoundly beautiful duet, hers threaded with flat notes and heartbreak. Her body swayed to the music, the whiskey glass in her hand, and John got up from the bed and took it from her. She stood up. "Dance with me, John," she said, slipping her arms around his neck, their weight featherlight, the touch of her flesh as intoxicating as any liquor. She was wearing a white T-shirt and shorts, and the feminine smell of her wafted through the whiskey fumes and filled him with an agony so intense he could no more have avoided what happened next than he could have raised his mother from the dead.

Closing her eyes, she crooned woozily to the

vocalists' pure, clear notes against a background of glorious orchestral sound while his and Cathy's steps and bodies moved in slow rhythm to the music, her body brushing his, her head snuggled against his chest.

"Cathy...maybe you'd better sit down."

She reached for the whiskey glass and finished it off, still moving in his arms to her humming. "We were going to share a lifetime, John, just like in the song. We were going to share every day and night...."

He slipped the glass from her hand. "Maybe you still will," he said, hoping he was wrong.

She nuzzled his chin. "I want to wake up to a morning with no more night, John."

She stumbled, and he caught her before she fell and lifted her up in his arms. *Oh, God.* Her eyes were closed. His groin was on fire. He laid her on the bed and made to move away, but she clutched his arm, her eyelids fluttering in a failed attempt to open. "Don't go."

"Are you sure, Cathy? We're drunk, very drunk."

"Say you love me," she whispered.

Were those her words, or the song's?

He answered with his own words, from his own heart, his throat raw from desire. "You know I do," he said. She continued crooning, her head moving from side to side on the pillow, as he slipped off his jeans and briefs and her shorts and panties, the blood pumping in his head, the music resounding, blinding him to all but her beauty and his need of her. "Cathy...Cathy, open your eyes and tell me this is what you want," he said as he straddled her, his erection hard.

She spread her legs, and the tip of his penis had barely touched the soft cleavage between her thighs when she murmured dreamily, "Trey..."

John was off the bed faster than if a rattlesnake had dropped from the ceiling onto her pillow. Cathy's mouth had sagged open in a deep, alcoholic sleep, and she did not stir when he slipped on her panties and shorts and covered her with the blue blanket he kept in his closet. He turned off the music and went into his bathroom to take a cold shower, noticing the whiskey bottle was almost empty. Five hours later, he woke her. She was still groggy.

"Oh, my God, John," she moaned, holding her head. "What happened?"

"You got a little drunk—a lot drunk, actually." He forced a grin.

"What time is it?"

"Six o'clock."

"Oh, my God. Grandmother's still at the

library." She covered her mouth with her hand. "John, I think I'm going to be sick."

"Right this way. Excuse the mess."

"If you'll excuse mine."

He wished he'd cleaned the toilet. He wished today had never happened. He wished for a lot of things. She returned, her face blanched the color of the dirty white bathroom tile. "I feel terrible," she groaned.

"Me, too."

He was standing, and with a sigh she wrapped her arms around his waist and laid her head tiredly against his chest. His hands stayed in his pockets. "I must have completely blacked out," she murmured. "The last few hours are like...gone. Did I say or do something stupid?"

"You practiced your singing."

"Ouch. Anything else?"

"You snore a little when you sleep."

"So I'm told. Anything else?"

"No."

"You're sure?"

"I'm sure. Believe me."

She lifted her head to look affectionately into his eyes. "I do, John, with all my heart. That's what I love about you. I can totally believe you."

"Why don't I drop you off at your house and go

pick up your grandmother? You're in no condition to drive."

"Oh, thank you. You're so good," she said, pulling away distractedly to look for her purse. He might have been a piece of furniture, endurable, reliable, always there, forgotten. She removed her car keys and gave him a weak smile as she handed them to him. "I'll get through this, John. When my heart understands it, my mind will accept it. Right now I just can't make sense of it. I've reserved the palomino for tomorrow, and I'm going riding after work. You and Bebe want to come with me?"

"Yeah, sure," he said, sorrow burning like a ball of fire at the base of his throat. "Sounds good. I'll call her."

But the next afternoon, he and Bebe rode out on their rented horses into the prairie alone. Trey was back in Cathy's life.

Chapter Twenty-Two

For the first time in his life, he'd crossed the line with his aunt, and she was in no mood to forgive him. She'd learned from Miss Emma what had happened, and the morning after she'd refused to look at him, even though a blind person could see how miserable he was. They'd never discussed personal things, mainly because he wasn't open to heart-to-hearts. She was his caregiver; he, her ward. Their conversations consisted of, "Trey, have you done your homework?" and, "Aunt Mabel, have you seen my brown belt?" and the like, and those exchanges were the extent of their intimate communication.

Now, though, Trey wished they were closer so

that he could confide to his aunt his reason for letting Catherine Ann go.

*I didn't do it because I no longer love Catherine
Ann, Aunt Mabel. I did it because I do. I didn't want
her to get even deeper involved with me, a guy who
may end up shooting blanks, when I know that someday she'll want children. If I tell her the truth, she'll
stick with me anyway. She would never abandon me
for any reason. That's the way she is. That's the reason
I love her.*

He'd tell his aunt about the glow he'd seen on
Cathy's face last November in Affiliated Foods
when she held a baby while its mother unloaded her
basket. *I might never put that glow there, Aunt Mabel.
We could eventually adopt, but God only knows what
we'd get. Catherine Ann deserves her own kids, blond
and blue-eyed—gorgeous, like her. At this point, don't
you think it's better to hurt her—and me—by letting
Cathy believe I was unfaithful to her* (he had been,
but not in his heart) *than by telling her the truth?*

He longed to explain all that to his aunt, get her
woman's opinion. It would be such a comfort to
him to have her understanding. She was likely to
agree with him and say that he and Cathy *were* only
eighteen, after all, awfully young to be tying themselves to one person, talking of babies and marriage

and forever. They had futures and careers—life!—ahead of them. But his aunt had thrown up a wall between them, and the air was so thick with judgment he could have ladled it into a bowl. Aunt Mabel adored Cathy, and he was now, in her mind, the biggest jerk of all times. He'd taken to making his own bed so she wouldn't see tears on his pillow, but his aunt had interpreted the deed as a means to get back in her good graces.

Even John had deserted him, and Trey missed him almost as much as he did Cathy. His best friend's disgust with him had reached unprecedented levels, and they'd never gone this long without speaking. He wished he could tell John why he'd gone "off the reservation," but he couldn't bring himself to share his secret even with him. A guy's private parts were just that—strictly off-limits for discussion—and there was just something about another guy, even your best friend, knowing you weren't as . . . manly as he was that made for an uneven playing field, not to mention the awkwardness and embarrassment the knowledge would bring to the relationship.

If he could just hold out from seeing Catherine Ann for two more months until he and John left for fall practice, he'd be over the hump. Meanwhile, he missed her with an ache so physical, it recalled the agony of the mumps, and there was no relief. He had no desire to date the girls who'd set the telephone ringing within days of his split with Cathy. Coach Turner's daughter, Tara, was one of them. *Jeez, what a brazen tramp! How could a man as great as Coach Turner have produced a daughter like Tara?* Trey wondered just how much Coach knew of her activities beyond his all-seeing eye. Out of respect to him, the football team had nothing to do with her. She'd come around to Aunt Mabel's on the pretense of getting Trey to sign her yearbook, thrusting out her big breasts and rubbing up against him. He'd signed it and seen her to the door.

He hadn't even called the telephone numbers he'd carried home in his pocket. All he could see was Cathy hurt and silent in her house from the trauma he'd caused. All he could feel was shame and guilt and pain. All that filled his heart and soul was the feeling he was giving up something he would never have again. He would never know anyone as faithful and steadfast as Catherine Ann. He would never feel as safe and secure with anyone else.

He'd never felt so alone since his mother had abandoned him.

It was his aunt's displeasure with him that led to his agreeing to drive out to the Harbison place to pick up her order of eggs and vegetables. This past year, since November, he'd adamantly refused to go in her place, his obstinacy not unusual since he'd always grumbled about the boring drive and then having to deal with Mrs. Harbison. The woman had never expressed it, but her manner left no doubt what she thought of Mabel Church's jock nephew who considered himself nose-bleeding heights above her horn-tooting son. But now, Trey didn't dare refuse. He'd give anything if John would go with him, but he wouldn't even *think* of inviting him to the scene of their worst nightmare, one Trey had engineered.

It was hot as an oven compared to that cold day in November, but otherwise everything about the Harbison place was the same. Trey approached the big front porch uneasily, the swagger gone. He heard Mrs. Harbison coming to answer the bell, and when she opened the door he couldn't help but blink in surprise. She'd put on a few years since he'd last seen her. He cleared his throat. "Hello, Mrs. Harbison. I've come to pick up my aunt's order."

She held up an arm that was bound in a cast, her hand and fingers strapped to a supporting device. "Well, as you can see, I'm a little handicapped. Had a fall the other day. You'll have to help me gather the eggs."

"The eggs? From where?"

"The barn. You'll have to follow me holding the basket."

Trey felt the blood plunge from his face. "Uh, maybe I should come back another time when— when you're feeling better."

"I feel fine. It's my arm and hand that aren't so good. Go on around the house. I'll meet you out back."

"Yes, ma'am," Trey said.

The stepping-stones and gate and backyard were exactly as he remembered. The concrete picnic table and ram's pen, looking deserted, were still there. The slam of the screened back door carried the same sound of that awful day as Betty Harbison came down the back-door steps and shoved an egg basket into his hand. She carried a knife as well. "Follow me. The door to the coop is in there," she said, pointing the knife at the barn.

Trey forced himself to enter. "We built the chicken pen next to the barn and the door inside, so poachers couldn't steal our eggs and stock from outside," Betty explained, catching his sickened expression. "In this heat, the smell's pretty pungent, but you'll just have to put up with it." She handed him the knife. "You'll need to help me cut some tomatoes, too, and I want to send your aunt a few sprigs of rosemary I've got drying up there."

She nodded to the beam where he and John had hung her son. The crucifix was still nailed on the far wall.

"Yes, ma'am," Trey said, gulping down a threat of nausea.

When all had been gathered, she said, "You'll have to come into the kitchen to help me sack up everything."

Trey was horrified. He'd expected to hand over his aunt's check for the amount and to wait outside until Mrs. Harbison returned with the sack of eggs and vegetables. He found himself snared by her gaze. It was the kind you couldn't get away from, and her tone was not one to say no to. She'd probably been strict with Donny, like a mama bear quick to swipe her cub, but prompt to hold and protect him, too. There was something missing in her that had been there before that November day.

"Yes, ma'am," he said.

Holding the basket, Trey followed her march to the back porch into the kitchen and closed the screened door softly, as if he might wake Donny's ghost. The room was huge and airy and smelled good, but its atmosphere reminded him of an empty auditorium with the audience gone. Two sets of silverware wrapped in napkins were in place on the large, round table. A school photograph of Donny smiling crookedly gazed from a shelf almost hidden by cookbooks and a vase of flowers. Trey stood, feeling tongue-tied and awkward until Mrs. Harbison took the basket from his hands.

"You'll need to wash the dirt off," she said. "Use the sink. I'll get a sack for these things." She ripped paper toweling from a dispenser and handed it to him. "And..." Her tone dropped to a shy level, and she did not look at him. "I expect you'd like a piece of pecan pie for your trouble. Just take a seat at the table, and I'll cut you a slice."

Eat at her table? Where Donny sat? "Oh no, ma'am, I couldn't do that," Trey said, his voice rising on a bubble of panic. He whisked the check from his pocket. "I'll just pay and be on my way."

She stiffened and her mouth set into a thin line. He could have shot himself. The poor woman had just wanted to feed a boy a slice of pie again, and his refusal had hurt the place where her hurt never healed. He could see it plain as day, though she wouldn't reveal it for the world. "I'll get that sack," she said, and went off to the pantry.

Should he tell her he was sorry about her son? If he did, he might give himself away. He could water up at the drop of a hat lately. He opened his mouth when she returned and began busily to sack the produce without help from him. "Mrs. Harbison, I—"

"There," she said, handing him the sack. She snatched the check from his fingers. "Tell your aunt thanks for me. You know the way out."

"Yes, ma'am," he said.

He drove away in his Mustang from the spot where he had parked it that fateful day, the crunch of the gravel echoing a sound he'd never forgotten. A terrible sadness worked its way up through his chest, his throat, his brain, and he pulled to a stop a distance from the house and threw open the door to get out for room to breathe. The hum of summer insects filled his ears—a waterfall of accusing sound. The prairie weaved and blurred. "Catherine Ann...," he sobbed. "Catherine Ann...Catherine Ann..."

When she opened her grandmother's door to him, his eyes were red and swollen and he could hardly get out the words he wished to say to the person he loved the most in all the world. "Catherine Ann, I—I'm so sorry. I—I don't know what got into me. I'm the biggest jerk in the world. I love you so much. Please, please forgive me."

Her stint at the clinic was over. Emma was at the library. Cathy took his hand and drew him inside the air-conditioned house. She telephoned the stable to cancel her riding reservation, then instructed an excited Rufus, "You stay here, boy," and led Trey into her bedroom.

Chapter Twenty-Three

Trey was at summer conditioning camp at the University of Miami when the drugstore pregnancy test confirmed her suspicion. A bomb exploded in her brain. *Oh no! Oh, God, no!* Then the bomb cloud lifted and the devastation was not as severe as she'd thought. She was even guardedly delighted. Pregnancy wasn't the end of the world. She and Trey would simply have to marry earlier than planned. The going wouldn't be easy, but then nothing of worth ever was. She'd have to forfeit her scholarships. They were for unmarried students only. Her studies would be interrupted, but there were other grants and scholarships she could apply for and they'd be in place after a year. Meanwhile, Trey's scholarship would cover their living costs and Aunt

Mabel would want to help. Trey would be of a mixed mind at first. A baby and marriage this early were not what they'd had in mind, but he'd eventually warm to the idea, might even be thrilled. He had never mentioned children, but she knew how much he valued family—how he treasured belonging to people who loved him—and who could give him greater love than a little son or daughter? Her grandmother and Aunt Mabel would be beyond themselves with joy. John would be excited to be an uncle! They would all pull together, and she and Trey would make it.

He returned from Coral Gables the following week, and in Aunt Mabel's parlor Cathy allowed him to tell her all about it—how the veteran quarterback had taken him under his wing, how much he liked Coach Mueller and his staff and the other team members, how well he and John had performed as rookies—and then she said, "Trey, I have something to tell you...."

"Before you do, I have something to tell you," he said, taking her hand. "I've kept something from you, Catherine Ann—something you may not forgive me for."

She stopped him by pressing a finger to his lips. "Too late for confessions," she said, smiling. "They won't change anything." Did Trey not realize she knew why he'd proposed they take a break from each other the last time he came back from Miami? This time, though, he'd called her every night to declare how much he loved and missed her and that he was so glad they'd be at Miami together so he wouldn't suffer the misery of not being with her every day.

"What I have to say is awfully important, Catherine Ann," he said, looking worried.

"So is mine."

"Okay. You first."

Snug against his calisthenics-hardened chest, she said, "I'm pregnant, Trey," and explained that it must have happened—*had* to have happened—the afternoon he came to her after their breakup and caught her unprotected. She'd thought it hadn't mattered, that she was still in her safe period.

She felt his body stiffen, grow absolutely rigid. His arms fell away.

"You're what?" he said.

She pulled back to look at him. His eyes were still as glass. Even his voice was expressionless, his lips pale as a mummy's, barely moving.

"I'm...pregnant, Trey," she repeated, a tremor chasing through her, the small of her back grabbing, the seat of her pain when she was anxious or afraid. "We're going to have a baby."

"Are you sure?"

Her smile flickered. "Yes. Isn't it...wonderful? I know this has come as a shock...."

"You can't be pregnant. You're mistaken."

"There's no mistake, Trey. I saw a gynecologist in Amarillo to make sure."

He pushed away from her as if she'd suddenly become infectious. "I don't believe it."

Her mouth had gone so dry, her tongue felt like sandpaper. She moistened her lips. "Believe what? That I'm pregnant? That it could happen to us?" She forced a small laugh. "Well, considering that afternoon you came to the house, you shouldn't be surprised...."

"I trusted you, Cathy. Even more than John, I trusted you." His voice collapsed, his gaze burned with what she could only interpret as the hurt of betrayal. He staggered up from the couch.

"Trusted me to take the pill?" she said, astonished. "But Trey, darling, why would I have needed to continue them? You'd broken off with me—"

"Get out," he said, so quietly and deliberately she hardly heard him through the growing roar of her terror. "Leave. Right now."

"What?"

"You heard me. *Get out!*" He looked around wildly, and she realized he was searching for her purse. He located it and threw it at her while she stared at him, speechless. "We're through. Get up!" He grabbed her arm and yanked her to her feet.

"Trey... What are you saying?"

"I'm saying..." His voice crumpled to a whimper. "How could you do this to us?"

"Well, I didn't do it by myself," she said, beginning to get angry. "I had a little help, you know. These things happen. A baby isn't the end of the world."

"It is for me. Get out!"

"You can't mean that."

"The hell I don't."

He pulled her by the arm to the front door and pushed her roughly out onto the porch. Feeling paralyzed, unable to grasp what had happened, she stood with her mouth agape as he slammed the door in her face and shot the bolt in place.

Mabel woke the next morning to find him gone, his sheets folded on top of the made bed, a note on his pillow. "I love you, Aunt Mabel. I'm going back to Miami. Thanks for everything. Trey."

Cathy flew to John. Trey had not said good-bye even to him. "Explain it to me, John," she begged. "Why is having a baby so horrendous to him?"

John was as flabbergasted as she. This time at Miami, Trey hadn't so much as glanced at another girl. He had been full of his love for Cathy, beating himself up to John over his notion that he could live without her. John had thought that now nothing could separate them. Trey was made of a complex mass of twists and turns hard for John to fathom at times, but he never shocked him. It was Trey's mode of operation to blast off in a storm of huff when he was angry with those he loved—John, his aunt, Coach Turner—but when his rage blew out he reentered the atmosphere, disarmingly apologetic, as he'd been with Cathy after their one and only separation.

But John had the terrible feeling this time was different.

"What are you going to do?" he asked.

"Wait it out. He'll change his mind. I know he will."

"What if he...doesn't?"

"He will, John. I know him."

John took her by the shoulders. "If he doesn't, will you consider marrying me, Cathy? I'm sure you know how I feel about you. I love you. I always have. I'll love your baby like my own. We can have a good life together."

She stared up into his handsome face, so like Trey's they could have been brothers, which they were except for blood. "I know you do, and I love you too much to let you marry me when you and I both know my heart belongs to Trey—whose *child* belongs to him. He loves me, John. It may take a while, but he'll come back to me. I'm certain of it. I must be available when he does."

No word came from Trey in the next two weeks before Cathy was to leave for Miami. Having no idea where he was staying, none of them had a way to contact him. John suggested that Mabel telephone Sammy Mueller, who assured her that Trey had arrived on campus safe and sound and was staying in the athletic dorm. John and Cathy wrote letters and Mabel sent telegrams and left telephone messages, but all went unanswered. Cathy's world fell black. She and Trey had been joined at the breast, moved to the same heartbeat. She felt as if she'd been torn from his flesh and left with no organs of her own to sustain life.

She and Emma—her grandmother's face reflecting her deep worry and disappointment—sadly discussed her options. Abortion was never even considered, and Cathy had to wonder why Trey, if he had still wanted her and had been so opposed to children, had not demanded that she have one. That would have been like him, but he also knew she would never destroy their child. There was the alternative of putting the baby up for adoption and going on with her life, but that, too, was unthinkable. How could she give away the child conceived out of love for the father?

John repeated his offer to marry her, but again Cathy refused. "Cathy, do you know what you're facing? I know it's the eighties and people don't look on unmarried pregnant girls like they used to, even on a college campus, but...they will look at you differently. There will still be a stigma. Think of the baby...."

"I am, John."

"You're sure there's no chance that you would marry me?" he asked.

"I'm sure," she said. "You deserve better, John."

"There is none better, Cathy."

The day before John was to leave for Florida in his pickup, he telephoned Sammy Mueller.

"Then you haven't discussed your decision with your buddy?" the coach asked him.

"I'll leave that to you, Coach Mueller."

"We were counting on your coming to us as a set."

"Trey will do fine as a single."

"We'll see. The game is going to miss you, John."

He gave Cathy his new address. "This is where you can reach me, if you need me," he said. "Don't hesitate to do so, Cathy. Promise me."

She read the slip of paper in dismay. "You're not—you're not—"

"No, Cathy. I've changed my mind."

He had already applied and been accepted into Loyola University in New Orleans. His binding letter of intent to the University of Miami was forgiven only because he would not be playing football for another college. At Loyola his plan was to apply for the Jesuit Candidacy Program with the hope of becoming an ordained priest.

PART TWO

1986–1999

Chapter Twenty-Four

At his desk in the Hecht Athletic Center, Frank Medford, the offensive coordinator and quarterbacks coach for the Miami Hurricanes, chewed gum furiously, disappointment burning a path to his belly. A little while ago he'd been informed that John Caldwell had turned down his scholarship to play football for Miami to enter Loyola University in New Orleans with hope of becoming a priest.

Frank had come close to having cardiac arrest. "He did *what*?" Frank, a Catholic, had yowled to the bearer of bad tidings. "That son of a bitch! Are you kidding me?"

When Sammy Mueller, as shocked and disappointed as Frank, had assured him he wasn't, Frank had pulled his hair and cursed and stomped around the head coach's office demanding why the hell they hadn't known of John Caldwell's religious predilection before.

"We didn't think to ask, and he didn't mention it," Frank's boss said, a droop to his normally rosy cheeks. "You got to admit, the kid's reason to withdraw from the program is one for the books." He sighed mournfully. "We could have signed the wide receiver from Oklahoma."

Frank paced himself out and fell wearily into an office chair. He'd had these disappointments before but never one that had so thoroughly shaken him. "This explains why Trey Hall came back to campus early," he said. "I knew something was gnawing at him. He's not the same kid who left here after summer conditioning. But why in God's name didn't he tell us that John planned to defect?"

"Apparently, he didn't know, Frank. You're going to have to tell him."

"He must have had some idea what his buddy was up to. What else would explain why Hall's been in the Dumpster since he got back?" Frank felt his neck grow hot, still rocked to the soles of his Nikes by the news. John Caldwell was to Trey Don Hall what fuel was to a rocket. They'd been best friends since their pabulum days. Could Trey get airborne without him?

"Lots of possibilities when it comes to eighteen-year-old boys," Coach Mueller said. "I want you to have a talk with the kid, find out what's going on with him and if you think this blow will affect his playing. Without John, Trey might fold on us."

His boss had put in words the fear that had now destroyed the high Frank had allowed himself ever since seeing the Kersey film clips of Trey Don Hall and John Caldwell and observing the dynamic duo during summer conditioning. Frank had been in the coaching business a long time and had learned to reserve his opinion of all blue-chip quarterbacks and receivers until they proved themselves when and where it counted. The rookies from the Texas Panhandle—especially Trey Don Hall—gave evidence of becoming one of the rare exceptions to the tried-and-true rule that had spared Frank the kind of grief he was experiencing now.

When they'd arrived for their first tour of the campus, Trey Don had appeared typical of the tall, good-looking, cocky quarterbacks Frank had seen as his duty to shoot down from their high school pinnacles.

"I prefer to be called TD," he had announced when he was introduced to the coaches, his grin inferring the meaning of the initials.

Frank had drawled, "Around here, you have

to earn that moniker before it's applied. For now, you're just Trey Don Hall."

But there was no *just* about TD Hall. It was becoming clear that he might live up to the dazzle of his game clips showing him all gold—arm, feet, hips, and brains. The offensive coaches had been impressed by his focus and conduct during summer conditioning when everybody would have bet he'd be out to the clubs in Coconut Grove every night undoing the day's physical training, John going along to keep Trey out of trouble. His dedication and abstinence from the frivolities he'd indulged in on his first visit to the campus had surprised them, as had his unexpected reappearance on campus within days of his departure back to the Texas Panhandle. Frank had known right away that something had gone wrong at home when the boy had asked if he could pay for his room and board in the athletic dorm for the remaining weeks before his scholarship kicked in. Since his return, he'd lived in monkish isolation—no girls or nightlife— in complete contrast to the outgoing, sociable kid they'd first met. He hung around his room alone, ate his meals apart at the training table, and turned in early. During the day he studied game films, worked out, and practiced throwing passes at moving targets he hit nearly every time. He drew spectators on those days—never members of the coaching staff, since the NCAA (National Collegiate Athletic Association) forbade coaches from any interaction with their players that could be construed as "preemptive instruction" before the season began. But they had watched the perfection of his spirals through binoculars trained on him from office windows and high in bleacher seats and imagined him standing tall in the pocket, effortlessly flicking deep cuts to his wide receiver, John. Their two-man combination was every offensive coordinator's ultimate fantasy.

Now one half of that fantasy was over and the other may be, too, if Trey Don Hall's exceptional skills and supreme confidence in his abilities were inextricably linked to John Caldwell's. Game films clearly showed their faith in each other and their almost telepathic connection that had powered Kersey High School to win a state championship. Could Trey function as successfully without his teammate?

"You wanted to see me, Coach Medford?" Trey asked from the open door.

"I do. Come in and have a seat." The boy had come from a workout and was still in his gym shorts and jersey. It was another pleasant surprise that Trey Hall consistently lifted weights. Most quarterbacks did not like to pump iron. They thought weights were for the big linemen and linebackers, but the rookie believed that great quarterbacks had to be strong and fast. At six foot three and carrying close to two hundred pounds of conditioned muscle, he was both. Frank felt another jab of anxiety. What if the kid proved a bust?

"I'm afraid I have some bad news, Trey."

Trey lowered himself into the proffered chair apprehensively. "It's not my aunt, is it?"

"No, not your aunt. It's John Caldwell. He's not coming to Miami."

Frank had deliberately dropped the news without preliminaries. How Trey reacted to it would reveal if he'd known of John's decision and maybe gotten used to the idea of suiting up solo.

But clearly Frank had thrown a grenade into the kid's lap. Trey's face washed of color. "What?" he said. "What do you mean he's not coming to Miami?"

"I mean he's changed his mind about joining our ranks this fall. He's declined his scholarship."

"But he can't do that, can he? Legally, I mean."

"He can if he doesn't play football for another college or university for a year."

"Not play football..."

Clearly another shock. "You know any reason why he'd pull out on us?"

"No...I...thought he'd probably get married, live off campus, but never give up coming to Miami, playing football. The girl he's...marrying has a scholarship here, too."

"Well, he certainly isn't getting married," Frank said, "at least not to a woman. He's going to Loyola University in New Orleans to become a priest."

Trey gazed at Frank like someone who'd taken a bullet to the chest, shot by a friend. It was several seconds before Trey reacted to its impact. He pushed back his chair and stumbled to his feet. "No, he wouldn't—he couldn't! *God, John—!*" He swung away from Frank's desk and covered his face with his hands, hunching forward as if taking blows. He held the position a few minutes before he turned back, wiping angrily at his tears.

"I'll be honest with you," Frank said. "I feel like crying myself. John Caldwell could have been the best wide receiver in college football. Did you have any inkling he'd do this?" He took a box of Kleenex from a drawer he kept on hand for his sneezing fits during allergy season and offered it across the desk. Trey snapped a tissue from the box and swiped his eyes.

"No...not now. Like I said, I...guessed he'd be getting married."

Ah, Frank thought, *so that probably explained it.*

John Caldwell and his girl had had a blowup. But, my God, at eighteen to renounce everything going for him because of a girl to enter the priesthood and become a celibate? "Well, look," he said, leaning forward. "It's not too late to get him back here. We'll track him down and you can have a talk with him, convince him to get his butt back here—"

"No."

Taken aback at the immediate response, Frank said, "Why not?"

"Because I wouldn't be able to change his mind."

Frank knew boys. Trey was keeping the lid on something he had no intention of sharing with him, a painful secret he thought too private to discuss. But there was nothing too personal Frank hadn't heard. He adopted his fatherly pose. "TD, what happened when you returned home? I know something did because you turned around and came back to us a different person and now John's taken off to join the priesthood. I appreciate that it's hard to talk about, but whatever it is, I might be able to help. You told us that you two have had a dream to come to Miami since junior high. When you were recruited, you never even considered another school. So what happened to change all that? If it's only a girl that's involved, then, by all that's holy, we've got to talk to John. He's too young to make this kind of decision right now. He can take his vows later. Lots of priests do."

The boy's eyes were now dry, though grief lurked in their darkness. He pushed himself out of his chair. "I've got to go," he said.

Startled—it was for Frank to decide when a recruit left his office—he said, "Very well, but all may not be lost. John might come back to us next year when he gets a taste of what his vows will entail. I once thought of becoming a priest until I spent a little time in what's called the discernment period. I didn't last. Poverty, chastity, obedience—those are the vows. I can see John dealing with two out of three, but chastity—?"

A twitch of the boy's facial muscle indicated Frank had hit a nerve. "Discernment period?"

"The preliminary time a candidate for a religious order is required to go through to determine if he's cut out for the priestly life."

"He's cut out for it," Trey said, and turned toward the door.

"Before you go, Hall, be honest with me." Annoyed at the feeling the kid had gotten the upper hand, Frank's tone was insistent. "Is John's defection going to affect what we brought you here to do?"

Trey wadded the tissue and lobbed it into the

trash can by Frank's desk. Minutes ago, he'd looked like any vulnerable eighteen-year-old boy. Now he'd taken on the stature of a full-fledged, bitter man. "No, Coach. Football's all I've got left."

BACK IN HIS ROOM, Trey dropped down hard on his bed and pushed his fingers through his hair. *John, going into the priesthood? Good God!* He should have seen something like this coming. Ever since last November he'd watched John gravitate toward his Catholic leanings, but he could never have dreamed that John would go to these lengths to redeem himself—certainly not *now*. Where would that leave Cathy? He was supposed to have married her with nobody the wiser about her pregnancy. How could John go off and leave Cathy in her condition unless...unless...

Trey stood and wrenched open the bureau drawer containing Cathy's letters, five of them, unopened, and one received from John a week ago, also unread. He tore it open, and the neatly written, one-page letter confirmed his suspicion.

Dear TD,
I'm writing to ask you—beg you—to come home and do your duty to Cathy and your baby. She's going to keep it because she says she

*can't give away a child born out of her love
for you. For the same reason, she's not going to
marry me. I begged her to, TD. I love her, too.
I always have, and not as a brother, either. She
refused because she says she can't marry anyone
else when her heart belongs to you. She's convinced you feel the same and will come back for
her and you can be married before school starts.
You've done a lot of things that I don't understand, TD, but this one has really stumped me.
What's got you so set against becoming a father?
Married to a girl like Cathy, I'd think having
a family with her would be the most wonderful thing in the world. Won't you please come
home and marry her, and we can all go to
Miami just as we planned?*

We miss you, buddy.

John

Trey balled the letter in his fist, tears streaming. *He doesn't know...hasn't even guessed...Cathy,
either. If she had, she'd marry John, not wait for me.*

He sat down again and clasped his head, reliv-
ing, as he'd done many times, the moment of
Cathy's announcement, feeling again the swamp
of shock and anger and disbelief and...abandon-
ment. It had taken only seconds for the certainty

to hit his heart—like lightning striking a power source—that he'd never, *could* never, feel the same for her again. She'd destroyed the one essential element that had bound him to her.

He still remembered the feel of her tanned skin when he took her arm and shoved her out onto the porch and out of his life. He'd braced himself against the locked door, his lungs on fire, and heard her small fists pummel the wood and his name cried over and over. *"Trey… Trey…!"* she'd cried, his fallen little angel, storming heaven's gates to open to her once again, but he was deaf to all but the voice of Dr. Thomas delivering his verdict in his office in May.

"What are you trying to say, Doc?"

"Your semen analysis shows that your sperm cells are abnormally shaped and cannot swim."

"And that means?"

"It means that you are presently sterile…."

Each blow on the door had driven a spike through his heart, but she was guilty of the one sin he could never get past. She had betrayed him with his best friend. He would rather have died than to think of Cathy in John's arms—the two of them copulating—and in only a week of their split. Fairly or unfairly, he'd trusted her to remain faithful to him even in the storm. She should have known it would blow over. She knew him better than he knew himself. She should have perceived that something had gone horribly wrong with him to break up with her. She should have trusted his love enough to consider his actions might have something to do with her welfare.

Her pleas had finally stopped. He'd heard her move away from the door and off the porch, her footsteps hesitant and slow, sounding like fallen leaves brushing stone, rifled by the wind. Tears had scalded his eyes. John would marry her, he'd thought, seeing the irony in the whole miserable mess. He had loved her since the sixth grade, same as Trey. He'd kidded himself in believing John thought of her as a sister. He'd marry her and raise the kid who at the moment she thought was Trey Don Hall's.

He had planned to tell her and John the truth about his...condition when they arrived on campus—the truth he would have spilled to Cathy just before she dropped her bombshell if she hadn't pressed her fingers to his lips. *Too late for confessions*, she'd said, and he'd thought she was speaking of his escapades at Miami, which of course she had suspected. Later in the confusion that had raged like hornets in his brain, he'd wondered if his capers were the reason she'd cheated on him, like most girls would have out of vengeance, but that didn't sound like Cathy, so he'd had to believe she'd simply gone to John for comfort and one thing had led to another and they'd ended up in bed together.

Too sad, too bad. She should have kept her panties on. She should have waited.

He couldn't have confessed his secret before he left Kersey. His pain was too great. Cathy and John had orphaned him again. They'd destroyed the family they'd built, and they deserved to feel the abandonment and loss they'd inflicted upon him. He'd expected them already to be married by the time they reported to campus—or would shortly after they heard his news. *Guess what, guys? I'm not the father of your baby, Cathy. You are, John. So you all have a good life—without me.*

And now John had gone off to study for the one vocation that would make his and Cathy's marriage impossible. *Christ!* How could everything have skittered so far off course? How could all their dreams and hopes and plans have changed as quickly as a fumble on the goal line and blown the winning score?

The drawer containing Cathy's letters was still open, begging to be read, her handwriting conjuring up her trim, small figure, but her memory brought only the bitter resurgence of his feeling of betrayal. How stupid he'd been to believe she was different from any other girl in the world. *Women!* You couldn't trust a one. Even John's mother had strayed, and look at all the damage her adultery had caused.

He would never read Cathy's letters. He would not be tempted by sympathy or guilt—or remorse for his own part in the breakup—to take her back, because now there was no way he and Cathy would ever work. But what should he do? Should he tell her and John the humiliating truth about himself before it was too late or... wait? What good would the truth do anyway? As much as John's loss to the game was nothing short of a tragedy, he had made up his mind to enter the priesthood. What right did Trey Don Hall have to interfere with John's plans to atone for that day in November? And as for Cathy... she was only eighteen. She would get over him. She was beautiful and smart and determined. Despite the baby, she had a promising future ahead of her. And... as much as she cared for John, she did not love him. Wouldn't it be wrong to condemn her to marry him for the sake of the baby when later, down the line, she might fall in love with someone she really did love and want to marry?

He was aware of what his silence would cost—temporarily. Aunt Mabel and Miss Emma would feel some disgrace. They were of the generation where nice girls didn't get pregnant out of wedlock, but the younger people would shrug. So what? It happened all the time—just not to smart girls like Cathy. He felt a special kick of guilt when he thought of the stigma to the baby. His aunt's friends would never forget it was born a bastard, and her nephew would be considered one, too, for deserting Cathy, but in time the town would forgive him. It always did its star football players. John probably never would. The priest might forgive him for leaving Cathy to face her situation alone but—though he had no room to point—not the boy who loved her. John should have known his best friend would wake up and reconcile with Cathy, but how could he not have answered the call of his gonads when she was available and willing?

Trey got up from the bed and closed the drawer. He'd give it a year. If John found he couldn't stick it out at Loyola and if Cathy was still carrying the torch for him, he'd tell them the truth. The rest would be up to them. If neither was the case, he'd keep his secret and let be what would be.

He felt better instantly. His tears had dried. The void in him was still there, a painful emptiness that brought back feelings of his days at Aunt Mabel's parlor windows, but other friends and other girls would come along to fill the space. It would just take time, and he had plenty of that.

Meanwhile—he picked up a football from his bureau, the feel of the pigskin comforting and familiar in his hands—he had the game.

Chapter Twenty-Five

In his room, John heard the television come on, his father's first order of business when he entered the house, followed by the thump of his boots hitting the floor beside his La-Z-Boy, the second indicator he was home. Next came the solid thud of his socked feet to the kitchen for a beer—to which he felt entitled after his sobriety during football season—and then the pad back to his chair, where he settled with an audible sigh of contentment.

"John! You in your room?" he called loudly.

"Same!" John yelled back.

"You getting packed?"

"Same!"

"Come out here when you're through. I've got a surprise for you!"

It was the way they'd always communicated—hollering through walls, from different rooms. John had yet to inform his father that, rather than to the University of Miami in Coral Gables, he'd be leaving for Loyola University in New Orleans in the morning.

He'd already made the rounds to say good-bye. He'd gone first to see Bebe Baldwin at her father's gas station, where she was manning the cash register for the summer before she and Cissie Jane Fielding left for the University of Texas in the fall. Bebe was behind the counter when he walked in, her face lighting up at his unexpected visit. He felt the usual twinge that he was unable to return her feelings. Now he had an excuse. Her face dimmed when he told her the news.

"You can't be serious," she said.

"But I am, Bebe."

"But you're too . . . virile, too sexy, too *gorgeous* to be a priest!"

He'd grinned. "Being a priest doesn't make a guy less those things, Bebe."

"But it's such a *waste*! You'll never be able to beat the girls away from you."

"I guess I have to find that out."

She'd sighed. "Well, thanks for the memories, John. If you change your mind and want to make more of them, give me a call."

Next, he'd driven to Aunt Mabel's house, an empty and echoing place without Trey, then on for a final visit with Miss Emma at the library, and finally to see Cathy at her grandmother's. Cathy had stood at the front door with tears in her eyes when he'd left and Rufus had followed on his heels to his pickup, jumping on him before he could get in, his whine begging John to stay. His throat had closed as he'd knelt to bury his face in the collie's ruff. *Take care of them for me, Rufus.*

"Have you heard from Trey?" Aunt Mabel had asked.

"No, ma'am," he'd said, noticing the brownish circles beneath her eyes, symptoms of worry and shame. "He's probably not had time to answer my letter."

"Sweet liar," she'd said, and patted his cheek.

He'd answered the same to Miss Emma's similar question and noted the deeper crevices in her lined face. "I just don't understand it," she'd said.

Cathy had not mentioned him. She'd said in French, "Dieu être avec vous, mon ami." *(God be with you, my friend.)*

And he had answered, "Et avec vous aussi, mon cher amie." *(And you as well, my dear friend.)*

He'd telephoned Coach Turner to inform him where he was headed. His change in plans had not had time to get around town. Coach would be surprised and saddened but not shocked. He had been aware of John's deeper involvement with St. Matthew's the past year, and he would figure that Trey's desertion of Cathy had been the deal breaker that had led his All-State wide receiver—"our moral compass" as Coach had described him in the *Dallas Morning News*—to follow his heart, not Trey's rear end to keep him out of trouble.

But John had not expected Coach Turner's vehemence. "He's a piece of work, that boy," he'd said, surprising John by the personal bitterness in his tone. "You're better off without that Judas."

Now the only person remaining on John's farewell list was the man who, for real or imagined, called him his son. Already John found himself wondering if he could ever completely think like a Jesuit and embrace the sanctity of all human beings as children of God, no matter their embarrassment to their Maker, but he would try. Bebe had asked, "When did you slip away from us, John, and none of us saw?"

He could have said it started the November evening he'd gone to St. Matthew's to beg God's forgiveness for his act of that afternoon. He had lit a candle and knelt before the altar and prayed. A lot of afternoons after football practice in the following weeks, he'd driven back to St. Matthew's without telling Trey. By then his onetime constant companion was with Cathy for the rest of the day. But Trey had guessed. "Say one for me, too, when you're at St. Matthew's, will you, Tiger?"

Father Richard had noticed his comings and goings and sat down beside him on the pew one afternoon before the state play-off game.

"Are you praying to win the game?"

The thought had never occurred to him, but rather than offer another explanation, he had remained silent.

Father Richard had given him an understanding smile. "There's nothing wrong with asking for direction around and through the obstacles that would prevent us from reaching our goals."

Father Richard had been speaking of John's opponents, but he had taken the larger meaning and had begun to pray for a direction in his life that would allow him to atone for what he had done and bring him peace. He began to feel a pull toward the priesthood and the Order of the Society of Jesus, in particular—the Jesuits—but he had read enough of the formation steps to ordination to realize that he might not be cut out for the ministry. At Loyola, he planned to get his bachelor's degree in business and go through the candidacy program that was designed to help the candidate decide if he wanted to become a Jesuit. Acceptance into the program carried no obligation, and he could withdraw from it at any time.

His last bag packed, John walked to the door of the living room and stopped short. His father was sitting in his easy chair wearing a green and orange and white baseball cap with MIAMI HURRICANES stitched across the crown. A huge grin spread across his face. "I've got one for you, too," he said. "It's in that box on the table. I ordered two. I figured we could wear 'em when I take you out for a little celebration supper tonight."

"Dad…" He hadn't called Bert that since he was eight years old. "I have something to tell you. Maybe you'd better turn off the TV."

"Well, sure, Son." Bert hurriedly clicked off the remote, John wincing from shame at his father's eagerness for the chance to chat with him. He withdrew his socked feet from the ottoman and pushed it toward John. "Have a seat and tell your old dad what's on your mind. But first, are you all gassed up to get off to Coral Gables in the morning? It's a long stretch between filling stations until you get out of the Panhandle."

"I'm all gassed up, but I'm not going to Coral Gables, Dad. I'm driving to New Orleans."

Bert blinked. "New Orleans? But aren't you supposed to be at Miami for fall practice two days from now?"

"I was, but I'm not going to Miami. I'm enrolling at Loyola University in New Orleans."

"What?" Bert's eyes bulged. He wriggled to a straighter position in his chair. "To hell you are! You're going to Miami, where you have a scholarship, and play football!"

"I've turned down the scholarship. I'm going to Loyola to consider preparing for the priesthood."

Bert gaped at him like a landed fish. Furiously he pushed himself up from his chair and glared down at John. "It's that goddamned fuckin' Father Richard that's done this to you, hasn't he?"

"He has nothing to do with this."

Bert punched the air with his fist. "He has *everything* to do with this. Johnny, listen to me—" Bert sat down again and drew toward John. "Do you realize what you're giving up: the chance to be one of the greatest receivers in college football, to go to the NFL, to make tons of money, to live the kind of life that most of us can only dream about—"

"Yes, Pop, I know," John said, getting up from the ottoman, "but I don't want that anymore. I need something else. I'm going to Loyola."

Bert looked up at him, his lip curling contemptuously. "To live without sex the rest of your life? What's wrong with you?"

"Lots. That's why I'm considering the priesthood. The first step to becoming a Jesuit is to know you are a sinner."

"Oh, hogwash! Johnny—" Bert's face twisted from his effort to get through to John. "You're a good boy, the best I know. You don't need no 'freshening up.' You don't need to sacrifice yourself to make yourself better."

"I wouldn't do it for that reason. I'd do it to make other people's lives better."

Bert scowled at him, disgust and disappointment molding the look he'd wear when he thought of him from now on, John suspected. "I don't suppose we're going out for that celebration supper," he said.

"Hell, no!" Bert sailed the baseball cap across the room. "I'm going to get drunk."

John spent the rest of the evening with Father Richard in his study going over details for his admission into Loyola University.

Chapter Twenty-Six

I'll sell the house," her grandmother declared. "The money from Buddy's insurance policy will give you more than enough to see you through until the baby comes, and by then the house will have sold and you'll have another grant. I'll move to Miami to look after the baby while you go to school. I have to retire at the end of the year anyway...." They were huddled around the kitchen table a few days before Cathy was to be at the University of Miami to register, their anxiety hanging in the air like smog. "Cathy, honey, there is no other solution—"

Cathy put up her hands to end the argument. "No," she said. "I'm not going to allow you to sell your house and move from your friends and the town you've known all your life because of my dumb mistake—make that *two* dumb mistakes."

The first was getting pregnant. The second had to do with her decision at the beginning of the year to accept the full four-year scholarship awarded her through the First Baptist Church. Upon its acceptance, the recipient had to forfeit all other scholarships with the exception of the National Merit Scholarship, which, while prestigious, would cover only a fraction of her college costs. As a result, Cathy had relinquished several she'd been offered that would have made a considerable difference in the financial dilemma she now faced. Because of a morals clause, the full scholarship from the church she'd attended since she was eleven years old had been rescinded.

It had been the hardest decision she'd ever made to report her condition to her pastor. She'd weighed the pros of waiting to disclose her unmarried state until she was at Miami and her pregnancy became obvious (there was always the chance that Trey would come around once they were on campus together), but if he didn't, she'd be in a deep financial pickle and forced to come home if the church yanked her scholarship in the middle of the first term.

The minister had bestowed a word of warning

after he'd asked if her predicament was generally known. When she'd told him no, he said, "I'm afraid that once I inform the board of deacons of the change in your...er, status, news of...your situation will come out, Cathy. People talk, you know, no matter that they're charged to silence. The board meets the middle of September. You have a few weeks' grace period before it does."

In her panic, every bit as mind numbing as Cathy's, her grandmother had overlooked several obstacles to her resolution of the crisis—one that Cathy had even thought of herself until she realized that selling the house offered no salvation even if she'd been selfish enough to agree to it. The house needed costly, unaffordable repairs before it could go on the market, and with its limited appeal and lack of house buyers in Kersey it could sit for a year, probably longer, before it sold—if ever. Her grandmother's old Ford was on its last wheels and would soon have to be replaced. There would also be medical bills to pay. Financially, there was no choice but for Cathy to remain in Kersey and get a job until she could apply for grant money that would allow her to go to a school in state next year—that is, if Trey did not come for her.

Her expectation that he'd come in time to save her from the discovery of her pregnancy lessened each day. But late was better than never. The more she thought about it, the more she found hope and comfort in the fact that Trey hadn't asked her to have an abortion or put the baby up for adoption. That surely meant he was giving himself time and space to come around to the idea of marriage and fatherhood.

"I'll ask Dr. Graves for a full-time job and stay here until the baby comes," she said. "That will give me enough time to figure out what to do and make plans. Meanwhile, I'll make the best of it." Cathy took her grandmother's hands, speared once again by guilt for the extra worry lines she'd put on her old face. "I'm so sorry for putting you in this predicament. I know it's what you always feared...."

"Yes, I did, but I believed that even if it happened, what was the problem? You and Trey would marry, raise your baby. Life would go on, not in the way you'd planned, but maybe even better." She shook her head. "I don't understand it. As crazy as Trey has always been about you, I never dreamed he'd behave like this. I look back on the way he looked at you the night of the junior prom, and— even as young as you were..." Her voice trailed off.

"You thought we'd be together forever," Cathy finished for her. "I did, too." Her throat burned. Of all the memories, the night of the junior prom was the best. Only a year ago last May had Trey promised to return her more beautiful than ever, and he had. Now it felt like a lifetime since the boy in the tuxedo had given that assurance to the grandmother of the girl in the blue chiffon.

"The baby will be fine here until I can get us on our feet," Cathy said. "Then she and I will move before she's old enough to feel...shame."

"She?"

Cathy allowed the wisp of a smile. "I have a feeling it's a girl."

Rumors flew at the breakup and questions arose when Cathy did not leave for college as expected.

"Cathy, what in the world are you still doing here?" Dr. Graves asked when she appeared in his clinic on the day she was supposed to leave for Coral Gables. "I thought you'd be on your way to the University of Miami by now."

"I'm not going to college this year, Dr. Graves. That's why I've come, to ask for my job back—full-time, if that's possible."

"Not going to college! Why not?"

"I...It's personal," she said, hardly able to meet his gaze. She'd caught a knowing streak of perception in it, though the board of deacons would not meet until next week.

"Come back to my office," he said quietly.

He closed the door and said, "I heard that you and Trey had a pretty serious tiff. Would that have anything to do with your decision not to go to college and honor your scholarships?"

"Dr. Graves, forgive me, but that's my business."

"I ask, Cathy, because... when a girl like you— who has everything going for her and no reason in the world to refuse the opportunities she's been given—suddenly cries off from them, well... that can mean only one thing, unless your grandmother is ill and you must stay behind to care for her."

"She's not ill."

"I see." Silence fell. "Cathy, you've put me in an awkward position...." Dr. Graves gestured toward a chair and Cathy sat on its edge while he explained. If it were up to him, he'd hire her without a second's thought, he said, his tone genuinely sorrowful. She was the best assistant he'd ever had, but he had to consider his wife.... She wouldn't take kindly to an unmarried pregnant girl in her husband's clinic. She'd feel Cathy's presence would send the wrong kind of message to other young girls, and... well, in this economic climate, he had to think of his business, that others might view the situation in the same light. Cathy understood, didn't she? He wished it could be different, but... he lifted his shoulders regretfully.

Cathy did understand. She thanked him for seeing her and left, and only when she'd driven Emma's car around the corner did she stop and allow herself a good cry over the steering wheel.

Dr. Thomas, to her surprise, was the first to show his overt disappointment. A kindly man, he didn't seem the sort to pass judgment, but he examined her without his usual warmth. "You're two months along, I'd say. The sonogram will tell us for sure. I'll send my nurse in to perform the procedure and to instruct you in prenatal care." He pulled off his gloves and threw them into the waste bin in patent disapproval. "I suppose one never gets too old for surprises," he said, and left the room.

By letter, she notified the chairman of the National Merit Scholarship committee that she would not be attending college in the fall as planned and received a courteous reply of regret that the scholarship would have to be withdrawn.

Mabel, bewildered, appalled at her nephew's behavior, said, "Now, see here, Emma, you must let me help. That's my great-nephew Cathy is carrying, and I have every right to meddle and interfere. At least let me pay the medical bills, and you can use Buddy's insurance money to buy a new car. You're going to need a good set of wheels. What if the time comes for Cathy to have the baby and that old Ford of yours won't start?"

Emma refused. The bottom had fallen out of Texas's petroleum industry, and her old friend's oil stocks had taken a hit. Emma would not allow Mabel to sell them far below their value and lose the dividends that supplemented her Social Security. They would get by, Emma assured her. One of the jobs for which Cathy had applied in town was bound to come through.

None did. The advertised positions for a bank teller, secretary in a local insurance agency, and receptionist in the county agent's office were filled by other applicants, presumably because they would not become a social embarrassment to their employers. Weeks passed and hiring possibilities in the county dwindled or dried up because of the slump in the oil-based economy.

Cathy's small, narrow figure showed evidence of her pregnancy early, further condemning her chances of "white-collar" employment, and at the beginning of her fourth month she parked Emma's dilapidated Ford in front of the HELP WANTED sign she'd noticed displayed for several weeks in the window of Bennie's Burgers.

She shut her eyes and swallowed hard at the

thought of working in Bennie's. She liked the proprietor, a short, burly, jovial man in his fifties who wore a beard and was rarely seen without his prominent middle covered by a food-stained chef's apron. He had inherited the business from his father, Benjamin, who'd established Bennie's Burgers in the fifties, and took great pride in calling it the only "family-owned" hamburger place in town. Unmarried, Bennie lived with his reclusive mother and her cats in a house behind his establishment, but he regarded his place of business as his home and its customers as his family.

But Bennie's Burgers was what her grandmother called a dive—dark and smoky, loud with jukebox music, the tacky menu limited mainly to greasy breakfast fare and hamburgers and fries. "A haven for cockroaches," Emma would sniff, disapproving of the high school's senior crowd (the only members of the student body allowed off campus for lunch) preferring Bennie's to the more modern and clean Whataburger across town. Some of Cathy's fondest high school memories had been made with Trey and John and Bebe in the scarred pine booths of Bennie's—but as a student, not an employee.

"You want a job *here*, Cathy? As a *waitress*?" Bennie Parker looked thunderstruck.

"I know I haven't any experience, but I'll learn fast, and—"

"Whoa!" Bennie held up a dishwasher-roughened hand. "You don't have to sell me. I know you learn fast. You're the smartest girl in town. That's why I'm going to say no. This job isn't for you."

"Bennie..." Her voice dropped out of hearing of several coffee drinkers at the counter. "It's...the only one I can get."

His glance dropped to her abdomen, the denim boyhood shirt her grandmother had kept of Buddy's hiding its telltale bulge for now. Emma had cut the sleeves to elbow length and trimmed the hems and shirttail in white rickrack to make a maternity smock. It went perfectly with Cathy's white cotton slacks.

"Is that so?" Bennie said, his tone indicating disgust. "Then I guess it's no use telling you to try the First Methodist Church. I hear the pastor's secretary is moving to Ohio."

Cathy continued in her undertone, "The job's already been filled."

Bennie made a face. "Their loss. Okay, you've got the job. I wish it were something more your speed, but we'll be good to you. When can you start?"

It was September. Classes had begun at the University of Miami and Loyola and the University of

Southern California, where Laura had enrolled in premed. By now, she and Trey and John would have bought their books, met their professors, settled in to get on with their futures. Tomorrow, Cathy would begin hers as a waitress in Bennie's Burgers.

Chapter Twenty-Seven

Fall football practice began. The University of Miami's athletic dorm filled up, football jocks occupying one end; participants in other sports, the other. Returning gridiron players—the starters—shared rooms with starters, the rookies with rookies. As everyone settled in, Trey was surprised that no one showed up to take John's berth. He kept quiet about it in case the dorm proctor brought up the oversight to the housing department. In his ever-present mood, sharing the room with a stranger—having to adjust to his habits and ways (what if he played rap music?)—was abhorrent to him. Trey found himself craving privacy and solitude and peace to cry and mope and throw things without consideration for anyone else.

From the get-go, even from the starters, he was accorded a respect not shown the other freshmen. The Miami Hurricanes had recruited only one quarterback to add to its roster, and Trey knew if he did not prove himself, that respect would vanish as quickly as footprints in a sandstorm. It was strange walking out onto the field without John at his side. The feeling of being without an essential piece of equipment persisted during the first week of pre-season practice, but it did not affect his performance, a concern of the watching coaches he laid to rest in one of the first morning sessions. Trey and a veteran center, along with a skeleton crew of freshman backs and receivers—"Seven on Seven"—were pitted against the starting corner backs, linebackers, and safeties. After the summer break, the drill was to help the veterans regenerate their confidence and timing at the rookies' expense.

"Okay, Trey, show 'em what you got," Frank said, smacking his bottom as he sent him out onto the field.

Trey complied by showing an uncanny ability to lay back, observe what was happening on the field, then, with no more than a flick of the wrist, let fly the ball to the exact spot the play called for. The freshman pass receivers sometimes dropped the ball, but through no error of Trey's execution.

The most spectacular demonstration of his accuracy came when he dropped back to elude a linebacker's serious intent to rush him, bounced up on his toes twice, and threw the ball sixty yards, a long, arching spiral that settled like a baby into his receiver's hands in the end zone.

Attempts to break Trey's concentration failed. He was not seen to blink when he was in charge of the action. He refused to fall for the veteran defense's most sophisticated "disguise coverage"—tricks to deceive him into throwing the ball to the wrong spot. In the huddle, trust grew in his ability to execute the play as planned and in his aptitude to figure out exactly what man was covered and who would be open to receive his pass. The tension of competition mounted as the chain marker advanced for Trey's group, and more than once a starting defensive back exchanged a look of surprise from behind his face guard with another veteran. The seasoned center grinned from across the scrimmage line and taunted, "You boys enjoying your lunch?"

On the sidelines, Frank let slip his cautious reserve of blue-chip quarterbacks and pumped his arm in jubilation. By the start of the season, the recruit from the Texas Panhandle had completely put at ease the offensive coordinator's anxiety that he could not make it without John Caldwell. Privately, though, and a little sadly, Frank sensed Trey Don Hall had learned to play his position with a missing limb. The boy had still not recovered from whatever had gone amuck back in Kersey, Texas.

FROM HIS FIRST IMPRESSIONS of the place in June, Trey was finding that little he'd expected to enjoy about the University of Miami and the surrounding area was panning out. The school was a private research university set in a tropical garden located in what was touted as one of the most beautiful and exciting cities in the country, but the tightly packed high-rises, blocked horizon, and noise and traffic gradually began to get under his skin. The weather was all he'd hoped for, but despite the open green spaces of the magnificent campus and the occasional breezes from the Atlantic, the humidity of the summer days induced a mild but persistent form of claustrophobia. The feeling had started after he'd left the treeless plains traveling south, alone, on Interstate 40. As he worked his way down through Louisiana, Alabama, Mississippi, the horizon he'd grown up seeing was eventually lost in the dense pines and kudzu-covered trees crowding the road, finally becoming tunnels that forced him to take deep gulps of air and gave him the sensation of drowning in a swamp. The Miami beaches were great and the girls gorgeous in their bikinis, but he'd never felt so alone or desolate as when he walked on stretches of sand along a never-ending body of water, and he'd discovered he disliked the cling of salt on his skin.

The University of Miami was expensive, its tuition one of the highest in the country, and most of the students came from wealth. Trey had believed, during his and John's initial visit to the campus, that it would be exciting and interesting to make new friends among those who could introduce him to the material delights of worlds he'd never known. Now, for reasons he couldn't explain, he was indifferent to the idea of "experiencing the rich," perhaps because he still longed for the simple pleasures he and Cathy and John had enjoyed in their relative poverty.

Even the climate affected Trey in a way unexpected. The first bite of fall was in the air in the Panhandle, but in this part of Florida, land of palm trees and hibiscus, the temperatures remained mild and steady, the sunsets the color of pink cotton candy and robin-egg blue. "Wind riders" rode the evening skies over his hometown of Kersey this time of year, cloud formations of powerful horsemen streaming bandanas of gold and purple and magenta behind them as they streaked across the heavens over the boundless Panhandle prairies.

At least those were the images that he and John and Cathy had found in the clouds.

"Doesn't it ever get football weather around here?" Trey asked one of his teammates, wiping his face with a towel on the sidelines during a game.

The boy was from Miami. "What are you—a freaking comic?" he asked.

Trey had spent most of his savings from his job at Affiliated Foods to pay for his stint at summer conditioning camp and now, for the first time in his life, found himself worrying where he'd get the money for his next tank of gas or a pizza to eat at midnight. He would have gotten a part-time job, but an NCAA rule forbade athletes on scholarships from working during the fall and spring, and while his scholarship paid for everything, it did not include spending money. He was not embarrassed by his lack of funds. The attraction of his looks and talent and brains, his potential to be a football great, made money unnecessary to be accepted into any circle he chose. He minded only because he hated to continue taking money from his aunt. He was aware that her income had taken a dive, and more often than not he returned her checks—out of guilt, shame, sorrow, feeling undeserving of her generosity, he refused to determine—and went without the extras the money would have provided.

But there was an upside to his financial situation. It gave him an excuse to decline invitations from his new pals—recruits like himself—to hit the local hangouts on Sunday, Tuesday, and Thursday nights, the big party night when everybody let loose before tightening up for the game on Saturday. He couldn't afford the evenings of throwing back beers and raising hell, and they would have done nothing to lift his mood.

Though he didn't understand it (he'd expected to be immersed in the glories of becoming another Jim Kelly by now and to hell with John and Cathy), Trey chalked up his atypical desire to be alone, to study by himself, to walk without company to class, to pretend ignorance of the signals he received from girls, as a tunnel he was going through until he came out the other end into sunlight and blue skies.

To add to his low-grade depression, the middle of October Cathy's letters stopped coming. Until then, he'd drawn a weekly blue envelope—her favorite color—from his mailbox. The letters gave him a small diabolical pleasure. He had never read a single one, but as long as she continued to write, she still cared for him, and he wanted her to care— to suffer—as just punishment for her betrayal. Still, it left him with a caved-in feeling when day after day the rest of October he found no blue envelope in his cubicle. He experienced an especially hollow moment when one day he saw a blue envelope among his mail and discovered it to be an advertisement. He'd thrown it vehemently into a trash container and vowed never to subscribe to *Today's Young Athlete.*

He'd kept her letters in chronological order, unable to throw them away. He'd pull the rubber-banded stack out of his drawer occasionally and run his fingers over their blue surfaces, but within minutes his heart would freeze, his jaw harden. She was history. The campus was running over with tall, voluptuous beauties only waiting for him to crook a finger. The problem was he was not yet ready to beckon, but he would be. "Time is a great healer" was a favorite expression of his aunt, and—like he kept telling himself—he had plenty of it ahead of him and the most exciting years of his life to get over Catherine Ann Benson.

He'd been shocked when Aunt Mabel had written that Cathy had lost her full scholarship from the First Baptist Church and would not be coming to Miami. He'd gone into a deep funk, not knowing whether he was relieved she wouldn't be on campus or deeply distressed she'd had to forfeit her dream. He'd run so many laps that day that Coach Medford had come out on the track and ordered him to stop.

At first, his aunt's letters had filled him in about Cathy, along with pleas to come home and "do your duty"—that phrase again. When he did not respond, his aunt had changed her strategy and framed her letters to stir his conscience.

Cathy has gone to work at Bennie's Burgers as a waitress. It's the only employment she could find. Milton Graves wouldn't take her back at his clinic because that self-righteous wife of his would disapprove. There were other openings in town, but they were "up-front" positions, and the county agent and Douglas Freeman at the bank and Anthony Whitmore at his insurance agency couldn't see their way to hire an unmarried girl in the family way. I'm sure you can appreciate the desperation that led Cathy to apply for the job at Bennie's—so many levels below her abilities, intelligence, and dignity— but she's willing to take any job to help support her and the baby.

Emma tells me that Cathy has had to endure a few snubs and pitying remarks from some of our more upstanding citizens as well as a few inappropriate advances from men customers at Bennie's. Mr. Miller, your biology teacher, who used to call her Dr. Benson, now addresses her as Cathy.

I just thought you'd like to know.

Rufus is getting older. He'll be eight years old this January. Remember when you and John snatched him from Odell Wolfe for Cathy? Seems like yesterday. You never knew, did you, that I deliberately sent you to your room that night because I was certain you'd sneak out your window to be "in on the action" when John presented that puppy to Cathy. Emma said she'd never seen you so excited—or cold! That sweet dog has been a great comfort to Cathy.

Trey had crushed the letter in his fist and his whole upper body had felt ready to explode, but again he had not replied and eventually his aunt had come to realize that if she expected him to correspond with her, she'd better lay off the guilt-and-sympathy trip. They spoke by phone seldom and then awkwardly, Aunt Mabel's conversations carefully modulated to navigate the mines that would put an end to the call and the rare opportunity to hear her only relative's voice. Afterwards,

Trey felt bad that he could not be more the loving nephew she deserved, but her silent, irrevocable disappointment in him erected a barrier he could not surmount.

Thanksgiving loomed next month. Aunt Mabel assumed he'd come home—"it will be just the two of us, a quiet holiday this year"—but Trey wouldn't have even considered returning to Kersey, despite his desire to see his aunt and his sadness at hurting her. To avoid prolonging her expectation, he wrote early to say he'd accepted an invitation from a buddy to spend Turkey Day with his family in Mobile, Alabama. Trey composed the note with an ache in his throat, knowing it would be the first of many that would disappoint his aunt. His former life was a thing of the past, and most likely he would never spend a holiday in his old home again.

Chapter Twenty-Eight

Are you hoping for a girl or a boy?" the ultrasound technician asked, spreading gel over the mound of Cathy's abdomen. She lay on an examination table in her obstetrician's office in Amarillo, her pants slipped to the top of her thighs in preparation for a three-dimensional sonogram that would determine the gender of her child as well as detect birth defects and other abnormalities. After her first prenatal examination by Dr. Thomas, she'd preferred to consult an obstetrician out of the county. It was the middle of November, and she was in her twentieth week of pregnancy.

Cathy winced. The gel was cold. "It doesn't matter, but from all indications, the baby is a girl," she said.

"Indications?"

Cathy grinned despite her nervousness and the discomfort of a full bladder, advised by her obstetrician in order to get a clearer computerized picture of the fetus. "Old wives' tales," she said. "I was really nauseous during my first trimester. That's a sign I'm having a girl, so I'm told, and my face is full and rosy, another sign." She would not divulge to this member of the medical profession the experiment that Aunt Mabel had insisted on conducting. She'd suspended a ring on a string over Cathy's abdomen and declared that if it swung back and forth, she was having a boy; in a circular motion, a girl. The ring had twirled like a top.

The technician looked amused. "I hope you didn't fall for the one that says if you carry high, you're having a girl. If you carry low, get ready for a boy. Nobody can ever remember which applies to which, but I will say this: Your baby is going to be a mighty big little girl if those wives' tales are correct—and a mighty pretty one if she looks like her mama." She turned on the wand or transducer in her hand, an instrument that would feed the image of the fetus into the computer behind her. "Ready?" she asked.

"Ready," Cathy answered, her head turned toward the computer screen to fix her eyes on the first pictures of her unborn child.

The technician began the slow glide of the wand over Cathy's stomach and eventually there emerged a fuzzy picture on the screen. The technician pointed to details in the body image, the heart chambers, blood in circulation, and individual organs. "Oh, my...," Cathy whispered in shocked wonder.

"Yep. Looks like the signs were wrong," the technologist said. "Congratulations. You're going to have a boy."

Cathy dressed while she stared dazedly at the set of sonogram pictures she'd been given of the infinitesimal human being carried within her. She'd been expecting—hoping—for a girl who might manage to grow up her first years in Kersey without the instant recognition that she was Trey Don Hall's daughter. After that, it wouldn't matter. She and her child would be moving to any city in Texas with a university that offered premed courses. But a boy...Was that TD's nose on the tiny profile... his brow? *Oh, God.* What if her son was born in the unmistakable image of his father?

She was now convinced that Trey was not coming for her. Their baby—a son—would be no lure. In November, looking over the baby-care magazines in Affiliated Foods, her eye had caught the title of an inside feature on the cover of *Today's Psychology*: "Why Certain Men Reject Their Children." She had gone immediately to the page listed and found an article written by a psychiatrist that explained Trey's puzzling rejection of her. A study had led to the discovery that certain males orphaned as children cannot tolerate sharing the love of a mate with their offspring. The introduction of a child into a household where such a man must have the undivided attention and loyalty of his partner will most likely result in rejection of the one who has, in his mind, violated and betrayed the trust of the union.

The article went on to state that men diagnosed with this rare emotional disorder who were deserted by parents in their formative years and who had found mates who loved them in the way they needed and desired to be loved were particularly exigent to sever the relationship. "Their feeling of irrevocable abandonment by someone to whom they felt enduringly secure and safe and exclusive is not unlike the emotion experienced at the time they became conscious that their parents had forsaken them."

Cathy recalled that the only time she'd seen Trey in the presence of an infant had occurred one day when she'd stopped by Affiliated Foods while he was working. A young mother with a baby in her arms had wheeled her cart up to the checkout stand where Trey was sacking groceries, and Cathy had offered to hold the child while she placed her items on the belt. Cathy had cradled the baby—a tiny newborn girl swaddled in pink—in her arm as naturally as if she had been born to her, and she'd given Trey a smile. "Nice," she'd said.

He'd ignored her smile and meaning, and she'd noted a clenching of his jaw muscles and an increased concentration on his business. She'd felt slightly rebuffed but figured he thought her attention to the baby was holding up the grocery line. It was November, and the store was crowded with Thanksgiving shoppers. Now she realized those tightened jaws had been her first clue to how he'd feel about having a child in their lives.

She had bought the magazine and gone at once to show the article to Mabel. "Was Trey aware that he'd been abandoned when he came to live with you and your husband?" she'd asked.

"Oh, my dear, yes," Mabel said. "He was only four but old enough to know he had no father and that his mother was not coming back for him. He came to us skinny as a newborn lamb with hardly enough clothes to keep him covered, not even a winter jacket, and nothing whatsoever to play with. His uncle and I fattened him up, bought him a smashing wardrobe and more toys than he could say grace over. He'd been neglected and probably abused, but he stood at the living room window day after day waiting for his mama to come home, and I've tried not to think of the nights I heard him crying for her in his sleep. Every year he expected her to return at Christmas and to remember his birthday, but she never did. Thank goodness, he had John for a friend. It was that period more than any other that forged their bond."

Deeper research had borne out the article's study, categorizing Trey's irrational aversion as a form of narcissism. It had even helped her to understand his complete rejection of John. They'd lived as give-and-take brothers. Despite the differences in their nature and temperament, they had made an equal and complementing pair, but this latest behavior of Trey's had tipped the scales—at least in Trey's eyes. He could not continue a friendship in which he'd proved himself to be less a person—a man—than John.

Cathy had been staggered by an overwhelming sadness, but her findings had supplied the answers she'd been searching for. She imagined Trey alone and lost on the campus of Miami, looking for another pair of arms to hold him exclusively as she had, going from girl to girl, searching for that light in the darkness that would shine only for him and him alone. She was no longer that light. She was now free to do what she must do.

In the waiting room of the obstetrician's office, Emma's eyes popped when she saw the copies of the sonogram images. "Would you look at that!" she said of the child's genitals, the joy in her tone giving away the private wish—which Cathy had long perceived—that her great-grandchild would be a boy. Cathy's silence caused her to look up from the pictures. "Sweetheart, you're not...disappointed, are you?"

"No, of course not. I...was surprised, that's all. I'd had my expectations set on having a girl and now I have to change gears. All I want is for my baby to be born healthy," she said, *and not to be in any way like his father.*

She wrote immediately to John to tell him the news, and he answered by return mail. "A boy!" his letter began, the exclamation mark punctuating his pleasure. "Have you thought of a name? Could I be called Uncle John, because I plan to love him as if he's related to me...as I still love and feel related to his father, and in your heart, Cathy, I'm sure you do, too. We must forgive Trey. He's his own worst enemy. He'll never know anything is missing in his life until he has it all, and by then, it will probably be too late."

Cathy folded the letter and slipped it into the family Bible as she had all the others from John.

Forgive Trey? She did not know if that was possible. It was enough that she did not hate him, but how could she hate him as long as love for him still burned in her heart—as long as memories of the two of them before that last afternoon in Aunt Mabel's parlor were like flames she could not snuff out? "Time heals everything," people said, but Cathy imagined time no more able to diminish her pain than the daily swipe of an eagle's wing could reduce the size of a mountain.

That day, the local paper had featured a picture of Trey—a rookie—released by the *Miami Herald*, firing a pass to a wide receiver during the fourth quarter of a game already in the bag for the Hurricanes. LOCAL STAR SHINES IN MIAMI'S GALAXY read the headline above a shot of Trey in his flawless passing pose, his features familiar behind his face guard. Cathy had caught sight of the photo as she turned the pages looking for grocery coupons and stared at it, dazed to the point of dizziness, stunned by the rush of warmth between her thighs.

Bennie frowned when she told him the results of the sonogram, his unspoken concern the same as hers. A thoughtless remark had already been thrown out at Bennie's by a male member of the Bobcat Booster Club speculating that maybe Kersey had another quarterback in the making. "Sure hope so," his coffee-drinking buddy had agreed. "The boy will have an uphill climb if he doesn't have that going for him."

Bennie said with a lilt of hope in his voice, "Maybe the boy will have the fine blond hair and blue eyes of his pretty mother."

"Maybe," she said, but her son's likeness to Trey wouldn't matter. Trey wouldn't matter, for when John came home for the Thanksgiving holidays she would ask him to marry her and be the father of her child.

Chapter Twenty-Nine

Other than an occasional letter from his aunt and sundry throwaway junk mail, Trey's mailbox remained empty. There were days when he did not even bother to check it. Gil Baker at Texas Tech and Cissie Jane Fielding at the University of Texas would have loved to start a correspondence with him (Bebe Baldwin, Cissie's roommate—never!), but they'd only make hay out of Cathy and he wasn't interested in Gil's braggadocio or Cissie's meaningless prattle. Trey would bet John received lots of mail—from Cathy, Bebe, Gil, Miss Emma, Aunt Mabel, Father Richard, some of their team-mates, and girls from their class. They'd all been crazy about John more than him because John was a gentle tease whereas his kidding could have a sharp edge. Everybody had felt safe with John. Apparently no one from his hometown had asked for his address. Trey felt a warm sense of injustice at the snub. *If only they knew!* He was lonely to hear from someone from Kersey in whose estimation he had not foundered—at least as a football player— and he decided to write to Coach Turner.

Miami had opened its 1986 season as the third-ranked team in the country and had climbed to number two after winning its first three games. Trey relished relating to his former high school coach how the starting quarterback was teaching him things that only a great player of the game could know and share. "I'm learning what he said he learned by sitting on the bench watching guys like Jim Kelly, Mark Richt, and Bernie Kosar," Trey wrote.

> *I'm learning to wait my turn and watch somebody else play, and there's none better to watch than this guy. It's a humbling experience, but it's teaching me humility and how to be patient, the most important attribute a quarterback can foster in himself, I'm learning—that and to continue to work hard to be prepared so that when the time comes, I'll be ready. I've been assured my time will come.*

They run a system here you trained me for,
Coach, so whatever success I may have in the
future, I owe its start to you. I'm in the hands
now of other great coaches, but none are greater
than you, and for all your own patience and
hard work with me I thank you with all my
heart.
   Say hello to the guys for me and keep me
posted with news of you and the team.
   Sincerely,
   Trey

Trey reread the letter and, satisfied with its contents, posted it. He waited four days for the letter to arrive, imagining Coach Turner's pleasure when he slit open the envelope with the return address of his All-State quarterback. He gave it another four days before he started haunting his mailbox for a reply. None came. Frustrated, puzzled, he wrote again out of fear that his first letter had gone astray. Again, no response. Worried that something had happened to Coach Turner, he telephoned his aunt to express his concern.

"Oh, Trey, I'm sorry I didn't let you know," Mabel said. "How thoughtless of me."

"Know what?"

"Tara died about a month ago."

"What?"

"Of a burst appendix. Of course, it was quite sudden. The Turners are bereft. That's why you haven't heard from Ron."

"I'll...I'll send him a condolence card, and when you see him, tell him I'm...thinking about him."

"I'm sure he'll be glad to hear that, Trey, and I know he'd appreciate the card."

The card and another letter went unanswered. Trey tried to mitigate the feeling he'd been dropped from his coach's A-list. A daughter's death took a long time to get over, but considering how close he and Coach had been, Tara's loss didn't explain why he couldn't at least drop him a line like he'd asked him to. Trey finally had to accept that Coach had not replied to his letters because of his bad treatment of Cathy. Coach had really liked her. She'd been his top student in history class, and it had been easy to see he wished his daughter were more like her. His father's sympathy had overridden his affection for his All-State quarterback, and he no longer thought of him as a son.

If only the man knew the truth.

At the first of November, Trey was astounded to draw an envelope from his box with the return address of Loyola University, only the second one he'd received from John. Apprehensive, he ripped it open with no intent to reply, but he read the enclosed letter hungry to hear John's voice talking to him from the page, because he wrote like he spoke. In his dry style Trey expected John to admonish and further plead with him to rescue Cathy from her demeaning existence, but he did not. Instead, the letter provoked another kind of dread.

Dear Trey,
I am writing from my room in Buddig Hall,
a residence dorm that is the tallest building on
the Loyola campus. I live in a two-bedroom
suite that's supposed to be shared with three
other guys, but right now there are only two of
us, another candidate like myself, and we each
have a room to ourselves. I love the place. The
food is great. You buy meal plans that offer
high-quality, nutritious meals with no gro-
cery shopping, cooking, or dishes to do. It beats
washing up after Pop's chili and goulash any
day. We're in walking distance to everything—
the student center, dining hall, library—and
so I decided to sell my pickup for money to tide
me over until my scholarship comes through.
It hurt me to let Old Red go, because of the
memories, and I have a feeling it's headed off
with someone—a Cajun who runs a fishing

camp—who might not treat it with the respect I did, but I needed the cash.

I've enrolled in the College of Humanities and Social Sciences and plan to go for a double major in philosophy and Spanish. Jesuits are required to write and speak Spanish fluently, so I thought, Why not? Giving up the major and the career I thought I'd pursue was hard, too, but I don't believe I'd have made it in the business world. To live the life I want to live, I need to live the life of Saint Ignatius, founder of the Jesuits, and in corporate America that would be as impossible as trying to breed a lion from a lamb.

I thought I ought to write and let you know that while I'll never understand why you ditched Cathy, your decision had nothing to do with my decampment to Loyola rather than Miami. Ever since that day in November, TD, when I went back to the Church, I've felt a call to make my life count for something beyond playing football for the NFL or making money in the business world. In my heart I knew that even if I was successful in accomplishing both, they would not bring me the peace I crave. Here at Loyola, going through the candidacy program, I am finding my way to that peace. Unless they kick me out, it's the place I belong.

I've been following the good fortunes of the Hurricanes and watch every televised game. The camera catches you every so often on the sidelines, and it's good to see my buddy wearing the orange and green and white. I can see from your face how eager you are to play, and all I can say is, "Wait'll next year, Miami!"

Write me when you can and let me know how you're doing. I miss you, buddy, and hope to see you over Thanksgiving break.

Blessings,

John

Fear balled like a cold fist inside Trey. The letter reminded him of how much he missed his old buddy. The longing for John's company and comradeship followed him around like a shadow he couldn't shake. But this new peace John craved... Would living "the life of Saint Ignatius" someday move him to make a clean breast of what had happened "that day in November" to Sheriff Tyson and put the hearts of the Harbisons finally to rest?

Would he, TD Hall, have to go through college, the NFL, waiting for the other shoe to fall?

Chapter Thirty

John put a shoulder to the front door of his house and pushed. His key worked, but the door had stuck from disuse. Apparently his father had not had occasion to open it in a long time. The wood creaked, and the immediate smell of a house long closed up assaulted him as he stepped inside. He left the door open to allow in a draft of cold November air and called, "Pop?"

No answer. John set down his duffel and walked through the living room past a small dining room that had not been used since his mother's demise and into the kitchen. He was surprised to find it relatively orderly. Dishes had been left to dry in the rack, the table was clear of newspapers and carry-out sacks, and the stove top looked wiped clean. A dish towel hung from its proper peg. The wastebasket contained no trash or liquor bottles.

Something about the absent air of the house different from other long spells his father had been away steered him into Bert's bedroom, a place John hadn't stepped foot in since the morning he'd found a strange woman on his mother's side of the bed. He opened the closet and was strangely unsurprised to find it empty of all but a few bent clothes hangers remaining on the rods. Bureau drawers were empty. The bed was made, but a lift of the spread revealed no sheets. He looked for a note but found none.

In his room, he discovered an envelope on his pillow on which had been scrawled:

I'm taking off. No need now to hang around.
You decide what to do about the utilities. Look
in the spot where your mother used to hide her
mad money.
    B.C.

Bert Caldwell. Not *Pop* or *Dad*. Now he knew.

Outside, he removed several bricks from the foundation of a gazebo, his mother's reading haven, the only attraction in the brown, weed-infested backyard, and found a small strongbox in her hiding place. Inside was an envelope containing ten one-hundred-dollar bills and the deed to the house, which his father had taken the trouble to have transferred to John's name.

John felt nothing for a moment standing there under the Panhandle sky, the wind tugging at his hair on this sharp but sunny Thanksgiving Day. The man who'd called himself his father was gone, perhaps forever, from his life. He held in his hand all of value Bert Caldwell had possessed. An odd sadness crept into his heart. The man had loved his mother once. John had fuzzy memories of his oil field–toughened father's tender embraces of her, his gruff affection for him. Their family had been happy enough. But all that changed after John turned four, and now he realized that his mother's confession of her infidelity had robbed Bert Caldwell of the husband and father he might have been.

How different life would have played out for all of them if she'd confessed only to her priest.

Peace go with you, Pop.

John reset the bricks and carried the packet of bills and deed into the house. He'd use the money for expenses and take the document to Loyola for safekeeping until time came to part with the sum of his worldly goods. He'd have to spend part of his holiday boarding up the house and arranging for the utilities to be turned off when he left—this time for good, he realized with another jerk of his heart.

In the kitchen, he realized how tired and sleepy he was and that he smelled. It had taken him over twenty-four hours to get home. After his final class yesterday, a fellow candidate had driven him as far as Shreveport, Louisiana. With the last of his funds, he had bought a bus ticket and, after a four-hour wait, caught a Greyhound to Amarillo that arrived at seven o'clock in the morning. He'd telephoned his father and got no answer, as there had been no reply to his letter stating his intent to come home for Thanksgiving. He'd reconsidered calling Mabel Church to pick him up. When it came to driving, Aunt Mabel had trouble negotiating traffic in Kersey. She'd never be able to manage locating the bus station in the heart of Amarillo during the morning rush hour. Cathy would be working at Bennie's Burgers and her grandmother would have closed the library for the holiday, but he wouldn't ask Miss Emma to put an extra strain on her rusty old Ford to drive fifty miles to collect him. He'd had no choice but to hitch his duffel to his shoulder and start walking, trusting God to keep him safe on the road and provide a ride that would get him home in time for Aunt Mabel's Thanksgiving dinner.

He hadn't minded. The early morning was

frigid, but it lost its bite as the day brightened, and the fresh air and prairie quiet were a relief after the hours he'd sat cramped and sleepless on the crowded, overheated bus listening to the racket of snores and hacking coughs and crying babies. He welcomed the opportunity to appreciate the handiwork of God in this vast, silent place of His creation. Autumn in the Panhandle was his favorite time of year. The sun shining through the turning grass transformed the prairie into a golden sea. Cathy, ever curious, had learned the names of all the fall flowers and shrubs of the Panhandle and taught them to him and Trey. Indigo bush, sand sage, desert bird of paradise, blue mist spirea...John wondered if Trey remembered. She had taught them so many things they'd never have learned. One day he was walking across campus past the music hall and heard the strains of Debussy's "Claire de Lune" drifting from an open window. He had stopped to listen, the earth suddenly stilled, and remembered the afternoons Cathy had played the composition for them on the piano in the First Baptist Church while he and Trey threw a football to each other in the center aisle. Sometimes she'd hit a crescendo just as Trey released the ball and it would soar high through the air and into John's hands as if borne on the chords of a symphony.

Did Trey, when reminded of her in some unexpected way, ever have one of those heart-holding moments? Did he ever recall the magic?

John missed his old red truck and having to hoof it wherever he went, but not on days like today. The serenity of the autumn fields and his sense of the presence of God in such a place filled him with a profound peace and confirmed his decision to enter the novitiate at the end of the year. When he enrolled in Loyola, he'd planned to finish college first, maybe even work in the secular world for a while before time to pronounce his vows, but he'd felt the call to take the first steps of commitment to a religious life now while still working toward his degree. He had talked it over exhaustively with his spiritual director, who had finally sighed and told him, "John, ordinarily I would try to dissuade you from burning any bridges that would prevent you from returning to your former desires, but for you, I see that choosing another path in life would be an existential mistake."

And so, he'd applied and been accepted into the novitiate program, the first rung of the ladder for a man considering life as a Jesuit. Acceptance carried no obligation. The goal of the first two years was to help the novice—through intense reflection, assessment, and discovery—affirm his desire to be incorporated into the Society of Jesus. At the end of the two-year period, only then did the novice take vows of poverty, chastity, and obedience to begin the next steps toward ordination. The whole formation process would take twelve to fourteen years.

"My goodness, John," Cathy had responded when he'd written her of the years involved, "in that length of time you could earn a medical degree."

The first semester of his training would begin in January. He could hardly wait.

He'd walked quite a distance and begun to tire when his prayers were answered and transportation arrived. A squad car pulled up alongside him and the driver's window slid down. "How about a ride, John?" Sheriff Tyson asked.

John's heart missed a beat, but he said, "Don't mind if I do," and gratefully climbed in.

"Home for Thanksgiving?" the sheriff asked.

"Yessir. Thanks for making it happen. I was beginning to think I'd be too late for Aunt Mabel's dinner. I sold my truck when I got to Loyola."

"Needed a little extra cash, did you?"

"Yes, sir."

"Your dad not much help in that department, I reckon?"

John blushed. Sheriff Tyson didn't think much

of John's father. A man like him wouldn't. "No, sir, but I manage."

"You fitting in all right at Loyola?"

"Yes, sir. It suits me just fine."

Deke Tyson glanced at him. "I can tell. It was a shock to most folks when you up and left for a Catholic school. A waste, they said, but I figured you probably knew what you were doing."

Uncomfortable with the tribute coming from the sheriff's ignorance of him, John studied the landscape. "I appreciate your vote of confidence."

"But I have to ask the inevitable question. Do you miss playing football?"

"I'd be lying if I said I didn't."

Deke Tyson's mouth crooked wryly. "We certainly can't have that now, can we?"

"No, sir."

"I imagine TD Hall misses you."

"He's doing okay without me, seems like."

"What do you hear from the boy?"

"Nothing, I'm sorry to say."

"Nobody else around here hears from him, either. I guess with Trey, once out of sight, out of mind. I don't believe I'm alone in saying I'm disappointed in the young man. His aunt Mabel has lost ground in the few months he's been gone and so has Miss Emma. Cathy Benson is keeping her head up, proving to be the trouper I always took her for, but it's got to be damn hard on her. Those women are going to be mighty glad to see you, John. At least they'll have *your* company to look forward to for holidays."

"It's nice to have them to come home to," he'd said.

Looking at the deed in his hand, John sighed at the irony. It was a little after eleven o'clock. His stomach rumbled emptily and he ached for a hot shower and a nap, but he was disturbed by Sheriff Tyson's comments regarding Cathy. He'd let Aunt Mabel know to expect him for dinner, then telephone Miss Emma to get the straight skinny on how her granddaughter was doing. Cathy's letters never mentioned the hardships of her situation. They were entertaining accounts of local people and happenings. She'd written recently: "Two weeks ago, somebody cut the padlock on Hubert Mason's gate and stole his crazy Irish setter out of his backyard. We all wondered why anybody would want to steal him since Sprinkle is the most incorrigible mutt there ever was. Well, yesterday Hubert came home to find his dog back in the yard and a new padlock on the gate."

The only negatives in her letters were the state

of the local economy, the Bobcats' next-to-none chances of winning the district championship, and Rufus's arthritis.

"No, Trey is not coming home for Thanksgiving," Mabel answered John's question. "A buddy on the team invited him to spend Thanksgiving with him and his family. I'm terribly chagrined, but I guess it was to be expected, and we'll have the joy of having you with us."

Disappointment plunged through him, in it a jab of something else. *Another buddy on the team...*

"I'll be there, Aunt Mabel," he said, "but Pop won't be coming. I'll explain later."

"Well, then, it will be just you and Emma and Cathy, and we're having a surprise guest at Emma's insistence."

"Who?"

From her tone John could picture Mabel's grimace when she said, "Odell Wolfe."

John hung up grinning, his newly fledged candidate's heart warmed. *Good for you, Miss Emma!* "*Unto the least of these, my brethren, you have done it unto me*"—the credo of the Jesuits. He dialed Emma's number.

"To answer your question, John, Bennie has been wonderful to her, making every allowance for her pregnancy. His kindness, of course, makes her work that much harder so it will not seem she's taking advantage of her condition. He worships her, and everybody knows it, so the customers mind their tongues. The reactions of some of our other citizens are hard to take, especially some of the mothers of your classmates. Pity is as bad as condemnation, you know, and of course there's been a slip in the respect she once enjoyed, but she keeps her chin up."

John bit down hard on his lip, imagining the type of snubs Emma described. Cissie Jane's mother had long resented Cathy usurping her daughter's place in beauty and brains, and she and her like, whose daughters had gone on to college, would take a natural delight in Cathy's predicament. "I understand Odell Wolfe is coming to dinner. How did that happen?"

"Well, part of it had to do with me. For years, Odell has cleaned himself up and come to the library on Monday to read in a corner carrel. I found him hanging around the back door one morning and could tell he expected me to shoo him away, but I asked if he wanted to come in. From then on, I'd find him back there every Monday soon as I opened up, so I started leaving the door unlocked—only morning I ever do—and a little something to eat on his special table, and it wouldn't be long before I'd see him hunched over magazines or newspapers or reference books in his corner. He comes and goes through the back door and leaves whenever anybody else comes in. He doesn't say much, and I've learned absolutely nothing about him, but I always find a thank-you note on the table."

"You said there was another part," John reminded her.

"That has to do with Cathy. She found Bennie giving food to Odell out the back door of his place and took over the job, taking pains with his plate and adding scraps for his dog. He thinks the world of her, and I have a feeling that if anybody ever tried to mess with Cathy, they'd feel the business end of his whip."

"How is Cathy feeling?"

"Fat, she says, but otherwise just fine. She'll be so glad to see you, John. She has something to discuss with you that I believe you'll want to hear."

John detected a trace of suppressed excitement in Emma's voice. "Can you give me a hint?"

"No, I've already said too much, but it will make you very happy."

"Can't wait."

John replaced the receiver, feeling his despondency lift like a dispelled ghost. What was the wonderful thing Cathy wanted to discuss with him that would make him very happy? Maybe someone rich—Coach Turner's wife?—had offered to send Cathy to medical school. Maybe there was someone new in her life. He couldn't imagine her falling for anyone else so soon, but he supposed it could happen. Or—praise God!—maybe it had to do with Trey. Had Trey approached her about getting back together?

The last *maybe* edged out the other possibilities and made him want to hum in the shower. It was only as John turned on the water that his hope dampened. If he'd guessed right about Cathy and Trey, why wasn't TD coming home for Thanksgiving?

Chapter Thirty-One

Cathy turned the CLOSED sign of Bennie's Burgers toward the street and shut the lock. Closing her eyes, she cradled the bulge of her abdomen and pressed her back tiredly against the door to relieve the lumbar pain shooting to her legs. She had thought the place would never clear of customers, and there were still dishes to wash and tables to clean before she called her grandmother to pick her up for the rest of Thanksgiving Day.

"I heard that sigh, Cathy girl," Bennie said.

Cathy snapped open her eyes. Bennie had come in from the kitchen, his apron-covered stomach leading the way. "Just taking a breather," she said.

"I want you to take more than that. I want you

to take off. Go home and put your feet up. I can finish here."

Dear Bennie. The kitchen was a mess. He'd fired his dishwasher a few days ago for stealing a week's worth of hamburger patties, and Romero, the other waiter, had not shown up for work this morning. The HELP WANTED sign was back in the window, and though Romero's disappearance was good for Bennie's bottom line, her body sagged at the possibility of the two of them handling the eight-to-nine crowd by themselves.

She resisted pressing a hand to her back, but God, she was tired—her son had been especially rambunctious today—and her throbbing legs felt on fire. "If I don't help, you'll miss the Texas-Aggie game on TV," she said halfheartedly.

"I don't need to watch the game on TV. I got a radio, don't I? Go call your grandmother."

"I'll clean the tables until she gets here," Cathy said, too grateful to be off her feet soon to further debate the issue.

She would miss Bennie and worried how he could continue running his business without her help once she was gone. He barely broke even now and was so mired in the daily grind of keeping his place afloat that he had no time or energy or money to consider improvements that might increase his profits.

But she couldn't consider Bennie's predicament over the necessity of providing a better life for her child. Her son's welfare was her most important—and only—concern right now. She'd have to put her personal aspirations aside. Children needed both parents in the formative years. Trey was a prime example of that. Sons needed a father to love and nurture and teach them in the way only a man could, and what better person to do that than John Caldwell? John loved her, and there was no doubt in her mind that in time she would come to love him in the way he deserved. It would be impossible not to. She was concerned only about her abilities to serve as a minister's wife because, even though marriage would prevent John from becoming a priest, he would certainly want to pursue a career in the ministry. When she and her grandmother had discussed the subject, Emma had asked, "What if John does not want to give up his plans to enter the priesthood to marry you?"

Cathy had given her the pitying look of the enlightened for the ignorant. "Grandmother, John made plans to enter the priesthood *only* after I refused to marry him."

Cathy had not shared the article explaining Trey's behavior with John, nor did she plan to.

"I don't understand," Emma said when Cathy

told her she'd keep the information to herself. "What prevents you from showing the article to John now that you've decided to marry him?" She'd emphasized the question with one of her pointed looks.

"I don't want him to think that's the reason I'm marrying him," Cathy said.

"Isn't it?"

"I don't know. I know only that John is a good man who will be a good father to my son."

Of course they would be unable to keep the truth of his parentage from the child when he was old enough to hear it. It would eventually come out that his father had left his mother when he was still in her womb. But John would handle the situation with his special wisdom and knack. How Trey would handle his version of the story when the press got hold of it was anybody's guess.

Cathy decided that the best time to propose to John was tonight after dinner. She'd have no time to see him before she and Emma were due at Aunt Mabel's. She had to work tomorrow, and John would be at mass in the evening. She'd wait until they were alone later at her grandmother's house to pop the question on the front porch swing.

Through the large front window, she saw the Ford drive up as she wiped the last of the tables clean, set the catsup bottle and salt and pepper shakers in place, removed the "Thanksgiving Day special" insert from the menus. She should be filled with relief that John would soon take her away from all this, but her heart couldn't quite manage the leap to joy. How different her life was turning out from the direction she'd planned. Laura Rhinelander was now thoroughly entrenched at USC and wrote of her premed studies with sensitivity to Cathy's misfortune but with obvious satisfaction that her chosen field was everything she'd dreamed. There might still be a chance to pick up the road further along, but Cathy doubted it. John's work would come first—God only knew where—with little money and opportunity to work toward a doctor's degree.

EMMA CUT THE PUMPKIN PIE while Mabel poured the coffee. Never had she endured a more miserable Thanksgiving occasion, and more misery was yet to come at the end of the day. She could feel it in her bones.

"Do you suppose everybody wants whipped cream on their pie?" Mabel asked, her tone flat, indifferent.

"Does it matter?"

"Absolutely not. Slap it on."

They were such good friends, in the privacy of

Mabel's kitchen neither had to pretend with the other. Masks slipped when overcome by fatigue, and at seventy-three, after a long, tense day, Mabel had reached the limits of her cordiality. This year, because she was watching her pennies, she'd managed her Thanksgiving preparations without help from the woman she usually hired to assist at special occasions. Emotional pain, too, figured into the tired lines of her face. Emma knew Mabel was suffering from the disappointment that Trey had not come home for Thanksgiving. How could that boy be such a horse's rear to the woman who'd done so much for him? They all understood why, of course. Trey Don Hall hadn't the guts to face Cathy and John—or Emma Benson!—so to hell with his aunt Mabel.

"I'll stay after everybody leaves and do the dishes and put up the food, Muffin," Emma said, using the nickname she'd dubbed her friend in childhood. "You've done quite enough to make this a grand Thanksgiving gathering."

"You know darn well you're lying like a rug, Emma Benson. This *gathering* is a disaster."

Emma had to agree. The meal aside (Mabel was a terrible cook), it was all Emma's fault, mainly because of the guest list. They should have simply prepared a plate to take to Odell Wolfe. They'd tried to make him feel welcome, but he could not be having a good time, unaccustomed as he was to wearing a necktie and a badly fitting suit unfit for a rummage sale. Since his arrival, the poor man had sat looking in fear of breaking one of his hostess's whatnots if he moved or—as Mabel trenchantly put it—"passing gas."

Inviting Father Richard had been another mistake. The women had been shocked to learn of Bert Caldwell's up and leaving Kersey without so much as a "see you around" to his son or friends. In Bert's place, Emma had suggested they ask Father Richard, and to their surprise, he'd accepted readily. Emma suspected he had plans but had canceled them when informed his neophyte would be at Mabel's table. The women of the parish would never have permitted their priest to dine alone on Thanksgiving Day.

She'd regretted her suggestion the minute Father Richard walked through the door. He'd been the last to arrive. Everybody had already greeted one another, John endearing as ever in his attempt to make Odell feel like one of them and so tall and glowingly handsome that Mabel said, "I declare, John, when you become a priest, I'm calling you Father Whatawaste." But a chill had rushed into her heart when he and Cathy embraced.

"Hello, Cathy," he'd said in the nostalgic tone of someone reuniting with a long-lost love but whose heart now belonged to someone else. Emma had hoped it was her imagination, but no, there was a difference in the way John looked at her granddaughter now from when he left for Loyola four months ago. He'd been bathed in the blood of the Lamb. A discernible ecclesiastical aura hung about him, pronounced when Father Richard arrived in his clerical suit and collar and monopolized John all through the cranberry juice and artichoke-dip stage of the evening. The two had shaken hands and clapped shoulders like conspirators who'd pulled off a successful coup.

Emma observed that Cathy had noticed the change in John, too, and when he enthusiastically announced he would be entering the novitiate in January, Emma saw her granddaughter's hope for her future fade in her eyes like bluebonnets at the end of spring. Cathy had little to say after that. Now and then, during John's energetic exchanges with Father Richard, she'd return an understanding smile to his apologetic look for "talking business." The good father and John politely tried to draw the rest of them into conversation, but Emma felt they were like outsiders indulged by members of the club.

She took the tray of pie into the dining room. "Will I get to see you later?" she heard John ask Cathy.

"Yes, of course. I'll save you a spot on the front porch swing. Rufus will be so glad to see you."

"And you're going to discuss something with me that's going to make me very happy?"

Her granddaughter leveled an accusing gaze on Emma. "Grandmother, what did you tell John?"

"I told him only what he just said to you," Emma admitted, returning Cathy's pointed stare as a reminder of her intention, but as she set a slice of pie before her she had a feeling that John would never hear the words her granddaughter had meant to convey on the front porch swing.

It was late in the evening when Emma finally revved up her old Ford. After the last Baccarat goblet and Lenox plate had been washed and dried and placed back in the china cabinet, she and Mabel had put up their feet and finished off a bottle of wine. Father Richard had dropped Cathy and John off at Emma's house and left the Ford for her. Emma was in no hurry to get home.

"At least one good thing came from this evening," Mabel said.

"What's that?"

"Father Richard's offer to sell you the parish car, and Odell's promise to arrange for the Ford to be sold for scrap metal. You're going to get a new set of wheels and a little cash to boot."

"A *used* set of wheels, Mabel."

"Gift horse, Emma."

"Right. It was awfully nice of Coach Turner's wife to make a present of her current Lexus to the parish. She buys a new one every year, I understand."

"I wonder if Flora will make another year. Her daughter's passing has been awfully hard on her. I hate to speak ill of the dead, but in death Tara may achieve the early grave for her mother that she nearly caused her in life. Hard to figure how parents as good and fine as the Turners could conceive a child like her," Mabel said. "She's an exception to our gene theory."

"Maybe not," Emma said. "Tara might have been a throwback to a grandparent responsible for her promiscuity." It was the only theory that explained Cathy. Emma had finally figured out where her granddaughter got her surprising fortitude, determination, and integrity. She wasn't a chip off her father's block but his mother's. Cathy had escaped the curse of her grandmother's acerbic tongue, thank goodness, but Emma believed she could take credit for her granddaughter's brand of internal strength. Emma didn't consider it bragging, simply an acknowledgment of the truth.

That's how she knew what Cathy wouldn't say to John Caldwell tonight.

"SO LET'S DISCUSS WHAT'S GOING to make me happy, Cathy. I can't wait any longer."

They sat on the porch swing with Rufus cushioned between them on his blanket. He'd been so happy to see John that he'd aggravated his arthritic hip. His eyes were closed from the bliss of John scratching his ear.

"You've been asking me what I plan to name the baby," Cathy said.

"Uh-huh."

"I'd like to call him John, if that's all right with you."

John turned to her with an astonished drop of his mouth. "Why, Cathy...I don't know what to say. 'I'm...honored' doesn't seem enough. Are you sure?"

"I'm sure. I can't think of anyone finer to name my child after than you, but..."

"But what?"

"I didn't take into account you might not like to have...Trey's son named after you."

He dismissed her concern with a wave of his hand. "Forget that. I'm thrilled. I'll feel he partly belongs to me, the closest I'll ever come to having a son."

"And will you be his godfather?"

"A double honor. It will be the nearest I'll ever come to being a father." He reached across Rufus to hold an open hand above the swell of her pregnancy. "May I?"

"You may."

He placed his splayed fingers on her abdomen and bent his head close. "Did you hear that, little guy? I'm going to be your godfather."

She gazed down at the curly brown crown, aching to draw his head to her breasts and say, *Don't go, John, don't go. Stay and marry me and raise my child as your son.* "John...," she said, "are you sure you want to give up having a wife and children to...do this thing you're going to do?"

He straightened up. "These next few years will tell the tale, Cathy. That's the purpose of the novitiate—to learn what life and ministry in the Society of Jesus involve, what sacrifices I must make. Right now, all I know for sure is that I've never been more certain of anything in my life than that I've made the right decision for me. I've never been happier. Whether I make the grade to become a Jesuit or not..." He shrugged. "I'll have to wait and see."

"Oh, you'll make the grade," she said.

He heard something in her tone that prompted him to put his arm around her shoulders. Rufus glanced up questioningly at the sudden cessation of the ear scratching. "What is it, Cathy? I detect something's wrong. Aren't you happy for me?"

In the darkness, she blinked furiously to hold back tears. "Of course I'm happy for you, John. It's just that...I suppose I'm sad, too. When will we ever see you again now that you have no father or house to come home to? You say that you'll be doing mission work this summer...and all the summers after that until your ordination."

"You'll see me whenever I have a chance to come back, Cathy. This is my home. You are my family— you and your grandmother and Aunt Mabel and the baby. Never forget that, no matter where my work takes me or for how long. I certainly won't."

She turned to look at him. In the darkness, the outline of his face, the set of his shoulders, could have been Trey's. "The baby is due in February, around Valentine's Day," she said. "Put us in your prayers then?"

He hugged her shoulders. "You're always in my prayers."

Finally it was time for him to go. The night had gotten colder, and she must rise early to open up for the breakfast crowd. She'd be at Bennie's until closing. John had a full day tomorrow shutting up the house. He would attend Friday night mass at St. Matthew's and had reluctantly accepted an invitation from Lou and Betty Harbison of Delton for dinner. It had been they, and not Father Richard, John told her, who'd ordered the University of Loyola catalog mailed to him. He would see her Saturday at Bennie's before Father Richard drove him to Amarillo to catch the bus back to New Orleans. With Rufus beside her, she stood on the porch and waved as John rounded the corner. The dog did not run after him. It was as if he, too, knew that where John was going he could not follow.

Chapter Thirty-Two

Bennie, we must talk," Cathy said. She maneuvered her heavy body onto one of the rickety table chairs and patted the seat next to her. At eight o'clock the Monday evening following Thanksgiving, Bennie's Burgers was empty. Romero had shown up on Friday and announced he'd accepted a job as an oil-field roustabout and Saturday would be his last day. His cousin Juan was available if Bennie wanted to hire him. The proprietor of Bennie's Burgers had no choice but to take Juan on. He would start Monday.

"Oh, oh," Bennie said. "This doesn't sound good."

Cathy came right to the point. "Bennie, I don't have to tell you that this place is losing ground. We have to do something to attract a better-paying

crowd than teenagers and the coffee and doughnut club."

"And just how do I do that, missy, without a
bankroll and the people to do it?"

"That's what I want to talk to you about." She'd
provoked a rare note of testiness in his tone. Bennie
was about his place of business like mothers were
about their children. It was all right for *him* to point
out its faults, but no one else better take the liberty.

"Forgive me, Bennie, but if something isn't done
to increase your business, you're going to go under."

"We'll get by. We always have, but...I take it
you wouldn't have brought up the problem if you
didn't have a solution."

She paid him a small smile. He had come to know
her well. "I'd like to propose a few suggestions."

"I'm all ears."

She'd hit upon her vision yesterday while watching her grandmother fry corn bread to go with
the pot of ham and turnip greens simmering on
the stove. Sunday was the only day they sat down
together to a meal. Cathy had always been amazed
that such simple ingredients and preparation could
produce anything as delicious as her grandmother's "hot-water" corn bread. It was made by pouring boiling water over a bowl of salted cornmeal
and stirring until the mixture looked like mush,

then dropping it by spoonfuls into hot fat and frying it. The result was a pone-shaped morsel with a crunchy outer crust and soft center that was sheer bliss to eat.

"Your grandfather used to say he'd walk a hundred miles to eat my hot-water corn bread," Emma had recounted for yet another time. "Fact is, it wasn't my loving but my cooking that lured that man to marry me."

"Everybody knows you're the best cook in the county," Cathy remarked dutifully, and recalled Trey hoping she'd learn to cook like her grandmother.

Cathy had observed her taking the corn bread from the skillet when the new image for Bennie's Burgers had implanted itself in her head. "Grandmother, I have an idea to pass by you," she'd said. "Tell me what you think."

Emma had listened. When Cathy finished, she said excitedly, "This could be an answer to prayers, Cathy. What do we have to lose? Let's *do* it! I have a whole month of sick days accrued at the library and can start right away."

"I'll see what Bennie says."

But first, she'd thought, she must work on another flight of fancy. Finished with the meal, she had said, "I think I'll take a walk. It's such a perfectly golden afternoon, and I need the exercise."

"As if you don't have enough exercise during the week," her grandmother commented.

"I won't walk far," Cathy said.

Her destination was over two streets, two empty lots down. If Mabel was in her kitchen, she'd see Cathy walk by and wonder where in the world she was going, since there was only one house at the dead end of the road, and not one to attract visitors.

When Odell Wolfe answered the knock on his door, his bushy eyebrows disappeared beneath the overhang of his uncut hair. "Miss Cathy! What are you doing here?"

"I came to see you, Mr. Wolfe. May I come in?"

"In? You want to come inside my house?"

"Yes, please. I have a proposal to put to you."

Odell Wolfe backed up, clearly unnerved by the word *proposal*.

Cathy smiled. "It's not what you think."

"Oh, no ma'am, I wasn't thinking anything—"

"It has to do with a job offer."

"A job offer? Who would want to hire me?"

"That's what I've come to discuss with you."

Cathy would now see what Bennie had to say about her scheme. She launched right in. "What if we expand the menu to include home-style lunch and dinner specials such as meat loaf, fried chicken, roast beef with all the trimmings—that kind of thing?"

Bennie eyed her with a tinge of disappointment. "And while we're at it, why don't we serve French wines and imported beer?" He swung a pudgy hand about his dingy establishment. "And why not petit fours and cream puffs?"

"I'm serious, Bennie. Aren't you getting tired of meager returns and unreliable help?"

"The only way to solve that problem is to sell the place."

"And who would buy it?"

Bennie shrugged his shoulders, his mouth arching downward. Cathy pressed on. "What if we can find a cook who can provide those home-styled meals and branch out from serving only breakfast food and hamburgers?"

"And who might that be?"

"My grandmother."

Bennie shot back his chair to accommodate his astonishment. "Emma Benson—cook *here*?"

"She said she'd love to. She'll be forced to retire from the library at the end of December, anyway, and she's been worried what she'll do with her time until the baby arrives. We've got it all figured out. We'll bring the baby to work with us. We can put him in your office off the kitchen. And one other suggestion. I'd like you to hire Odell Wolfe as a dishwasher and janitor."

Bennie's jaw fell. His eyes distended. Finally, he stammered, "And...h-h-ow will I p-p-ay these people?"

"You won't—at least not at first. My grandmother is willing to work for free for a few months. If business turns around, you pay her a commensurate wage with increases as your profits grow. The same for Odell Wolfe. Until then, he'll work for three meals a day and scraps for his dog."

"You've talked to him?" Amazement filled Bennie's stare.

"I have. He's all for it—thrilled, as a matter of fact. Don't worry that he'll show up looking like an alley bum. He cleans up nicely. You should have seen him last Thursday at Miss Mabel's."

Bennie scraped a hand down his beard. "Well, that all sounds mighty fine, Cathy, but how can we compete with Monica's Café? She's got the market cornered on home-cooked meals. This town's not big enough to support two cafés that serve the same things."

Bennie was referring to Monica's Café across the courthouse square. Its draw was based on the claim that it was the only eating place in town that served "home-cooked meals," a misnomer in Cathy's view. Discerning taste buds could tell that the café's self-touted baked goods, sauces, and gravies were prepared from a box, its "hand-breaded" fish and chicken-fried steak were prefrozen, and its "charcoaled sirloin steak" came with prepackaged grill marks and was cooked in the microwave.

"The only thing 'home-cooked' about their meals," Cathy said, "is that they open their processed foods on the premises. Ours will be made from scratch. We'll use fresh produce, fresh meats. Believe me, people will know the difference. And second, we'll change our business hours. Let Monica's feed them breakfast. We'll open for lunch and dinner—"

"Hold on just a minute there, sweet face." Bennie put up his hand like a jaywalker halting traffic. "What about my morning coffee drinkers?"

Cathy sighed, knowing she was about to tread on touchy ground. After the trickle that came in for breakfast, the rest of their customers were men, mainly retired, who lined the counter for half a day to shoot the bull with their cronies and rarely spent more than the price of a cup of coffee and a doughnut. It was a ritual they'd enjoyed for years, and Bennie considered them his friends.

"Bennie, for this to work, we have to close in the mornings in order to give my grandmother time to prepare the food. It will also give you extra hours to work on receipts, to tidy up the place, run errands for the business—all sorts of things that go undone around here because there's no space in your day to do them."

"What about the high school seniors? The place won't be the same to them."

"True." Cathy realized she was fooling with tradition. Heading to Bennie's for hamburgers and fries at lunchtime was a time-honored, long-established custom Kersey High School students looked forward to on becoming seniors that no parent's argument against its unsanitary conditions had been able to stem. "But what will you do without their business in the summer?" she countered.

Bennie rubbed his bearded chin, and Cathy could see that her arguments were making headway.

After a contemplative silence, he said, "What do you get out of this, sweet face, besides tips from a minimum-paying job?"

"If things improve, a higher salary and a say in the business, which means I want your guarantee that you'll listen receptively to all my other suggestions to turn this place around."

Bennie looked doubtful. "Like what other suggestions?"

Cathy struck while the iron was hot. "The place needs a thorough cleaning. I propose that we close it for one week and give it a good airing and washing from the ceiling down—windows, floors, walls, the kitchen and bathrooms. If Romero's cousin helps, there will be five of us. Even Mabel Church might lend a hand. Bennie..." She laid a hand on his arm and said gently, "We want this to be a place where people will want to bring their *families*... where couples can come on *dates*." She left it to him to deduce why currently they did not flock to order prefrozen hamburgers from grimy menus served on tacky tabletops before dirty windows.

"A week will also give us time to contact vendors and vegetable growers and for Grandmother to set up her menus," Cathy continued. "It will mean a sacrifice of income for those days and may cut into your bottom line, but in the end, I'm confident you'll see the time as an investment that will pay big dividends. This town *needs* the kind of eating establishment I'm talking about."

Bennie leaned back in his chair to consider, folding his hands over his food-daubed apron. "I suppose I can afford to close the place for a few days, but..." He looked at her woefully, "I'm to be kicked out of the kitchen when we reopen?"

"You're to be the *proprietor*!" Cathy said. "You're to walk around, greet people, make them feel welcome."

"I don't have to wear a tie, do I?"

She laughed. "No, but the apron should go. And one other thing…" Cathy paused. The next suggestion would be the trickiest. "Would you consider changing the name to simply Bennie's?"

She expected an argument, but to her surprise, Bennie said, "I guess I can go with that, too."

Her heart swelled with the thrill of victory. "You mean you'll agree to everything?"

He lifted his shoulders. "What else can I do? I don't have much of a choice, do I? But just so you know, little miss smarty, the deal maker is the part about leaving the baby in my office."

Chapter Thirty-Three

A day after Cathy's proposal, a sign was posted on the front of Bennie's Burgers: CLOSED FOR REPAIRS. WILL REOPEN DECEMBER 1. The labor force set to work. Cars slowed on Main Street to observe the moveable furniture of Kersey's only family-owned hamburger establishment piled on the sidewalk and a flurry of cleaning activity going on behind the large plate-glass windows. New menus were drawn up and encased in clean plastic folders. Booths, tables, and chairs were scrubbed down to the visible wood. An advertisement publicizing the additions to Bennie's bill of fare was placed in the local paper alongside the editor's interview with the owner, who was quoted as saying, "It was time for a change."

Bennie surprised her with a new sign in the window—No Smoking. "For the sake of the baby," he explained.

There were naysayers, among them Mabel Church. "Emma Benson, have you lost your senses? You know I've never been one to mind too much what people say, but this time they'd be right in thinking that the Bensons have succumbed to the lowest depths possible with Cathy working as a waitress and her grandmother slinging hash."

"Now, Mabel, that's not so," Emma said. "The next level would be begging on the streets."

"And *who*, pray tell," Mabel went on, "will want to eat food from an eatery with Odell Wolfe in the kitchen?"

"Those who want to eat my hot-water corn bread."

When the place reopened, a curious stream of customers were greeted with fresh scents of recent cleaning and table displays of poinsettias in honor of the season. Emma's prediction to Mabel proved correct. Baskets of her hot, crunchy corn bread—"manna bread"—came standard with every meal and alone drew patrons who had never before been inside Bennie's. By the end of January, the ledger books showed that the formerly named Bennie's Burgers had enjoyed the best fiscal month in years.

Mabel's concern that Emma would be "looked down upon" in her new line of work did not take into account the other side of the Panhandle character that deemed folks who worked hard to do their best with the hand they were dealt deserved respect. The Benson women found their stock gradually returning to their former heights in the eyes of Kersey County. The awkward situation of her nephew's abandonment of the mother of his child prevented Mabel from having a baby shower for Cathy, but Paula Tyson, the sheriff's wife, was bound by no such embarrassment. She hosted a Sunday afternoon party attended by classmates of Cathy's still in the area, a sizeable number of the town's elite, including Coach Turner's wife, and Bebe and Melissa, who drove in from their colleges.

Trey had not come home to spend the Christmas holiday with his aunt. The town frowned over his neglect of the woman who had done so much for him. It did not matter that he had asked Mabel to Coral Gables to join the family whose invitation he had accepted. The feeling was that Trey's place at Christmastime was at the fireside of his loving and lonely aunt. The tide of public opinion slowly turned in Cathy's favor and against Trey, who, so local judgment went, "was showing he wasn't man enough to come home and face the music."

As February rolled toward Valentine's Day, Cathy wrote John that "the way people around here are keeping a watchful eye on my due date gives me some idea of how the world awaited the birth of Mary's son—no comparison intended." She realized that much of the town's anticipation was as much out of curiosity as concern. Would her son look like Trey Don Hall?

Cathy believed the material she read that said women's bodies were designed to grow, birth, and nourish babies, but she was prepared for a difficult birth. Her pelvis had been diagnosed as small, and the sonogram indicated the baby could weigh as much as ten pounds. Against her obstetrician's advice, Cathy had elected to deliver her son naturally rather than agree to an early induction or a C-section. She'd thoroughly educated herself on the complications of both and believed the benefits of a vaginal delivery outweighed the pain and risks involved.

"You understand that your baby can be injured in the birthing process," the doctor warned her. "For example, big babies can fracture their collarbones. It's rare, but it does happen."

"Are sonograms always correct in determining a baby's weight?"

"No."

"And wouldn't I have to have an MRI to determine the size of my pelvis?"

"I see you've been doing your homework."

By her doctor's calculations, Cathy was a week away from her first labor pains. Her one piece of luggage was packed and in the Toyota Camry Father Richard had sold to her grandmother, its gas tank full and tires checked for immediate departure to the hospital in Amarillo. If all went well, Cathy would be hospitalized for no more than two days, the financial reason for opting for a natural delivery. Her main worry was the weather. Freezing high winds and ice accumulation on the highways were not uncommon in the Panhandle in February. As a precaution against the worst possible scenario, they had packed the trunk with blankets and food and emergency medical supplies.

Cathy could now feel the full weight of her baby, especially when she turned over in bed. Their game-playing days were over. She could feel her son was cramped and wanted out. From the minute she'd felt him kick (*Hi, Mom*) she'd press her thumb on the spot (*I'm here, Son*), and as he got bigger, when she pressed he'd push back. She'd tickle his foot and he'd move in a way that made her think he was giggling just beneath the skin of her muscles and nerves. She'd call him John, sing to him, talk to him, and no one could have convinced her that he wasn't listening.

She would expect no less sportiveness from Trey's son, but his frolics unleashed the ache for his father she'd managed to control. How could Trey turn his back on the baby they had made? In moments when her guard was down she'd fantasize that Trey would rush into her hospital room after the delivery, find their baby in her arms, begin to cry, and say as he had that day in June, *Catherine Ann, I'm so sorry. I don't know what got into me. I'm the biggest jerk in the world. I love you so much. Please forgive me.*

Once she left the hospital, she hoped to be back at work after a couple of weeks, since she could bring the baby with her. Bennie had ordered her to take even more time. "We can manage," he said. "You are not to come back until you and the baby are completely well."

"We're not sick, Bennie, just neonatal. Women used to drop their babies in the fields, put them to their nipples, and keep on working."

Bachelor Bennie blushed from the image. "The café ain't no cotton field and I'm no Simon Legree. We can manage, I tell you."

But how? The staff of five ran their feet off now. Juan was turning out to be better help than expected, but he attended Canyon College three evenings a week. Her grandmother would be in and out attending to her, and with Cathy gone, Bennie would have to wait tables and man the cash register while Odell would have his hands full in the kitchen dishing up orders. Word had spread of their new look and menu, and diners were driving over from Amarillo and Delton and towns in the adjoining counties. Cathy hated to disrupt the flow of customers who might not try them again if things were not as advertised or—God help them—Bennie had to resort to serving his hamburgers and fries.

Within days of believing her baby was turning in position to be born, a godsend walked through the door. The staff was between lunch and dinner. Bennie was at the cash register, chatting with a customer.

"Bebe Baldwin, what are you doing here in the middle of the semester?" Cathy said in surprise when she saw her friend from high school take a seat at the lunch counter. They had visited over the Christmas holidays and at her baby shower, and Cathy had listened like a diabetic craving sweets to Bebe's wails of discontent with her professors and classes and higher education in general.

"I quit," Bebe said. "I gave it a go, but college isn't for me. No sense in wasting my dad's money.

Cissie Jane is lapping up the life, of course. She's majoring in Kappa Kappa Gamma."

Cathy chuckled. "Sounds like her." She set a cup of coffee for her friend on the counter. "So what are your plans now?"

Bebe shrugged. "I'll be looking for a job. I wish it could be around here, but with the job market the way it is..."

"Would you like to work in Bennie's?" The question popped from Cathy's mouth before she could think about it. "As you can see, we've spiffed up the place, and I'm expecting my baby—" A sudden gush of liquid warmed the inside of her legs. She clasped her abdomen and caught the smell of a musky odor. "Like...like...right now."

Bebe shot off the stool. "Oh, my God, what do I do?"

"Call my grandmother. She's in the kitchen." At the cash register, Bennie whipped his head around and let out a bark of dismay. "Bennie, meet your new waitress," Cathy gasped when he rushed over. "Right, Bebe?"

"Right," Bebe said.

The weather threatened but held off as Emma drove the Camry out of Kersey. The afternoon had lost the little sun that had managed to penetrate the low-cast clouds. A winter storm was expected to roll in at midnight. "How are you doing, sweetheart?" Emma asked, her hands clenching the wheel, her body pitched forward as if the tense position might help her better navigate the road.

Cathy's eyes were on the stopwatch she held to time her contractions. "So far so good," she said. Her cramps were regular in duration and spacing, but she had no doubt that labor had begun. She rubbed her abdomen, determined to remain calm and relaxed. *It's all right, John. Mom will have you out in no time.*

They were a mile out of Kersey when, "Oh, shit!" exploded from Emma's mouth. Cathy looked at her grandmother in surprise, then behind her to see what horrible thing in her rearview mirror had provoked the unprecedented outburst. "'Oh, shit!' is right," she groaned. A squad car, blue lights twirling, siren released, had drawn up close behind them.

"What the hell is he stopping me for?" Emma said furiously. "I was driving the speed limit."

Through the precipitation collecting on the back windshield, Cathy could make out only the outline of a broad set of shoulders in the leather jacket of a law-enforcement officer and the dull glow of a medallion on the crown of his western hat. He stuck his hand out his window and motioned they were to follow him. Cathy went limp with relief. "It's okay, Grandmother," she said, feeling the stab of another contraction. "It's Sheriff Tyson. He's come to lead us to the hospital."

Chapter Thirty-Four

Frowning, Trey took a seat next to the girl he'd agreed to meet for coffee in the University Center. They'd been dating since December, and he'd spent the holidays with her and her family in their mansion in Coral Gables, where her father owned an important advertising firm.

The glow that had heightened the loveliness of the girl's face when Trey walked up faded when she saw his ill-humored expression. Beside her pastry plate was a small gift-wrapped box tied in red and white ribbon. "What's the matter?" she asked. "You look...put out."

"Put out?" Trey's frown deepened. "I'm worried. Can't you tell the difference?"

"Worried about what?"

"Nothing important. I have...a friend who's supposed to be going into the hospital today."

"Who is it? I thought I knew all your friends."

"Well, you thought wrong. Not from here. From home."

The girl's face instantly grew wary. "A him or a her?"

Trey hesitated. "A her. I'm hoping someone will let me know how she is."

"What's wrong with her?"

"She's going to have a baby."

She noticed he'd not removed his jacket and had made no move toward the coffee bar. "Yours?" she asked.

His dark eyes snapped. "Why would you say that?"

She hiked her shoulders in an attempt to make light of her obviously unfortunate remark. What was *wrong* with him today? "I don't know why I said that, Trey. I suppose because love is in the air—"

"Are you saying it would be okay for me to walk out on a girl having my baby?"

She rocked back from his cold stare, the censure in his tone. "Of course not. That's not what I meant."

"What did you mean?"

"Trey..." She leaned forward and drew his hand

362

to the red heart on the front of her white sweater. "This is Valentine's Day. I didn't mean to start an argument."

"I don't feel like going to the dance tonight," he said. He pulled back his hand from the familiar swell of her breast and pushed back his chair. "I'm sorry, Cynthia, but I need some breathing room from us for a while."

Cynthia watched him go without undue regret. She couldn't keep up with his moods lately, and they'd become a bore. Gazes from the other students trailed after him. He'd been picked as next season's starting quarterback, and at the University of Miami that made him top dog on campus. The information her father's investigator had gathered on Trey Don Hall must be correct, she thought. Her father had all her boyfriends investigated. She was, after all, the heiress to a fortune when she turned twenty-one. The dossier stated that when Trey Don Hall went off to college he'd left his longtime girlfriend pregnant and had had nothing to do with her since. Her baby would be due about this time. Cynthia had shrugged the information off to her father. What did that have to do with her and Trey's relationship? But she should have known better than to let herself fall in love with TD Hall. There was something cold and indifferent about him once you got past the sex. He would only hurt her as he apparently had that poor girl he'd left high and dry. Yet Trey must still feel something for her to be worried about her having his baby. "Nothing important," he'd said. *Like hell.* She slipped the gift into her purse. He hadn't even noticed it. It was a framed photograph of her and Trey posing before her family's enormous Christmas tree. She would keep it among her mementoes of her college days and decide whether to let his boo-boo back home be known. Not that it would make the least difference to his status at Miami.

IN THE POST OFFICE ATTACHED to the student center, Trey checked his box. No mail from Aunt Mabel. Since November, she'd written him only twice, punishment for his not going home for the Christmas holidays, he assumed, and her letters contained no news of Cathy or John. He hadn't heard from John in a long while, either. It was just as well, he told himself. The greater distance he put between him and his two friends, the easier it would be to assimilate into his new life, a world away from the windswept little prairie town he'd left behind.

In the dormitory, he asked at the proctor's station if he had a message. The student assistant handed him two envelopes, but they were not from his aunt. Today was Cathy's estimated delivery date and he would have telephoned for a status report, but he couldn't risk Aunt Mabel misinterpreting the call. She might take it as a sign—and report it to Cathy—that he still cared for her, and he did not. He simply wanted the baby and his... onetime valentine to come through all right.

He read the contents in the envelopes and dropped them in the nearby trash receptacle provided for junk mail. One was from a student reporter of the school paper requesting an interview and the other from a men's clothing store wanting to know if Trey would be interested in modeling their line of clothes at an alumni event. Six months ago, he'd have been eager to accept, but now he thought such affairs a waste of his time. He was finding it liberating not to give a damn about anything or anybody but his studies and football. He ought to mind that somehow Cynthia had found out he'd left his girl pregnant back home and worry that the gossip would tarnish his image, but he didn't. What did image matter to how a quarterback played the game?

"HE'S OUT, AND HE'S PERFECT!"

The doctor's relieved announcement resounded like a symphony in Cathy's ears. Exhausted, she fell back against the pillow and gave a weak smile and thumbs-up to the miracle he held in his hands. *You did it, Son. You did it!* In the eleventh hour of her labor when she thought she could no longer bear the excruciating pains of her contractions, she'd felt the strong will in her son to be born. He would not let her give up, consider a caesarean. Through the blur of her pain and nausea, the assault of harsh, bright lights, machine sounds, loud laughter and conversation, the indignity of being exposed to strangers walking in and out of the room, he had fought her urge to cry for relief from her agony. *We can do it, Mom!*

"Will," she whispered at one point to her grandmother swabbing the perspiration from her face. "I want my baby's...middle name to be...Will. John Will Benson. We're...going...to call...him Will."

"I'll make sure the name gets on the birth certificate, sweetheart."

After a preliminary exam of the baby, the doctor placed her newborn in her arms, still slippery from the birth canal. "Ten pounds and one ounce, and all high marks on the Apgar score," he announced. "Congratulations."

Emma, who had never left her bedside, began to weep softly. "Talk about a labor of love," she said.

Cathy touched her lips to the soft cranium, plastered in a crown of dark-brown hair. "And worth every second of it. He's beautiful, isn't he?"

Emma daubed her eyes. "How could he not be?"

Yes, how could he not be? Cathy thought, recognizing Trey's forehead, nose, chin.

"I'd better go call Mabel before she has a conniption fit," Emma said. "She'll let the others know."

By *others*, Cathy knew she meant Bennie and John and possibly Sheriff Tyson, to whom she'd owe an eternal debt of gratitude for leading them, patrol lights flashing, through sleet and Amarillo traffic directly to the emergency doors of the hospital. With the care and consideration he would have shown his own daughter, he had helped Cathy out of the Camry into a wheelchair and hung around until she was in the hands of the medical staff. But would Aunt Mabel telephone Trey? His aunt had cooled her relationship with him. His refusal to come home for Christmas had been the final straw. Trey was aware of Cathy's due date. Would he be waiting anxiously for word that mother and son were doing fine? Would he call if he did not hear from his aunt? Would he want to know if the baby looked like him? When he learned of his son's birth, would Trey be able to stay away?

Emma left to make the calls, and Cathy felt a

sudden emptiness when the baby was taken from her for a bath. When she was back in her room, freshly bathed and dressed in a clean gown, a nurse entered carrying Cathy's son. Cathy held out hungry arms. "How is it possible to barely remember my life without him?" she said as the baby immediately found her breast, and she felt the sweet, urgent tug of his tiny mouth on her nipple.

"I don't believe that question falls in the realm of the answerable," the nurse said. "Are you ready to receive your first visitor as a mother? There's a young man waiting to see you."

Cathy's heart flew to her throat. "Who is it?"

"I don't know his name, but he's tall, dark, and handsome if that gives you a clue."

Cathy pushed up in bed, cradling the baby's head. *Oh, my gosh! Trey!* "Send him in!" she said, breathless from a flood of joy and relief. She looked down at the sleeping face of her son. "You are about to meet your daddy, John Will."

But when the door opened, it was John Caldwell who walked into the room.

Chapter Thirty-Five

At the end of two weeks, Cathy was back waiting tables at Bennie's. She had hoped for a quiet return, but a well-wisher had sent a blue and white floral arrangement with balloons bobbing: "It's A Boy!" that sat on the checkout counter for days and invited requests to see the baby in Bennie's office. Customers brought gifts and cards—justifiable grounds to see for themselves if the baby sleeping in his bassinet looked like Trey. The tacit consensus was that he did. There was no doubt at all. The dark, curly hair, the shape of the facial features, could have come from no one but Trey Don Hall.

The next week, Cathy set the helium-filled balloons free and drove to the cemetery to lay the still-fresh, dyed-blue carnations on the grave of an infant who had lived only a few minutes after birth.

The icy days that gripped the Panhandle in February eventually warmed into spring, and the year passed. The baby grew. He was quiet and curious and displayed a level of intelligence uncommon in a child his age. He drew forth the first laughter that none who knew Odell Wolfe had ever heard and provided such pleasure to the working environment from his playpen that Bennie—a bit cocky from the profits that allowed him to increase wages—laughingly declared he ought to put the boy on the payroll.

Bennie had come to think of Cathy Benson as the best thing that had ever happened to him. She had saved his business and brought joy and pride into his life, not to mention the people he had grown to love. He didn't mind that more and more it was becoming a question of which of them was in charge. Her ideas were good for business. They gave class to the place. The waitstaff now wore black trousers and white shirts. The barbequed ribs were served with finger bowls. Cloth napkins were used instead of paper.

The only worry that shadowed his good fortune was the inevitable realities he must face. The day would come when Emma would grow too old to work. She was a woman of amazing energy, but he'd seen it with his own mother when she entered the season Emma was in now: one day, hale and hearty; the next, frail and gaunt, and then gone.

What a black day that would be! When Emma was in the kitchen, all was well with the world. In her light, Odell had found his way. Bebe, too, would leave in time—why would she not? She was a pretty girl, young and lively. Working for Bennie was just a stopgap until she got the itch to move on. He dreaded most the moment some handsome stranger walked through the café door, won Cathy's heart, and took her and her son away. It was bound to happen. He hoped he was too old to work himself by then. He would sell the place before the buyer realized the primary reason for its success— and Bennie's happiness—was gone.

On New Year's Day, 1988, as a sophomore, Trey led the undefeated Miami Hurricanes to the national championship. Throughout the season, all eyes in Kersey had been on the highly limelit quarterback it had bred, and details of his exploits appeared frequently in the sports section of the town newspaper in reprints of articles from the University of Miami's campus publication. No tidbit pertaining to the star was unworthy of being mentioned. One such morsel buried in a feature on the homecoming activities of the university caught Cathy's eye and broke her heart. A tradition at the university—equivalent to the lighting of bonfires at other schools—was the setting on fire of a wooden boat in the middle of Lake Osceola, around which the campus was built. Legend had it that if the mast stayed upright as it burned and sank, the Hurricanes would win the game. As part of the ceremony, starting players were to throw a personal article into the flames. It was reported that TD Hall had tossed in a quilt.

After the final game in the Orange Bowl in which Miami defeated the country's number-one-ranked team to win "The Game of the Century," the national media discovered Cathy.

A stranger strolled into the café between lunch and dinner days after the victory and ordered coffee. He was young—mid-thirties, Bennie guessed—pleasant looking, and well dressed. He carried the camera of a serious photographer around his neck, which he placed on the counter while he drank his coffee. Bennie's brows drew together when he saw him studying Cathy over the rim of his cup. His gaze was not predatory but investigative. She had carried the baby into the dining room to give him a few minutes' change of scene, since the man at the counter was the only customer that time of day.

After a while, the man strapped the camera back on, lined it up, and said, "Miss?"

Cathy, engrossed with her son, turned toward the voice, and the camera clicked.

"Hey, what are you doing?" Bennie demanded, roused from his station. "She didn't give you permission to take her picture."

"Are you Catherine Benson?" the photographer asked, ignoring Bennie.

"What's it to you?" Bennie said.

Dandling the baby, Cathy said, "What if I am?"

"Is that Trey Don Hall's baby, and are you its mother?"

Cathy whitened, and the man raised the camera again.

Bennie hollered into the kitchen, "*Odell!* Come out here and bring your whip!"

Aghast, shielding her son's face with her hand, Cathy asked, "Who are you?"

"I'm a freelance photographer. I've been hired to take pictures of you and your baby. I'll make it worth your while. I—"

Odell's whip cracked on the floor beside him. The photographer jumped, but brazen gumption or professional reflex kept the camera focused on Odell drawing the whip handle back to lash forth again. The whip struck over the man's head, lifting hair. Clicking furiously, the photographer backed away and out the door before Cathy could close her astonished mouth.

Within days, the scene was splashed on the front pages of a grocery store tabloid under the headline SUPERSTAR'S LOVE CHILD. Pictures of Cathy's shocked white face above the dark curly head of her son vied with Odell's ferocious brandishing of his whip featured alongside inserts of a victorious Trey Don Hall after the Orange Bowl game.

Publishing interest in the indiscretions of a nineteen-year-old football star and his teenage girlfriend died quickly, but the damage was done. Mabel Church nearly took to her bed from the shame, and in Coral Gables the scandal sheet tarnished somewhat the pride the Hurricanes took in their quarterback. Frank Medford called Trey into his office to account for himself.

"Have you seen this?" the coach asked, pushing the tabloid feature on his desk toward Trey.

Trey lifted it, puzzled, and his heart stopped when he saw the picture of Cathy, his first sight of her since he'd thrown her out of his aunt's house a year and a half ago.

"Oh, crap!" he said, reading the article accompanied by pictures of him and Cathy in happier days during their senior year. The photos had been copied from the school yearbook.

"Any truth to the story?" Frank asked.

"Cathy Benson was my girlfriend, but the baby's not mine."

Frank looked at him like a judge hearing an automatic *Not guilty* from a defendant caught red-handed. "I didn't call you in here to pry into your personal affairs, Trey, or to lecture you. I called you in here to advise you to keep your mouth shut about this. Say nothing—zip—to reporters that try to worm a reaction out of you. Your answer will be 'No comment.' You're to go on about your business and ignore them. Got that?"

"I got it, Coach."

Frank tapped the tabloid. "This kind of thing casts a long shadow, Trey, and can follow a player his whole career. It's the sort of stuff that reporters love to file away and haul out as it suits them, especially when there's a kid involved. Be prepared to be questioned about this situation from now on and for the girl to cause trouble later when you're rich and famous."

"She won't cause any trouble."

"She won't wave a paternity test over your head for child support?"

"No."

"How can you be sure?"

"Because I know her."

Frank's brows lifted. For two years he'd looked for clues to explain what had gone haywire during those few days Trey was home after summer conditioning that had reversed his affable, if sardonic, personality and sent his best friend into the priesthood. Frank remembered that Trey had mentioned a girl was involved, and now he'd bet his mother-in-law's schnauzer that the beauty in the tabloid figured into a love triangle featuring him and John Caldwell.

"When you're financially able, do you plan to... do anything about the baby?" Frank asked.

As usual when Frank trespassed into private territory, Trey remained silent, his impassive face and direct gaze implying his plans were none of his coach's business.

Frank sighed. "The papers will paint you as a villain."

"Let them. If I support it, I'm saying I'm his father, and I'm not."

Frank dropped the tabloid into the trash can by his desk. "Well, then, I guess my final advice is let your conscience be your guide. Remember what I said about long shadows."

Trey left his coach's office, his last words replaying in his ear. *"Let your conscience be your guide."* Coach Medford did not believe him when he'd said the baby wasn't his. Nobody would, but so what? He'd known this story would crop up, and he'd thought over the issue from front to back, side to side, and decided that if he was going to be branded a "villain" he'd rather it be for failing to do his duty by an illegitimate child than for his real sin. Last fall, he had intended to tell Cathy and John that he was sterile. The only stipulations were that John had changed his mind about entering the priesthood and Cathy still carried the torch for him. The first had not happened. John was in his second year of the novitiate, happy as a pig in mud, according to Aunt Mabel, and Cathy had...moved on. She'd transformed Bennie's Burgers into something of a culinary wonder, and Trey was presumably dead to her. John was the baby's godfather. It wasn't as if the kid wouldn't have a father figure in his life— a twist of irony there. Everybody seemed happy enough. What would happen if Trey suddenly confessed the truth and upset the applecart? John would have to leave the novitiate to marry Cathy, and—if Trey remembered anything about Catherine Ann Benson—she would always feel guilty for taking him away from his chosen calling.

If the media gave TD Hall's run-of-the mill screwup this kind of attention, what would it make of the deception he'd perpetrated on his best friend and the girl he'd professed to love? The public—and the Heisman committee—might forgive him for not taking responsibility for his child, especially since he claimed it wasn't his, but not when they learned of the knowledge he'd deliberately kept to himself and the consequences that followed. He'd stood by and let his best friend become a priest unaware of the fact that the baby was his, and he'd prevented his girlfriend—also ignorant of the baby's paternity—from marrying the real father of her child.

What was even worse—much worse—was allowing the kid to grow up believing Trey Don Hall was his father.

When the media got wind of that, and they would, what kind of shit would they make him out to be? His career would be over, maybe not the game but the parts of it he loved—the respect from coaches and fans, the camaraderie and loyalty from his teammates. Talk about a long shadow! It would follow him all the days of his life.

For a minute, looking at Cathy's picture, the baby so cute, Trey had felt a pang of conscience. He'd tried to forget her face and figure, but the photo brought every lovely detail back to him. She looked out of place in a café with a jukebox in the background. She ought to be wearing a white coat in a lab somewhere, studying to become a doctor. He never passed the medical campus with its renowned Jackson Memorial Hospital but that he didn't tamp down the memory of how much she'd looked forward to attending classes there. Sometimes he felt a spike of anger at the career she'd screwed herself out of—literally. It was still a wonder to him that—because of his unaccountable behavior—she and John had not figured out that the baby wasn't his and could only be John's. They'd gone to bed together, hadn't they?

It was that gall Trey still tasted that locked his conscience back into its dungeon. Cathy and John had destroyed all he'd loved. Football was the only thing in his life true and steady. It was all that was left for him to care about, and he wouldn't sacrifice it for anything or anybody. He already had one shadow trailing after him, one he could easily outrun if Novice John Caldwell did not listen to *his* conscience.

Chapter Thirty-Six

The invitation arrived in May when the Panhandle's last cold front yielded to the first mild day of a late spring. From the post office Emma immediately drove to Bennie's for Cathy to read it, and asked the inevitable question as her granddaughter drew it from its thick envelope, "Where has the time gone?"

Yes, indeed, where? Cathy studied the richly embossed Jesuit logo on the invitation's cover, but the question wasn't where time had gone but what it had left in its wake. For John, it was the fulfillment of his dream.

WITH GREAT JOY AND GRATITUDE TO GOD

THE JESUITS OF THE NEW ORLEANS PROVINCE

INVITE YOU TO JOIN US IN PRAYER AND
CELEBRATION

AS THE CATHOLIC CHURCH ORDAINS TO THE
PRIESTHOOD

JOHN ROBERT CALDWELL, S.J.

THE MOST HOLY NAME OF JESUS CATHOLIC
CHURCH

6363 ST. CHARLES AVENUE

NEW ORLEANS, LOUISIANA

AT TEN O'CLOCK AM, SATURDAY,
JUNE 5TH, 1999

For Cathy, the thirteen Mays since she and John and Trey had graduated from high school had brought blessings, but not the ones she'd planned to enjoy nine springs shy of forty.

But this invitation was not about the short circuits of her life but about the man who had persevered in spite of his. She stood before the window of her office, swelling with pride for John's accomplishment. She lifted her face to the spring sunshine and sent her thoughts skyward as if she were releasing a bird to carry her congratulations to his ears. *I'm so proud of you, John.*

"I'll be on my way," Emma said, relying heavily on her cane as she rose from a chair in Cathy's office. "I knew you'd want to see the invitation as soon as it came. I imagine Mabel and Ron Turner and, of course, Father Richard received theirs. What would you say to having a little party to celebrate the event and discuss the possibility of all of us carpooling to Amarillo and flying to New Orleans together? We'll need two cars to accommodate the luggage."

"I'd say that was a great idea."

"We can all stay at the St. Charles. That's where your grandfather and I honeymooned."

"Sounds good."

"I'll call everybody when I get home and see what they have to say about the idea."

"Splendid."

"Catherine Ann Benson, I'm reading your mind like a large-print book. You're wondering if Trey Don Hall was sent an invitation."

Cathy's sheepish smile admitted her grandmother's perception. "And Bert Caldwell, too," she said.

"I'm sure John has no address for Bert, but I do know that he asked Mabel for Trey's. What will you do if he shows up?"

Cathy gave her grandmother a wry look. "You have a suggestion in mind?"

"Oh, my, yes, but I wouldn't want the mother

of my twelve-year-old great-grandson arrested for assault."

"I don't think we have to worry. Trey will not show up."

Cathy was certain of that. After her grandmother left, Cathy remained at the window overlooking the staff parking lot to watch her grandmother get into her car. Emma, now eighty-three, had been the reason Cathy had laid her final dream of becoming a doctor forever to rest. There had been a window of opportunity six years ago when Bennie, having his late-afternoon caffeine fix and chatting about the day's receipts, had let his cup slip to the floor and grabbed his chest. Despite all efforts from her and Odell and Bebe to revive Bennie, he had died of heart failure within minutes. Cathy had been shocked to learn that in his will, but for his family home, Bennie had named her the sole beneficiary of his worldly goods. The house he bequeathed to Odell.

By then, Emma had retired her apron and a local graduate from the culinary school at Canyon College had taken over her cooking duties. Cathy's son was six years old, a perfect time in his young life to introduce him to a new home before his father's fame sullied his school years. She would sell Bennie's and move to Dallas, where she would take premed classes at Southern Methodist University. It was possible that she could graduate with a medical degree before she reached her fortieth birthday.

But Emma, too, was diagnosed with heart disease, within the month of Bennie's demise. In despair, Cathy watched the window close. She could not go off and entrust her grandmother to the dubious attention of the local caregivers, and moving her to a small apartment in an unfamiliar environment with her six-year-old grandson while Cathy worked toward a degree would have been even more detrimental to Emma's frail health.

Sadly, Cathy withdrew the FOR SALE ads from commercial publications, perversely comforted by the fact she'd received no interested buyers of the property anyway.

Emma, knowing Cathy's habit of standing at the window until she'd gone, waved as she pulled out of the parking lot. Cathy never missed an opportunity now to say good-bye. She went back to her desk, disgusted at her increased heartbeat that occurred whenever she thought of Trey in a certain way. Most times, he was a blank figure in her memory. She had trained herself to give him no face, voice, figure, mannerisms, even when she looked at her son. From the moment he was born, she'd looked beyond the obvious physical characteristics of the man with whom she'd conceived Will to those uniquely their son's, and she'd discovered an abundance of them. To her amazement, she'd found that Will—in every way that counted—was very much unlike his father.

But sometimes, when Trey's name cropped up or she caught a picture of him in the newspaper or on the TV screen, heard a scrap of gossip about him, her breath would catch and a certain feeling would plunge right through her. He was suddenly inside her head as if he'd never left her—*"dance with me, my funny valentine."*

She read the invitation again. What *would* she do if Trey showed up at John's ordination? She hadn't seen Trey in the flesh in almost thirteen years. He had never laid eyes on their son, not even from a photograph. She had Mabel Church's word on that. "It breaks my heart not to show him a picture of my great-nephew, but I declare, Cathy, I'm afraid that if I did, Trey would never speak to me again, he's so determinedly indifferent to the child."

Not to wonder, the narcissistic jerk. The question was what *his son* would do or say—how would *he* react?—when he came face-to-face with Trey. Will had first learned who his famous father was at four years of age. Cathy had always thought it ironical and terribly sad that Will had felt the abandonment of a parent at the same age as Trey. Until then, though his visits were few and far between, John had filled the man role in Will's life, bolstered by Bennie and Odell Wolfe.

"Where does my daddy live?" Will had asked.

Cathy would never forget the Sunday afternoon in November at the height of football season when he posed the question. He had come in from playing with a group of boys a few years older, and his question had made clear the topic of their sandlot talk. The moment she'd dreaded had arrived. Her son's dark hair was tousled, his cheeks were a rosy pink from the cold, and in his windbreaker and jeans and tennis shoes with the laces untied he had never looked more like the poster child of every parent's dream of a perfect little boy. He was too big for her to pick up, so she'd patted her lap and he'd crawled into it, smelling of the exertion of play, heavenly to a mother's nose, and she'd enclosed him in the safety of her arms to deliver the hurt to come.

"He lives in California," she said. "He plays football for the San Diego Chargers."

Will quizzed her with his luminous dark eyes, round and innocent beneath thick, curly lashes. "Why doesn't he live here?"

"Because he chooses to live there."

"Doesn't he love us?"

"I believe he would if he could, but he lacks something inside him that would make that happen." She'd swiped Will's nose playfully with her finger, fighting the swelling in her throat. "You know your Hess toy truck that we had to buy special batteries to make run? Well, that's what's lacking in your father—a special kind of battery."

"Can we buy him one?"

"No, darling. That kind of battery is not for sale."

His little-boy face had grown reflective. He bit his lip. "Will he ever come to see me?"

She'd coughed to keep her windpipe from closing. "Maybe someday...when he grows up."

The day had never come. Trey's star rose in the NFL, and Will, a natural-born athlete, grew up in the shadow of his father's fame under the watchful eyes of those in town who hoped to see him take the field as quarterback in the spitting image of Trey Don Hall. Cathy would always be grateful to Ron Turner for influencing Will to concentrate on his real love—baseball. From the time he could pick up a bat, he had headed for the baseball diamond, leaving it to his buddies to suit up in pads and helmets for the Pop Warner league. At twelve, he had established quite a local reputation as hitter and right fielder.

"Why don't you take a paternity test and sue

the son of a bitch for child support?" Bebe said, the heated suggestion also voiced by Bennie and even her grandmother. Cathy had refused. She wanted nothing from Trey that had to be coerced, and she was beginning to detect in her son a streak of his mother's pride. Odell summed it up best: "Better for him to do without now than be in debt to his father later."

Reporters nosed around occasionally, one catching Will on the playground with questions of how it felt not to be acknowledged by his famous father. A quick-thinking teacher had telephoned Sheriff Tyson, who showed up before the reporter could make his getaway and cited him for disturbing the peace.

At those times, Cathy hated Trey Hall and would have wished she'd never laid eyes on him if those she loved were not in some way connected to him.

Chapter Thirty-Seven

Trey set the invitation aside on his desk, a stinging sensation behind his eyes. *Damn, Tiger, you did it!* It had taken John—what?—twelve years to get his name on that invitation. Aunt Mabel had kept him informed of John's whereabouts and activities after his letters stopped coming. The last one had been mailed from Guatemala in the summer of 1990, in which he'd described the squalor of the massive garbage dump on the outskirts of the capital where tens of thousands of children and their families lived. "You would not believe the poverty," he wrote. "My mission here is to assess how best the Church can serve these people—get them food, medicine, fresh water, while ministering to their spiritual needs." It had been a time when the world news section of the

San Diego Union-Tribune was reporting the ruling regime's unconscionable acts of terror against Guatemalan citizens, priests and nuns in particular. In that year alone two hundred thousand Guatemalan citizens were slaughtered, and while John was there, a number of indigenous people were massacred in the plaza of Santiago Atitlan, where he was temporarily staying in the rectory of a priest who had been murdered for opposing the death squads.

"I'm doing my best to keep my head down and my faith up," John's letter had stated. "It's not an easy balance, and I have my anxieties, believe me. It's sort of like the feeling I used to get when I was reaching for a first-down ball and knew a two-hundred-pound linebacker was a grunt away."

Trey had yearned to write him back and tell him to get his damn butt out of there, but of course he didn't. He wrote a check instead and sent it anonymously to the Catholic Relief Fund for Guatemala. After that he searched every mail delivery for a letter from John and when none arrived, crazy with worry—surely Aunt Mabel would have told him if something had happened to John?—Trey had telephoned her for news. John had managed to get out of Guatemala with his hide, she'd told him, and next summer he was to be sent to India, where he hoped to meet Mother Teresa. Meanwhile, he was teaching at a Catholic high school in New Orleans and coaching football.

Trey had felt a deep loss when John stopped writing and could guess at a number of reasons why he had. One, John had given up trying to lure him back into the fold, presumably to Cathy's side. She was still unmarried, and her baby was almost four years old. Maybe John had come to realize that the friend he'd sacrificed so much of his soul for wasn't worth his effort and time. That thought made Trey's nerve ends stand on end. If that was the cause of John pulling out on him, what was to keep him from going to the authorities—and the Harbisons—with the truth of that November afternoon? Or maybe John had simply grown tired of receiving no response from him, or he'd gotten too busy to write, or he thought he didn't care to hear from him. None of his speculations quite fit the friend Trey remembered. Once in John's heart, always in John's heart. He was tenacious when it came to holding on to people he loved.

At the time, Trey had just signed with the San Diego Chargers and was looking forward to living the lifestyle of the rich and famous or, rather, the grossly overpaid and notorious. He'd lost all contact with home except for the tidbits Aunt Mabel fed him of local happenings and people, including

Cathy's childhood friend from California, Laura Rhinelander. She had entered medical school. He could imagine how the information had affected Cathy. He'd felt for her feelings, and the blues had trailed him around all day like a bad dream he couldn't shrug off.

Rufus died that year. The news opened the floodgates. It was like a lever had been pulled, and all the sadness Trey had kept dammed up poured out in his grief for the dog. He'd always thought of Rufus as belonging to him, and Aunt Mabel had told him that the dog never failed to perk his ears and run from room to room looking for him when he heard his voice on television. What bothered Trey the most was not being with Rufus to say good-bye. As the years passed, Laura Rhinelander graduated from medical school, Cissie Jane married and divorced, Bebe Baldwin stayed on at Bennie's but was promoted to manager. Gil Baker came home to help his father run the family's feedlot, Ron Turner, who'd not had a championship season since 1985, retired under duress, and Miss Whitby, thirty-seven, unmarried, and still a scatterbrain, was killed in a car accident.

A vortex of memories had spun through Trey's brain at the report of her death. "Hall, what the hell is the matter with you today?" his quarterbacks coach had yelled at practice the day he learned. "What's eating you, son?"

His coach had caught him emotionally and mentally in the back row of Miss Whitby's home-room the January day in 1979 when Cathy walked into the room. "There's been a death in the family," he'd said.

It was 1995, and he was twenty-seven. No female connection had worked since Cathy. He'd been married briefly to a model who grew tired of the walls she'd failed to scale and in and out of relationships with women he dumped as soon as he grew weary of them, a frequent occurrence. He had established a reputation as one of those high-profile bachelor athletes to steer clear of if a girl didn't wish to be chewed up like a delicious plum and tossed away like a pit. Those who traded in gossip of famous sports figures never bothered to examine the possible cause of his fickleness that other super-stars who attracted girls because of their fame and money understood. Only Cathy had loved him for himself alone.

Aunt Mabel had not mentioned her or her son's name to him since Trey's freshman year in college. When she'd visit him in California, the Bensons were never brought up, but in regaling him of the latest goings-on in Kersey their exclusion was as conspicuous as the missing page of a book. He forgot the faces and bodies and names of the girls who flitted in and out of his life, but Cathy's remained inerasable, as persistently stuck in memory as the lines of a poem he'd memorized in grade school.

Cathy's son would be twelve by now. He and Cathy were sure to attend the ordination service.

"Mind if I come in?"

Trey batted the moisture from his eyes. Yes, he did mind, but she was nicer than the usual girls and she'd been thoughtful to make coffee. "Reading your mail?" she asked, setting a cup before him. She wore a loose robe over a teddy, and he hoped she didn't invite herself to sit on his lap and play with his hair.

"Uh-huh. I didn't get to it last night."

She grinned at him. "You did have other things on your mind."

He did not rise to the insinuation, and to his annoyance she picked up the invitation. "What an impressive cover. What do the initials *A.M.D.G.* and the dissecting cross mean?"

"They're Latin for *Ad Majorem Dei Gloriam*, which means 'For the greater glory of God.' It's the motto of the Jesuits."

She cocked a surprised brow. "You know about stuff like that?"

Her meaning was clear. His hedonistic image did not jibe with someone who would have knowledge of religious matters. When the Internet first became available for home use, Trey had researched the Order of the Society of Jesus and read countless testimonies from ordinands explaining what had drawn them toward the priesthood. It was the celibacy issue Trey couldn't understand. It wasn't normal for a man to deny himself his God-given urges. John had as strong a libido as he, if more restrained. Bebe must have thought John had lost his mind when he told her he wanted to become a priest. Or maybe... after Cathy no other woman would do.

A search through the Internet yielded an answer. Catholic priests were called to be "espoused" to God and the Church, Trey read, "because it frees the individual to concentrate solely on the concerns and needs of the larger family of God without the distractions associated with marriage. This spiritual concept is the reason why family words—father, brother, sister—are used to refer to those in a religious vocation." One priest wrote: "People don't choose celibacy because they don't want to get married. Quite the contrary. They choose to live the celibate life in order to give an undivided heart entirely to God and man." Trey remembered Aunt Mabel writing emotionally that when John took his first vows he'd said he was aware of the sacrifice of a wife and children of his own for a much larger family in the Church.

But if John had known the truth, would he have made the sacrifice of his son and the girl he loved to set out on his journey for atonement?

The years-old question usually kicked in late at night when Trey couldn't sleep, and there were times he'd be at his computer in the study reading of the order of John's calling when the sun rose through the window behind him and lit the screen.

She opened the invitation. "My goodness," she said in admiration when she'd read it. "Who is John Robert Caldwell?"

He retrieved the card. "An old friend."

"You've never mentioned him to me."

"I suppose not."

"There's no *suppose* to it, Trey. You never have."

He swiveled his chair away from her and got up. This was the point where his girlfriends accused him of shutting them out. He would lay money on what she would say next.

"Trey, why don't you ever share anything about your past with me?"

He'd have won his bet.

"Look, Tangi, why don't you get dressed? There's no point in hanging around here. I'm going for a run, and the rest of the day I've got things to do. I don't know about tonight, either. I'll have to give you a call."

The look came on her face he'd left on many a girl's when she knew it was over. "Was it something I said?" she asked, her voice small and hurt, like a child's.

"No," he said gently, drawing her into his arms. He pressed a kiss to her forehead. He'd liked her and they'd had a good time. "Nothing you said or did or didn't do. It's...just the way I am...who I am."

"A very hollow man," she said, pulling away, closing her robe. "I'm sorry for you, Trey."

"Me, too," he said.

Chapter Thirty-Eight

Turning her neck with difficulty, Cathy glanced across the aisle to give Will a smile. The aircraft's wheels had popped down in preparation for landing at the New Orleans International Airport. It was his first plane ride, and he was one year older than she'd been in 1979 when, at eleven, she'd taken her last trip by air. Her son returned her smile and leaned toward her. Nearly six feet in height, he blocked Mabel's view behind him.

"How's the neck?"

Cathy kneaded the area of her left carotid. She'd awakened with a painful crick in her neck. "Sore, darn it. Let's hope it unkinks by the time of the ceremony."

She did not want to miss a single detail of the

ordination service. John would be entering from the rear of the church and she hoped to follow his every step in the procession. She and Will were to be seated in the first row, and to see everything would take quite a bit of neck craning.

Beside her, Emma said, "John is going to be surprised at how much his godson has grown since the last time he saw him."

It had been a year, and in those months time had begun to refine Will's facial features and physical build. Cathy saw Trey's chromosomes at work in her son's dark hair, deep brown eyes, and athletic grace, but missing were the chameleon temperament and cocksure manner that had set his father apart at that age. Though he was already catching the eyes of the girls, was an exceptional student, class leader, and baseball stand-out, there wasn't anything remotely swaggering about Will. He possessed what his father never had—a rare combination of humility and confidence.

The June before, John had come home for a couple of weeks between completion of a Masters of Theology degree and a summer assignment to gain pastoral experience at a parish in Chicago. Will had not been able to get enough of his company. Out of school for the summer, he and John had hung out in the school gymnasium shooting hoops and on the baseball diamond, where Will practiced hitting John's fastballs. John had bunked at Father Richard's, but he'd spent his days with Will while Cathy ran Bennie's, the two of them stopping by the café for a hamburger at noon, then taking off again on some outdoor expedition—horseback riding and hiking in Palo Duro Canyon, fishing and sailing on Lake Meridian, the type of pursuits John and Trey had enjoyed at Will's age.

The two had turned brown as saddle leather and were thoroughly played out by mealtimes when they sat as a family around Emma's table, then watched television together until it was time for John to leave for Father Richard's.

Will had pined when John had gone, and Cathy had recognized in him the kind of loneliness that only an abandoned and orphaned child can know—the sundown blues, she and John and Trey had called it, because they felt their forsakenness the deepest at dusk. It was another one of those times when she would have gladly wrung Trey's neck. His name had not been brought up among them for some time, not even by Mabel, and Cathy wondered if Will ever thought of him or fantasized what it would be like to grow up as the wanted son of TD Hall.

"Will knows that you and Trey grew up

together," she said to John. "Does he ever ask you about his father?"

"Never. Not once."

"Do you ever speak of him?"

"No."

Others remarked to Will on his father successfully leading the San Diego Chargers to the NFL play-offs season after season—some to get a reaction—but Will stolidly added no comment of his own, and after he turned nine Cathy never heard him speak Trey's name again.

"He's come to a realization and accepted it," Emma had observed.

"I wish I knew what was going on in his head. He feels deeply and says little. I don't want him to hate his father or become embittered by him, but what can I say to defend Trey's denial of him?"

"All you can do is what you're doing—adding no fuel to the fire and making him understand that in the long run a person becomes who and what he is because of himself, not his parentage."

"I hope it's working."

"It is."

There were times Cathy was not so sure. When Will was ten, she'd found a *Sports Illustrated* magazine hidden under his mattress. The cover featured Trey Don Hall in a classic quarterback pose, arm back to pass, the other outstretched, his uniform showing the ravages of a hard-fought game. One-third of the four-page article was devoted to his phenomenal staying power and luck in having survived seven years in the NFL without injury. Chronicled were his verbal run-ins with the news media as well as examples of his satirical exchanges with female TV reporters who stuck a microphone into his face at halftime and after a game. It was Trey's opinion that "women have no business on a football field unless they're shaking ass and pom-poms."

"TD, can you tell us how you feel?"

"About what?"

"Uh, about the score." (Losing or winning.)

"No. Can you?"

"On that last play, TD, what was going through your mind?"

"Beats the hell out of me. What was going through yours?"

In spite of herself, Cathy chuckled.

Another part described his freewheeling lifestyle, love of sailing, and penchant for brunette models. It had detailed features of his $5 million condominium in Carlsbad, located thirty-five miles north of San Diego, among the most expensive places to live in the United States. Her son had read of Trey's three sailboats and multiple cars and seen pictures of him in the company of an assortment of beautiful women. She'd discovered the magazine when the café had begun to afford an increase in their standard of living, but Will could not help but compare his father's affluence to the years of his mother's financial struggles when he'd wake in the night to find her worrying over the ledgers at the kitchen table. Out-of-pocket expenses for his great-grandmother's medicine, car repairs, a new roof for the house, and renovations to Bennie's left little room for bikes at Christmas and trips to Disneyland.

And Cathy was sure he had not missed Trey's preference for tall women. She'd felt a maternal tightening of her chest. How could Will not feel resentment toward a father who favored arm candy in such contrast to his mother and who was earning millions while she'd labored to make ends meet?

She'd wondered if Will had paid much attention to the rest of the article that depicted Trey as "a heads and tails kind of guy." Cool thinking, total self-control, and exemplary conduct described him on the field. "Off the gridiron," the reporter wrote, "he could rival the back end of your most cantankerous farm animal." However, from a long observation of Trey Don Hall, the writer stated, he had gotten the impression that the San Diego quarterback had gotten tired of his fame, riches, and women but never his game. "On the football field you see a person. Off, you see a persona. It's like he's posing for the cover of a glossy, glamorous, in-your-face magazine—*this is what it's like to be me, folks!*—about as real a portrait of himself as a woman wearing makeup. One wonders how authentically the Armani suits, Berluti shoes, and diamond-studded Rolex project the image of a man relishing a full and happy life."

Cathy had remembered John's words: "He'll never know anything is missing in his life until he has it all…"

She had slipped the magazine back in place and never mentioned it. Afterwards she'd regretted allowing the chance to slide by that might have gotten Will to open up about his father. There had not come another opportunity to penetrate her son's obstinate silence on the subject of Trey Don Hall.

The flight attendant came down the aisle for one last pass to collect trash. She was young and pretty and gave Will a special smile. Turning painfully to check if his seat belt was fastened, Cathy caught an amused grin from Ron Turner in the seat beside him, a pleasant sight for a change. Coach Turner hadn't had much to smile about since his team won the state championship. He'd taken the death of his daughter terribly hard the following fall, and within a few years his wife had died from the heart disease she'd battled for years. His coaching duties began to suffer, and after a number of losing seasons he'd been forced to retire rather than be let go. Loss of income was no problem, but his sense of personal failure and disappointment with life showed in his sour demeanor and devitalized posture. This trip to New Orleans to celebrate the ordination of his favorite player to the priesthood might be just what the coach needed to restart his engines.

John was waiting for them in the reception area as they deplaned. His tall figure was easy to spot in the crowd awaiting arrivals, and Cathy's heartbeat stopped when, for the first time, she saw him dressed in the black suit and shirt and Roman collar of his calling.

"Oh, my goodness," Mabel said in an awed whisper. Loaded with bags, they all stopped several feet short of him, halted by his priestly beauty.

Cathy laughed teasingly. "We don't know whether to genuflect or throw our arms around you," she said.

John's grin broadened, lighting his deep brown eyes. "Hugs will do. Welcome to N'orlins, y'all." He and Cathy embraced, holding each other without speaking for an exclusive, personal moment before John hugged Emma and Mabel and shook hands with Ron and Father Richard, whom he'd asked to "vest" him at his ordination. Will stood silently behind the group to wait his turn, looking shy and wary of John as if he'd suddenly become a stranger.

"Hello, Will," John said in a quieter octave.

Will seemed not to see his extended hand. "What do I call you?" he asked, shooting an uncertain glance at his mother.

"What you've always called me—John."

"Not Father?"

"Only if you want to. And only after my ordination."

"Father. I want to call you that," Will said, his voice catching, and without another word flew into John's arms.

THE MOST HOLY NAME of Jesus Catholic Church was an imposing neo-Gothic structure erected in 1918 and inspired by the Canterbury Cathedral in Kent, England. Cathy believed the altar one of the most impressive things she'd ever seen—which wasn't saying much for someone who had hardly been outside Kersey, Texas, since she was eleven years old, she allowed wryly. Still, the most jaded world traveler would appreciate the ornate sculpture of the pure white marble communion table. John had told her the stone had been chosen by the primary benefactor of the church to represent sugar in honor of his family's sugar-planting heritage. Surrounded by such gold and red opulence, Cathy imagined Father Richard must think the place a cathedral compared to his modest church back home. Hanging conspicuously from the altar rail was the white stole that he would later place over John's shoulders.

She heard a growing swell of voices behind her, a testament to the regard in which John was held. They belonged to his Loyola classmates and professors, scholastics and novices, members of the clergy, parishioners, his students, and their parents. There would be the homeless among them, sitting beside the sheltered; the unwashed, sharing a pew with the freshly showered. They would all come, his spiritual director had told her last evening at a small gathering in John's honor. John had touched many in all walks of life. He was beloved. "He's a very gifted scholar," the director said, "but it's not academics he's known by, but his ability to relate to people, to connect with them, whether they're student or faculty, clergy or laity, lowly or exalted. He has the touch." With the exception of Father Richard, who would be participating in the processional, the contingent from the Panhandle occupied the first row on the right side of the aisle. Cathy would have liked to sneak a glance at the filling church for someone in particular, but her neck was too sore to make the effort.

A door opened and the provincial superior of the New Orleans Province, richly clad in the vestments of his office, took his place by the altar. The choir filed in and stood in their nook at the right side of it, an impressive body in white robes and mantles adorned with a gold cross. The members lifted their maroon music folders as the director stepped to his position, and with the sweep of his hands a chorus of voices lifted in the ancient hymn "Soli Deo Gloria" (Glory to God alone) to the resounding chords of the grand organ. The ordination service had begun.

Cathy glanced at her watch. In two hours, John would be lost to her forever, married to God. From time to time through the years, she had allowed herself to imagine what her life would have been like if she'd accepted John's proposal the day before he left for Loyola. Of course she did not feel then what she felt now, and in the ceremony today there would be no moment when the provincial would instruct: "If there be any among you with reason why this man should not be joined in holy matrimony to his God, speak now or forever hold your peace."

She would hold her peace.

The procession began. The assembly rose. Cathy saw Will's eyes grow wide. This was his first time to witness such a display of liturgical pomp and splendor. Followed by the bishop, John was the second to the last in line, simply dressed in an alb, a long, white garment representing the baptismal dress of a new Christian who "puts on Christ." How handsome he was! Cathy had noticed him draw the eyes of women at the airport as he strode along, curiosity in their gazes as to why such a man would willingly remove himself from the pleasures of the flesh that would naturally be his for the taking.

At her pew, John stepped from the line and winked to the group as he took his place beside her until an altar server would come to escort him to the bishop to be ordained. Cathy held the order of the service in her hand, and all through the long reading of the Scriptures, the sermon, and the recitation of the Apostles' Creed she fought the crazy urge to grab his white-robed arm and cry as she'd wanted to do on her grandmother's porch that Thanksgiving evening in 1986: *Don't go, John. Stay and marry me...*

Her hold tightened on the program when the altar server, a young man in an alb and white surplice, approached John to lead him to the provincial superior, who would present him to the bishop.

Do not turn and look into my eyes, John. You will see my heartbreak. He did not. He followed the server without a glance at her or a gentle squeeze of her arm. It was as if he had stepped forth into a new light and left all former things on the pew behind him. Before the bishop, the provincial placed his hand on John's right shoulder and intoned, "I present for ordination to the ministry of word and sacrament John Robert Caldwell, who has been prepared, examined, and approved for this ministry and who has been called by the Church to this ministry through the Society of Jesus."

TREY HAD EXPECTED to tear up. He had to fight to keep his eyes dry during intensely emotional moments. Though most times he subdued it, his tendency to cry had a will of its own. Reporters called it an anomaly, since it appeared contrary to his cynical nature. He sat at the far end of a middle row on the right of the church where he had a clear view of the front-row seats and refused to surrender his vantage point, even stand, to accommodate arrivals. They'd had to step over his feet, casting him dark glances, not a flicker of recognition in them. In the off-season, he wore his hair longer. Its length and a month's growth of beard and tortoiseshell-framed reading glasses were all the disguise he'd needed to grab a flight to New Orleans, rent a car, book a room, and slip into a seat of the Most Holy Name of Jesus Catholic Church unrecognized.

His eyes had begun to water when he'd spotted the complement from his hometown spread along the first row—John's adopted family. His heart had turned a painful somersault at the physical changes in the dauntless Emma, now shrunken and dependent on her cane, and his hero and father figure, Coach Turner, prematurely aged almost beyond recognition. Even his aunt, whom he'd seen at Christmas, seemed frailer, but his greatest shock of feeling came when his gaze landed on the blond head of Cathy Benson. She was seated next to her son, the other side of her presumably reserved for John. The years had strengthened her beauty, but Trey recognized with tender amusement that the straight posture she'd forced on herself since before he met her was unchanged. By now those petite shoulders were so disciplined, they wouldn't have dared sag.

He had watched her through his glasses, risking she'd feel his watery stare and turn her head. Cathy would not be fooled by his appearance. She had once been able to sense his eyes upon her. Was she wondering if he was somewhere in the congregation and had her in his line of sight?

During the many points in the program when the assembly was instructed to stand, he was surprised and disappointed that she did not once cast a look over her shoulder searching for a familiar brown head. Her interest was focused on the star of the show, as was Trey's when his attention wasn't on Cathy. It wasn't too hard to reconcile the man in the white robe to the boy of their letter-jacket days. He'd stayed virtually the same—older, of course, seasoned, but he was still John, tower of quiet strength, purposeful, focused, confident, at home with himself and everybody in the universe. So different from the man who watched him now.

The emotional moment arrived that he'd read of and prepared himself for. As the choir began to chant the Litany of the Saints, a beautiful centuries-old prayer, John walked to the center aisle. Trey's vision blurred as the figure in the white robe lay facedown in front of the altar and stretched out his arms in the form of a cross, a symbol of his submission to God.

Only Trey knew what had brought him there. He hoped it would bring his friend the peace he craved.

Trey steeled himself during the rest of the ceremony but wiped his eyes again when the bishop and the other priests laid their hands on John's head in a ritual that declared him now one of them, a recipient of the Holy Spirit with the sacred right to pursue his ministry—and which now put him forever beyond his old life's reclaim. Trey thought the service would never be over, but there was still the stirring vesting rite where Father Richard's former altar boy knelt before him to accept the stole and chasuble drawn over his head like a knight receiving his battle armor. Not a sound disturbed the hush of the moved congregation. Trey was not so touched. He blamed Father Richard for taking John from the game, playing on his vulnerability that had been as obvious as an open wound after that day in November. Had John ever confessed his part in it to the good father? he wondered.

As he watched Cathy's face turned in profile toward the proceedings, a sharp twist of bereavement caught him just as he'd dried his eyes. Her brow and nose, the strong-willed little jaw and upward sweep of her lashes, were as they were stored in memory. Already her son—a good-looking kid—had overshot her by a foot. He held his shoulders straight, his head high. His gaze was fastened on John. A muscle grabbed beneath Trey's breastbone. What would have happened—where would he be in his life today—if he'd played the final minutes of the last quarter of his childhood differently? Would he have been able to love the boy as his own or would he have rejected him like Bert Caldwell had John? He would never know. It had been a mistake to come, but he could not have stayed away. He'd had to assure himself that his and John's secret was safe. John had now been given the authority to act *in persona Christi*—in the name of Christ. For whatever it had cost him in personal pain to be here today, Trey was convinced that in a moment of stricken conscience John Caldwell, ordained to the priesthood, member of the Order of the Society of Jesus, defender of the faith, would never reveal the truth of his one and only sin.

With a last look at those he would likely never see again, Trey slipped away when everyone stood for the Acclamation of the Assembly and before John turned to be presented to the congregation like a groom at his wedding ceremony.

When he got back to Carlsbad, he decided, he'd get himself a dog.

Chapter Thirty-Nine

His ministry began. "Where do you wish to serve, my son?" the provincial superior asked John. *At St. Matthew's to be near Cathy and my godson,* he wished to respond. Next winter, Will would enter his teens and need a father figure, and Emma and Mabel, both frail and ailing, were at the tail end of their lives and would soon be gone, leaving Cathy alone but for the few years remaining before her son took off for college.

But he had committed himself to the larger family of God and to Ignatius Loyola's mandate directing Jesuits to "travel throughout the world" to help those in need. And so he replied, "Send me where I am needed."

He was needed first at Pelican Bay State Prison,

billed a "super-max" penal facility, near Crescent City in Del Norte County, California. It housed some of California's most dangerous criminals and was located in a remote forested area close to the California–Oregon state line, far from California's major metropolitan areas. The weather averaged sixty to seventy degrees in summer, a welcomed change from the stifling heat and humidity of New Orleans. His digs in Crescent City, located on the beautiful Northern California coast, were comfortable, and the area, utilizing the proximity to the Pacific Ocean and state parks, offered an abundance of the outdoor activities he loved. Within a week of reporting for duty, he thought he'd been assigned to hell.

The uniformed guard who'd been asked to show John around the prison asked, "Have you ever been in a SHU, Father?" using the acronym for the Security Housing Unit—the modern name for solitary confinement. They were standing inside an eight-by-ten-foot cement cell with no windows. The only light filtered in through a high, barred skylight as gray as the concrete walls, unmoveable sleeping slab, stool, and writing platform, and combination stainless-steel sink and lidless toilet. Nothing penetrated the deep, enforced quiet of the isolation cell but the sound of a few muted voices and the occasional flushing of a toilet. The inmate confined to these quarters would be able to see the outside corridor only through the widely spread, nickel-sized perforations in a solid steel door. The metal was set with a small, knee-high portal through which his meals would be served on plastic trays—twice a day, John had been informed.

A shudder ran over him. He was a Texas Panhandle boy. No matter to what dingy, teeming city his formation years had taken him, he'd carried the big skies and wide prairies of his home region in the forefront of his brain. It was a mind trick he'd developed to ward off the hemmed-in feeling he got from inescapable throngs and squalor and poverty. He could imagine no sentence worse than to be locked up in this starkly efficient place of electronically operated doors and sterile concrete and steel, unable to move more than eight feet in one direction, denied for years on end the sight of grass and trees and blue sky.

The guard's smirk clearly indicated he knew his visitor's answer from his appalled expression. John asked, "This...*pod*, so I understand it's called, is where the offender eats, sleeps, and exists for twenty-two and a half hours a day. Where does he spend the other one and a half hours that I assume are allotted for leisure?"

"Out here." The guard showed no offense at the sarcastic tone of John's question. John got the impression he was accustomed to the objection that do-gooders like him took to the facility, where there wasn't a prayer's chance in hell of rehabilitating a man forced to live in these conditions. He followed the uniformed figure through a remote-controlled door that slid open to a bare concrete courtyard the size of a dog run. The walls were twenty feet high and covered by a metal grate allowing the inmate to see a patch of sky. It looked as inviting to John as an abandoned mine shaft.

"This is the exercise area," the guard explained.

"No athletic equipment is allowed and the offender is to have no contact with any other prisoner in here?" John asked to confirm his reading of the rules.

"That's right. Isolation is strictly enforced. Most of 'em do sit-ups or walk from wall to wall. Mainly this is just a place to stretch legs and get fresh air." At John's look of distaste, the guard added, "And, Father, I wouldn't call the men who are sent here 'offenders.' As a matter of fact, the one who's going to find a home in the pod I showed you murdered a family of five, including a two-month-old baby."

"How do I address the spiritual needs of these men, hear their confessions, administer the sacraments, without human contact?"

The guard grinned, mockery in his eyes. "If you have any customers, through the food portal."

He had customers. The draw was not spiritual guidance, John was aware, but that he afforded the SHU inmates their only source of human contact, the opportunity to slip a little finger through one of the small holes in their cell doors to exchange a "pinky shake" with him. From his days of counseling inmates and hearing soul-sickening confessions from prisoners in the SHU and general population he learned much about the depths of evil and depravity to which a human being can descend that John's psychology textbooks had not addressed. His clerical involvement with murderers and rapists and child molesters tested his belief in the Ignacian concept that God could be found in all things.

"Do you believe man is made in the image of God, Father?"

John considered the shackled serial killer of little girls before him, the derisive curl of his mouth, the mocking glint in his eyes, as he asked the question. He saw not a ray of redeeming light in the man. He was a monster. For some reason, unfairly, John thought of Trey, a servant to his nature. "He begins there," John said.

If the iniquity he encountered daily shook his belief that man's essential goodness would prevail over evil, his trust that God could make it happen never trembled. All was certainly not right with the world, but God was in His heaven. It was John's mission to lead men to see that through God's grace and if they were willing, they had the power to change the wrong inside them, even in a violent, gang-infested prison where goodness was as hard to make thrive as a sunflower in toxic waste.

He had been about his priestly duties for almost a year when his landlady announced a surprise visitor.

"A doctor," she said. "She's in the living room. Are you sick, Father?"

John read the business card: LAURA RHINE-LANDER, NEURO-ONCOLOGIST. The name rang a familiar bell. *Ah, yes:* Cathy's childhood friend from Santa Cruz. He was aware they still corresponded, and he'd been proud of Cathy for keeping in touch with the friend who'd gone on to achieve the dream she'd had to abandon. He remembered that Laura was a doctor trained in the specialty of diagnosing and treating brain tumors—had become quite well known in her field, so Cathy had told him. She'd suggested he try to see Laura, since she practiced in San Diego, but the very name of the city where Trey played for the Chargers left a bad taste in John's mouth. Cathy must have given her his address. She would be thrilled that Laura had taken the initiative to look him up.

He thought of taking off his Roman collar and changing his shirt, but he was eager to see someone who knew Cathy and was not associated with the prison.

"No, I'm not sick," he told his landlady. "She's simply a friend of a friend."

He entered the living room warmed by a flush of anticipation. "Laura?" he said.

She turned from the window, and he recognized the woman grown from the chestnut-haired, hazel-eyed little girl with a flair for fashion he had met when they were twelve years old. She tendered an uncertain smile. "I hope it's all right to spring myself on you like this. I didn't know I'd have the time off until yesterday morning."

He recognized burnout when he saw it. He guessed she may have suddenly decided she needed to get away from sick people for a couple of days and thought of him. "I'm happy to see you," he said, reinforcing his joy with a big smile. "Thoroughly delighted, as a matter of fact." She was wearing sensible shoes despite her outfit that called for more stylish footwear. "Let's take a walk," he invited, "and you can fill me in on the last nineteen years."

She was associated with a cancer center in San

Diego, she told him, and had been practicing four years.

"So Cathy informed me," he said. "Do you ever see Trey Hall?"

"Only on television when the Chargers play, and once in a restaurant. He was with a group of friends. He did not recognize me, and I didn't reintroduce myself. I was afraid I might stab him with a table knife. How about you? Have you tried to reconnect with him since you've been in California?" She smiled an apology. "Cathy told me of your falling-out."

John shook his head. "I thought about it, but that's as far as I got."

When it came time to be reassigned, his only regret in leaving Northern California was Laura. They had become friends. It was a two-day drive from San Diego to Crescent City, but he served as her excuse to get away from the numbing despair of her work, as she offered a break from his. She was one of the most sensitive and thoughtful people he'd ever met. One February afternoon, she drove straight to Crescent City from San Diego after a racially charged riot broke out in the prison yard the day before that had made national news. Guards had been forced to use assault rifles to subdue the thirty-minute melee in which one prisoner was fatally shot, thirty were wounded, and at least fifty had been stabbed. Among them were a number of John's "parishioners." In helpless and appalled resignation, he had witnessed the devastating scene through the prison fence.

"Thought you could use a friend," she said, holding up a basket of his picnic favorites when he entered his landlady's living room.

Laura had introduced him to surfboarding, clam bakes, sourdough bread, and California wines. He had provided a listening ear and broad shoulder in the gloomy gap left by her divorce from a concert pianist whom she still loved. "We simply couldn't mesh," she said. "Our careers got in the way."

There followed a relatively peaceful stint in Jamaica, where John lived in community with other Jesuits who, over the years, had built extensive schools and churches on the island and where he worked with the government to improve education and housing for the poor. Afterwards, in 2002 he was sent back to Guatemala to engage in activities for social justice, the same ministry in which he'd been involved before his ordination that had helped lead to the signing of Guatemala's Peace Accords ending the country's thirty-six-year civil war. Despite some progress, he found Guatemala as violent as ever and his face and former advocacy work for human rights well remembered by some still in power in the military. Assassinations, kidnappings, theft, drug trafficking, prison uprisings were prevalent "with 426 deaths registered in December alone—13 a day," he wrote to Father Richard with a strict warning that he was not to share news of the dangerous situation with Cathy or the others. To Cathy, John described only the extreme misery of poverty "in such a beautiful land the world has forgotten."

He longed to be assigned somewhere in the United States, but he was sent to the seaport parish of St. Peter Claver in the tiny neighboring country of Belize to assist Jesuits of the Missouri Province in meeting the humanitarian needs of a Mayan population who had been left even more destitute from Hurricane Iris. His jobs included the never-ending task of feeding and housing the teeming indigenous poor, facilitating their training and education, and working for their social and economic improvement. In an area that postcards depicted as a balmy tropical paradise, he badgered and begged for help from medical institutions to combat the illnesses inflicted by a high disease-carrying insect population, lack of clean drinking water, and unsanitary hygienic conditions. He hammered and sawed, planted and tilled, taught and preached, and resisted and argued against the tyranny of the privileged few over the deprived many. By the summer of 2004, he could speak and read the native language of Kriol fluently, spear fish like a Mayan, build a canoe, and detect the presence of a venomous, tree-dwelling eyelash viper lying in wait to ambush an unsuspecting victim below. His skin reflected the color of burnished wood, and he was twenty pounds below his normal weight. He had not been home in five years. He was thirty-six years old.

And then one day he received a communiqué from the provincial superior of the New Orleans Province. Father Richard was retiring. Would John like to assume his duties as pastor of St. Matthew's Parish in Kersey, Texas?

Chapter Forty

On New Year's Eve, 1999, Mabel ran a bathtub of extra water, set out flashlights with a supply of batteries throughout the house, double-locked all the doors and windows, and placed one of her late husband's hunting rifles cocked and ready by her bed. She had packed a pantry full of nonperishable food goods, cases of distilled water, bags of charcoal briquettes, and cans of lighter fluid. Her safe was stuffed with cash and jewelry, and the tank of her Cadillac was full—to be replenished from the five-gallon drums of gasoline stored in the garage.

"You and the children need to stay with me tonight," she said to Emma, referring to her thirty-two-year-old granddaughter and a great-grandson on the cusp of becoming a teenager. "My house is safer."

"Your house is a firetrap," Emma said, "and you might shoot me when I get up to go to the bathroom."

"It never hurts to be prepared," Mabel sniffed. "And you'll be sorry you didn't stay with me if what is expected to happen tonight happens."

It was the quietest New Year's Eve in Kersey's recorded history. The world did not end and the Y2K bug did not materialize, but in the early-morning hours of 2000 Emma Benson died in her sleep. The café had closed for the holiday, and Cathy was home. She had gotten up early to make a French toast casserole for breakfast prior to her and Emma and Mabel settling down to watch the Rose Bowl Parade on television. Will would be off at the baseball diamond with friends.

After a while, when Emma, always an early riser, did not respond to the aroma of freshly brewed coffee, Cathy knocked on her door. "Grandmother, coffee's ready," she called.

No response. Cathy held her breath. She realized she had not heard the toilet flush. Quietly she opened the door to find the scene she'd long dreaded. Emma lay in her bed with her eyes closed and her hands interlocked peacefully on the coverlet, eternally beyond the reach of her granddaughter's voice.

A large black wreath was hung below the

CLOSED sign of Bennie's. The courthouse flag was lowered to half-staff. Cathy, her grief like a stone in her chest, held herself together for her devastated son and Mabel, who overnight seemed to have been robbed of most of her remaining years. Cathy suggested she call Trey to come home, but Mabel shook her head. "It would be a sacrilege to Emma's memory for him to show up now," she said. The morning of the funeral, Cathy discovered a magnificent arrangement of white gladiolas, Emma's favorite, beside her casket with a card bearing Trey's name and a simple inscription: *Rest well, Miss Emma.* John flew in from California but was able to be with them for only a few days. He'd promised a prisoner who had been transferred from Pelican Bay to San Quentin's death row that he would walk with him to his execution.

Drawing upon the legacy of Emma's guidance and wisdom, Cathy concentrated on the future.

"I HAVE TO SAY, Cathy, you've done one hell of a job with the place," Daniel Spruill, president of the Kersey State Bank, said in praise of his mortgagee's remodeling of Bennie's. "What a contrast from the days when Gloria used to spit on her handkerchief to wipe off a tabletop before she'd even sit down."

He spoke of his deceased wife. Daniel had grown

up in Kersey and graduated from high school seven years ahead of Cathy. He and Gloria had returned to his hometown after college and his marriage, Daniel to serve as vice president in his father's bank and Gloria to assume a prominent role in society, such as it was in Kersey, Texas. Upon the senior Spruill's death, Daniel had inherited his father's position as president, becoming a widower when Gloria had died of cancer three years before. He and Cathy had been seeing each other since the day she'd sat across from his desk and explained her plans for the expansion of Bennie's.

That had been six months ago. It was December 2000. Cathy had been afraid that the slowdown in the economy owing to the dot-com bubble burst would affect her chances of a loan, but the bank president had assured her that his institution was only too grateful to accommodate her financial needs.

"I couldn't have done it without your faith in me," Cathy responded to Daniel's compliment.

"Yes, you could have. Your faith in yourself would have been enough. I'm just happy to be a part of all this." He swept a hand about the enlarged dining room, new buffet facilities, and expanded counter space before encircling her waist with his arm. They were alone in the dining room. Bennie's had not yet reopened for business after the renovation. An open house was scheduled for tomorrow. "Do you have any idea what you mean to me?" he asked, his voice quiet, his lips close to her ear.

Yes, she did. He was moving a little too fast for her, but as he'd put the question when he'd first expressed his feelings, "Who has time for the waiting game?"

She did not love him in the way she'd hoped to love again, but he was kind and good and thought the world of her son. He had two of his own, college students, nice boys, and Daniel imagined them sharing holidays, going on trips and outings together—"having fun as a family!" He was handsome in a professorial way (his glasses had left permanent indentations on the sides of his nose) and was an adoring and adroit lover. He cherished in her the things that had been missing in his wife. Gloria had been described as emotionally insecure, spending money to atone for her deprivation as a handyman's daughter, jealous and controlling, a woman who felt the need to acquire enviable possessions so that she would not feel inferior to her husband's friends. She'd had no wish to travel and no curiosity outside the world of Kersey. She'd doted obsessively on her sons, to whom Daniel had taken a backseat.

"I was simply the guy who paid the bills," he said.

There was a polite cough from the door of the

kitchen. Cathy peered around Daniel's lanky shoulder. "Yes, Odell?"

The delivery truck is here, Miss Cathy."

"I'll be right there."

She extracted herself from Daniel's arms, her mind back to business. "I'm just hoping that now that I've built it, they will come."

They came. Wall Street's panic did not deflect a steadily increasing customer base of local diners, travelers along Interstate 40 who'd read of Bennie's, and Panhandlers inclined to drive long distances from occupying the tables and booths of the highly touted café in Kersey, Texas. Framed food critics' reviews and menus autographed by celebrities began to appear on the wall. Cathy settled into her relatively prosperous life, disturbed only by the question of whether she was willing to give up the hard-earned, growing success of her business to marry. Daniel would expect her to sell Bennie's. From his description of the life they'd lead, there would be no room for the day-to-day demands of running a restaurant. Their first and only argument was over the café.

"New York, Cathy. We're talking *New York*! Plays, restaurants, walks in Central Park, art galleries, the Waldorf-Astoria. Think of it—autumn in New York!" He waved Fodor's *Guide to the Big Apple* before her.

Cathy sighed. "I know."

"No, you don't know!" Daniel slapped the Fodor's down onto his desk. "How could you possibly know? You've hardly been anywhere outside Kersey County since you were eleven years old."

They were sitting in Daniel's office in the bank discussing—or, rather, arguing—the prickly topic of Daniel's upcoming trip to attend a banking conference in New York City. He wanted her to go, but the dates in question collided with bookings for events to be held in Bennie's party room. Bebe couldn't handle the number alone, and the special-events reservations were what kept Bennie's in the black. It simply wasn't possible for Cathy to be gone at such a time.

She could feel the frustration and disappointment he must have felt many times when his wife refused to accompany him on business trips because of the children. "I mean," Cathy explained, "that I know how wonderful it would be to go to New York. So what about this idea? Why don't we go there on our honeymoon?"

"What?" he said, his frown beginning to dissipate like a thundercloud when the sun breaks through. "What's that?"

Cathy smiled. "I accept your proposal. I'd love to marry you." She was now sure. She loved Daniel, if not with the whole heart she'd given Trey, at least enough for her to know she was making the right decision for both of them. She was thirty-three. Her grandmother was gone, and Will would be leaving for college in three years. John was in Jamaica, and Trey was never coming home. The years stretched long and empty before her with only the café to fill her days. Marriage to Daniel would mean a move to the big house on the hill, the possibility of having another child, and relief from having to provide a living for her and her son. Most important, it would mean sharing her life and growing old with a man she respected and admired.

He came from behind his desk, his face glowing with happy astonishment. "You won't change your mind while I'm gone?"

"I won't change my mind."

"Hallelujah!" He grabbed her up into his arms and swung her around, her feet a foot from the floor. He kissed her.

"Now," she said laughingly when he set her down, "will you please have your secretary make a copy of the conference schedule so that I can at least be with you in my thoughts wherever you are?"

On the first day of his conference after he left, she dutifully checked where his meeting would be held. The World Trade Center, she saw, ninety-second floor in the North Tower. The date was September 11, 2001.

Chapter Forty-One

The gloom had moved in and settled, Trey reflected back, when Emma died on New Year's Day, 2000. She'd been eighty-three and had suffered from a bad heart for years, so her death was not unexpected, but somehow the knowledge of that tough old lady being no longer around still made him sad. He could only imagine her loss to Cathy and his aunt. Miss Emma's death had reminded him that Aunt Mabel's days were numbered as well, and that made him sadder.

"Why don't you move your aunt here to live with us?" his second wife had suggested, the offer taking him aback. Mona's usual preoccupation was with herself.

"You'd go along with that?"

"I'd go along with anything to make you fun again, less of a drag."

So it had been about Mona after all, but his aunt had turned him down.

"No, dear, my home is here," she'd said. She no longer asked him to visit, and she'd reply to his invitation to come for holidays that she was too old to fly by herself anymore, so the last time he'd visited with Aunt Mabel was the Christmas before John's ordination. There had been moments after that, with a longing like a lump of coal burning in his chest, that he'd have given everything he possessed to go home again, hug his aunt and Miss Emma, put his arms around Cathy and John, and scatter a magic dust that would erase the past and they could all start over again. But Emma had died, his aunt had given up on him, John was off in Central America doing his priestly duty, and Cathy had fallen in love with a bank president. Every door that had once been open to him had closed.

Why was it that he never saw things until it was too late?

"Trey, are you listening to me? I just told you that you're almost broke."

"I heard you," Trey said. He was sitting across the desk from his wealth management advisor in the Carlsbad office of Merrill Lynch. It was September

2007. He did not have to look at the review his advisor had prepared to know the state of his finances or how they got that way. In his first five years in the league, he fell into the trap of most rookies who were suddenly paid five hundred thousand dollars every two weeks. It was difficult to maintain a financially conservative lifestyle, even though he was aware that the average career of a pro football player was three years and his salary was guaranteed for only a short time if he could not play.

For the first four seasons, after taxes and his agent's 6 percent cut, he'd spent money at a maniacal level, buying fancy cars, sailboats, his condo in Carlsbad, and one in Santa Fe, not to mention the tailor-made clothes, lavish parties, sky-high restaurant tabs, jewelry, and the cost of his first divorce.

But after that, he began to invest his earnings. His goal was to have enough money when he retired to sail the world and never have to work again. He studied the stock and real estate markets and carefully analyzed the offers to invest in everything from restaurants to clothing lines to oil leases. He did everything right when it came to doing his homework, and still he blew it. Against the advice of the man before him, he transferred the millions in his blue-chip portfolio to stocks in computer software, telecommunications companies, and the

Internet. In 1996, he saw his starter Yahoo! stock jump 155 percent on its first day of trading. His thirty-thousand-dollar investment in one company's stock increased to a million in one year. How could he go wrong? The future was technology and the Internet, engines of wealth on the par of railroads, electricity, and the automobile. He did not foresee the danger of companies going public with only the prospect of future profits. Before the bubble burst and he witnessed shares that had been worth $244.00 dropping to $7.00, Mona sued him for divorce, cashing in her half of his investment portfolio when it was at its peak.

In 2001, after his eleventh season with the Chargers, his contract was not renewed. The blow had come before the events of 9/11 and the stunning news that Cathy's fiancé had perished in the North Tower of the World Trade Center. The San Francisco 49ers picked him up as their second-string quarterback, but on his first play he lost his concentration and held the ball too long before catching a nearly paralyzing blow to the head that sidelined him with a concussion. Because of knee problems, he limped, literally, through the rest of the season, when San Francisco bid him adieu at the end of his one-year contract. He was thirty-four years old.

For him, the game was over. He refused to make

the pro circuit as a second stringer, sitting on the sidelines, competing for playing time like a hungry rookie, and he dusted off his business degree from the University of Miami. His name alone gained him interviews with executives of top corporations in the San Diego area, most of whom were tightening their belts because of the Silicon Valley debacle and the following terrorist attacks that sent the stock markets tumbling again. None of the positions he tried suited him until finally he was hired within the last year as a fund-raiser for a nonprofit organization. He liked the charity work and people, mostly dedicated volunteers, and for the first time unashamedly enjoyed using his star status and charisma to pump money out of the well-heeled to relieve the suffering of the less fortunate. There were times, after a successful campaign, he wished John could see him accept the check that had resulted from the employment of his magnetic powers. *What do you think of these apples, Tiger!*

"At least you have no debt," his broker was saying, "and if you sell your condo—"

"I'm not selling my condo," Trey interrupted. "That's not an option."

"Well, if you continue to work, you should be

able to live in... reduced but certainly satisfactory circumstances."

If he continued to work. He had an appointment with a doctor in San Diego right after he left here today. He'd been having headaches, blurred vision, for some time, and they seemed to be getting worse. He hoped the problem was not the result of that last doozy of a concussion he'd suffered. If so, he'd deal with it. Headaches, dizzy spells, memory loss were the price of admission to play on Sundays in a sport built on and driven by violence.

Rain slashed at his car windows when he drove into the office parking lot of an internist he'd researched on the Internet. He'd chosen to go to a stranger rather than to his old sports medicine doctor, where members of the media hung out to catch and snap famous athletes on their medical visits. He chose for his to remain unreported.

When he turned off the ignition, he sat a few minutes watching the rain through the window of his BMW, his hands tight on the wheel. Then he drew a deep breath and pushed open the door. To hell with an umbrella. If getting soaked was the worst that happened to him today, he'd welcome it.

A physician's assistant took a history of Trey's symptoms followed by a neurological exam that tested his vision, balance, coordination, and mental status. After that he was sent for a CT scan and MRI of his brain. When it was explained that in order to assure accurate pictures, he would have to lie absolutely still and strapped to a moveable examination table that would slide through a closed-sided imaging chamber, his issues with claustrophobia came surging back. He would have turned and walked away if not for the technologist who treated the famous San Diego quarterback—*"you're my hero, Mr. Hall!"*—with such respect and reverence.

"Think of the most beautiful time in your life, and it will all be over before you know it," he said to Trey as he injected a special dye into his vein.

Trey thought of the night he'd spent with Cathy after the junior prom.

When it was over, he waited an hour before the technician returned to the sitting room. "A radiologist will analyze the images and send a signed report to your primary-care physician, Mr. Hall," he said. "You'll hear something in about three days."

It was less than twenty-four hours before he was summoned back to the internist's office. The doctor explained the results of the tests and said afterwards, "I'm giving you a list of the finest physicians in our area specializing in the treatment of your disease, Mr. Hall." He pushed a sheet of alphabetized names across his desk. "As you can see, there are ten, all located at the cancer center here in San Diego. Personally, if I were you, I would choose the second from the bottom."

Trey looked at the name he indicated with the tip of his pen: Dr. Laura Rhinelander, neuro-oncologist.

PART THREE

2008

Chapter Forty-Two

Father John Caldwell woke abruptly from a bad night's rest. He had not been able to get to sleep after the brief, cryptic, out-of-the-blue midnight telephone call from his onetime best friend, Trey Don Hall. He had gone to bed feeling the shock of having picked up the phone to hear the voice of a man he hadn't heard or seen personally in twenty-two years. What was more, Trey would be arriving in Kersey today. John had tossed and turned all night wondering what could be bringing Trey back to his hometown after so long an absence. John still couldn't buy that it had anything to do with the sale of Mabel Church's house. Finally, toward morning, he had fallen asleep, only to drop into the morass of a nightmare that had jolted him awake with his mouth dry and his heart pounding. He realized that part of the drumming in his ear was due to his housekeeper, Betty Harbison, knocking on his bedroom door, bringing him his morning coffee.

"Come in, Betty!" he called, too sluggish to get out of bed.

"Father?" Betty stuck her head curiously around the door. "You're not up?"

John rubbed his eyes. "Not quite. I had a sleepless night."

"You mean the part of it when you finally got to bed?" Betty set the tray on a table and poured a mug from a carafe of extra dark roast brewed just for him, her disgust plain. "I heard the phone ring around midnight. Don't people realize you've got to get your sleep?"

"I was awake," John said. "I'm sorry if the ring disturbed you."

"I didn't mention it out of concern for myself, Father."

"I know," John said, propping himself up to take the mug. "You worry about me too much, Betty."

"And who else will?" She favored him with a hairline smile as she drew open the draperies, the most anyone could usually pry from her. John had rarely heard her laugh. Only he and her husband and those who had known her for many years understood why.

"We're going to have a guest with us for a few days, an old classmate of mine," John said. "He's arriving today and says he'll be here in time for lunch. I hope the short notice won't be a problem. I only learned he was coming last night."

"The midnight caller," Betty said. "No, it won't be a problem. The women's auxiliary is sending out Eunice Wellborn and Bella Gordon to help me this morning. An old friend, you say?"

"An old *classmate*," John corrected. "I haven't seen him since we graduated from high school. At least you don't have to bother with breakfast for me. I have an early appointment in Kersey."

Betty waited to be told more, the name of the visitor at least, but she recognized that Father was waiting patiently for her to leave before getting out of bed in his boxers and T-shirt. "It would be no bother," she murmured. She took the tray and quietly pulled the door shut behind her. Whoever it was, Father didn't seem too keen on seeing him. A freeloader, she'd bet. Father let people impose on him too much.

John threw off the covers and pushed his feet into slippers to go out onto his balcony. The coffee did not set well on his soured stomach, and his balcony presented a soothing view. It overlooked a large vegetable garden and livestock pens and corrals beyond where the children of Harbison House raised the animals for their FFA (Future Farmers of America) project. Felix, the orphanage's pet dog, was eating his breakfast on the back porch steps, and all around the prairie, now in bloom, flowed toward a quiet, pastel infinity. An idyllic setting, but John had the sense of something building at a distance, unknown and unseen, that would soon threaten its tranquility, like a storm gathering just over the horizon.

He remembered the last contact he'd tried to make with TD Hall. It was the summer of 1990, in Guatemala. John was working with the Jesuit Refugee Service at an especially dangerous time when the brutal government security forces had escalated its slaughter of political dissidents and their suspected supporters, among them the Jesuits. Thousands had had to flee their homes and country, and his task was to assist refugees in completing documents for political asylum and to record human-rights abuses. After days of hearing their appalling stories, of eluding death squads and battling the jungle's steaming heat, mud, snakes, and mosquitoes, it had come as a respite in the evenings to write to his old buddy back in the States. John had not given up hope that eventually he and Trey and Cathy would reunite. Father Richard had told him that a sizeable check arrived yearly from an anonymous donor to be deposited in the scholarship fund set up in Donny Harbison's memory—an indication that his old pal was still recoverable. Trey had not forgotten his promise made to John the night of their heart-to-heart after the district game. But one night John had risen straight up out of an exhausted sleep on his cot and from then on had never written to Trey again.

It was one of those inexplicable moments when the subconscious reveals a truth that has heretofore been buried beneath a pile of denial. Trey was never coming home. He was as lost to him and Cathy as the origin of the Mayan civilization. Perhaps some night his subconscious might kick out the reason Trey had abandoned them and his child, but whatever the cause—real or imagined in that capricious head of his—it was enough to guarantee they'd probably never see Trey again. It was simply something John was certain of, like a twin knows instinctively that a mishap has befallen his womb mate. His letters, and even his prayers, sent with the hope that Trey would return to them, were pointless. He wrote at once to let Cathy know. She'd written back: "It's all right, John. I let Trey go a long time ago."

So why was he coming home now?

"Don't bet on it, Tiger," he'd said when John had told him it would be good to see him. Now what did Trey mean by that? What threat lurked behind those cryptic words?

Loose ends to tidy up, he'd said. When had TD Hall ever cared about loose ends? Mabel Church had been a loose end, the aunt who'd raised him and done her best by him, and Trey hadn't even come to her funeral. He hadn't bothered about the loose ends of leaving a girl pregnant in 1986 with the son he'd never acknowledged. When Trey had been halfway into his celebrated career, a reporter had gotten hold of a school picture of him at eight years old that showed a remarkable likeness to a boy of the same age in his hometown rumored to be his son. Trey was quoted as saying: "The Texas Panhandle breeds a bunch of us long, tall, drink-of-water look-alikes. We're as common as tumbleweeds."

Though she'd held her head high, John knew the implication had crushed Cathy and no telling what it had done to Will, but in the county it had boomeranged against Trey. It was one thing for a man to refuse to support his illegitimate child but another to deny the kid as his when everybody knew from his looks and the timing of his birth that he could only be the son of TD Hall. No wonder Trey hadn't shown his mug in Kersey in twenty-two years.

So why now? Was he coming home to claim Will at last? To woo Cathy again? The possibility of it turned John's stomach. Cathy's "past indiscretion" had been forgiven, as she sardonically referred to it. John liked the way she'd once phrased her restoration to the town's good graces: "If you keep your head up long enough, eventually the floodwaters will recede, and you can walk to shore on dry land."

And indeed she had, as Trey would soon discover. Cathy was a vital contributor to the community, serving as president of the school board, a member of the city council, and a committeewoman on civic boards. Everybody adored her. She was lovelier than ever and owned a prosperous café hailed as one of the top small-town finds in the Southwest.

The town took as much pride in her son as it had in him and Trey. John Will Benson had batted his baseball team to the state finals, losing in the last nip-and-tuck inning. "He'd have been a natural on a football field," Coach Turner once confided with both regret and relief that Will had not followed in his father's footsteps. Will could have gone to most any college on a baseball scholarship, but his academic achievements had earned him a free ride to Rice University. He had recently graduated with a petroleum engineering degree and had accepted a job in Delton at a regional office of the oil company for which he'd interned. While John and Cathy were thrilled to have the boy close by, she'd hoped her son would have selected a position in the company's other offices scattered around the country and the world. "He needs to expand his horizons, to experience life beyond Kersey County," she had said, but Will loved the Panhandle and planned to buy a ranch in the county someday and raise horses.

So was Trey, forty, divorced, the glory days over, coming home to warm his backside at Cathy's hearth?

Another surge of unease, like an electrical shock, made John go inside, and he caught sight of himself in the glass door. He stepped back from it, running his hand through his hair, and inspected his reflection for the first time in years. He had regained much of the weight he'd lost in Central America. He'd come home looking as if a wind had raced through his body and sucked his skin to his bones, but his muscle tone had been good and his body strong. Despite the years showing in his face, the gray in his sideburns, he could still see a trace of the looks that used to vie with Trey Don Hall's. Overall, time had been relatively benevolent to him, but the rigors of his avocation had definitely left their mark. He wondered if the same was true of TD Hall.

Going in to take his shower, John speculated what toll the years had taken on Trey after two failed marriages, messy divorces, legal battles, money problems, a serious concussion that took him from the game, and a nonstop life in the fast lane. Not much, John was willing to bet. Trey Hall had always lived a life impervious to consequences, and at forty his face and body probably proved it.

As John always did when leaving Harbison House, he stopped by the kitchen to say good-bye to Betty and leave word where he could be reached. He knew she expected and appreciated the courtesy. It satisfied a certain maternal need when he told her where he would be for the day and when he would be home. "I'm going by St. Matthew's to hear confessions after I leave Kersey, but I'll be back in time to meet our guest," he said.

"And you'll be where in Kersey, Father?"

"At Bennie's. I have to speak with Cathy Benson."

Betty's lips cracked open in her thin smile. "So that's the reason you won't be eating breakfast here."

"Guilty," he said. He heard the usual boisterous breakfast noise coming from the big dining room where the residents of Harbison House—ten children aged six to twelve, abandoned all—ate their meals. He was anxious to see Cathy and decided not to step in to say good morning. They would be all over him, begging him to play ball, check out their vegetable plots, animals, achievements at the easel, piano, and archery range. Felix, a mutt adopted from the highway, had been let in. John gave him his morning pat and headed out.

He steered his truck down the drive that in June was littered with lacy white blossoms from two ancient mock orange trees flanking the gate. They fell like lazy snowflakes on the hood of his pickup as he passed under them, their gentle drift normally lifting his spirits, but they had no effect this morning. Trey had probably had a laugh years ago when Aunt Mabel told him that the Harbisons had turned their farmhouse over to the diocese as a home for unwanted children with the stipulation that Father John Caldwell be appointed its director. John had heard the sardonic amusement behind Trey's remark last night, "That must be nice for you," when he mentioned that the Harbisons helped him run the place.

He'd been the pastor of St. Matthew's less than a year when Lou and Betty Harbison made an appointment to speak with him. It was November, almost to the day they had found their son in the barn nineteen years before. John had dreaded the month's arrival ever since, so ushering them into his parish office on a golden afternoon of the anniversary of their son's death had increased his melancholia. He couldn't imagine why they'd asked to see him. They lived devout lives.

"How may I help you?" he'd asked.

They'd presented their proposal, asking only that they be allowed to stay on in their home as housekeeper and overseer of the property.

John had been dumfounded and struck with the blasphemous image of God in His heaven, observing the scene below in smirking amusement. "Why?" he asked. "Why would you give up title to your family home and serve as employees there?"

"It's for Donny," they answered.

"Donny?"

"Our son," Betty said. "Don't you remember him, Father? You used to lay flowers on his grave. He...died when he was seventeen. His death was...an accident. He'd...be your age now."

She'd spoken haltingly, in obvious pain and embarrassment.

"But he was a good boy," Lou avowed in a tone urgent for John to believe him. "He was a devoted son."

"I have no doubt," John said, clearing the obstruction from his throat. He pushed some papers aside and leaned forward, deciding in the flash of a second to risk everything—his reputation, his calling, his and Trey's freedom—to give the Harbisons the assurance their grief cried for. "Your son needs no absolution for anything he may have done upon this earth," he told them. "Let your hearts no longer be troubled. Donny died in a full state of grace. You do not need to sacrifice your home to atone for him."

They had stared at him in wonder, astounded by his insight into the root of their pain and the authority with which he spoke of a boy he'd barely known. John's breath had held while he waited for the question that would have led him to confess everything.

How can you be so sure?

But they had accepted his pronouncement as typical of something a priest would say, and Betty had said, "Thank you for your confidence, Father, but we've made up our minds. If the bishop agrees, we wish to bestow our property to the diocese in memory of our son."

The bishop had agreed, and John had moved to the upper floor of the sprawling farmhouse while the Harbisons kept their old room and turned the rest of the space over to "Father John's children," the little castoffs who trooped in and out of their lives yearly.

The change in his quarters and the enlargement

of his pastoral duties had occurred almost four years ago. John had never been happier or more at peace in his life and work. The shadow of his old sin still lurked in the background, but he hardly felt its chill anymore. Some days he thought he was almost too happy, too at peace. Had TD Hall come home to change all of that?

Chapter Forty-Three

From the living room window of her former home, Betty Harbison watched Father John's Silverado pull away. The almost-like-new pickup had belonged to a parishioner, now deceased, who had bequeathed it to the home. In years past, the parish vehicle had been a Lexus, donated by the late Flora Turner, but that was long before Father John's time. Betty observed the truck passing under the mock orange trees and out the gate with relief that it had replaced Father's old station wagon clunker. At least that was one prayer for his safety that God had answered. Others for his well-being she could not be sure of. She'd glimpsed the scars Father John had brought home from his days in Central America.

Lost in nostalgia and memory, Betty remained

at the window long past the disappearance of the pickup onto the road leading to the highway. How many Junes ago had she stood right here and watched her teenage son drive off in his father's pickup and vanish behind a cloud of white, her heart in prayer for his safe return? He'd had his driver's license for a year when he died. She'd had only one June to stand staring at the empty space where his truck had disappeared.

"Father John off somewhere this morning?" her husband asked behind her.

"To Kersey," Betty said, blinking the wetness from her eyes and assuming her stoic expression. "We're going to have company for a few days. He didn't say who. I better go air out the guest room."

Lou caught her arm gently. "That feeling come over you again, Betty?"

There was no hiding anything from Lou. He could sense when she was having one of those spells that could pierce as sharp and sudden as a knife thrower's blade. "You'd think that after all these years...," she said.

"Sweet darling, time makes no matter mind to a sorrow like ours, but at least we've got Father John, same age as Donny would have been. God was good to give him to us."

Lou was right about that, she would have said,

had the old wedge not lodged in her throat. At least they had Father John, a son to them in every way but one of birth. He had come to them as their parish priest after the nineteenth summer their boy had been gone. She and Lou had noted his concern for deserted and abused children and the lack of a facility in which to shelter them. One day they had come home from mass to their huge and empty house ringing with loneliness since Cindy had moved away to California with her husband and their children. Betty had said to Lou, "What if we offered this place to the Church as a home for unwanted children and asked for Father John to be its director?"

Lou's face had brightened as she hadn't seen it in years. "Why not?" he'd said.

So it was done. Father John had moved in with them and, together with the children, they had made a family. Gradually the ache in her grew less, the emptiness in her filled. A day did not arrive but that she didn't think of Donny, but never a day passed that she did not give thanks to God for giving them Father John.

JOHN HAD CALLED AHEAD to make sure Cathy would be available to speak in private with him. This time of the morning, she and Bebe were usually in a huddle to discuss the day's business before supervising serving lunch to a packed crowd.

"Of course, John, but what's the occasion? You sound...mysterious."

"I'll tell you when I see you, Cathy. In your office about nine?"

She'd agreed and told him to tell Betty to go easy on his breakfast, that she'd have fresh cinnamon rolls and coffee waiting.

A few minutes to the hour, he drove around to the back of the café and parked next to Cathy's white Lexus. He'd driven past the front, taking in Bennie's through Trey's eyes, and wished he could see TD's face when he saw the changes in the place. Even the partially walled-in rear entrance was a far cry from the days when Odell Wolfe used to come scrounging for a meal at the back door. In those days, the staff parking lot had been a storage area for overflowing garbage cans and old café equipment and a catchall for anything the wind blew in off the street.

"The junk and smell keep other cars out," Bennie had defended the looks of his personal parking space, but Cathy had cleaned it up, built an attractive shed for the trash cans, and put up a polite sign that read: PLEASE...STAFF AND DELIVERY ONLY, and the lot had been respected as off-limits to all other vehicles since.

Except for his.

John climbed the short flight of stairs and rang the bell. Multicolored snapdragons in large urns on each side of the stoop waved in the mild June breeze. He stuck the tip of an index finger into a velvety throat, but there was no easing of the apprehension that a simple creation of God's usually induced. He sensed a gathering of shadows—those long, reckoning shades cast by old sins that time cannot disperse.

Cathy opened the door. As always, the sight of her stirred something tender inside him. Once it had been desire, unrequited and unrevealed, a secret between him and his groin, but he had expunged that longing years ago. Now, only the deep and abiding love of friendship remained. She wore the day uniform of the café: a cornflower-blue denim painter's smock embroidered with yellow daisies, the trademark colors of her dining establishment.

"Come into this house, Father John," she said, using her grandmother's old form of greeting that held just a hint of the teasing she couldn't seem to resist when calling him by his title. "I'm dying to hear why I've taken precedence over the homily you usually write on a Friday morning."

He could not lift his mood to match her bantering tone. "What have you done with Bebe?" he asked, entering an office whose sunny yellow walls, abundance of houseplants, and white window shutters gave it the pleasing charm of a morning room in a southern mansion.

"She's taken a deposit to the bank. I told her to take her time." Cathy eyed him, looking puzzled. "I can see you're going to keep me in suspense."

He could not bring himself to tell her yet. He took a seat before her desk, where neat stacks of paperwork had been laid aside to make room for a coffee butler and plate of the café's famous yeast cinnamon rolls. "I see from the number of cars out front that the coffee wing is a success," he said, alluding to the new addition set apart from the dining room that Cathy had built as a place for local retirees and businessmen, farmers, and ranchers to congregate for mid-morning coffee. Cathy had explained it as a gesture to make up for the time she had to kick Bennie's cronies to Monica's and the courthouse benches. Bullshitters, Bebe called them. They served and cleaned up after themselves and were on their honor to pay for the coffee and cinnamon rolls they consumed. The only other stipulation was that they were to be gone by eleven o'clock, when the café opened and the space was needed for an overflow lunch crowd.

"It's one of the wisest business decisions I've ever

made," Cathy said, sitting down behind her desk. "I had no idea the room would be in such instant demand as a meeting place. It's been booked through December and should pay for itself in a year." She set their cups into saucers. "You'll have to pop your head in and say hello before you leave. The men will love it."

"If I have time," John said. "I'm a little pressed for it this morning."

Cathy unscrewed the top of the coffee butler to release its pressure, and steam poured from the spout. "Why is that?"

"I'm hearing confessions at ten and then I'm meeting a guest at Harbison House for lunch."

"Oh? Who?"

He reached forward and took the thermos from her to prevent a spill burning her hand. "Trey Don Hall."

Her lips parted. Her face went still, and he wondered what thoughts would flow into that sensible head once the shock cleared. Did she still care for Trey? John did not know—hadn't wanted to know. He'd wondered if she'd been disappointed two years ago when Trey had not come for his aunt's funeral.

"Trey called last night, late, or I would have alerted you then," he said. "He told me he was coming to dispose of Aunt Mabel's things and to meet with the Tysons about the sale of her house. Deke is retiring to Kersey and wants to buy it."

Cathy retrieved the thermos and poured two cups. "He has to come in person to do that?" she asked, the pot only barely shaking. "He couldn't send one of his minions?"

John shrugged. "I asked myself the same question."

"Did he have anything else to say?"

John repeated the brief midnight conversation.

Cathy handed him his cup, her demeanor calm, but...below the serene surface the turbulence of hidden rapids? John wondered. "Loose ends... What do you suppose he meant by that?" she asked.

"Your guess is as good as mine."

John watched her get up, still slim and desirable at forty, her straight posture and the denim wedges making her appear taller than her given height. He and Trey had towered at her sides, a pair of over-substantial bookends with a small volume of verse slipped between. She adjusted a set of shutters to allow in greater light, but more to compose her feelings, he thought.

"The bastard, John," she said quietly, staring out the window. "No telephone calls, no response to my letters, no birthday or Christmas cards, no money sent for our care, no acknowledgment of his son's achievements or graduations, no inquiries concerning our welfare. It was as if Will and I never existed. If we're the loose ends he's come to tidy up, he's twenty-two years too late."

"Are you sure, Cathy?"

She turned from the window, the sunlight setting her hair aglow. His breath caught at her loveliness, and he saw her beauty as Trey would see it—irresistible. "You think I'm still in love with him, don't you—that all he has to do is crook his little finger and he's back in my pants."

"The thought had occurred to me."

Her eyes flashed, allowing a glimpse behind the mask. "He hurt my son. I could never get past that, John."

"Even if... the desire is still there?"

She turned back to the window. "A fair question. I'll repeat what you said to Bebe when you told her you were going to Loyola to become a priest and she warned you'd have a hard time beating off the girls."

He frowned, trying to recollect his words. "What did I say?"

"You said: 'I guess I have to find that out.'"

It was not the reassurance he'd hoped for. "Bebe has a loose tongue, and you have a long memory," he said.

She returned to her desk. "Exactly. That's why

you don't have to worry that I'll ever let Trey Don Hall hurt me or Will again."

"I don't suppose you and Will could go away for a few days...."

She gave him a look that made him wish he hadn't offered the suggestion. "No, of course not," he said, and sighed. "A bad idea. Not your style at all." Bebe had returned from the bank. He could hear her joshing with the coffee drinkers who were clearing out for the lunch crowd. He stood, realizing he had not touched the plate of cloud-light cinnamon rolls he'd have usually wolfed down. "I'll call you when I learn Trey's plans."

"They may not include Will and me at all," she said.

He caught a plaintive note in her tone, and his heart constricted. Cathy might try to deny it, but Trey was still in her blood. "Stay close to a phone," he advised.

Chapter Forty-Four

When John had left, Cathy remained at her desk and took several deep, rhythmic breaths just in case there should be a mild recurrence of her early mutism. She'd researched the disorder and learned that the symptoms—fast heartbeat, tense muscles, queasy stomach—are a part of a "fight-flight" response caused by a rush of adrenaline and other chemicals throughout the nervous system that prepare the body to make a quick getaway from danger. The trick for coping with it was to allow time for the thinking part of the brain to process the situation and evaluate whether the perceived threat was real and, if so, how to handle it. There were techniques for that—cognitive and physical exercises—but she didn't need them.

Trey Don Hall presented no threat. She must believe that. He could not hurt her or her son again. Trey's charm would not win them over. She hadn't experienced the symptoms of her childhood condition since her first day of attending Kersey Elementary School, and she wasn't about to start now. The sensations she was feeling were related only to her fantasy coming true of Trey Don Hall one day strolling into the café they used to call the grease bucket to find it transformed into the spotless dining establishment of rave reviews it was today and her its highly respected owner. She'd imagined his astonishment as he tried to reconcile his last memory of the shattered, penniless, pregnant girl he'd left behind to the successful businesswoman she was today, but it had been some time since she'd pictured their encounter. When Trey hadn't come home to attend Mabel Church's funeral but sent flowers instead, she'd put that image out of her mind for good. Enraged at his indifference to his aunt's death, his total disregard for her memory, Cathy had looked at her nineteen-year-old son standing next to her at the burial and been thankful he'd been spared his father's utter callousness. Wishing the bastard to burn in hell was the last thought she'd had of TD Hall.

Now suddenly, at the very mention of his name,

her heart was beating fast, her stomach had tied in knots, and she was wondering what she should be wearing when he walked through the café door. *Not smart, girl, not smart at all.* Whatever on-the-road-to-Damascus light Trey may have seen back in San Diego, it had happened too late for her and Will. They didn't need or want Trey's used-up life. She was way beyond having to accept the dregs of an empty cup.

Still, though, she'd like to see him again. She'd like him to see Will. Not to start anything or to make up for the years lost. She wanted Trey to see what he'd missed, what he could have had, what would have endured after the victories were over, the money spent, the knees gone.

Because to this day, despite his narcissistic tendencies, she thought the two of them would have made it if she hadn't gotten pregnant when she did. He had loved her, selfishly perhaps but entirely, and she still believed that given time, he would have accepted children into their lives.

Or maybe not. Aunt Mabel had once remarked, "Looks like our Will is the only great-nephew I'm ever going to have." Her implication had been clear: In Trey's two marriages, both of his wives had remained childless.

But still, Cathy couldn't let go of the feeling that

she and Trey would have been different. Theirs was not the typical high school romance. Even those disapproving of their teenage intimacy had seen something special, almost spiritual, in the way they were together and had been since the day she'd walked into Miss Whitby's sixth-grade homeroom and stood mutely to be introduced. *"Let her sit here, Miss Whitby."* Cathy had never been able to forget that boyish command cutting through the charged silence, the intense gaze, the long arm in the flannel shirt pointing to the seat next to him.

Was Trey arrogant enough to believe she'd never married because her heart still belonged to him? Aunt Mabel would have told him of her engagement to Daniel, but would Trey have thought she had merely settled? Cathy let out a short, ironic laugh. He might have been right about that, but she was sure it would come as a shock to Trey Don Hall to learn that the only man she loved now and would want to marry wore a priest's collar.

There was a soft tap on the door. "Cathy? Okay to come in?"

"Yes, Bebe, come in." When her manager entered carrying empty money pouches, Cathy said, "You'll have to do without me for an hour or so, Bebe. I'm driving out to Morgan Petroleum to see my son."

*   *   *

GLANCING OUT THE WINDOW of his boss's office, Will Benson halted in his report of the test samples he'd taken of oil-bearing rock layers at one of the company's drilling sites. He had just watched his mother's white Lexus pull into the Morgan Petroleum Company's parking lot. His boss looked out the window to see what had arrested Will's gaze. "Why, there's your lovely mother," he said. "What do you suppose has brought her out here? I hope nothing's wrong."

"Me, too," Will said, his heart leaping. His mother was still in her café smock. "I'd better go find out."

"Sure enough. We can take care of this later."

Will hurried to meet Cathy in the reception room. His first thought was that his mother had come to tell him the bad results of her annual physical last week. Each year he held his breath until she telephoned to say she'd been given a clean bill of health. This time she had not called. He could think of nothing else that would draw her thirty miles from Kersey to the place he worked, and shortly before the noon rush at Bennie's.

She was talking to a geologist who'd held the door open for her, and Will searched her face for a preliminary sign to prepare him for his worst fears.

He saw none. His mother was asking the man about his wife and his new baby. Her face and voice were unstrained, but that could be misleading. His mother never gave away anything in public.

Before his co-worker could haul out his wallet to show her pictures, Will crossed his arms over his chest and stared at him so pointedly, the man took the hint and moved on.

"Mom, what are you doing here?" he said when the man had left.

Cathy smiled, standing on tiptoe to kiss his cheek. "John Will, is that any way to treat a new father or a tone to use with your mother?"

He looked worriedly into the face that meant the world to him. "What's wrong?"

"May we go into your office?"

"Sure," he said. Something was definitely wrong. If it was cancer, it should have been caught in time. His mother took care of herself and was in otherwise excellent health, and nowadays the medical world could perform miracles. Whatever it took, he'd see that she got it. His voice tense, he said to the secretary, "Linda, will you call rig six and tell them I'm going to be a little late getting out there?"

"Of course, *John* Will," she said, with a teasing emphasis on his first name. "Anything for you."

"Pretty girl," Cathy commented as she followed

her son down the narrow hallway to his broom closet, he called it, in the rear of the building. New to the company, he had yet to earn his stripes for one of the larger offices boasting picture windows. She loved the grace with which he carried his long-legged frame and wore his clothes—mostly khakis and denim shirts for his job but always immaculately starched and ironed. "Is she married?"

"Yes, Mom, she's married," Will answered, his jaw taut, and opened the door. "Now tell me what's wrong."

Reading his concern—only then realizing what he must be thinking—Cathy pressed her hand to his cheek. "Oh, Son, it's not what you suspect. If I were any healthier, they'd have to preserve me in formaldehyde. I got the results of my physical only this morning and didn't have a chance to call. I've come about another matter."

Will let out his breath. "Okay, then what?"

"Maybe you'd better sit down to hear this, darling. I've come with news that may shock you."

Oh, God. His mother was getting married—to that twice-divorced oilman from Dallas who'd stopped by the café last spring and instantly gone crazy over her. Will liked him well enough, but there wasn't a man in the world good enough for his mother unless it was Father John.

"Your father is coming back to town," she said. "He called John last night and told him he'd be in Kersey at noon today. He's come to close out his aunt's house. Deke and Paula Tyson, Melissa's parents, want to buy it."

Everything temporarily went fuzzy, as if a flashbulb had gone off in Will's face. At six, when he was fully aware of who his father was, he'd dreamed of a day when TD Hall would appear out of nowhere, collect him and his mother, and take them back to San Diego to live with him. His great-grandmother would come, too. It was a secret hope he went to bed with at night and held close like some kids did their baseball gloves and stuffed animals. By the time he was ten, he'd learned all about his father's high-living escapades, sexual exploits, astronomical salary hikes while his mother worked long hours trying to make a go of her café, worried she couldn't afford his great-grandmother's prescription bills. By then, too, he'd been informed of how his father had abandoned his mother when she was pregnant with him, gone off to college in Florida, and never come home again. By thirteen, he'd vowed that if the son of a bitch ever showed up, he'd shoot his balls off with the old .30-30 rifle his mother kept under the bed.

He had his mother's trained knack of showing

no emotion in times that called for it. He blinked once and asked, "Is that all he's in town for?"

"As far as I know."

"How long is he staying?"

"A couple of days, John said."

"That doesn't sound like he's come to hook up the RV for a while."

"You're right. He'll be staying at Harbison House until his business is through, he told John, but that's all we know at the moment."

"Did he ask Father John about us?"

"No, but he may be testing the waters, and that's why I'm here. I came to ask you to see him if he wants a meeting, because if I know my son, he'll take off hiking with his dog this weekend until his father goes back to where he came from. I'm advising you not to do that, Will. If you don't like what he has to say, then kick him out, spit in his eyes, slam the door in his face. That's up to you, but I believe if you don't see him, you'll regret it later."

"What if he hasn't come to say anything to me, Mom? What if he's come simply to sell his aunt's house? What if we're not on his agenda?"

Cathy shook her head. "He didn't have to come here in person to clean out his aunt's house and take care of the house sale. That could have been done from San Diego. Father John and I both agree on that."

Will concurred. He studied his mother in a new, frightening light. He half-suspected she welcomed this visit, had been expecting it for years. Looking at her now, still youthful and beautiful, he wondered what she would do if TD Hall—washed up, divorced, reputedly broke—should show up again at her door, beg her to forgive him and grant him a second chance? She was well thought of, a pillar of the county. What would it do to her reputation if she took back the bastard who had left her and her son high and dry?

"Tell me," he demanded. "What you would do if the guy walked in right now, says he's sorry and that he loves you and wanted to make it up to us? What would be your reaction?"

She granted him a smile understanding of his anger. "Your godfather asked me basically the same question, so I'll tell you what I told him. It will take more than sweet talk and self-flagellation to win me again, Son. For twenty-two years, he's ignored your existence. Forget mine. Mine pales to a mere snub compared to his rejection of you. I can never forgive him for the shadow he cast over your childhood, but I don't hate him for it, either. That's because, amazingly, you grew into a man you never would have been if your father had been around."

"I'd have been okay, Mom," Will said. His pride in her roughened his voice. "I'd have had you."

"Not the mother you know. If TD Hall had married me, I wouldn't have been the woman I am today."

He conceded that was probably true. His mother had overcome a different, and more commendable, set of odds than the ones she'd have faced with his self-centered, womanizing father. You could tame a tiger only so far.

"All I'm asking is that you give him a chance to say what he's come to say," she said. "I plan to. I have a feeling it will convince me we were fortunate he abandoned us."

"All right," Will said. "I'll do it for you. But don't be disappointed if he's only here to sell his aunt's house."

Cathy stood and removed her car keys from her purse, her movements calm and resolute. "I don't think it's possible for Trey Don Hall ever to disappoint me again."

If only he could believe that, Will thought, as he escorted her to the parking lot. His jaw felt so hard he could barely feel his mother's lips when she kissed him good-bye. As usual, she read his thoughts.

"He'll try to charm the hate out of you, Will, and that would be a good thing," she said. "Don't be afraid to let it go. Releasing hate does not make you forget what you want always to remember. It does not mean reconciliation."

Will watched her drive off, shaken that she'd been aware all along of the fear he'd tried to hide since he was old enough to analyze it. As much as he hated his father, Will was afraid that if he ever met him, he'd fall victim to his charisma, his star shine, and despise himself for his vulnerability, his neediness, when he'd had the love and attention since the day he was born of the best father figure ever to walk the earth—Jesuit priest John Caldwell.

Yet what else but a need for his father would explain why, on the sly, he'd made a study of TD Hall? There wasn't a word about him Will hadn't read, not many of the man's football games he hadn't seen one way or the other. Will told himself he was on a quest to find out how much like him he was, what tendencies he recognized in himself. He had made up his mind early that he didn't want to be like Trey Don Hall in any way, and as far as he could tell, he wasn't. He'd inherited his mother's innate courtesy, calm temperament, and sense of commitment. He wasn't a skirt chaser or a practitioner of casual sex.

But really, his object had been to get to know his father, to share time and be with him even if it was only through published interviews and the TV screen. Will would never let his mother know that, until he graduated from high school, he still looked for a package at Christmas, a card for his birthday, a telephone call out of the blue, some sign that his father knew he was on the planet.

But that was then, and this was now. His yearning days were over. He despised Trey Don Hall. If he'd come to worm his way into their lives when he'd made such a mess of his, his son would make sure the man regretted it.

Chapter Forty-Five

He slid open the grill between him and the penitent three times that morning.

"Forgive me, Father, for I have sinned."

"How have you sinned?"

"It's my father. I have no respect or liking for him. He lies; he gambles; he cheats on my mother; he does not keep his word. I wouldn't trust him as far as I could throw a bull. He's overweight, smokes like a fiend, and drinks. He doesn't give a damn about me."

"Do you love him?"

"Yes, that's the thing. I care about him, and I don't want to. I know it's a sin to want to hate somebody, especially your father, but life would be so much easier and my pain gone if I could only hate him, and I'm furious with myself because I can't."

"Do not be angry with yourself. You have demonstrated the greatest love of all. You love someone unworthy of your love. This cross you bear is a burden now, but such crosses, faithfully carried, are the wings that fly us to heaven."

"Can people change, Father?"
"In what way?"
"The genes we're born with."
"Not your genes, but the behavior they generate. We are given the power to be in control of what we do because every person is born with free will. With the help of God, we human beings can choose to disobey the dictates of our baser natures. The original self will always be with us, like the alcoholic's inborn proclivity to drink. The struggle against our nature is never ending, but it can be overcome."

"Bless me, Father, for I have sinned."
"So have we all, my friend."

Chapter Forty-Six

⟨

Trey Hall slowed down his rented BMW as he turned off Interstate 40 onto the road leading to Kersey. His plane had landed in Amarillo with minutes to spare. He had no luggage to collect, and there had been no waiting line at the car rental office, giving him time to kill before meeting the Tysons at eleven o'clock. Except for the wind turbines—mammoth energy-producing structures that looked like sculptures of gigantic white albatrosses lined to the horizon—the prairie in spring was as he remembered. For a while he drove with his window down to let in the fresh smell of Panhandle grasses, but he found the wind nippy and raised it. He had been warned against getting chilled.

A mile from his destination, he spotted the water

tower of Kersey, and memories flooded over him of the times he and John used to climb the darn thing. They'd been too respectful of its important place on the landscape with its proud claim CITY OF KERSEY written on its girdle to deface it, but mainly they'd been too scared of Sheriff Tyson finding out they were the culprits. But they were definitely not above leaving a physical reminder that they'd scaled the ladder to the catwalk that ran around it. They completed a successful rite of passage when, in the seventh grade, they finally reached their goal and left a scarf of Cathy's tied to the railing. It blew in the wind for some time until one day it was no longer there.

Like a lot of other things that had blown away, Trey thought.

As he entered the city limits, he noted some new signs and a few unfamiliar shops—a hair salon, an antique place, a game-processing plant—but the old automotive repair garage and feed store and junkyard rusting away behind a Cyclone fence were still in place. There was nothing much about the entrance to his hometown to distinguish it from other widely scattered prairie communities except the weathered, faded billboard that greeted visitors at its city limits: WELCOME TO KERSEY, HOME OF THE BOBCATS, WINNER OF THE 1985 HIGH SCHOOL

FOOTBALL STATE CHAMPIONSHIP. The sign echoed a time long past its glory like a boarded-up hotel in a ghost town.

The gate into the Peaceful Haven Cemetery was up ahead, and he turned in and located the grave site of his uncle Harvey from memory. As Trey had expected, Aunt Mabel had been buried beside him. Their memorial stones were identical, with a hand engraved on each reaching toward the other. Aunt Mabel never did get over the death of Uncle Harvey, Trey had realized long after it was too late for him to be of much comfort to her. He'd known his uncle only a few months before he died, but Trey remembered him well, and he'd grown up thinking the two of them married—Aunt Mabel a small, shrinking-violet type and Uncle Harvey robust and rugged, a big-game hunter—was something of a joke. But back then, what the hell had he known?

He'd bought a bouquet of spring flowers at the airport and laid the perky arrangement of carnations, stocks, and daises before her name. The burning sensation he hated flamed in his throat. "I'm sorry, Aunt Mabel," he said. "I wanted to come, but I didn't have the guts. Now that you're in heaven and know all, I hope you can forgive me."

He glanced about at the other memorial plates in the area and noted the familiar names of those who had died since he'd been away. For one, their old school bus driver he'd given undeserved grief, and for another, a woman who'd worked in the school cafeteria who always added extra helpings of mashed potatoes on his plate. He now wished he'd shown her more appreciation. Cathy's Baptist minister had bitten the dust, a sanctimonious ass who'd slammed the door shut to her future when she turned up pregnant. Trey looked around for Miss Whitby's grave and Emma Benson's but didn't see them in the vicinity, and it was time to go. Before leaving, he kicked a clump of cockleburs on the Baptist minister's grave and headed for his car.

The high school and football stadium were on this side of town, and he took the improved road to the entrance of the place where he'd spent the happiest years of his life. A digital billboard had replaced the old wooden structure that had announced school events. It wished students and teachers a safe vacation and informed the unlucky ones that summer school would begin in a week's time. With the exception of a few cars in the expanded parking lot, he had the place to himself.

He got out, the opulent slam of the BMW door carrying in the quiet, almost still, prairie air. The school had been modernized to a degree, but the feel of it was the same. With the close of his eyes, he could imagine being a school kid again, arriving in the bus in the junior high years, then in his Mustang or John's old pickup when they hit their teens, Cathy wedged between. The intrepid trio of Kersey High, they'd been called.

Trey walked the distance to the fence that enclosed the running track and football field. The gate was probably locked, but he heard young male voices like his used to be and figured students were working out on the track. His guess was right, and a padlock hung unfastened on the gate. He pushed it open and saw three boys at the far end of the track in running shorts and T-shirts, stretching their hamstrings and rotating their arms. Trey heard the field house door creak open and turned to see a man step out wearing a ball cap in the school's colors and a whistle around his neck. A coach obviously. "May I help you?" the man asked.

"No, not really," Trey said. "I graduated from here and thought I'd stop by to see what the place looks like now. Mind if I look around?" The man was middle-aged but still looked too young to have been on the coaching staff when Trey ran track and played on this field.

"No, go ahead. Happy to have you." The man peered at Trey, his forehead moving back as recognition dawned. "You're . . . TD Hall, aren't you?"

"I am."

"Well, Christ almighty!" He stuck out his hand. "Tony Willis. Track and special teams coach. It's an honor to meet you. They should have named the place after you for all the trophies you won for the school. Is this the first time you've been back since you graduated?"

Trey shook his hand. "I'm afraid so. Anybody around who coached when I was here?"

"Bobby Tucker. He's the head football coach and athletic director now."

"Can't say that I remember him. Did he replace Coach Turner?"

"Bobby followed a couple of replacements in between. Coach Turner didn't last but about another five years after your class graduated. When his daughter died unexpectedly, he just sort of lost interest in football and everything else." He squinted at Trey quizzically. "You...know what I'm talking about?"

Trey nodded. "My aunt kept me informed. Some sort of infection, wasn't it?"

"Yeah. So sad. His wife passed away a few years afterwards. Ron became an alcoholic, lives like a hermit now, but I'm sure he'd be glad to see the best player he ever coached."

"If you don't count John Caldwell."

"Well, yes, there's Father John. A great pair of

hands and feet, judging by the old film footage. Football lost a good one when he went into the priesthood, so they say."

"They say right." Trey fished his car keys from his pocket.

Coach Willis looked perplexed. "Aren't you going to look around?"

"I'm afraid I don't have the time, after all. Nice to have met you."

"Well, uh, wait—" Looking flustered, the coach stepped in front of him. "Where are you staying? Maybe we could meet for a beer...."

"At Harbison House with John, but I'm only in town overnight. I'll catch you next time."

Trey left the man puzzled, but he'd lost his nostalgic itch. The news of Coach Turner had sickened him. An irrational fury at Tara bloomed and then died. Laura—*Dr.* Rhinelander—had cautioned him as well about the dangers of impotent anger. "Let's not rush things," she'd said. But why the hell had the slut gone and died on her parents when she had already made them miserable enough? What he wouldn't give to clear the slate with Coach Turner, explain to him why he'd cut out on Cathy, but Coach would still consider him horse manure for not manning up to the truth when it would have made a difference.

The next stop would depress him further, but at least it would be one change for the better. He wouldn't go in. He'd merely drive by Bennie's to see if he could catch a glimpse of Cathy's blond head behind the windows. John would have told her Trey would be in town today, and he wondered if she was expecting him to walk through the door of the café any minute. His heart beat faster and his mouth went dry at the very thought of it. When Laura told him he was dying, in his frantic need for comfort his first impulse had been to fly home to Cathy's arms for the months he had left, stay in his old room in Aunt Mabel's house, have the spiritual consolation of the only true friend he'd ever had.

But after the initial shock of the prognosis, he'd laughed at himself for his outrageous arrogance. Considering the wreckage he'd left in his wake, what had made him think that Cathy and John would take him to their bosoms again?

So he'd had to consider another way to ease out of this world into the next, and he'd decided to make a clean breast of his deceptions that had marred the lives of two loving parents and aborted the life journeys of his best friends. He'd kept his mouth shut out of a false sense of injury and betrayal, ego and pride, the self-destructive demons he'd allowed to destroy his soul. Facing death shed a light on things he'd refused to see before. Now he'd come to tell the truth and maybe undo some of the damage he'd caused. He'd leave this earth hated by the two people he loved and who'd loved him, but he could not die with a lie upon his soul.

He turned down Main Street, curious if anybody would recognize him as the driver of the unfamiliar BMW. Coach Willis would have to tell only one person about meeting him today for the news to make it around town.

A big Lincoln Navigator was tying up traffic waiting for a pickup to back out of a parking space in front of Bennie's. The delay gave him an opportunity to note the revamped storefront with its blue-checkered awnings and bright flower boxes, a front door painted yellow. He strained to see Cathy moving about beyond the immaculate windows, but he recognized instead the dark-headed figure of Bebe Baldwin taking charge of the customer line. Again, teenage memories surged, and he was back in a fun-filled moment with Cathy and John and Bebe eating greasy hamburgers and fries and drinking Cokes that went down his throat like carbonated fire. Finally, the Navigator pulled in, clearing the street, and it was then he saw Cathy in a white Lexus stopped at a red light at the intersection.

He stared, not daring to blink for fear of losing

a second of her face taking shape like a photo in a developing solution. She had not seen him. He recognized the small frown between her brows as a sign her mind was clearly on something else as she waited for the light to change. What would he do if she should suddenly snap out of her concentration and turn those big blue eyes on him? The motorist behind him gave a prompting little toot of his horn and Trey accelerated, but the traffic light remained on red and he was caught at the intersection a few feet away from where the white Lexus waited for a turn signal.

It came within seconds, and Cathy, still preoccupied, passed in front of him, the sun glinting off the swirl of her short blond hair, illuminating the remembered features of her profile. Riveted to his seat, he watched her drive a short distance before turning into the back of the café where stray dogs used to paw through garbage cans for scraps. In the seconds before the trailing motorist tooted his horn again, Trey was tempted to follow her. There might still be a chance that, in the time he had left, she'd take him back and his secrets would be buried with him, but he couldn't do that to Cathy—cause her to love him again when he'd have to leave her once more. He pressed the gas pedal and gave up his last chance to see face-to-face the only woman he had ever loved.

Chapter Forty-Seven

Deke Tyson lowered his body gingerly onto the ancient swing of Mabel Church's front porch before subjecting it to his full weight. It appeared sturdy enough, and he relaxed to wait for Trey Don Hall while his wife, Paula, was off taking a last look at the house before finalizing the deal. At her urging, they'd arrived early to look over the property again before the owner arrived and bird-dogged their steps. Deke didn't think they had to worry about the owner bird-dogging their steps. He'd gotten the impression from Trey Don Hall's attorney that it didn't matter to Trey one way or the other whether they bought it. The lawyer had named a price, and he and Paula had dealt with him in working out the details for inspections, repairs, and documents.

Which was the reason Deke was surprised and oddly moved when Trey, after not being home since he graduated from high school, had written to say he'd fly out to deliver the deed in person and they could settle up.

Deke placed his hands on the overhang of his belly, a change from the last time TD Hall had seen him. In 1986, when Trey and Melissa had graduated from high school, Deke's stomach had been hard and flat and he hadn't cut too bad a figure in his western-styled uniform that Paula had kept pin sharp. Now the once solid mass of his chest muscles had sloped down to settle at his midriff as Paula's ample, round bottom had traded shapes with her level stomach. Age was nothing if not humbling. He wondered how much TD Hall had changed since the last time he'd seen him on television. Eleven or so years ago, was it? Melissa and her friends had called him the Heartbreak Kid in high school, but that was mainly because of the female hopes he disappointed by going steady with Cathy Benson. Who would have figured he'd go off and leave her like he did? No other permanent attachment had worked for him, apparently, and he still had no children. Did Trey have regrets about Cathy and the wonderful son they could have raised together?

Deke had just stretched out his legs and tilted

his Stetson forward to doze in the spring sun when he heard a car drive up to the curb. *Son of a gun! The kid was on time.* Somehow, he'd expected him not to be. Deke recognized the famous but older and thinner face instantly and went down the steps feeling the thrill that used to come over him when he watched Trey play in high school, then later in college and the NFL. Trey Hall might be a reputed horse's behind, but he was one hell of a great quarterback.

"Hello there, TD," Deke said, meeting him on the walk. "Welcome back to your hometown."

"Looks like I can say the same to you, Sheriff Tyson," Trey said, shaking Deke's hand. "Amarillo doesn't suit you?"

"Not for the golden years. It's gotten too big and noisy. And Melissa lives here now with her husband and our grandson."

"Melissa?"

"Our daughter. You and she were classmates. Graduated the same year."

"Oh, right." Trey looked about ready to smack his forehead. "I went blank there for a second."

"And it's not *Sheriff* anymore," Deke said. "Just plain ol' Deke Tyson."

"Well, just plain ol' Deke Tyson, let's go inside and see what we can work out."

Still a smart-ass, Deke thought, remembering the crooked grin, but for some reason Trey's cussedness had endeared the boy to him. "After you," he said, to allow Trey to go first into his boyhood home.

Deke was curious to see what Trey Hall's reaction would be when he stepped inside the house he hadn't visited in twenty-two years. Surely the bric-a-brac, framed photos, his aunt's hand-stitched pillows, the treasures she had loved, would have some meaning for the boy who had grown up here. Deke held back at the threshold to give him time for the memories, the ghosts to rush out to welcome their long-lost boy, and for a moment, he thought they had. Trey stood still in the musty living room, his body tense as if he heard voices from long ago.

"It's smaller than I remember," he said.

"Places we come back to after we're grown nearly always are," Deke said quietly, hearing Paula exclaim over some find in another part of the house. "Excuse me, and I'll go get my wife. She's around somewhere."

"You can have any of this stuff you want," Trey said suddenly, sweeping his arm about the room. "I won't have a use for it."

"Oh?" Deke said politely, his policeman's ear catching *won't* instead of *don't*. "Does that mean you're moving to another place out there in San Diego?"

"That's right. I'm not taking much with me."

"Sounds like you're downsizing."

"You could call it that."

"Well, that's awfully generous of you," Deke said. He glanced around the room, saddened that the boy placed no value on the things that had been such a part of his life. "There are some fine items here, and you haven't been through the house yet. There might be something you want to keep."

"No, there's nothing," Trey said, "and I'd appreciate your taking it all off my hands. Whatever you don't want you can sell or give away."

Paula stood in the doorway, wearing the expression Deke understood well. She disliked the rough-and-tumble game of football and placed no stock in professional athletes with bad manners and worse morals who were paid fortunes for their talents while her daughter drew a paltry salary as a public school teacher. Never on Paula's good side, Trey Hall had zoomed to the top of her bad list for his treatment of Cathy. She looked at him now as if he were a dead bug in her soup.

"What about the attic?" she asked, her tone cold. "Boys' things are usually relegated to the attic when they leave home. I imagine Mabel did the same with yours. You might find something up there you'd like to have."

Trey flashed his devilish grin, apparently amused at his cold reception. "Hello, Mrs. Tyson. It's nice to see you again. No, I can't think of a thing. The only items I remember stored in the attic were my uncle Harvey's stuffed hunting trophies. I imagine they're in pretty bad shape by now and ready for the trash heap."

"Whatever," Paula said, ending the discussion with a dismissive wave of her hand. "But just remember. What we don't keep we toss or sell. Don't change your mind a year later and ask for something that's not here."

"I believe I can assure you I won't," Trey said. "Now, Sheriff Tyson, why don't we go out on the porch and finish our business?"

It was done in less time than it would have taken to drink a cup of coffee. Deke handed over the check and Trey the deed. A muscle worked along Trey's jawline, and Deke was glad to see some visible sign that the boy was sorry to see the place go. "Will you be going back to San Diego or staying around for a while?" he asked when Trey slipped the check into his shirt pocket.

"I'm planning to take off tomorrow morning after I finish taking care of a few things. I'm staying with John Caldwell at Harbison House."

"That's nice," Deke said, wondering if Cathy

Benson and her son were among the few things Trey would be taking care of. "You'll be a treat for the kids. They've never seen a real, honest-to-goodness superstar."

Trey threw a mock punch at his arm. "You're dating yourself, Sheriff. Those kids are too young to have a clue of who I am." He put out his hand. "You and Mrs. Tyson enjoy the house. I'm glad I'm leaving it in your care. My aunt would be pleased."

"I wish you'd reconsider and look through the house, son. I imagine your high school trophies are still in your room."

"History," Trey said. "I couldn't take them with me to my new digs anyway. So long, Sheriff. You've been a good man to know."

Hands in his pockets, his Stetson pushed back, Deke watched Trey go down the steps to his car, oddly depressed. Trey Don Hall impressed him as a very sad man. It wasn't an enviable position to be in at his age with the career over and the money gone and no loving wife waiting at home, no child to give him grandchildren, at least not the son he'd left Cathy to raise. Will Benson wanted no part of Trey Don Hall, so county gossip went, and Deke found that especially tragic, since the boy had made one mighty fine young man.

But...as with his aunt's treasures, Trey seemed

not to mind leaving behind the valuables that would have been his to keep.

Sighing, Deke went back inside to accompany Paula on a tour of the attic. It was the one area of the house they hadn't explored, since they'd turned that inspection job over to their son-in-law, who was a building contractor. Paula wanted her husband with her in case spiders and other unwanted visitors had taken up residence in Mabel's absence. By a miracle, one bulb in the overhead fixture still worked and added to the light cast from Deke's flashlight.

He almost didn't see it. As Trey Hall had stated, his aunt had stored in the attic mainly the stuffed trophies of her late husband's hunting expeditions, and they lay piled in a dried-out, forgotten heap gathering dust in a corner. Deke passed the beam quickly over the glass-eyed creatures and was about to move on, then threw it back.

"What is it?" his wife asked as Deke grunted and left her side to investigate.

Without responding, Deke reached into the pile of taxidermist specimens and drew out a large gray bobcat mounted in a pouncing position, its eyes wild and teeth bared and claws extended. Only one problem detracted from its menacing pose: a missing foreleg.

Chapter Forty-Eight

Upstairs at his study window, John observed the gray BMW take a slow turn at the gate and make its way at a sedate speed up to the house. He had been expecting to see something on the order of a red Corvette tearing up the drive, sending gravel flying and shattering blossoms from the mock orange trees, arriving late for the lunch Betty had prepared. That was the vision his childhood memories evoked of his long-ago best friend.

John's stomach tightened. Had Christ felt this clenching of his muscles when he saw Judas enter the garden the morning of his betrayal? he wondered.

He watched the car draw into a visitor's space, the door open, and the man he'd once thought of as a brother get out. He looked the same TD Hall, a little older, hair a little thinner on top, his clothes a few notches above the ones Aunt Mabel had provided. But he still hitched up his pants the old way, glanced around with the same cocky turn of his head. In spite of John's feeling that a serpent had entered Eden, he could not suppress his joy. By all that was holy, it was good to see Trey again.

John had stepped out onto the porch before Trey climbed the steps. The two men halted, stared, then laughed and embraced, slapping each other's back as if they'd shared a hard-won victory.

"Hi ya, Tiger," Trey said, his voice cracking with emotion. "How the hell are you?"

"I can't complain," John said, as hoarsely. They broke away to look each other over through tear-glazed eyes that neither bothered to hide.

"You never did," Trey said. He ran his gaze mockingly over the plaid shirt and jeans John had changed into. "What? No cassock and cross for the returned sinner?"

"What would be the use?"

Trey laughed. "You look good, Tiger. A little undernourished, maybe, but then all you zealous clerics do. Proof of your sincerity, I guess."

"And you look like you could still knock the girls dead. How about a beer before lunch?"

"Love one. Want me to bring in my carry-on?"

"Leave it until later. My quarters are upstairs. We'll go there. It gets a little noisy down here. The kids are out of school now. They'll be playing the TV in the next room at full volume. Go on up, and I'll get the beers from the kitchen."

Trey did as directed, and John found him standing before the group pictures of the 1985 football team when he joined him.

"Quite a team, weren't we?" Trey mused.

"Well, we had a good quarterback."

"And a great wide receiver. You were the best, John."

"So were you."

Trey shrugged. "At playing football, not much else."

John returned no comment as he handed Trey the beer. "I would have brought mugs, but I remembered you like your brew straight from the can, or has that changed?"

"No, that's stayed the same."

The men sat down, John at his desk, the light of the window behind him. Trey chose an easy chair with an ottoman. The sound of popping tabs echoed in the sudden silence of their faltered conversation. John noted Trey's ironic interest in the room's book-lined walls, fireplace, bedroom beyond, and outside balcony.

"Fancy you living here," Trey said.

John took a swallow of his beer. "I lived in the St. Matthew's rectory when I first arrived, then moved here when the Harbisons offered their house to the diocese as a home for abandoned children, and I became its director. We house ten children who'd otherwise be in foster care. The extra duty stretches me thin, so I find it easier to work from here."

"That's not exactly what I meant."

"I know," John said softly. "I only wanted you to know what we're about here. Why are you back, Trey?"

Trey lifted the beer can to his lips. After a lengthy swallow, his lips glistening with residue, he said, "I told you. I came to unload Aunt Mabel's house."

"Is that all?"

"Is that long, ecclesiastical look supposed to suggest I have something else in mind?"

"Don't play games, TD. This is John, remember?"

"I remember." Trey closed his eyes for a moment. When he spoke again, his voice sounded tired. "I remember you could read me like a book, knew what I was thinking before I said it. I could never put one over on you, and that was somehow my greatest consolation growing up, knowing my best friend knew me through and through and cared for me anyway. And you always did know when I was about to play a card from under the table, didn't you, Tiger?" He shot John a fleeting grin before it vanished in the gloom that settled over his face. "Well, here it is. I'm dying, John. I have it on the word of none other than Cathy's old friend—and yours, I understand—Dr. Laura Rhinelander. I have a brain tumor, stage four. Laura gave me about eleven months when I was referred to her. I've already used up half of them."

Several long ticks of John's desk clock went by before comprehension penetrated his shock. Trey dying? It wasn't possible. He was TD Hall, superstar, invincible, indestructible. He was only forty years old, for heaven's sakes! He couldn't be dying. But he was. The dark shadows under Trey's eyes told him it was so. Pain spread in his jaws, mingling with the acrid aftertaste of the beer. "Is that why you came home—to tell me?"

"I came home to confess."

"To me as a priest?"

"No, Padre. To you as a friend. And to others, too. I have to clear my conscience so that I can die in peace. I'm sure you know what I'm talking about."

John did. Trey's meaning loomed like a long-buried specter rising from the grave. Alarm swept through him, swamping his compassion, displacing his grief of a few minutes ago. His uneasiness at Trey's return had not been unfounded. Trey had come to buy peace at the cost of his.

"Funny, I always thought you'd be the one to squeal on me," Trey said. "At the beginning of my career, I lived in fear you'd have an attack of conscience and bare all, but I stopped worrying after you became a man of the cloth."

John observed him coldly. "Why?"

Trey seemed surprised that he did not understand the obvious. "Why... because of all this." He swept a hand about the room. "You'd have as much to lose as I would if you hadn't kept silent."

"Yes, I would, but did it ever occur to you I kept silent because of my promise to you?"

Color rose to Trey's cheeks. "Of course it did, but you'll forgive me if I felt better protected when you took your vows." After a moment's embarrassed silence, he said, "Tell me, John. Has it worked?"

"Has what worked?"

"The priesthood. Has it given you... the peace you craved?"

John hesitated to answer. There was no mockery in Trey's eyes, only plaintive hope. He had to disappoint him. "It has had its moments," he said.

"Ah. I'll take that as a 'sometimes,'" Trey said, reaching for the beer can. "Well, let me strike that look off your face, Tiger. I didn't come to undo your good work. I don't intend to involve you in my confession to the Harbisons. Father John and what he's about are safe. This is all on me and only about me. My conscience, not yours. As far as the Harbisons will know, I acted alone that day. You were back in Kersey, sick in the home economics room." He took a swig of the beer as if his throat had gone dry. Restored, he patted his wet lips with the back of his hand and continued. "Don't be afraid that Lou and Betty Harbison will say anything to the authorities. Why would they and let the world know the condition in which they found their son? It will be comfort enough to know their son isn't burning in hell. I'm guessing they probably cut the boy down and dressed him and made his death look like an accident. Otherwise, Sheriff Tyson would have been all over the case."

John should have felt enormous relief. At last, the Harbisons would know the truth of their son's death. Their grief would be lifted, and they could live out their years in peace without ever knowing of John's part in the crime—without having to lose a second son—but he had lived long enough to know that once a light was shone on part of the truth the other half would soon be revealed.

"What's the matter, John? I thought you'd be happy and relieved to have this burden off your soul."

"Your share, yes. Mine still weighs heavily."

"I'd say you've more than made up for it."

Betty's tap came on the door, and John, feeling slightly sick to his stomach, called for her to come in.

"I'm sorry to interrupt, Father, but lunch is ready. Should I bring it up?"

Trey looked around, gave a sound of surprise, and got to his feet. "Hello, Mrs. Harbison. How have you and Mr. Harbison been?"

Betty gazed at him as if having trouble with her recollection.

"Trey Hall, remember?"

"I remember. You used to pick up your aunt's order for eggs and vegetables."

Her tone did not match the warmth of his.

"Yes, I did," Trey said. "Is that all you remember?"

"All I've a mind to," she said. She turned to John. "Father, should I serve lunch?"

"That will be fine, Betty."

When the door had closed, John explained. "She and Cathy are friends, and Betty is crazy about Will. Every year for his birthday, she bakes him her famous butterscotch cookies."

"And she hates my guts because of what she thinks I did to Cathy."

"Well, didn't you?" John said.

Trey turned to sit down again, a little slower, his

silk shirt defining his thin shoulder blades, reminding John of his illness. When he was settled, he said, "I saw Cathy a while ago, but only for a few minutes. She didn't see me. She was stopped at the traffic light next to Bennie's. Damn, John, she looks good. Better than ever."

"She's survived well. So has her son."

"Will Benson? He's another reason I've come to town."

"Oh? Another wrong to put right in your final days?"

"I'd call it a *misperception* to put right."

"What do you mean?"

"I mean that all these years, everybody, including you and Cathy, has believed that Will is mine. He isn't."

"Oh, for the love of God, Trey!" John swiveled his chair away from the sight of the figure in the easy chair. The gall of the man, steps from death's door, to continue to deny the wonderful son who would make any father proud. "Whose else could he be?"

"Yours," Trey said.

Chapter Forty-Nine

John spun his chair around. A chill ran through his body. "What?"

"You heard me." Trey unscrewed a prescription bottle and shook two pills into his palm. He threw them into his mouth and washed them down with the beer. Illness pulled at his lean, handsome face.

"That tumor has made you crazy, Trey. I hope what you just said stays in this room—that you won't spread that crazy lie around town."

"It's no lie, Tiger, believe me."

"Why would you say such a thing? The boy looks exactly like you."

"Does he now?"

"The same build, hair, eyes."

"No, Padre, he's got yours. Everybody expected

him to look like me because they knew I was screwing Cathy. They searched for what they wanted to find and found it, but they were wrong. Look closely at you and me, or rather, the way we were then." Trey nodded toward the framed pictures of the Kersey Bobcats on the wall, he and Trey seated together in the center of the front row. "See if you and I don't look enough alike to be brothers. Next time you and Will are together, look at his face without superimposing mine over it and I think you'll see your own." Trey raised the can to his mouth. "And, of course," he added, "there's always my DNA to prove I'm telling the truth."

Stiffly John turned his gaze to the picture and studied it. Growing up together, they'd often been told they could have easily passed for brothers, but Trey was suffering from a cancer-induced delusion to claim he wasn't Will's father. The boy could be no one else's. Had Trey forgotten the time he crawled back to Cathy, begging her to forgive him? They didn't come up for air for a week.

"What makes you think the boy isn't yours?" John asked.

"Because I'm sterile," Trey said calmly. "I have been since I was sixteen. If I'd ever fathered a child, your Virgin Mary would have nothing on me."

John's mouth slowly dropped. He recalled Trey's

collapse during spring training the end of their sophomore year, his inflamed and swollen jaws, Aunt
Mabel's eyes popping when she took his temperature, the swagger gone from him when he returned
to school after his two weeks' confinement.

"That's right," Trey said. "I see you remember.
The mumps hit me in both testicles. They were
swollen the size of lemons by the time Aunt Mabel
got me to Dr. Thomas and had to be packed in
ice for days. When I was eighteen, I got my sperm
tested. No swimmers then or forevermore. So you
see, I couldn't possibly be the father of Will Benson."

"But...the condoms, the pills Cathy took..."

"To be on the safe side until I got the courage to
have myself checked out. I was going to tell Cathy
the results of the tests the day after we got back
from summer conditioning, but before I could, she
dropped the bomb on me that she was pregnant. I
figured it could only have been by you."

For a delusional moment, the sense of detach-
ment came over him he adopted in the confessional.
The grate between him and the penitent and his sin
removed him from personal involvement and liber-
ated him to offer wise counsel. He was listening to
Trey as if his revelation pertained to someone else.
It wasn't possible he'd gotten Cathy pregnant. He'd
hardly touched her....

Dear Mother of God...

"I know how this must hit you, John—as hard as it hit me when my best friend, the guy I loved like a brother, hell, more even than myself—boffed my girl behind my back. I've always been surprised that you and Cathy never suspected the boy could be yours. I figured it happened during the time I broke up with her, right after you and I got back from our first visit to Miami. Do you deny it?"

The pump of blood to his head was almost blinding. He could not draw breath. "I admit that Cathy and I...one afternoon came close to what you're accusing me of," John said, Trey's face growing fuzzy. "She was devastated when you dumped her, out of her mind. She came to me desperate for comfort. We started drinking and got very drunk, but nothing happened. Cathy passed out instantly. She has no memory of it—"

"No memory of what?"

"That I almost took advantage of her. But I didn't, TD...that is, I...well, you see, I...never penetrated her."

"Were you wearing a condom?"

"No, I—it happened so fast—"

"Were her panties off?"

John blushed. "Yes."

"Why didn't you go through with it?"

"Because—" He had never forgotten Cathy's sleepy, contented murmur. "Because she said your name, TD. She thought I was you. I backed off immediately, so I see no way Cathy could have gotten pregnant by me."

Trey gripped the arms of the chair and drew to a taller sitting position, staring at John as if he'd had a glimpse into heaven—or hell. "What? She said my name? She thought you were me?"

"Yes. Clearly. She was out of it—totally plastered. She loved you, TD, and only you. Cathy would never have knowingly slept with anyone else but you. How could you believe she would?"

Trey dropped back in his chair, his face stark with the anguish of horrified realization tinged with the cast of cancer. "Catherine Ann...Catherine Ann," he moaned, closing his eyes. "Oh, God, John. If only I'd known..."

"You would have if you hadn't run out on her."

"I couldn't...have hung around, Tiger. Not then." He lifted his head, his eyes feverish in their sickly sockets. "Didn't you ever wonder why I... went 'off the reservation,' as you put it, on that first visit to Miami—how I could do that to Cathy?"

"You know I did!"

"I found out my test results the day before we left. I couldn't tell Cathy; I just couldn't. She'd have pitched her tent with me no matter what, and I thought it was the perfect time to break us up. It was better to leave her thinking I couldn't be faithful than that I couldn't father children. . . . She'd get over me easier, I thought. . . ."

John shook his head. "Good God, TD . . ." Trey's voice came to him muted, as if he were speaking through glass. *He . . . Will's father? How he wished it was true, but he couldn't be. . . . It wasn't possible.*

"You know I could never go by the books, Tiger—that I could never play anything straight."

"Well, you've called the shots wrong this time, too, TD. I couldn't be Will's father. I barely touched Cathy."

"You still impregnated her, Tiger. You and Bebe may have got it on, but you were still a virtual innocent at eighteen. You didn't know that you didn't have to penetrate her for her to become pregnant. Cathy was off the pill then, and your semen only had to touch her skin . . ."

"But I didn't ejaculate!"

Trey's voice gained volume. "You didn't have to. Your fluid alone would have done the job. Most guys have no control over it and cannot feel it coming out. That's why the withdrawal method you Catholics preach as a means of birth control doesn't always work. Because of that, I thought somewhere along the way you'd have figured out the kid could be yours."

"How do you know so much about this subject?" John demanded.

Trey's mouth twisted into a sad, wry grin. "Believe me, I've researched everything ever known about sperm." He gazed into his friend's appalled gaze. "You're Will's father, John."

A full picture of Will Benson popped into John's mental vision, and the faint paternity traces he and Cathy had taken no notice of were suddenly accented: the slant of Will's right eyebrow, the slight slope of his left shoulder, a certain swing to his walk, a particular resonance in his laughter... all characteristics of John Caldwell. How could he and Cathy have not noticed them? They had searched only for likenesses to Trey.

John heard Trey's voice crack in remorse. "I'm sorry, John. I know that makes no difference to you and Cathy and that you'll never forgive me for not telling you the truth right away. I don't expect you to, but as God is my witness, I expected you and Cathy to marry and come on to school as planned. I had no idea you were considering the priesthood."

Astounded, still trying to absorb the marvel of the impossible, John cried, "But later, why did you keep the truth from us, Trey? Why did you let the boy grow up thinking his father had abandoned him? You knew what that was like. Cathy and Will—do you have any idea the shame and hardship you left them to suffer?"

The questions caught Trey like a ball thrown too hard at his midsection. He clutched himself— a house caving in upon itself. "Because I thought you *betrayed* me!" he said, his eyes suddenly blazing with anger and illness. "You were my family—all I had in the world. All I cared about. Do *you* have any idea what it was like to believe that the friend I would have died for fucked the love of my life—my *heart*!—and had fathered the son I never could! At that time, you could have all gone to hell, for all I cared. I wanted to hurt you as you'd hurt me, but then, as the years passed…" His voice weakened, his eyes dulled. "It was too late. The boy had his mother and great-grandmother and…you. You and Will were as close as father and son could be. You were on the path to righteousness and Cathy was… settled. There would have been a scandal involving all of you. Was it better for the boy to believe his father was a bastard than that his mother conceived him with his best friend behind his father's back?"

He was still good at it, John thought. Trey could find a vein of glitter and sell it for a gold mine— and John would buy it.

Still holding his stomach like a cradled football, Trey lifted tormented eyes. "I did what I thought was best when it was too late to change things," he said. "It was rotten of me, but I...didn't know what else to do."

"Coming in!" Betty called, opening the door, and John, thankful for the interruption, rose to take the tray from her and place it on a table earlier set for the meal. At the waft of food, his stomach turned over. Betty's wide gaze of surprise told him he must look as white as the table linen. She threw a glance at Trey, still bent over, and set a grim face as she unloaded the tray without a word.

"Thank you, Betty. It looks delicious," John said. "We'll serve ourselves, and I'll bring the dishes down when we're through."

"Very well, Father," she said, cutting Trey a warning look he did not see as she left the room.

When the door closed, John asked, "When do you plan to tell Betty and Lou?"

Trey roused himself. "You tell me when would be a good time. I have a flight out of Amarillo tomorrow at noon, so I'll be leaving early in the morning. I don't want you with me when I tell them. You'll squirm and look guilty as sin, and it wouldn't take but a look at your face for that sharp old Mrs. Harbison to know you were involved."

A weakness in his legs forced John to take one of the chairs at the table. "Tonight when Lou returns from mass with the kids," he answered. "Betty stays behind to look after the ones who don't go. She and Lou settle down in their room to watch TV around eight. It's at the other end of the hall. I won't be home until late. Now come to the table and try to eat something. The food will give you strength."

With a labored effort, Trey pushed out of his chair and took his place at the table. "Am I going to hell, John?"

The hardest duty of his office was at times like these when he was called upon to offer assurance to the morally corrupt facing death that their sins would be forgiven. He would remind himself that he spoke for God and not for John Caldwell. "Nobody goes to hell who truly repents of his sins and asks forgiveness from those he has injured, Trey. Your heart knows the truth, so it is there you should look for your answer."

It was the best comfort John could give. Trey alone knew whether he'd be here today if he weren't dying tomorrow.

John picked up a spoon to take a stab at eating the luscious cream of vegetable soup Betty had taken pains to prepare along with a salad of greens picked that morning and tossed with her tangy strawberry dressing.

"When are you going to tell Cathy?" Trey asked.

John looked up from his soup. "When am *I* going to tell her?"

"I can't face her now any more than I ever could, Tiger. I don't want to die remembering the look in her eyes. The only saving grace will be her relief when she learns that Will is your son."

Will was his son! He was the boy's father! It was almost impossible to believe, but he would keep his eye on that one inextinguishable light. "I'll have to decide," he said.

"There's no point in telling the world the boy is yours. It should stay between you, Cathy, and Will. Think what would happen to your reputation if the news got out." Trey made a visible effort to smile. "Let me die with my public believing the worst of me. I deserve it, and I'd like to leave with yours still thinking the best of you."

"That will depend on Will and the will of God," John said.

Chapter Fifty

Deke Tyson fidgeted, hardly able to swallow the lunch Melissa had prepared to celebrate the purchase of the house. His mind was miles—years—removed from the conversation around the table where he and Paula sat with their daughter and her husband and son.

"What's the matter, Daddy?" Melissa asked. "You're not eating. Don't you like the casserole?"

"Oh, I do, I do," Deke assured her. "It's just that I've got my mind on something else."

"I hope you're not having regrets about the house," Paula said.

"No, no, I like the house. I think it will be fine for us." Deke forked up a mouthful of the chicken casserole with feigned eagerness and considered how to break the news that he would have to cut the weekend short. He had to get back to Amarillo to have the crime lab check out something in the evidence bag related to the Harbison boy's death.

"If I didn't know better," his daughter remarked, "I'd say you're wearing the kind of look you used to get on your face when you were working on a case."

"Does it have anything to do with that stuffed bobcat you put in the trunk?" Paula asked.

"Paula, be quiet!" Deke ordered. "You don't have to tell all you know."

Everybody at the table looked astonished at this uncharacteristic outburst. Paula, recognizing that something was going on with her husband since he'd pulled the bobcat out of the pile of disintegrating hunting trophies, recovered first. "You're right," she said, taking no offense. "Sometimes I blab too much. This casserole is delicious, Melissa. What does your mother have to do to get the recipe?"

Deke asked suddenly, "Melissa, do you remember Donny Harbison?"

Melissa's brow elevated at the question. "Donny Harbison? Wasn't he that boy from Delton who died from an accident when I was in high school?"

"That's him. You kids were seniors. Do you know if Trey Hall knew him?"

Her brow still hiked in surprise, Melissa said,

"I doubt it. They went to rival schools, and Trey was a jock. He hung out with other jocks like John Caldwell. Donny played in the band. Even if he'd gone to Kersey, he would have been invisible to Trey."

Paula put her hand on her husband's arm. "Why are you asking these questions?" she asked, curious about his concern. But then, he'd always been disturbed by the Harbison boy's death.

"Oh, no reason," Deke said. His answer wouldn't satisfy Paula, but she would let it be. At this point he didn't want to betray the drift of his thoughts, especially to his wife and daughter. In a town like Kersey, where gossip was the mainstay of conversation among the womenfolk, they might have trouble keeping their mouths shut.

"Well, I'm sure he didn't," Melissa said. "The Bobcats and Rams didn't mix in those days."

Deke let out an exclamation and jerked the napkin from his collar. *Bobcats . . . Rams . . . By God, that was the connection!* He shot up out of his chair. "I'm sorry, everybody, but we're going to have to get back to Amarillo."

Deke's son-in-law made a sound of objection and his grandson let out a wail of dismay. His grandfather was supposed to be taking him fishing that afternoon.

"We do?" Paula said.

523

"Oh, Daddy, why?" Melissa protested. "You just got here!"

"Because your father said so, dear," Paula said, getting up. The glance she gave her daughter cut off further objection. Paula cupped her grandson's chin. "We'll be back over during the week, sweetheart. Now give your grandma a big kiss, and we'll be on our way."

In the car, Paula said, "And why do we have to get back to Amarillo as if we've got a lynch mob after us?"

"I need to get to the forensics lab before it closes," Deke said. While Melissa had packed them a part of the chocolate cake she'd made for dessert, he'd called in a couple of markers. First, he'd telephoned Charles Martin, now chief of the Crime Laboratory Service for the Department of Public Safety in Amarillo. During his tenure as county sheriff, Deke had met Charles as a fledgling technologist. Yes, he told Deke, he remembered the case from years ago when Deke had asked him to process the fingerprints on some lewd magazines and extension cord and compare them to a set taken from a teenage suicide victim. Charles had never forgotten the look on Deke's face when he told him that the victim had never touched either item.

Deke now had an idea why Donny's prints weren't on the magazines or the extension cord.

His next call was to Randy Wallace, current sheriff of Kersey County. "I'm to look for what?" the sheriff asked.

"If it weren't important, I wouldn't ask, Randy."

"Yeah, I know. Okay, give me the name on the evidence box again, and I'll go look."

"You're a good man," Deke said.

"Glad you think so. That opinion got me elected."

Every nerve in Deke quivered like a dog back in the hunt. From the get-go, he had not been convinced that Donny Harbison was alone the day he died or even that his death had occurred the way he was discovered. The later hair-raising discovery that Donny's prints were not on any of the items collected from the scene substantiated Deke's doubt. Another pair of hands had handled them. That proved to him that the person who spread the magazines had also tied the ligature, as either a perpetrator of Donny's death or a participant in the experiment.

In his discreet investigation later at Delton High School, Deke could find no likely suspect to support either theory. Donny had no known enemies, and neither he nor any of his friends seemed the type to experiment with kinky sex. The boy checked out to be as his parents described him, a well-liked, fairly sexually naïve kid who ran with others of the same ilk, band members like himself whose only passions were their trombones and a fetish for peanut butter.

According to attendance reports, Donny was in school on Monday, the day his parents left for Amarillo. He was marked absent the next three days, with his body found late Thursday afternoon. From the degree of decomposition and the consensus that Donny wouldn't for the world have missed marching practice after school because of the band's intricate routine to show up Kersey's band Friday night, Deke guessed the boy had died late on Monday.

Deke had investigated the whereabouts of the few Delton High students listed as absent the days in question and found nobody out of pocket, and none of Donny's friends admitted to visiting him after band practice.

The missing shirt was another unresolved mystery. It never turned up. When Betty was able to go through her son's things, Lou reported to Deke that she could not find the blue chambray shirt Donny had recently received for his birthday.

Deke's research into autoerotic asphyxia gave him further cause to question the death as an accident. He learned that in the practice of AA the ligature is usually tied in a complex manner to provide easy escape. Donny's had been clumsily arranged. Also, practitioners usually wear padding around the neck for comfort and to prevent telltale bruises and abrasions. None was under the rough rubber cord.

Of course it may have been the first time for the boy, Deke had told himself, and despite the instructions given in the magazine, Donny hadn't known the finer points of such a practice.

Deke's taped and written interviews were in a box in the evidence room of the Kersey County Sheriff's Department, along with copious notes, the cat's limb, magazines, cord, and forensics reports. It was this sealed box that Randy Wallace had agreed to bring to the forensics lab to prevent contamination of the evidence, thereby ensuring it would be admissible in court. Still plagued by professional guilt that he had covered up what may have been a homicide, Deke had made sure to secure the box when he did not stand for reelection, writing: **Do Not Remove!** in huge black letters on its face. Since the death was ruled an accident, the department considered the case closed. But not Deke. Hardly a day went by during his tenure in office and for a long time afterwards that he did not regret his decision to forgo an autopsy to determine the time and exact cause of death. Eventually, the guilt was rationalized away. What good would come of an autopsy anyway? It couldn't reveal who may have strangled Donny and arranged his death to look like a sexual act gone wrong or—if he did die from autoerotic asphyxia—the name of his accomplice. There were no suspects and no motives. Everybody in Delton would have to be fingerprinted to find the match Deke was looking for. And in the meantime, the lurid details of Donny's death would become known, the Catholic Church might revoke his Christian burial, and the Harbisons would be subjected to the shame Deke had agreed to cover up.

And so he'd done nothing, said nothing, merely hoped against hope that someday, somewhere, something would turn up to provide a clue to what really went down at the Harbison place the day Donny died.

And now, by God, Deke had found it. He could hardly believe the miracle. He was trembling, he was so excited, even if he was shocked that it implicated, of all people, Trey Don Hall, dubious pride of Kersey County, as different from Donny Harbison as pabulum from T-bone steak. Until today, Deke could never connect the cat's paw with the other items found at the death scene. Even when he discovered the bobcat in Mabel's attic and felt certain the foreleg in the evidence box would match its stump, he could make no association. But when Melissa commented that Bobcats and Rams did not mix, a light had flashed on. He remembered Donny's other high school distinction that hadn't seemed relevant at the time: The boy was keeper of the Delton football team's mascot, a little ram called Ramsey. It was easy then to guess what had happened in the Harbisons' backyard during the week of the Kersey-Delton football game to decide the district championship.

"Why are we stopping here?" Paula asked when Deke pulled up to the curb in front of Mabel Church's house.

"Won't be a minute," he said. "I'll keep the motor running."

He ran up to the porch, inserted the house key into the lock, and within minutes found what he was looking for. He lifted it with his handkerchief and carefully slipped it into a paper bag he found in the pantry, then hurried back to his car.

"What in the world is going on, Deke?"

He leaned over and kissed his wife's cheek. "I'll tell you when I'm sure, honey bun."

But he was sure. It had started in the fertile imagination of Trey Don Hall, star quarterback of the Kersey Bobcats. Trey got the idea of sawing off the foot of his uncle's stuffed bobcat to claw the hide of the little ram as a statement to his opponents. Somehow Trey had known the Harbisons would be out of town, maybe through Mabel, who bought her eggs and produce from Betty. Deke would have to work out the time on Monday when Trey pulled off the deed, but it had to have been when Donny was home after band practice. The boy was eating a snack at the kitchen table when he saw Trey at the pen's gate, the hoop already off. Donny ran out to investigate and a scuffle ensued. Trey got the better of the smaller, less fit boy and either tried or succeeded in his attempt to strangle Donny in a fit of the temper for which he was known.

To hide the evidence of finger marks, Trey had staged the body to simulate death by AA, familiar to a kid of his precocious sexual sophistication. He spread the magazines, got rid of the shirt, and raked the ground to eliminate signs of struggle. In a hurry to leave, he'd overlooked putting the hoop back on the gate and either could not afford the time or could not find the cat's limb concealed in the shadows under the picnic table.

Deke could imagine no other scenario. What other reason would explain why that cat's paw showed up in Donny Harbison's backyard? Of course, everything hinged on the unidentified fingerprints on the two items of evidence matching the ones on the athletic trophy he'd taken from Trey's old room. If they checked positive, Deke had sufficient cause to ask Randy to reopen the case. Deke knew that would open a big can of worms. As the investigating officer of the incident, he'd have a lot of explaining to do. An exhumation—if one was agreed to—would reopen wounds from which the Harbisons had never fully recovered. The couple would be scarred even further because of their guilt in covering up the facts of their son's death, in the eyes of not only the authorities but also the Catholic Church. The contribution of their house to the diocese would be seen more as an act of atonement than a generous gesture to provide a home for unwanted children. And in the end, most likely a smart defense attorney would get Trey off.

But none of that mattered now. Deke's intent was to gather as much evidence of the truth as he could before deciding whether to go to Randy Wallace with his findings.

His foot hard on the gas pedal, Deke's jaw clamped tight as he remembered how Donny's body was found, what the boy's death had done to his parents. Since 1985, the Catholic Church had mitigated its stand regarding suicide, but the Harbisons' Catholic convictions had never let them rest from the fear that their son was burning in hell because he died by his own hand from a twisted sexual act. Deke hoped for the chance to prove to them once and for all that their boy was innocent of causing his death and that he'd died trying to protect a harmless animal from a cruel high school prank.

What a stupid, conscienceless act for someone of Trey Don Hall's indisputable ability and intelligence to try to perpetrate the week of the big game—a game the Bobcats handily won by a margin of *thirty-five* points. By God, if that boy was guilty of causing Donny Harbison's death, Deke would see him brought to justice if it was the last thing he ever did. There was no statute of limitations on murder or manslaughter, and in Texas a seventeen-year-old charged with such offenses was tried as an adult. *Don't go making too many plans for that new move, TD. Your new digs may be a jail cell.*

Chapter Fifty-One

Trey Don Hall was taking a nap. John had insisted on it after Trey threw up his lunch. When John checked on him, Trey lay in a deep sleep, his eyelids tinged a faint blue, his pale, thin hands crossed over his chest in a position that looked like a dress rehearsal for the real thing to come. John adjusted the blinds against the noon sun and left the room quietly, his breath still shallow from the shock of Trey's revelations.

He returned to his study and sank into his desk chair, joy and fear fighting for dominance of his feelings—joy that the boy he'd loved like a son was really his flesh and blood and fear that tomorrow all he'd given his life to might be over. Trey was convinced the Harbisons would be so relieved to learn the truth of their son's death, they'd bury their grief and live the rest of their days in the sunshine of their new knowledge.

But John wasn't so sure. Yes, the Harbisons might be satisfied with their newfound peace and content to let sleeping dogs lie, and, yes, they probably wouldn't want the embarrassment associated with pressing criminal charges. They would also want to keep the secret of their cover-up from the Church to assure Donny's burial in consecrated ground.

But John knew Betty well, and she might not be so relieved that she would willingly bury her twenty-three-year-old grief without exacting retribution. Lou would be satisfied to let the matter go, but Betty might not be so forgiving. When John came to live with the Harbisons, he'd prayed for a release from his burden without hurting them or implicating Trey, but as the years had gone by, he'd rationalized that God had made a present of him to them. He'd been uncomfortable under their love and devotion, but he'd grown to understand their need to love him like the son they'd lost. Love was never misspent, no matter how unworthy the recipient.

But to this day, Donny's picture—a shrine— remained partially hidden among flowers on a back shelf in the kitchen, and John would catch Betty standing before it, head bowed in prayer continuing to ask God to have mercy on her son's immortal soul. Many afternoons, she left to light a candle in the church. Those were the times John was tempted to throw himself on *her* mercy and confess all, but of course he never had.

Her general dislike of Trey could flare to hatred, and she might want him exposed and punished for what he had done, the torment he'd put them through, and report him to the authorities.

If that should happen, an investigation would unearth Father John Caldwell's part in the crime.

John got up from his desk, his unease roiling in his stomach, and went out onto his balcony. He had considered laying out to Trey the possible ramifications of his confession, but as a priest he could not. He would not deny Trey this last opportunity to redeem himself and cleanse his soul. A while ago, as he was drawing a blanket over him, Trey had grabbed his hands and begun to cry, the tears trickling into his gray sideburns and filling the sick lines around his eyes. "Please forgive me for what I did to you and Catherine Ann and the boy, John. I've suffered a penance, too. After I left for Miami, I was never able to make anything like you and Cathy happen again—nothing as good and sweet and sure. Nobody else came along to save me from myself."

John knew that to be true. "I understand," he said.

"I left my heart back here. That's why no one was ever able to find it, not even me."

"I know, TD."

"And will you let Cathy know?"

"I will."

"And will you tell her that I didn't come to Aunt Mabel's funeral because I didn't want to embarrass her and Will. I'm not that much of an asshole."

"I'll tell her, TD."

"You're going to her now, aren't you?"

"Yes."

Trey's hands slipped away. He crossed them over his chest and closed his eyes. A small sigh escaped his pale lips. John turned to go. "Tiger?"

"Yes, Trey?"

"I love you, man... you and Catherine Ann. I've loved you always, no matter how it seemed."

"I know," John said, patting Trey's crossed hands. "Go to sleep now. Rest."

"And do you forgive me?"

"I do."

"You're my man, John."

John looked out on the vista where he had so often found wisdom and peace. Would these be the last hours he would perform his duties as the

Father John that all those who loved and believed in knew? He was not worried how his flock would take the surprise of Will's parentage or how Will would receive the news. His son loved him, and he'd be thrilled to be rid of TD Hall for good. The uneasiness in the pit of his stomach he could shrug off if God had not warned him that another scandal was approaching far more staggering than that he was Will Benson's father. From it there would be no recovery, not for him as pastor of St. Matthew's Parish and as director of Harbison House.

Well, so be it. He'd always known there would be a reckoning, but in the presence of God after his death. How naïve of God's ways he'd been to think he could leave this life untainted with his sin undiscovered and his work completed without blemish. The shadows had gathered at last. He felt their presence like dogs circling for the kill. He made the sign of the cross. *In the name of the Father, the Son, and the Holy Ghost, Thy will be done.* He stored up a last look of the unbroken prairie and went inside to make several telephone calls. The first was to Cathy at the café.

"We have to meet," he said.

"Oh, oh, I don't like the sound of that."

"It's best if we meet at your house."

"I'll give you a half-hour head start and be there by the time you arrive."

The next call was to St. Matthew's associate pastor alerting him that he might have to conduct the weekend masses. "You're going out of town?" Father Philip asked on a note of surprise.

"Something unexpected has turned up, Philip. You may be required to fill my shoes for a while."

"Impossible," Father Philip said.

The next was to the bishop of the Catholic Diocese of Amarillo.

"Yes," the bishop said, "I can see you at three this afternoon. What's this all about, John?"

"I'll tell you when I see you, Your Grace."

John looked into his bedroom to see that Trey was still sleeping peacefully, then went downstairs to the kitchen carrying the tray, embarrassed at the food uneaten. The rich smell of broth announced there would be chicken pot pies for supper. Betty stood at the counter removing the flesh from a pile of boiled carcasses, Felix at her feet vigilant for a fallout. From outside came the squeals of children splashing about in the watering tank.

A sudden attack of emotion made John's eyes water, and the tray tilted. Startled, Betty grabbed it from him. "Father, what's wrong?"

"Oh, a few things that should have been made right long ago, I'm afraid."

"It's him, isn't it?" She jerked her head toward

the ceiling. "He's gotten you upset. I could tell when I went up."

"Don't blame him. He's sick, Betty, and his visit is long overdue. I've left him sleeping. When he wakes up, will you see that he drinks a cup of that broth I smell? He couldn't keep down his lunch, good as it was."

Rinsing the remaining soup from the bowls, Betty said, "I see you didn't eat much, either, good as it was. Are you going out?" She'd noticed he'd changed back into his clerical shirt, but there had been no call for his services.

"Yes," he said, "and I won't be home until late tonight."

Her worried eyes searched his face. "What's the matter, Father?"

"Betty—," he began, but he let die unspoken the words he wished to express. They would mean nothing to her anyway if what he feared came to pass. He pushed the bridge of her glasses higher on her nose, moist from working over the simmering pots.

"Yes, Father?"

"I was only going to say that Trey will be leaving us in the morning. He has a plane to catch at noon."

BETTY REMAINED at the kitchen counter after John had gone. Now she was sure of it. Something was afoot, brought into this house by Trey Don Hall. She'd lay a wager that it wasn't good, if she were a betting woman. It might have to do with his illness, but he had looked fine to her when she took up lunch, not much changed since he'd brought his insolent airs and handsome face to her front door, acting so put upon that his aunt had sent him to pick up her vegetables and eggs—as if he didn't owe everything to the aunt who'd raised him and then, when he was rich and famous, discarded like wilted lettuce.

Betty had been surprised, though, when he'd inquired after her and Lou. Trey was really asking how they were doing without Donny, but his sympathy didn't make her like him any better. He'd acted so superior around Donny on the several occasions they met at the house.

Her instincts were seldom wrong, and they were telling her now that something serious was bothering Father. Lou had sensed it, too. "Distant and distracted," he'd described Father when he went to the garage to get his truck this morning. She thought *worried* and *distraught* more like it, the kind of look a farmer gets when he's about to lose his land.

Cracking the bones she'd use for making gelatin, Betty cocked an eye in the direction of the upstairs bedroom. Sick or not, Trey Don Hall better think twice if he'd come here to cause trouble for Father John. Neither she nor Lou would stand for it.

CATHY STOOD at the front window of her house watching for John's Silverado. She unlocked the nervous clench of her hands and eased them down her smock. What was John coming to tell her that he couldn't say over the phone? Why hadn't he given her some inkling of Trey's plans? It wasn't like John to keep her in suspense, any more than it was typical of her to bombard him with questions when his tone had made clear he must speak to her in person. At least, though, she wished she'd asked if Trey would be coming with him. Just in case, disgusted with herself, she'd tidied her hair and refreshed her lipstick.

The Silverado swung into her driveway, and she saw only John in the cab. Her half second's disappointment was swept away at the sight of him getting out, still with a wide receiver's lithe grace, his black, short-sleeved clerical shirt and Roman collar inexplicably adding to his sexual attraction— the allure of the unattainable, she supposed. How could she still carry a smidgen of feeling for Trey Don Hall when she grew more in love with John Caldwell every year?

When she opened the door, a sudden wave of déjà

541

vu struck her. She had lived this exact, imperishable moment before. It was the afternoon she'd opened the door to find a dejected Trey Don Hall on her doorstep, his face wearing John's expression now, a look begging her to forgive him and to take him into her arms. It was the afternoon Will was conceived. A longing so powerful, it tasted like gunpowder, drove through her body, but she caught herself before she made the mistake she'd made then. "Hello, Father John," she said with her usual composure. "I know it's early, but you look like you could use a shot of whiskey."

"I believe I could," he said.

After she'd mixed the drinks, she sat next to him on the couch. It seemed the place to be. John stared down at his glass. "I recall drinking whiskey with you at this time of day once before," he said.

"We did?"

"Uh-huh. Once upon a time when our hearts were young and sad."

"Ah, yes," she said. "Trey had dumped me. I vaguely remember getting loop-legged drunk and falling asleep on your bed."

"Twenty-two years ago this month, as a matter of fact."

She had other reasons to recall that June of twenty-two years ago. "The things we remember after so much time," she said.

John sipped his drink. "Trey tells me that Will is not his child, Cathy. That's one of the confessions he's come home to make."

Her head spun from the fury that filled it. "The conscienceless bastard! You mean he *still* denies he's Will's father?"

"You remember that bout Trey had with the mumps at sixteen?" John asked.

Something ominous—confounding—was taking shape in her mind. "Yes...," she said. "I remember. He was...very sick."

"The mumps left him sterile. Trey could never father a child."

She set her drink down sharply, mindless of the water mark it would leave on the fine burled wood of her coffee table. "That's impossible, John. He's lying. Will has to be Trey's child. I'd never been with anyone else."

Calmly John picked up two coasters from an end table and slipped them under their drinks, then took her hands. "Yes, you had, Cathy. You had been with me."

Chapter Fifty-Two

In the forensics lab of the Department of Public Safety in Amarillo, before the eyes of Deke and Charles Martin, Sheriff Randy Wallace broke the seal and poured out the contents of the requested evidence box. "I don't suppose you're going to tell me what this burr under your saddle is all about, Deke?" Randy said.

"Not yet, Randy." Deke picked up the dismembered foreleg and joined it to the mounted bobcat he'd brought in. A perfect fit. "Aha!" he said, unsurprised. He then separated out two small plastic bags of unidentified fingerprints from those marked as Donny's, taken before the body was removed, Lou Harbison's and others. One bag, marked x, contained two cards bearing the same fingerprints found on the magazines and cord. The other sack, marked Y, contained one unidentified set of prints taken off the ligature but missing from the pornographic material.

Deke handed the bags to Charles. "Let's see if the prints in these match any on this trophy." With latex-gloved fingers, he lifted a brass football from the paper sack. Charles and Randy peered at the inscription commemorating Trey Don (TD) Hall as the Texas Sports Writers' most valuable high school player of the 1985 football season. Randy whistled. "Holy Toledo! Are you kidding?"

"I'm afraid not," Deke said. He had taken the trophy from a glass case with the hope that Mabel Church's dusting rag had never touched it.

"Well, let's go see," Charles said, and led the men into a room of computers, X-ray machines, and other analysis equipment. After conducting the procedure of transferring the prints from the trophy, he ran them through a screening device to compare them to the ones on the three cards. Within seconds, the system beeped: MATCH. "Looks like your guess is right, at least regarding X's prints," Charles said. "There's no doubt that the person who handled the magazines and cord handled this trophy."

"Hot dog!" Deke yelped.

"But also," Charles said, pointing to the card

bearing only the cord's fingerprints, "Y's fingerprints are on the trophy."

"What?" Deke cried.

"See for yourself." He stepped aside to let Deke and Randy study the images projected on the computer screen. The ridge characteristics of Y's fingerprints matched those taken from the trophy.

"Good lord!" Deke exclaimed. *So Trey had an accomplice—probably a classmate! He hadn't gone out to the Harbison place alone!*

"Come on, Deke, what's this all about?" Randy begged.

"Sorry, Randy. I can't afford to tell you until I'm sure of a few more details."

Charles, too, looked mystified. "Twenty-two years is a long time," he said. "If TD Hall was involved in something that happened back then, he'd have been...what? Seventeen at the time?"

"That's right," Deke said.

"Well, for goodness' sakes, Deke!" Randy exclaimed. "Short of murder, what could Hall have possibly done at seventeen that would have you call me to Amarillo on a Friday afternoon when I'd planned to meet the boys for a beer?"

Deke's face set in its noncommunicative mold as he returned the items of evidence to the box, and the other men exchanged shocked glances.

"My God," Randy said.

Back in his car, Deke formulated a plan of action, which now must include the assumption that Trey had not acted alone in the death of Donny Harbison. Deke was surprised he hadn't thought of two boys being involved, one to hold the animal, the other to mark him. And it wasn't the kind of prank a high school boy would pull off alone. He'd want a buddy to share the risk and danger, somebody who could bear witness to his daring when he bragged about it later.

So now, Deke had to find out who that somebody was so that he could track him down and obtain his prints. Randy had agreed to give him the weekend to work his hunches before he became involved. The accomplice was probably on the 1985 football team, a fellow player Trey could lead by the nose, which was the whole squad except for John Caldwell. Trey could never have talked John into participating in a stunt to hurt an animal. Deke would interview Ron Turner and get the names of players willing to do anything for their star quarterback. Most of the '85 team had long left Kersey, but he'd get the addresses from the roster Melissa had compiled for her twentieth high school reunion.

He glanced at the clock on the dashboard. Nearly three o'clock. At top speed, he could be back in Kersey in a little over an hour and catch Ron while he was still sober.

DEKE DREW UP BEFORE the Turners' redbrick house with its handsome Corinthian columns in record time and was saddened to see the changes in the place. At one time, the large, two-storied residence had sat like an architectural gem on manicured grounds and was the showplace of Kersey. Ron's wife had come with money when they married, inherited more afterwards, and it was her resources that allowed Ron to live in a house far above what he could have afforded on a coach's salary. Today, from the looks of the neglected lawn and flower beds, the untrimmed hedges and cracked drive, the place was going to ruin.

What a shame, Deke thought. Ron Turner had been one of the best high school head coaches in the business, but his life had crumbled when his daughter had died just shy of her nineteenth birthday of a ruptured appendix. He'd hung in the coaching business for another five years or so, doing what he could with mediocre teams, but then his wife had died and he gave up. The last Deke heard of him, he was drinking heavily and living like a derelict in the house where he once reigned as king.

Deke found Ron's telephone number in a Kersey directory he kept in his car and called ahead to make sure he was home. "Sure, come on, but don't expect the butler," Ron had chuckled, and answered the door almost the second Deke rang the bell. He saw little resemblance to the robust football coach his state championship team had once hoisted to their shoulders.

"Well, well, Sheriff Tyson, I can't imagine why you're here, but it's mighty good to see you."

"You, too," Deke said.

"Oh, now." Ron flung up a hand. "I look like a blown out retread, and you know it. Come on out to the kitchen. I've got us a couple of beers chilling."

Deke followed the shambling figure past dark, drapery-drawn rooms to a cluttered kitchen connected to a breakfast nook and a cozy sitting area dominated by a handsome fireplace. The smell was peculiar to a man living alone who forgets to take out the garbage. "Sit down, sit down!" Ron invited, brushing newspapers off a kitchen chair. "What brings you to see me?"

"Trey Don Hall," Deke said.

Ron slowly straightened. For an instant, his watery, alcohol-reddened eyes were as icy as chipped crystal. "Trey?"

"I have a few questions I'd like to ask you regarding him the week of the district championship game in '85, Coach."

"Why? That's ancient history, Sheriff."

"Indulge me. I bet you remember every minute of that week."

"You wouldn't be wrong there." Ron shuffled to the refrigerator and extracted two bottles of beer. "But I can't imagine why you'd be interested after all these years."

"I'm afraid I can't tell you, and I'd appreciate your keeping this visit and our discussion under your hat."

"Don't worry," Ron said. "I don't talk to anybody anymore. You were sheriff then. Is TD in some kind of trouble related to that time?"

Deke took the beer. "He could be. That's what I hope you can help me decide. Your information might help clear up an injustice that would ease the pain of some good people who've suffered a long time."

"They must be parents," Ron said, taking a swig of the beer. "Usually, the good people who suffer a long time are parents. What do you want to know?"

Deke set down the beer bottle and opened a notepad. "Think back to the week of November 4, 1985. That was a Monday. Now, during any of the days before Thursday, can you remember anything being awry with Trey Don?"

"I sure can," Ron said. "He and John Caldwell were sick on Monday. Came to practice that afternoon sick as dogs."

"What?" Deke gaped at Ron. "John Caldwell, too?"

"Both of 'em. Scared the liver out of me, I can tell you."

"What was wrong with them?"

"Something they ate for lunch. Seniors could go off campus then during their lunch break, and Monday was the only day I let my boys out with the rest of the pack. The other days they had to brown-bag it, and we met in the gym for a bull session during lunch. I always regretted that I didn't keep them confined the entire week. Trey and John picked up a stomach virus eating hamburgers at that greasy hangout Cathy Benson bought."

"You're sure it was a stomach virus?"

Ron shrugged. "That's what they thought it was."

Busily writing, Deke asked, "Practice began right after school?"

"Not a minute later."

"And Trey and John showed up on time?"

"No, that was the problem. They were late. Nobody knew where they were. Some of the boys said they'd cut their last class. Turned out they were in the home economics room lying down. It was set up with a bed for the girls to practice putting on sheets. Can you imagine that being taught today?"

Deke felt as if somebody had thrown ice

551

water down his back. *John Caldwell?* Father *John Caldwell, pastor of St. Matthew's Parish and director of Harbison House?*

"Was anybody else on the team sick?" he asked.

Ron shook his head. "No, thank God."

"Did anybody else eat at Bennie's Burgers that day?"

"Deke, how the hell could I possibly remember after twenty-three years? Come on. Tell me what this is all about."

"You recall the name of the home economics teacher?"

"Thelma something-or-other. Old maid. Moved to Florida when she retired."

Deke wrote down the first name on his notepad. Melissa would remember the rest of it. Maybe the woman's address was included on the twentieth-reunion roster. He'd track her down to confirm the boys' crumpling in her room that afternoon.

"Do you recall how long after practice began that the boys showed up?"

"A good hour, I'd say. We were well into practice when they came out onto the field, pale as silver dollars. I sent them home early."

Deke drew a sharp breath. He'd bet *his* last dollar that Trey Hall and John Caldwell were nowhere near that home economics room. They left school before their last class and planned to be back for football practice. They hadn't counted on a murder or accident to delay them, throw them off schedule, mess with their digestive systems. But one problem gummed up his whole theory. The time frame didn't work. It would have taken Trey and John no more than an hour to go and come from the Harbison place. Even allowing a half hour for the scuffle, to arrange the body in the barn and rake the ground, plus a few minutes to throw up in the weeds, the boys would have been long gone before Donny got home from band practice and prepared a snack. They'd also had time to change into their practice uniforms.

"Hate to challenge your recollection, Ron," Deke said, "but can you give me the name of anyone else on the coaching staff back then who can confirm your memory?"

"Bobby Tucker, head coach now," Ron said. "He was the line coach then, a rookie. Ask him if you don't believe me."

"I'm sorry, but I will."

Ron got up. "This beer sucks. I'm going to fix myself something stronger. How about you?"

"Beer's fine," Deke said, hearing Ron's empty bottle clink against others in a paper sack on the floor. "Did you ever check out their stories with the home economics teacher?"

Pouring himself a glass of Jack Daniel's from among other high-priced labels ranged on the counter, Ron said, "I saw no need to. Those boys weren't in the habit of cutting classes. They took their studies seriously, especially John. And you only had to look at 'em to believe they were genuinely sick."

Of course they were, Deke thought, but not from anything they'd eaten. He had to find a glitch in the time sequence to prove it. He rose to go, catching sight of a picture of Ron's wife and daughter over the fireplace mantle. "Thanks for your help, Ron."

"Wish you'd tell me what's going on," the coach said. "With Trey it could be anything."

"Did you like him?"

"Yes, I did. I tried to be a father to him. I saw some saving graces in him beyond his ability to play football, but the boy could betray you on the turn of a dime. Look what he did to his aunt and Cathy Benson and John Caldwell."

Deke nodded. "Yeah," he agreed, seeing the bitter close of Ron's mouth, the glint of long-banked anger in his eye. Best if he not mention Trey staying at Harbison House. In a drunken stupor Ron might call him up and chew him out, and Deke didn't want him spilling the beans that former sheriff Tyson had been by asking questions. He said his good-byes and let himself out, leaving Ron to get stoned before the cold fireplace under the gaze of his wife and daughter.

Chapter Fifty-Three

Cathy did not utter a word as John finished relating how John Will Benson had been conceived. He had not let go of her hands. "Stay with me, Cathy," he said, and she understood he thought he recognized signs of her old malady. "I know what a shock this is." He released one of her hands and she felt suddenly set adrift, but he meant only to pick up her glass. It was not her old nemesis threatening. Disbelief had paralyzed her beyond speech. "Drink this," he said, putting the glass to her lips, and she tossed down its entire contents, the liquid raw and prickling in her throat. She set aside the glass and took back his hand, dry and warm like a perfectly fitting glove, the fingers strong and familiarly shaped—like her son's.

"You and I...But I don't remember...," she said. "How could I not have remembered something like that?"

"You were definitely loop-legged drunk, and you fell instantly into a deep sleep," he said, failing at a grin. "I mean—like out cold."

"Even so, how could I never have suspected—"

"Why would you? You were with Trey the next day. If I'd been more...knowledgeable, I might have recognized the root of his behavior. I'd have recalled his bout with the mumps and suspected his problem. The indications were there, clear as neon signs shouting that something that had given meaning to his life had been destroyed, something irreplaceable."

Cathy waited to feel something for Trey's eighteen-year-old feelings, the devastation he must have felt when she told him she was pregnant, but nothing came, nothing at all. Her vision, her heart, were filled only with this man and the awe that he was the true father of her son. Never again would she have to worry that one day, years down the line, Trey's genes would kick in, pollute the integrity that had marked the difference between father and son since Will was born.

"John..." She took her gaze over the features of his face, the shape of his ears, recalling the way his hair—like Will's—curled in damp weather. How had she not seen John in her son? She said in wonder, "You're Will's father?"

"There's no doubt, Cathy."

"I should have known.... I should have guessed...."

His fingers tightened. "As Trey said, we looked only for what we expected to find."

"I can't begin to imagine how Will will feel when he learns the truth."

"He'll feel what I do."

They stared at each other, each reading all the what-could-have-beens in the other's eyes. "Good lord, John..." The enormity of Trey's lies, the camouflage of his deceits, rose in her awestruck mind like gigantic boulders blocking the sun. "How could he have done this to us... to Will...?"

"He believed we betrayed him," John said. "We shattered all he knew to be faithful and true, and he wanted to punish us."

A mother's fury began to shake her. She stood to get away from the rebuke of the liturgical shirt and Roman collar to the unholy rage she felt. She balled her fists. "But how could he let Will think his father had deserted him? How could he let that little boy suffer the same feeling of being unwanted he'd known? Somewhere along the way, wouldn't some decency in him make him come forward with the truth?"

"He thought it was too late," John said. "I was already in the priesthood, and he knew you'd never ask me to leave my vocation to marry you."

"I despise him," she said simply.

"You have reason to."

"You should despise him, too."

"I would if I didn't feel enormous pity for him. He's never stopped loving us, Cathy, and that has been his greatest torment. I believe if you saw him, you'd see he's suffered more from the consequences of his acts than we have. You and I, for all we've been denied, have had our friendship, and we have Will."

She swung around. "If I saw him, I'd shoot him, so help me God, I would. I swear if he walked in right now, I'd drag out my grandmother's old .30-30 and blast him to hell."

"He'll meet his death soon enough," John said.

"What do you mean?"

"He's dying, Cathy. An inoperable brain tumor— an astrocytoma. That's why he's here now."

An image of Trey on the tennis court their senior year in high school—tall, strong, tanned, reflecting sunlight—whirled out of the past. She'd carried that picture of him through the years like a secret photograph tucked away in a wallet secretly glanced at now and then. That Trey could be dying—that strapping paragon of male health, the man she'd loved nearly all her life—momentarily stunned her, but no sorrow or pity, no understanding, warmed the cold hatred she felt for him. "I see," she said, her voice soft with contempt. "And so he's come to buy some eleventh-hour peace with God, is that it? Trying for a Hail Mary. How typical of TD Hall."

"Sit down, Cathy," John said, indicating the seat next to him. "There's more I've come to tell you." He picked up his glass and emptied it.

Cathy's hopes tumbled. He was going to tell her they couldn't make Will's paternity public. There was John's work, his reputation, to consider as well as hers and Will's. But what was worse—correcting an old scandal based on a lie or raising a new one established on truth? She'd not had time to think it through. She sat down. "What is it, John? Do you feel we can't let it be known you're Will's father?"

"It's not that at all, Cathy. I'll be proud to announce to the world that Will is my son if that's what you and Will wish. He was conceived before I took my vows, and the Church would want me to do what's right by my child. In any case, when you hear what I have to tell you, Will may not want to acknowledge me as his father. *You* may not be all that eager to claim him as mine."

Goose bumps rose on her skin. "Why not?"

"Trey came home to make two confessions."

She put her hands over her ears. "I think I don't want to hear this."

"Do you remember Trey and me getting sick the week of the district championship game against Delton?"

She dropped her hands. "Vividly. It was a Monday. You and Trey looked green as stewed turtles from the hamburgers you ate at Bennie's."

"We weren't sick from Bennie's hamburgers. We were sick because we were responsible for causing Donny Harbison's death."

Cathy sat rock still, her jaw slowly dropping.

"Yes, you heard correctly," John said. "Donny died from an accident, but Trey and I caused it. That's the other sin he's come home to confess—to the Harbisons."

Cathy heard him as if a wad of cloth had been shoved into her ears. Household sounds faded. She thought of the school picture of Donny displayed on a shelf in the Harbisons' kitchen. She'd never seen it without a vase of Betty's flowers beside it. The photo was all she knew of the son they had lost. His name had never been mentioned to her in the years of her buying produce from the children's gardens at Harbison House.

John turned his head to the window, and Cathy could see memory float into his gaze like a tide bringing long-lost flotsam to shore. "Trey was convinced our scholarships to Miami were on the line if we didn't win district, and he got it into his head we had to do something to give us an edge...."

It took no more than five minutes to relate the events of that unalterable November afternoon. Listening in horrified silence, Cathy recalled that a razor had gone missing from Dr. Graves's clinic. She could remember the bruise on Trey's shoulder and how he had clung to her that afternoon as if she were a lifeboat in a stormy sea. She could remember thinking then that the two of them were forever and that nothing could drive them apart.

"Trey plans to tell the Harbisons the truth about their son's death tonight while I'm at mass," John concluded. "He says he'll keep my name out of it— that he'll take full responsibility for Donny's death."

She was still too appalled to form a response. She could imagine the depth of the Harbisons' pain and grief only through what she would have suffered if it had been Will strung up in the barn. To go off and leave their son like that for his parents to find... The act was almost too unconscionable to comprehend, and it had been John's idea. But he had been only seventeen and panicked beyond any thought but saving from jail a boy closer to him than a brother—and preserving his future for the girl they both loved. John's Catholic conscience had compelled him to choose the lesser horror of two evils.

And the act had driven him into the priesthood.

"Do you believe him?" she asked.

He diverted his attention to the window to watch a hawk diving and swooping high in the sky. The wistfulness in his gaze caused her to wonder if he was envying the bird its ability to spread its wings and fly away. "I believe his intention," he said.

"His intention?"

"Trey's a dying man making his confession. He's emotional, desperate for absolution, and on medication. It wouldn't take but a slip of his tongue to start the Harbisons questioning, wondering...."

She felt her scalp tingle. "What are you saying? Do you think somehow they'll learn you were involved?"

"The Harbisons are intelligent people. They're bound to wonder how Trey could have acted alone. It would have taken two to hoist Donny's body in the barn. Trey would never intentionally implicate me, but the Harbisons—Betty, especially—might decide to have their son's death investigated. She is not of a forgiving nature, and in Trey's condition he could never stand up to a police interrogation. Eventually, my name would come out. I was Trey's best friend in high school. We were inseparable...."

A cold panic whipped through her. "Oh, my God, John. Did you warn him he was risking your exposure?"

"No. I must let Trey do what he feels he must do."

"Oh, John!" She had the insane urge to rip his Roman collar from his neck. "How can you be so blasted priestly? You've got to stop him. Trey could ruin you—your life, your work, your reputation. Think of what it would do to the Harbisons if they learned of your involvement. It would destroy them."

"Believe me, I am thinking of it, but I have no choice but to let things ride out as they will." He stood, pushed his hands into his pockets, and stared out the window. "It may be that I'm worrying for nothing...."

"You don't believe that."

"No. I believe God has given me fair warning." He turned to face her, the light behind him throwing his broad-shouldered, dark-suited figure into relief. "Cathy, dear, it's been...very difficult for me to live with the knowledge of the lie I allowed the Harbisons to suffer all these years. It's a sin I've never forgiven myself for and neither has God."

She did not like where his priest's conscience was taking him. She hopped up. "Screw God!" she cried. "You've made up for your *sin* a thousand times over, if you want to call it that. You've done your penance. Betty will never, ever forgive you. Trust me, as a mother, I know. You've got to stop Trey!"

"Shush," he said softly, and held her by the shoulders. "I must leave this to God and trust His will. If worse comes to worst, I must be prepared to accept it. At least I'll be free of the shadows that have dogged my backside ever since it happened. I'm so tired of trying to outrun them...."

"But it's so unfair!" she cried. "That afternoon was all Trey's doing. He should take the rap for *all* of it—with God and the Harbisons. He *owes* it to you. You were only seventeen—a boy!"

His arms came around her, and she pressed her cheek to the black shirt like the time she dimly remembered from long ago when she'd rested her head against his chest after being sick in his bathroom.

"But as a man I could have put it right," he said, speaking softly above her head. "I'm not sure now whether I did not use my allegiance to Trey as my reason not to confess to the police and the Harbisons what happened that day. And as a priest, I convinced myself that God's work could be achieved only through people's faith in His priests and ministers and I had no right to relieve my conscience by destroying what I had accomplished in His name. But I was wrong. God's work will prevail despite the frailty of its priests. And all my efforts to atone for what I did have brought me no peace. Every time I look into the Harbisons' faces, I feel my guilt."

She lifted her head to look at him. "They must never know your involvement."

"I pray to God they won't."

"If Trey had not come, you would continue living with your guilt? You wouldn't be tempted, for the sake of your conscience, to break your silence?"

"God forgive me, I wouldn't." He drew away and glanced at his watch. "I have an appointment with the bishop at three. He'll advise me what to do." He smiled at her. "Let's talk about how we'll go about telling Will our wonderful news. I'd like for us to be together as a family before…whatever happens. Could I come back after mass?"

She nodded numbly. "We'll be here."

"It will be all right, Cathy. One way or the other, it will be all right."

"You could be kicked out of the priesthood," she whispered as he took his keys from his pocket. "You could face criminal charges. You could lose everything…."

He came to smooth his thumb gently across the ridge of her cheek. "Not everything," he said. "I will still have our friendship, and I will have my son. Now I must go." He kissed her forehead and left her staring numbly after him before the couch.

Chapter Fifty-Four

Deke pulled away from the Turner house feeling that a black cloud had dropped over him. *Good God! John Caldwell, an accomplice to the death of Donny Harbison!* He hoped to hell he was wrong and that Trey had talked somebody else into going with him on his mission that day, but Deke had a sick feeling that the other set of prints on the extension cord belonged to John. Deke wouldn't know until he acquired a set to match them to, but before he worked on that he had to be absolutely sure of the time the boys showed up for practice.

It was possible that Donny was killed at night and the food on the table was his supper, not an afternoon snack as assumed. Trey and John could have driven over after dark, done the deed, and returned home with nobody the wiser. But several things bothered him. One, would a boy alone in the house eat his supper on the kitchen table rather than in front of the television like every other kid in the country? And, if Trey and John were as sick as described, would they be in the mood to carry out such a stunt? He'd think it would be the last thing on their minds.

Also, the boys would have expected Donny and his family to be home in the evening unless they had reason to believe the Harbisons were out of town. That was another point he'd have to get cleared: how the boys knew they'd be alone to have a clear shot at the ram.

He'd start first with Bobby Tucker, the defensive line coach from those days. Coach Tucker might have a different recollection from Ron of the hour the boys appeared on the field.

Deke caught him working in his yard this first week of summer vacation. Bobby was grateful for the break, and he and Deke plopped down on the porch steps. Deke came right to the point without explaining the reason for his question or that he'd been to see Coach Turner. Bobby did not take long to reflect.

"Yeah, I remember the incident like yesterday," he said. "Coach Turner was about to have a stroke before they showed up an hour into practice. It scared the hell out of us, our quarterback and his best receiver coming out on the field sick as rabid dogs."

"You're sure it was an hour, not two?"

Bobby laughed. "Are you kidding? I'm telling you Coach Turner would be pushing up daisies now if they'd been a minute later."

"But still, how can you be so sure of the time?"

Bobby grinned. "We gave them an hour. If they didn't show up, we were going to call you at the sheriff's department to go look for them. They made it in the nick of time."

"I see," Deke said, but he really didn't. Donny was just coming home from band practice when Trey and John got to the field. "One other question before I let you get back to your mowing," he said. "It will sound strange, but do your best to answer it. Did you notice an emotional change in TD and John during and after that week? Maybe they were distracted, edgy...."

Bobby frowned. "I'm not the one to ask. That was my first year on board, and I didn't have much to do with Trey and John. They were Coach Turner's personal bailiwick. He's the man to talk to— that is, if he'll answer his phone." He shook his head sadly. "You know about his...addiction?"

"Melissa keeps us informed."

"A tragedy that Coach Turner now practices what he preached against. He's got everything—money, a beautiful house, a garage of fine cars."

"Except the things that must matter to him," Deke said. He looked at his watch. Fifteen until five. He'd stop by Bennie's and talk to Cathy Benson. If anyone could tell him about Trey and John's behavior the week of the district game, it would be Cathy. After that, he'd go by Melissa's and look for the name of the home economics teacher.

"Is it true you're buying Mabel Church's house?" Bobby asked as Deke got to his feet.

"Trey and I made the deal at noon today. News travels fast."

"Thank Melissa for it, Sheriff. She's made no secret of you and Mrs. Tyson buying the house and meeting with Trey. I thought I saw TD in town today around lunchtime. He didn't see me. Was it something he said to trigger your interest in the week of that district play-off game?"

Deke grabbed at the opportunity to pacify the coach's curiosity. "Something like that," he lied. "Melissa is tasked with writing a journal of her senior year for posterity."

Bobby smiled understandingly. "Like a time capsule," he said, walking Deke to his car. "TD Hall and John Caldwell. They were quite a team.

John could have had a shot at the pros, if you ask me. Did you ever figure him for the priesthood?"

"Not right out of high school," Deke said, having an idea why John had fixed on his avocation so soon. "Maybe later, but not at eighteen." He tipped his Stetson. "Much obliged, Coach."

Deke headed toward town with his heart still heavy. If he brought down Trey Don Hall, he'd also destroy John Caldwell, a man who'd spent his life trying to atone for a mistake he'd made as a teenager. Trey had gone on to riches and glory and probably never looked back on what he had done, but John had taken his burden with him on a path of poverty and chastity and obedience to God. Deke had no doubt that when he got to the bottom of this he'd find that John had gone along that fateful November afternoon to minimize the cruelty, maybe even prevent it. He'd bet his bottom dollar that Trey had decided on autoerotic asphyxia as the cause of death when John, a Catholic, had refused to go along with suicide as a cover-up of what had happened.

Was restoring Donny's good name to his parents worth annihilating John Caldwell's? The county had given him the status of a virtual saint, and justly so. Father John's exposure and possible arrest for obstruction of justice would have far-reaching and devastating effects to the Church, not to mention the Harbisons. He hated to think what they would feel when they learned the man they loved like a son had participated in their boy's death and the cover-up of how he died. The scandal would drive the most decent man Deke had ever known from the parish, maybe the priesthood, and the life he'd lived, the good he'd done, would be seen as a lie.

Did he, at this late date, with everybody's lives in place, the past almost forgotten, have the right to dig out and expose the truth at the expense of the destruction it would cause?

It was not for him to pose such questions. He believed the truth was always better than a lie no matter who it hurt, what damage it caused. The truth did not destroy; it built. And he was first and foremost a cop. The pursuit of justice ran in his blood, pumped his heart, even if he no longer wore a badge. And he was also a father. He would want his son to rest in peace cleared of shame. His honor would be worth the cost of the truth. Father John would have to accept his fate.

However, before he shared his allegations with the current sheriff sitting in the chair he once occupied, he'd better make damn sure of his evidence. Destroying the river to snare a couple of badgers would be a sorry trade. In town, he stopped by

Bennie's to speak to Cathy but was told she'd left early and would probably not be back. He got the impression from Bebe that a problem had come up at home. Deke had an idea of the name of the problem. Disappointed, he returned to his car and telephoned Paula on his cell, thankful that she wasn't home and he could leave word on the answering machine that he was back in Kersey and would be spending the night at their daughter's. He planned to attend six o'clock mass at St. Matthew's. He had an idea where he could get a sample of Father John's fingerprints.

Chapter Fifty-Five

Trey opened his eyes and blinked rapidly to orient himself. It had been a while since he'd awakened in a strange bedroom, and never one where his first view was of a crucifix on the wall. *John's room.* Black despair washed over him. He remembered that John had gone to see Cathy and now she hated him with all the passion with which she'd once loved him. He swung his feet to the floor, risking the dizziness and nausea from sudden movement caused by his disease. It was five o'clock. He'd been asleep over three hours. Good. He didn't have as long to wait before his confab with the Harbisons. In the bathroom he urged a trickle of urine, threw water over his face, and washed the rancid taste from his mouth. He avoided looking into the mirror, certain of what he would find. "Be sure your sins will find you out," his aunt had warned him many times, and he knew he'd see every one etched in the haggard, sick face of his reflection.

He went out into the hall to fetch his carry-on from the car, his medication-leached stomach reacting appreciatively to a savory smell wafting from the kitchen up the stairs. A small girl skipped past him, apparently answering a call to supper. He glanced into the dining room on his way to the front door and saw a group of youngsters around a long table. A teenage girl was distributing pot pies from a sideboard, one of the inmates, obviously.

He'd parked the BMW in front of one of the hitching posts still in existence in front of the house. A white blossom from a tree at the gate had caught in his windshield wiper, and he carefully freed and examined it. A little miracle of nature right here in his hand, he thought, fluffy and sweet smelling, perfectly wrought, like Cathy. An unexpected peace stole over him. Why had he never noticed things like this when they might have made a difference?

He slipped the blossom into the shirt pocket containing Deke's check and obeyed an impulse to follow a brick path round to the back, an improvement since he was last here. Somebody had taken care with the mortar and design, a first-class job, probably a landscaper's charity write-off. John was good at getting people to do the right thing. The barn where they'd strung up the son of this house still looked the same, though, and the quiet peace he'd captured a moment ago chilled like a sudden change in the weather. He set his luggage by the house and walked on past the barn and down another path that ran alongside a small orchard and huge vegetable garden soaking up the afternoon sun—all well tended—and came to a dead end at a layout of pens and outbuildings that housed animals and equipment. He heard sawing in one of the sheds.

Lou Harbison looked up from his work over a sawhorse when he saw Trey in the doorway and turned off the power of an ancient Black & Decker timber buster. "Howdy," he said, pushing up his safety goggles, straightening his back. "Anything I can do for you?"

"No, I'm only looking around at all you've got going out here—the garden and orchard, the stock. You guys still keep chickens?"

"There's a coop the other side of the barn. You remember that?" Lou's face turned pinkish— surprised pleasure, Trey interpreted, that after all his high-style living he'd remember a simple thing like his wife's chickens. Lou Harbison seemed a gentler sort than his wife, less scarred, but there was the same kind of something missing in him as in Betty Harbison.

"I sure do," Trey said. "Best eggs I ever ate. My aunt used to make pancakes with them. They'd turn out yellow as corn."

"That's because our chickens ate corn—no additives or hormones."

"Makes a difference—eggs not doctored with that added stuff."

"Sure enough."

Lou stood with the Black & Decker still in his hand, his expression politely wondering if Trey had more to say. He thought it time to move on. "Well," he said, "you've got a good thing here, Mr. Harbison."

"We've got Father John to thank for that."

"Is that so?"

"The place wouldn't be much without him. Betty and me...we wouldn't, either."

He spoke softly, with no hint of menace, but there was a mixed warning and plea behind his words. *Don't mess with John...please.*

Trey agreed with a nod and left the shed.

Betty Harbison came out on the back stoop as he drew near the house, her eyes sharp and suspicious. She must have seen him through the kitchen window, the one her son had spotted them through that fateful day. "I see you're up," she said.

Not for a long time, but thanks for the presumption, he was tempted to reply, but she didn't seem in the mood for jokes. "I thought I'd take a stroll around the fine place you have here," he said. "It's such a great afternoon"—*and the last I'll ever see in the Panhandle.* As usual when he thought such thoughts, terror broke through the calm surface of his acceptance of his coming death.

Her stiff expression relaxed slightly. "We think so. Father said you threw up your lunch and I'm to get a cup of chicken broth into you. Come on inside, and I'll see to it." She held the screen door open for him, her determined stance and set mouth brooking no argument.

Reluctantly he entered her lair, catching sight of Donny's framed photograph beside a vase spilling with flowers from the trees next to the gate.

"Could your stomach handle a chicken pot pie?" Betty asked. "You look like you could use something a little more substantial than broth. And there's Jell-O, too, made with peaches from our orchard."

"Break my arm," Trey said.

That goosed a faint smile from her. "You'll have to wait a few minutes until I get the kids off who are going to mass."

"Will happily do," Trey said.

Left alone, he strolled to the back screened door.

It was from here that Donny had shot out after them like a charging bantam rooster. He had been a ballsy little bugger. All these years, Trey had not forgotten that.

He saw Lou go by the house to get behind the wheel of an old van used for transporting the children of Harbison House. Outside in the hall and down the stairs came a scramble of footsteps and voices heading toward the front door. When Betty returned to the kitchen, he asked, "Did you ever get a new rolling pin?"

Her brow line vaulted. "Why, yes. Long ago. Right after the one I had disappeared. How did you know it was missing?"

"I guess I remembered my aunt saying something about it." He flashed his disarming smile. "The mention of pie made me recall it."

He chose a seat with his back to the photograph and ate as much as his shrunken stomach would allow, sneaking a few bites to the dog that had taken an expectant position by his chair. There was still a lot of activity in the house, and Trey was generally ignored while Betty oversaw after-supper duties and activities from her command post in the kitchen. She was in her element, ordering the children around in a motherly way, but he could see John's influence in their manners and attitudes.

"What would Father John say?" Betty remonstrated more than once when the dish drying got out of hand and a squabble broke out over which TV program to watch.

He folded his napkin and picked up his plates to take them to the sink. It was warm and cozy on this floor. The time of confession was several hours away, and he'd just as soon be lying in an ICU unit rather than wait upstairs in John's room for them to pass. "The pie and Jell-O were delicious, Mrs. Harbison. I've never eaten any better. Mind if I take a tour of the house?"

"Go ahead."

Right outside the kitchen was a long hallway, its walls lined with pictures of John and the children of Harbison House caught in moments of fun and play, success and achievement. Betty, drying her hands on her apron, stole beside him as he studied them.

"These are just a few taken over the years," she explained. "You won't find any of those glad-handed certificates like the kind the Rotary Club awards for exceptional community service or pictures of Father John posing with big shots displayed here. He's received dozens over the years, but they're stored in the attic."

"That's John, all right," Trey said with a wry

chuckle. His study in California was a virtual ego den filled with commemorations of his success.

"He's a wonderful man. I don't know what folks around here would do without him." A warning glint had come into her eye, more pointed than her husband's. "The children worship him, and he's like a son to my husband and me. You remember that we lost a son...."

"I remember," Trey said.

Her gaze was rock steady behind her spectacles. *Damn!* What did the Harbisons suspect he'd come to do—defrock Father John? Pinned to the wall by her stiletto stare, he drew an abrupt breath. *Oh, Jesus...* A horrifying possibility had just occurred to him. John's voice echoed in the sick caverns of his brain. *"Your part, yes. Mine still weighs heavily."*

He must have lost color in his face. He thought he may have wobbled, for Betty gripped his arm. "What is it? Are you going to be sick again?"

"I need to sit down," he said, "—in there." He pointed to the fairly quiet place of the living room.

"Should I bring you some water?"

Trey pressed his temples. "No, I just need a place to think."

She left him sitting in a stiff formal chair before the cold fireplace, and he heard her instruct her kitchen help to lower their voices. Trey felt that a bucket of ice-cold Gatorade had been thrown over him. Would John think that after his old buddy bared his soul to the Harbisons he'd be free to bare his? Once John no longer had to keep his silence, would he listen to that damn conscience of his and give up everything to square himself with God?

Oh, my God. He might. That would be so like John.

And…what if he inadvertently incriminated John when he related what had happened? His brain was no longer capable of quick thinking. His tongue was not as glib. What if he said *we* instead of *I*? What if that sharp Mrs. Harbison asked questions and he flubbed his answers, or—another possibility he hadn't thought of—what if they decided to report him to the police? He'd assumed the Harbisons would want to keep the embarrassing details of their son's death to themselves since they'd not made them public twenty-three years ago, but what if he was wrong? What if they wanted their pound of flesh for what he did? He had not planned to reveal that he was dying. His impetus for coming forward with the truth was not to be part of his confession. But…how could he be sure that, even if he told them of his terminal illness, Betty and Lou Harbison wouldn't still want justice for Donny? What if they wanted him charged with manslaughter! There would be an investigation. John could be dragged in....

Christ almighty! What had he been thinking?

He got to his feet and left the room. He picked up his carry-on and started up the stairs.

Betty heard him and came to the foot of the balustrade. "Are you all right now?" she called.

"Never better, Mrs. Harbison!" he called down.

Chapter Fifty-Six

At Melissa's, Deke declined supper and took over his son-in-law's study to make his calls. He had fifteen minutes before he had to leave for mass and would finish his list tonight when he returned. By another stroke of good luck, Thelma Goodson, the name of the home economics teacher, was among those on his daughter's reunion roster. He dialed her number in Florida but received no answer. Rather than leave a message, he'd try her again later. The next call was to Harbison House, hoping Lou had already left with the kids for mass. A mother was more likely to know the answers Deke was seeking, and he could trust Betty to say nothing to anyone at this point, even to Lou.

He breathed easier when she answered but

found her a little hesitant when he identified himself. She'd been that way with him since her boy's body was discovered. He asked if they could speak privately, knowing he sounded mysterious.

"One of the girls is in the kitchen with me," she said. "Want me to get rid of her?"

"No, that's okay," Deke said, "but I'd like you to keep this conversation between ourselves. Just you and me—okay?"

"I owe you that," Betty said, her tone terse. "I won't say anything to Lou. What's on your mind?"

His first question produced the perplexity he'd expected. "Did Trey Hall know Donny?" Betty repeated. "Well, he knew him, sort of. Why do you ask?"

"I wish I could tell you, Betty. What do you mean, 'sort of'?"

"They weren't friends by any stretch of the imagination. They'd see each other when Trey used to pick up his aunt's order."

Just as he'd guessed. That would explain how Trey had learned Donny looked after the school mascot. "What about John? Did they know each other?"

"Only to speak once in a while at St. Matthew's. Now you do have me curious, Sheriff."

"I can imagine. Now, prepare yourself for this

next question, Betty. Would Trey have known you and Lou were going to be out of town the week Donny died?"

Betty's startled surprise was palpable in her silence. Finally, she spoke. "I suppose Trey could have learned from Mabel that we'd be gone. She would have been one of the customers I'd have called."

Deke let out a breath of satisfaction. Another piece of the puzzle had slipped into place.

"It's...peculiar, your asking about Trey Hall," Betty said. "You may know he's spending the night here. He shocked me a while ago by asking if I'd replaced my rolling pin. It was the one I couldn't find when we got back that week."

Deke bolted upright in his chair. "Did you ever find it?"

"No. I know I used it Monday morning to roll out biscuits. I left some for Donny. The next time I went for it, it wasn't in the drawer."

A weapon! Donny must have gone for the rolling pin when he saw two strapping athletes from a rival school in his backyard and reckoned what they had in mind.

"He told me that his aunt had mentioned I'd misplaced it," Betty said, "but I can't see how I'd have said anything about it to her."

Chills were chasing up and down his backbone,

and Deke guessed they were Betty's as well. "Is Trey still leaving in the morning?"

"I understand from Father John those are his plans."

In the morning. That didn't leave him much time. "I have to ask you once more to keep this conversation between ourselves until you hear from me again," Deke said. "Promise?"

"I promise," Betty said, "but you're scaring me, Sheriff."

"I know, Betty, but it can't be helped. I appreciate your cooperation."

Deke hung up. The noose was tightening. The only problem was the conflict of the time element. He'd gone over and over the notes he'd jotted down from memory (the original ones were still in the evidence bag in Randy's keeping) to check for the one point he'd missed but could find none to put Trey and John in Donny's backyard after he came home from band practice. He'd find it, though. He closed his notebook. Time he left for mass.

But just as he reached the door, an idea hit him that sent a tremor down his legs. *God bless America!* He was guilty of breaking the first rule of police work: Never assume anything. He returned to the desk and rummaged through drawers until he located a county phone directory. The name he'd forgotten but might recognize began with a *P* and fit the man Deke remembered from his earlier investigation. Maybe he still lived in Delton. Ah, yes, there it was—Martin Peebles, band director of Delton High School. Deke recalled him as a prissy young fellow, full of himself, patently resentful of giving him his valuable time during their interview. Deke's luck held. Martin Peebles answered after an interminable six rings and wasted valuable minutes of Deke's time making sure he was who he claimed to be before Deke got him to concentrate on the afternoon in question.

"Ummm, November fourth...Yes, I remember that afternoon well."

"Do you recall if Donny Harbison attended marching practice after school? I know he was present in your last-period class that day because he wasn't marked absent, but did he report to *marching* practice?"

"A correction, Mr. Tyson," the man said. "Donny wasn't present in my last-period class."

Deke gripped the receiver. "What? He wasn't marked absent. Are you sure?"

"Of course I'm sure. The date of the birth of one's son is not something one is likely to forget. My wife went into premature labor that afternoon and I left my last class under the direction of a student assistant, but I gave the seniors a pass and canceled marching practice."

"Why didn't you give me this information when I asked for it?" Deke thundered.

"Because you must not have asked me, Sheriff. I believe you wanted to know if Donny would have played hooky from band practice, and I assured you he would not have missed it for the world."

Deke dropped back into his chair, the wind knocked out of him. Well, there it was. The missing piece. He'd collect the final bit tonight and disturb Charles's and Randy's Friday night happy hour to insist they meet him at the crime lab in Amarillo. He wouldn't be able to rest until Y's set of prints in the evidence box was compared to those he'd snitch tonight. It saddened him to think it, but he was sure the outcome would plug the last gaping hole in the puzzle.

CATHY TOOK A LAST LOOK in the mirror and drew on the bright blue cardigan that matched the print in her pique sundress. Trey had liked her in azure blue. She glanced at her watch again. It was five thirty. Finally! Time to go. She'd thought the moment would never arrive, but she had to make sure that John would be on his way to mass and out of the picture before she arrived at Harbison

House to talk with Trey. She was counting on the house being relatively quiet with Lou and most of the children at mass. The front door was always unlocked until bedtime. If Betty was in the kitchen and the kids in the TV room, she might be able to slip quietly inside and up the stairs to the guest room to conduct her business in private without being seen or heard. Later, when Trey disappeared, no one could report to John that she had been there unless her car was spotted outside the house.

Shadows of old sins... They only dogged the good, she thought. The wicked always escaped them. But not this time. She believed she could convince Trey Don Hall to die with the sin upon his conscience he'd come to confess.

UPSTAIRS IN JOHN'S ROOM, Trey sat down at his desk and pulled Deke's check from his pocket, the mock orange blossom coming with it. He took a pen from its holder and wrote his name on the back of the check, attaching a note that read: "For the kids. I'm leaving, Tiger. I've reconsidered and have decided not to go through with it. I'm trusting you to keep your silence as you always have. Spare me that blight on my name. I'd appreciate your prayers. Love to the end, Trey."

He placed the mock orange blossom on top. It

had wilted, only the fragrance remaining of its former perfection. When he was dead and gone, what would linger of him?

Without saying good-bye, he drove away from the house. The sun had set and left a sky striated with the colors of red and purple, orange and yellow that the region was famous for. He'd forgotten the magnificence of the Panhandle's sunsets in June, the quiet of the prairie at the end of the day. It would have been a melancholy time for him as a boy if it hadn't been for John and Cathy.

The slow fading of the light made him think of the days he had left, but the thought of his approaching death did not fill him with the usual suffocating panic. He felt calm and satisfied, the kind of deep gratification he'd known only during moments in a football game when—against the order from the sidelines—he called the right play. With one of those memory tricks his brain played on him these days, he found himself back at Miami his sophomore year. It is fourth down and Miami is on the six-yard line, seven seconds remaining in the game. The Hurricanes call their last time-out to discuss the final play of the contest. He and the coaches huddle on the sidelines, the season and any hope of a national championship riding on their decision. The offensive coordinator calls 76

Double Seam; the head coach wants 62 Topper Z Sail. They agree to go with 76. He returns to the huddle unconvinced. His team eyes him, trust in their stares. He goes with his gut and calls a different play that wins the game.

And so he'd done today. Last play of the game, and he'd called it different from what conventional wisdom—or self-interest—would have him do, but he couldn't jam up his best friend. He couldn't give John cause to fall on his sword. He'd have to die without the measure of redemption he'd hoped to earn by facing the Harbisons with what he had done. He was sorry for their pain, their brokenness, but he wouldn't take a second son from them. He'd burn in hell before he'd ruin John's life and his wonderful work to save his rotten soul. When he got home to Carlsbad, he'd take back the letter he'd given to his lawyer to be mailed after his death. He'd written it before he'd decided to come in person to face the music and seek forgiveness, but now he could not risk the danger it might pose for John.

A white car was coming toward him. It was almost abreast of the BMW when he recognized the driver. Trey couldn't believe it. With a happy whoop, he waved and blew the horn long and hard as the Lexus passed by, his heart filling with surprise and gratitude. He pulled over to the shoulder, and sure enough, the Lexus slowed and made a U-turn on the empty country road and headed back, pulling behind the BMW. Its door opened, and Trey got out of his car, a broad smile splitting his face. He held his arms wide. "Well, I'll be damned."

"I certainly hope so."

"What?"

"I said I certainly hope so—that you'll be damned."

When Trey saw the gun raised, his arms fell. "Catherine Ann!" he cried as the rifle was aimed and fired and a bullet ripped through his heart.

Chapter Fifty-Seven

The newest employees and the secretary of the Morgan Petroleum Company were expected to man its offices until six o'clock, even on a Friday night when the whole business world knocked off early, so it was not like Will Benson to log out at five thirty. Linda, the secretary, ever curious about details of the handsome young petroleum engineer's life, remarked, "Got a hot date, Will?" when he bid her and a fledgling colleague like himself good night.

"You might say that."

"*Might?* Don't you know?" his fellow worker chortled with a wink at Linda.

"I expect a cold reception," Will said, scrawling his name to the sign-out sheet.

From the office, driving fast, it would take him almost an hour to get to Harbison House, and, unfortunately, he'd have to stop for gas. That would put him at the front gate approximately a half hour after six, thirty minutes or so after his mother's arrival to have it out with his deadbeat father. He could think of no other place she'd take off to at this time on a Friday evening and leave Bebe to handle the crowd alone when the entire county ate out at Bennie's. His mother had fired up his worry a while ago when she'd called to ask him to meet her and Father John at her house after mass. She'd refused to tell him why, and her voice had sounded both tense and excited. "Just do as I ask, darling," she said, aware he'd have to break his usual Friday night date with his girlfriend, Misty.

"Has he contacted you?" Will had asked.

"No, Son, and now I don't expect him to. Believe me, you shouldn't, either."

The *now* had implied she had some new knowledge of his father, but she'd hung up before he could question her further. When he'd telephoned the café minutes later to have her explain herself, Bebe had said she'd left around one o'clock and had not been back or called in. He'd then dialed his mother's house and received no answer. He'd tried her cell phone and got her voice mail. That's when he'd left his desk and said to hell with it. He wasn't leaving his mother to face Trey Don Hall alone.

Will couldn't blame her for wanting to see him again, if only to confront him with the truth of what a shit he was. All afternoon, every time the phone rang or a car drove up he'd thought it might be Trey Don Hall attempting to get in touch with him. Curiosity alone might lead him to make contact with the son he'd never seen. Whatever his explanation, it wouldn't mean a damn to him, Will told himself, yet in a way it would mean everything. It would give him the chance to tell the jerk what he thought of him. He'd have the satisfaction of giving Trey Don Hall a taste of the rejection he and his mother had suffered all these years.

By late afternoon, just before his mother had telephoned, he'd realized his father was not going to telephone or come by. He'd leave town without ever laying eyes on him, and that likelihood made him feel a surprising dismay. Even before the call from his mother, he'd almost decided he would not allow his father to escape that easily. Trey Don Hall was going to meet his son, know what he looked like, learn how much he hated him. Now he'd made up his mind to drive out to Harbison House himself.

It was close to six fifteen when he saw his mother in her Lexus at the intersection of the road that led to the orphanage. He had filled the gas tank of his Jeep and was folding his receipt when he spotted her car stopped at the traffic light. He saw his mother glance both ways before turning onto the highway toward Kersey—furtively, Will thought, as if she didn't wish to be seen. He was shocked by her white, drawn face. She looked badly shaken.

Will let her go without hailing her down. She was wearing something in bright blue, and her hair was bouncy and shiny, done up in a perky way for her meeting with the man she supposedly no longer cared for. Heat warmed Will's neck. Why had she dolled up like that? Had his mother gone to Harbison House to make up with his father? Seduce him? Only it hadn't gone so well. Trey Hall had sent her packing and hurt her once again. Will's jaw clenched. He jerked his Jeep into gear. The bastard wouldn't send *him* packing.

He came upon the body five minutes later. He saw the gray BMW first, parked on the shoulder, and then the long length of a man lying faceup near the back wheels of the car. His heartbeat deadening the sound of his cry, Will pulled to the opposite side of the road, jumped out, and approached the figure on the ground. He stared, slack jawed, down at the still face of the legendary Trey Don Hall, his father. *Oh, God, no...*

He dropped to the sandy shoulder and folded the man's hand in his grip. It was stiff but not cold, enough life in it for Will to feel the touch of his father without his father feeling his. He began to cry, his tears falling on the gray silk shirt, adding splotches to the dark red circle where a bullet had entered. A wave of loss coursed through him. Now he would never know the man who was his father, the man his mother had killed with the .30-30 rifle she kept under her bed.

BACK AT HER HOUSE, Cathy hurried to the medicine cabinet to search for a bottle of long-expired tranquilizers she'd never taken. Her hands trembled so that when she finally pried off the childproof lid the bottle tipped and the contents spilled to the tiled floor. Laboring for breath, her heart beating so fast she thought it would lift her off her feet, she retrieved two pills and gulped them down with a glass of warm tap water to loosen the tensed muscles of her throat. The sight in the mirror made her gasp. Her face was as white as Sheetrock and her eyes stark and raw. Turning the water off, she was horrified to see a dark blotch on the sleeve edge of her blue sweater. Examining it, she realized it was a spot of blood she must have picked up from the wound when she felt Trey's neck for a pulse. Wildly she tore off the sweater and, unsure of what else to do with it, pushed it down among the other items in the clothes hamper.

She made a conscious effort to breathe in a lungful of air slowly through her nose and went into her bedroom to sit down in her reading chair. Slowly she exhaled. She sucked in her stomach—"try for your backbone," she could remember her grandmother instructing her from a manual on how to relieve the symptoms of selective mutism. Cathy held the position for ten seconds and continued the breathing and tension-release exercises she recalled from that time until she began to feel warm and limp. Finally, when her body had relaxed, she tried her voice.

"Dear God, Trey," she said aloud. "Who could have done this to you?"

She would have given all she owned to go back and undo her movements, but the shock of finding Trey murdered had aimed straight for her voice box and dictated her actions and thoughts from the second she'd spotted his body by his car. She'd cried his name as she ran to him, but no sound came. All her old feelings for him had rushed from their bolted rooms as she saw him lying inert on the road with the wind gently ruffling the collar of his shirt, his hair, the dust on which he lay. Frozen dumb, she'd stared into the familiar dark eyes, locked open in sightless astonishment, and wanted to shake recognition into them. *It's me, Trey. It's me!* She'd knelt on rubbery knees to press his neck for a pulse but could feel nothing through her numb fingers. He had utterly left this world, the boy who had been so full of life and the love of hers.

She'd fumbled for her cell to call 911, then realized with a feeling of helpless paralysis she could not speak. She could only cry powerlessly, tears wetting the useless instrument in her hand. She did not want to leave Trey uncovered and vulnerable to the elements, but she must get help. She heard the sound of a tractor in a far-off field but wasn't sure of its direction. She would drive to Harbison House, write out to Betty what had happened, and Betty would call the sheriff's department. Who could have done this? Who would have reason to kill Trey besides herself?

Oh, God.

From that point, the flight response of her condition had taken over. Cathy could hardly believe her actions. With robotic precision, she'd turned her car around, stopped, and brushed all evidence of the Lexus's wheel tracks from the shoulder with the whisk broom she used for clearing debris from her grandmother's and Mabel's graves. She'd driven off, leaving Trey's body where it had fallen, untended and exposed to the chill of dusk falling, but her foot was frozen to the pedal, and she could not breathe.

The tranquilizers were beginning to take effect. Calmer, she rose from the chair. What was done was done. She regretted her actions. They were those of a guilty person. She should have reported Trey's death and trusted in her innocence, but she'd avoided a lot of unnecessary hullabaloo by not being found at the crime scene. Once again Will's mother would have been the center of public scrutiny and gossip, and tongues would wag fast enough when it was learned that John was the father of her child.

Initially suspicion would fall on her anyway. Randy Wallace would have no choice but to question her, but he'd do it quietly and have nothing to tie her to the crime except his guess that at times she must have wished Trey dead. Once the police learned Trey had come back to tell John the truth of Will's paternity, what reason would she have to kill him? She could only be elated over the news and grateful that Trey had made his confession before he was killed. If need be, DNA would support Trey's claim. And Father John had told her of Trey's terminal illness. Why would she want to kill a man she knew was going to die anyway? Her gun would not match the ballistics of the bullet that had killed Trey. All she was lacking was an alibi, and she believed she could establish a credible story of where she was at the time of the murder.

Randy must never learn she was on that road or her reason for being there. She'd gone to prevent Trey from revealing a secret that could mean possible ruin for the father of her child and the man she loved, and now his lips were forever sealed. She must keep her whereabouts this afternoon from John, too. He would never believe her capable of murder, but he'd known there was murder in her heart when he left her. No need to give him worry that the police had reason to suspect her of the crime.

He and Will would be arriving in less than an hour, and she must look and act as if she did not know that Trey was dead. This was to be a joyous and memorable night when Will finally met his father. She would not let Trey in death—as he'd done so often in life—destroy this precious moment in their lives. When Randy came to question her she'd say she'd left the café early to prepare dinner for her son and Father John to celebrate a special occasion. How could he know that her famous lasagna and cheesecake that usually took hours to prepare had been put together and frozen on a winter day when she was in the mood to cook?

*   *   *

DEKE WAS SURPRISED TO FIND nearly a full house attending mass on a Friday night. He was of Presbyterian stock himself and couldn't imagine attending church at any other time than on Sunday, certainly not on the last night of the workweek. Friday nights were for kicking back and unwinding at home unless it was high school football season. It must be the June moon, he decided, having no choice but to take a seat in one of the front pews.

He was late, and the service had well begun. John Caldwell sat on the left of the altar in his white vestments, and Deke drew a surprised stare from him as he came down the aisle. For a long second, their gazes engaged, John's registering a small shock, Deke's open and candid. Deke thought he'd aged slightly since he last saw him.

Then Father John began his sermon—the homily, Deke believed it was called.

Immediately Deke understood that the full moon had nothing to do with it. What drew the crowd was the priest behind the pulpit and the relevance of his simple but eloquent message. In Deke's church in Amarillo, the congregation was restless, easily distracted, oftentimes downright noisy, but not here. In St. Matthew's, only an occasional soft cough disturbed the listening hush and

603

concentration on Father John's words, enhanced by the strong sincerity in his voice.

Deke stirred uncomfortably. How could Father John ever be replaced? How would these parishioners ever trust a priest again once they lost their belief in a spiritual leader like John Caldwell? These were faith-shattering times. The Catholic Church was already reeling from allegations of sexual abuse by its priests, not to mention the scandals of corruption and greed that had caused the loss of belief in the country's most revered government leaders and financial institutions.

Not for him to agonize over, Deke reminded himself, ignoring a spate of remorse. John Caldwell, however young he'd been, whatever his justification at the time, had helped to cover up either a murder or an accident and assigned a loving set of parents to a lasting hell on earth.

The moment came that he'd been waiting for. He watched Father John withdraw a water glass from a recess in the altar and drink from it. He slipped it back before raising his white-robed arms to the congregation. "The peace of the Lord be with you always," he intoned.

"And also with you," the congregation responded.

Deke recognized this part in the order of the service as the passing of the peace, the place where the congregation greet one another by embracing or shaking hands. To his surprise, Father John left the altar and approached him.

"The peace of Christ be with you, Sheriff."

Shaken a bit, Deke said, "And also with you, Father." The look in John's eyes made him think of Judas at the Last Supper. *"Is it I, Lord?"*

"You have spoken."

Finally, the mass drew to a close and Father John gave the blessing from the center of the chancel, then followed the altar boys down the aisle to greet his parishioners at the door. While they filed out, Deke waited by his pew until he was alone at the front of the church. No one saw the former sheriff of Kersey County quickly take the two steps to the altar, remove Father John's drinking glass, then as quickly let himself out the side door.

It was the next morning when the Women of the Altar Society came to clean the church that they noticed Father John's monogrammed glass was missing.

Chapter Fifty-Eight

Will arrived first. At his insistence, Cathy kept the doors locked, even when she was home. Since he was a child, Will had shown a somewhat irrational fear of something happening to her—natural, Cathy supposed, to a boy growing up with only one parent. His eventual wife might view his vigilance of his mother as an annoyance, but she would deal with that problem when it arose. She had poured a glass of wine and was trying to relax when he sat on the doorbell, sending the Westminster chimes into a furious jangling.

"Coming! Coming!" she called, going to the door on legs still shaky from the afternoon's trauma. Her heartbeat had gradually slowed, but it started to race again when she saw her son's face. His cheeks were flushed, and he looked as if he'd been crying. "Goodness, darling, what's the matter?"

"Mama—"

He hadn't called her Mama since kindergarten.

"What is it, Son? Tell me."

He scrutinized her with a look of anguish. "Where were you this afternoon? Bebe said you'd left the café around one o'clock."

"Why, here at the house, preparing dinner." She gestured toward the dining room where the table was set with her best china and a centerpiece of flowers from her garden. The aroma of bubbling lasagna filled the house. "We're having your favorites," she said. "Lasagna and cheesecake."

"Did you go anywhere else?"

Cathy felt herself go cold. It was as if he *knew*! "Why do you ask?"

"I called you here, and you didn't answer."

"Why, I—I suppose I was outside cutting flowers."

He squinted at her. "You didn't hear the phone ring?"

"How could I? I was in the far backyard."

"I left a message on the answering machine."

His tone implied that if she'd been home, she would have noticed. What was going on here?

"I wasn't expecting a call so I paid no attention."

"You always check your messages when you come in."

Her patience was at an end. It was true she listened to her messages first thing when she got home, but today they were the last habit on her mind. "Well, today I didn't," she said, her tone sharp. "Why all these questions, Will? What's got you so upset?"

Will pushed a hand through his hair—not for the first time, from the disheveled look of it. "I was afraid…you might have gone to Harbison House to see…my father," he said. "I thought— Oh, Mama, you didn't drive out there, did you?

He'd left the front door wide open. Closing it gave Cathy a second's opportunity to compose an answer. She had never outright lied to her son. Small fibs, yes, to avoid hurtful truths when he was a child, but never a deliberate lie. "Well, Son, you've caught me out," she said, turning to him. "Yes, I did, but before I got to Harbison House I lost my nerve and turned around and came back. I was reluctant to tell you because I…didn't want you thinking your mother was a fool."

She could see relief flood his face, and he reached out and hugged her roughly to him. "I would never think you were a fool," he said. "I was just afraid that…"

"I know what you were afraid of," Cathy said,

smothered against the blue denim. "I was, too. That's why I turned around and came home. I couldn't trust my feelings. I didn't know but that Trey could still throw his charm around like lightning bolts." She extricated herself. "Now let's have some wine."

"Don't mind me," he said. "I'm just having a problem with knowing my father has…left us without saying good-bye. It's got me crazier than I'd like to admit."

She brushed his curly forelock in place. "Well, I think Father John and I can make you feel better about that."

Cathy was relieved that Will preferred not to watch television while they waited for John. The local network had no qualms about interrupting a program to bring breaking news to its viewers. But they were both nervous as neurotic cats, neither able to sit still. Cathy unnecessarily busied herself in the kitchen and Will roamed about with his hands in his pockets, often peering out the big front window into the night. Cathy wondered with a skipped heartbeat if he was still looking for Trey to drive up. Conversation lulled between them, and Cathy constantly checked her watch. *What was keeping Father John?* To calm her anxiety, she concentrated on the wonderful moment Will would learn that John was his father.

Finally, she heard the Silverado and hurried to

the front door. What she wouldn't give to crawl between the sheets with John tonight, if only to be held and comforted against the horrors tomorrow was sure to bring. As it was, she could not resist throwing herself into his arms as she'd never done. Will, too, seemed unusually glad to see him, hugging him rather than shaking his hand, and they clung to one another in the foyer like a family reunited after a disaster.

"Well, that was quite a welcome," John said as they broke apart to adjourn to the living room and the wine carafe.

Cathy slipped her arm through her son's. She could wait no longer. They all needed relief from the tensions twisting their nerves into corkscrews— John from what he feared he'd face later tonight; she the dread of a police investigation tomorrow; and Will, his angry disappointment in being deserted once again by the man he thought was his father.

"Will is distraught tonight over Trey leaving without trying to contact him, Father John," she said. "Shall we put his mind to rest about that before we have dinner?"

"I think that would be a good idea," John said, grinning at Will.

Will glanced from John to his mother. "What are you guys talking about?"

"Maybe you'd better sit down, Son, and we'll tell you," John said.

"I'VE GOT BAD NEWS FOR YOU, Deke," Charles informed the former sheriff of Kersey County when he opened the door to let him into the Crime Laboratory Service of Amarillo.

"What's that?"

"Randy Wallace was on his way here with the evidence bag when he got called to a crime scene in his county. He'd have called you, but he didn't have your cell number."

Deke let out a tired sigh. "Damn. Now I'll have to wait until Monday morning for you to compare the prints on the glass in this sack to those in the evidence bag."

"I'm afraid so, and maybe not even then. Randy's going to be tied up investigating his homicide."

"Homicide?"

"Yep. Somebody got himself murdered. He didn't say who."

"Probably some victim of a barroom fight."

It was a few minutes till nine. Walking to his car from the crime lab, Deke felt he'd lived a lifetime since meeting with Trey Don Hall at eleven that morning. He was tired to the marrow of his bones, and his heart had never felt heavier. It didn't matter that he'd been unable to get the prints on the glass compared to the ones on the cord. He knew they would match, and the weekend would give him time to come to terms with what he had to do. His only regret was that TD Hall would be back in San Diego when Randy confronted John with the evidence—maybe arrested him—and Deke hadn't wanted him to face the music alone.

He had not let Paula know he was back in Amarillo because he'd expected to return to Delton to be with Randy when he approached John and Trey tonight. He expected a cool reception and no supper when he got home, but he longed for the solace of Paula's presence and a good night's sleep beside her in his own bed.

He rang the bell rather than startle her when he walked in unexpected, and she surprised him with a big hug and expressions of concern over his obvious fatigue. "Your daughter called to warn me that you've gone temporarily bonkers," she said.

"And what did you reply?" he asked, looking tenderly into her face, reminded once again why he loved her.

She laughed. "I said I considered myself warned."

She made him toast and an omelet while he drank a beer. She did not ask what he'd been up to since depositing her at the house in the early afternoon. Deke knew she recognized his behavior from the days of his police work and that he'd tell her in good time what it was all about and if he did not that was fine, too. She'd never been curious about or interested in the dark side of his work, not from indifference but from fear she would never let him out of the house if she were aware of the evil and danger he faced. It was her job to provide a haven when he returned home, which she did without being sure of exactly what she was sheltering him from.

So, after his supper, she sent him on ahead to take a hot shower while she tidied the kitchen and listened to the ten o'clock news. Deke had just lathered himself with soap when, for the first time since leaving their youth, his wife threw open the shower door and stared at her husband naked and streaming under the showerhead.

"Well, for goodness' sakes, Paula!" Deke exclaimed in astonishment.

"Not what you think," she said. "It's Trey Don Hall. He's been found murdered."

Chapter Fifty-Nine

Cathy poured herself a cup of coffee and waited for calls from Will and Father John. It was ten o'clock, and she expected the phone to ring any minute. She'd kept the television turned off until John left a few minutes ago, right before Betty called from Harbison House looking for him. Will had gone shortly before that to stop by his girlfriend's.

"Trey Hall has been murdered," Betty said. "Turn on your TV. It's all over the news."

She'd clicked on the remote and all major channels were covering the story. Tapes were being shown of the crime scene shot earlier when the EMS and a sheriff's deputy had responded to a call from Lou Harbison, who'd discovered the body when he was returning to Harbison House after mass with a busload of children. Viewers were informed that the NFL quarterback's body had been taken to the medical examiner's office in Lubbock, Texas. Later footage showed a team of forensics personnel out of Amarillo with DPS (Department of Public Safety) written on their vests photographing tire tracks on the shoulders of the road where Trey's BMW was parked. She had been judicious in wiping out those of the Lexus. Will would hear the news at Misty's, John—unless he heard it on his truck radio—not until he came upon the police tape and the remaining investigative crew on the road to Harbison House. Cathy could imagine their initial shock. At least Will would suffer no grief. John would mourn, but after his son's jubilant and moving reaction to their announcement tonight he must surely be relieved that his secret was forever safe. He would rather endure his conscience—and those shadows he had never outrun—than sully the image of the father Will had finally found.

They had not been able to get fully into the evening. Will's joy at their news on what should have been the happiest night of his life had been clouded. Some inner turmoil still dragged at him through dinner and the champagne, tingeing the loving banter between father and son.

"What do you want me to call you?"

"Anything as long as it's not Daddy-o."

"Pa?"

"No."

"How about Papa?"

"How about not?"

"Daddy?"

"No."

"Dad?"

"That sounds about right."

An awkward moment had come when they discussed when, how, and where to make Will's paternity public—or if they should. Cathy knew that for the time being John was troubled by the possibility of his exposure and how the scandal would affect Will. Will had balked, too. "I don't want people thinking my mother hopped from one best friend's bed to another," he said, reddening. "Let's wait."

They'd tabled their decision for a later time. "I'm happy enough," Will said, looking with unabashed love at John, "to know that John Caldwell is my father."

They were cutting into their cheesecake when Will asked, "What time did you learn that Trey Hall was dying, Mom?"

Surprised, she'd said, "Your father told me early this afternoon. Why?"

"Before you drove out to see Trey?"

John pinned her with a startled look. "You saw Trey this afternoon?"

"No. I drove out to have a talk with him, but changed my mind and came home."

"Did anybody see you on the road?" Will asked.

All forks were suspended. Will and John were staring at her. Her flesh prickled between her shoulder blades. Once again, she had the distinct feeling her son knew something of the murder. But how could he? And now John had learned she'd been on the road to Harbison House this afternoon.

"What a curious question," she said. "I don't recall seeing anyone. Why do you ask?"

Will took a bite of cheesecake. "I...wouldn't want anyone to have seen you who knew Trey was staying at Harbison House. They might get the idea he was the reason you were going there."

It was a lame explanation, but she believed him. Her son was very protective of her reputation.

"Actually, as far as I know, Son, no one in town but your mother and Deke Tyson knew Trey was staying with me," John said.

John's remark had not seemed to appease Will, and when they learned of Trey's murder both would be deeply disturbed she'd been in the vicinity. They would have to believe she'd be suspected of the murder.

As the phone shrilled beside her she jumped and lifted the receiver immediately. "John?"

"You've heard."

"I'm listening to a news report now."

"Randy is downstairs. He hung around to question me. I'm grabbing a few minutes in my study to call you. I found a note from Trey that I'll turn over to him. He had changed his mind, Cathy. Trey wasn't going to go through with it."

Her cheeks stung. "Really?"

"Really. He endorsed Deke's check for Mabel's home over to the orphanage and simply left the house. Betty says she didn't know he had gone. I'm guessing he was on his way to the airport when... somebody shot him."

So John would have been safe in any event. "Did he explain why he changed his mind?"

"No."

But they both knew. She massaged her tightened throat. "Does Randy have any idea who killed him?" she asked.

"Trey was shot outside his BMW. Randy thinks he got out to meet somebody in another vehicle— a friend or someone Trey knew or recognized he would have stopped his car for."

Somebody like her. "I'm so sorry it had to happen this way, John, but from the news report, death was instant, and now he won't suffer as he was likely to if he'd lived. Perhaps it's a blessing."

"Not to the person who killed him. Cathy... I have an idea Randy will want to question you."

"Because I'm their chief suspect? What's my motive? From the news reports, Trey was killed between six and seven. You'd already told me he was dying hours before. What would have been the point of killing him?"

She paused, expecting to be reminded that she had another motive unknown to the police.

"When did Will get to your house, Cathy?"

She stiffened in her chair. "Why do you ask?"

"I overheard Randy tell his deputy that the crime lab people had successfully lifted a clear set of Jeep tracks they found across the road from Trey's car."

Going cold, Cathy tried to recall who drove Jeeps in town. None with a motive to kill Trey Hall. The owners didn't even know him. Her terror building, she knew in her bones those tracks belonged to Will. She recalled Will's distraught face, his agitation all evening, the odd looks he'd thrown her, the questions he'd asked. *"Where were you this afternoon? What time did you learn that Trey Hall was dying, Mom?"*

Good lord! She'd misinterpreted Will's concern. It wasn't that he feared for her reputation if she was seen on the road to Harbison House this afternoon but that she had no alibi for the time of Trey's murder. But how could he have known she'd need one...

"Cathy? Answer me. I have only a minute before I have to talk to Randy."

"Oh no...," she whispered, rigid as the stone garden sculpture bathed in moonlight outside her window.

"Cathy—"

She replaced the receiver.

Her legs were too unsteady to stand. Will had parked over the wiped-out treads of her Lexus, the reason for the Jeep's clear impressions. He must have left his office early to go to Harbison House to confront Trey. He came along after her and found the body. Cathy pressed her fingers to her mouth. *Did her son suspect her of murdering Trey Don Hall!*

But the police would think he could have done it. If he signed out early, the log sheet and the Jeep tracks would be enough for Randy to suspect him, and she knew her son was innocent.

If they charged him, she would confess to the crime. She had blood on her sweater sleeve as proof she did it, and her motive to kill Trey was stronger than Will's. Her son was not aware that Trey wasn't his father until after he'd been killed, but she had known, and she'd murdered him out of an uncontrollable rage. Father John could confirm her fury. The authorities would have no choice but to believe her, but first, she must get rid of the gun. Its disappearance would be further proof of her guilt. She'd get rid of it so that if she was suspected of killing Trey, the murder weapon wouldn't be found.

The phone rang again. She glanced at the caller identification screen. *Will!* But she could not trust herself to speak to him now, and she must hurry to find a place to dispose of the gun.

Chapter Sixty

The shotgun killing of nationally known football celebrity Trey Don Hall took precedence over
other cases pending for the attention of the Lubbock Medical Examiner's Office as well as plans its
pathologist may have had for Saturday. The same
held true for Charles Martin in the crime lab of the
Department of Public Safety in Amarillo. In joint
efforts, an autopsy was performed and evidence
from the murder scene analyzed, and by noon
Randy Wallace was in possession of both departments' findings. Trey Don Hall had been shot with
a .30-30-caliber hunting rifle. Clear sets of fingerprints, other than the victim's, were found on his
leather watchband, probably made by the killer
when he or she folded Trey Don Hall's hands across

his chest. DNA had been extracted from tearstains found on the victim's silk shirt close to the entry of the bullet. In addition there was the mold made of the Jeep tracks found on the other side of the road from where the body was found. No results of the analysis reports were to be released to the press.

The news media descended immediately, arriving like rodents scuttling out of woodwork, filling up the county's few motels and milling about in Bennie's, the newspaper office, and the sheriff's department. To interview Will Benson, Randy and Mike, his deputy, both wearing baseball caps rather than their uniform Stetsons, drove out of the department's parking lot in Randy's personal car so they wouldn't be recognized and followed by "the paparazzi," as he referred to them in disgust.

The reason for his trip to question Will was simple. Will Benson was the only person in town who owned a Jeep with a motive to kill Trey Don Hall, weak as it was. His mother had a motive, but she did not drive a Jeep. Randy couldn't fathom either one of them killing anybody. Cathy Benson was one of the most levelheaded women alive, and Will was one of the few boys who'd grown up in the county who did not hunt and probably owned no gun. Success was the sweetest revenge of all, and both mother and son had certainly exacted that from the man who'd deserted them. They might let him choke on their accomplishments, but why kill him?

But he had to start somewhere, and he had a couple of reasons to drive out to Will's place this morning. The Jeep tracks constituted one, but earlier he had wakened Linda Hadley, the receptionist at the Morgan Petroleum Company, from a Saturday sleep-in to ask what time Will Benson had left work yesterday. He did it with regret, since Linda had the loosest tongue in town and was sure to start rumors that the sheriff was investigating Will. The boy had suffered enough from the slings of gossip in this county, but he was following Deke Tyson's line of thought. If Will had gotten off at his regular time at six o'clock, he could save himself the trip and eliminate him as a suspect.

But, by George, Linda had told him that Will had signed out at five thirty, unusual for him, since he followed company rules to the letter, she said. That would have given him plenty of time to be on the road at the time TD was killed. Linda had also volunteered one other interesting piece of information. She'd said that Cathy Benson had paid an unexpected visit to her son yesterday at noon. Now *that* was definitely unusual. Randy ate his lunch at Bennie's, and he couldn't recall a time, except yesterday, that Cathy wasn't overseeing the café at that time of day. When he'd asked Father John for the names of those who knew Trey was staying at Harbison House, he'd said he couldn't say for sure.

"Well, then, name the people you can say," Randy had told him.

"Deke Tyson and...Cathy Benson," he'd answered reluctantly. "Betty didn't learn Trey would be here until noon today."

"And when did Cathy learn the news?"

"This morning."

It sounded reasonably certain to Randy that Cathy would have gone in person to deliver the shocking news to her son that his deadbeat father was in town. It also made sense that Will would want to meet him. Also—Randy found himself thinking like Deke Tyson again—there was the way Trey Hall's hands had been folded over his body and the tearstains on his shirt. Folding those hands and crying—didn't that sound like something a son, still feeling something for his father, would do after he'd killed him?

"Fancy a handsome bachelor like Will Benson renting a place way out here when he could be living the party life in that new apartment complex in town," his deputy commented as Randy parked in front of a ranch house that looked to have been built in the days of Indian raids and buffalo herds.

"He wanted a place to keep a couple of horses and provide room for his dog to run," Randy said. The place suited what he knew of the boy from the years his son and Will had played on the high school baseball team. Will had seemed somewhat of a loner even then, favoring quiet and solitude and his animals to hanging out with his rambunctious buddies. As a father, Randy had deduced the boy's preference for his own company was formed by the circumstances of his birth.

Silently Mike pointed out the Jeep Wrangler parked in a leaning carport attached to the house. Randy nodded and climbed the worn steps to the weathered wraparound porch. The door opened before he had a chance to knock. "Come in, Sheriff," Will said. "I heard you drive up. I was...sort of expecting you."

The boy looked as if he hadn't had a wink of sleep. Randy hadn't, either, for that matter. "Sorry to disturb your Saturday, Will, but I've got a few questions to ask you."

"I figured you would."

"I'm sorry for your loss, whatever it was."

"Not much," Will said, sticking his hands into his jean pockets. "You guys want a cup of coffee?"

"Sure could use one," his deputy said.

Randy nodded agreement. "Sounds good."

The men sat down, and a dog padded up wagging his tail, a blue-eyed Siberian husky. He gave their boots a cursory sniff, then followed Will into the kitchen off the main room. When Will returned with three steaming mugs, Randy took his carefully; while aware he could not remove it from the premises without a warrant, he'd thought of another way he could legally get a sample of Will's fingerprints.

"Will," he began, pulling his handkerchief from his back pocket, "we've got to look at you and your mother as the only folks in town who might have a reason to kill your father."

"I can understand that, but my mother wouldn't kill a rattlesnake, and I'd be pleased if you didn't refer to Trey Hall as my father." Will sat down, his strong, finely shaped hands—his batter's hands—cradling the mug.

"Good enough. And knowing you, I have a hard time believing you were involved, but I've got to do my job and ask where you were yesterday between six and seven o'clock. Excuse me a second—" He set down his cup and sneezed hard into the handkerchief.

"I was at my mother's," Will said when Randy had recovered. "She made dinner for Father John and me."

Randy coughed deeply, covering his mouth with his fist. "The whole time?"

"Most of it."

"Oh? What time did you leave Morgan Petroleum?"

Randy, getting ready to sneeze again and ignoring his deputy's puzzled look, noted a small hesitation. "I took off early," Will said. "Around five thirty or so."

"Why?"

"I was upset. Mom drove out to tell me Trey Hall was in town, and I kept hoping he'd come by to see me or telephone, but he didn't."

"Did you go directly to your mother's from there?"

"No, I drove out here, fed my animals before I drove to Mom's. I'd guess I got there somewhere around close to seven."

Randy loosened his black uniform tie. "Can anybody vouch for you out here?"

Will shook his head and looked down at his dog, plopped on the floor beside his chair. "Nobody but Silva here. Sheriff, are you okay?"

"I'm fine," Randy said, clearly looking as if he wasn't. He blinked hard, as if his eyes were stinging. "And your mother? She was home then?"

"Of course. She'd been cooking all afternoon."

Over the handkerchief he'd plugged to his nose, Randy twinkled a friendly smile, "Didn't bring anything home from the café?"

Will returned a slight grin. "Everything made from scratch—lasagna and cheesecake—right in her kitchen."

"All right then, that should do it—" Randy started to get up, then clutched his chest, the coffee mug rolling to the floor. The dog and Will leaped to their feet. "No, no!" he gasped, thrusting out a hand to prevent the husky from jumping on him. "Stay back."

"Randy!" the deputy cried. "Are you having a heart attack?"

"No! No! I'm...allergic to dogs."

"Why didn't you say so?" Will demanded. "What can we do for you?"

Randy coughed loudly. "Water. I need water. My throat's on fire."

"Put Silva outside while I get him some water," Will ordered Mike, dashing for the kitchen. There was the sound of water blasting from the faucet, and Will was back in seconds with a Styrofoam cup, which Randy, standing, grabbed by its bottom and drank with great thirst.

Breathing heavily, Randy said, "I apologize, Will. I thought I'd gotten beyond it," and headed for the door as if in desperate need of fresh air.

"You want me to call a doctor?" Mike asked when they were outside.

"No, I just need to get away from the dog." He tossed Mike the keys. "You drive. Will, thanks for your time. I'm sure there'll be no need to bother you again."

As they drove away, the deputy said, "I didn't know you were allergic to dogs, Sheriff."

"Lots about me you don't know, son," Randy said, fully restored and carefully holding the rim of the cup by his handkerchief.

Chapter Sixty-One

Will watched the squad car disappear in a cloud of dust. Had he just been duped? Had Randy's allergic fit been a ruse to get a sample of his fingerprints? He'd given the Styrofoam cup to him willingly. His deputy would testify to that. The cup was not an object of an illegal search, but as long as he'd known Sheriff Wallace and his family, he'd never heard anything about his being allergic to dogs.

Silva came to sit beside him, his expression asking pitiably if he was in trouble. "No, boy," Will said, bending down to scratch his ears, "but I may be."

Like a fool he'd left his fingerprints on the wristwatch, his tears on the shirt. He should have removed them both. He had no alibi for the time of the murder. Sheriff Wallace had known he was lying when he accounted for his whereabouts. His regret and sadness for a longtime friend of his son's were unmistakable in his eyes.

Well, better he than his mother, Will thought, patting his leg for Silva to follow him back to the house so he could telephone his father.

They met at St. Matthew's in John's office. "What's this all about, Son?" John asked, hoping—praying, as he'd done all night—that he hadn't already guessed. The Jeep tracks and Will's generally known antipathy for Trey were enough to draw attention to him as a suspect. John had been in a sweat all night going over the names of every possible person who had the cold-blooded nerve and motive to kill Trey after so many years. Who besides Cathy and Will and Deke knew where Trey was staying? Who would Trey have known and stopped his car for? He wouldn't have recognized Will unless Will had flagged him down.

"I believe I'm going to be charged with the murder of Trey Don Hall," Will said.

John was preparing to pour coffee. Carefully he replaced the pot to its burner beside the empty cups. Images of Pelican Bay Prison flashed into his mind.

"Confessions given to a priest, even if he's a suspect's father and the son's not a Catholic, can't be used in court, can they, Dad?" Will asked.

God have mercy, John thought, his ear picking up on Will's natural use of *Dad* through the boom of his heartbeat. *Was his son about to confess to the murder of Trey Don Hall?*

"No, Son," he said.

"Then let's go into the confessional."

Behind the wine velvet curtain of the confessional, through the grill, Will blurted, "I didn't kill him, Dad. You've got to believe me."

"I do, Son. I do," John said, for a moment dizzy from relief, "but why do you feel you have to assure me of your innocence in the confessional?"

"Because I think I know who did."

"Really? Who?"

"Mom."

"*What?* Why on earth would you think that?"

Will's face darkened. "I don't want to think it. I can't *bear* to think it, let alone say it out loud."

"Okay, Will, take a deep breath, and tell me why you suspect your mother."

Will described his discovery of the body, which satisfied John's worry over the presence of the Jeep tracks, a detail not yet released to the press. He could imagine the boy's shock and despair, his pain when he knelt beside the still form of the man he'd thought was his father. At such a moment, he would not be thinking of fingerprints or tread markings or DNA. "But why didn't you call nine-one-one?" he asked.

Will averted his eyes. "Because...because of Mom."

"Because she was on the road where Trey was killed?"

"Because I thought she may have been involved."

John struggled to subdue his panic. "And what made you think that?"

Will's tone grew bleaker. "I...saw her yesterday evening about six fifteen at the intersection to the road to Harbison House. She had come from that direction and was stopped at the light. I was at the gas station across the street. She didn't see me."

"But she admitted she'd gone to see Trey and changed her mind."

"Yeah, well, if that were all, she wouldn't have looked so strung out. She looked like she'd seen... a murder. I thought that maybe she'd gone to start something again with Trey. She'd changed out of her smock and was all dolled up, but from her face I thought he'd rejected her again, and that's when I went to have it out with him and...came across the body. The bullet hole looked like a rifle shot to me—like the kind that old .30-30 of Great-grandmother's would make."

The confessional was suddenly too confining

and stuffy. "How do you know she didn't turn around before she came to the body?"

"Because I know my mother. Her public expression is trained. It takes a lot for it to slip. She'd been crying and looked pale as a lily."

John reflected back on the evening. Cathy and Will had not seemed themselves. He'd attributed their agitation to the emotional upheaval of the day, but they'd been going through travails deeper than his.

"Have you spoken with your mother since last night?"

"No. I telephoned right after the news broke, but she didn't pick up, and her cell was off. I had to leave a message. I've been worried about that ever since. She may have simply not wanted to talk to me right then. I can't imagine why she'd leave the house unless...it was to get rid of her grandmother's rifle."

Will had reason to be worried. After Randy had left, he'd called Cathy, too, and gotten the answering machine. Concerned out of his mind, he'd gunned the parish truck back to her house, but the place was dark. There was no answer to the bell and no way to tell if her Lexus was in the garage. He'd left, hoping she'd closed herself away to deal with Trey's death in her own way. It was completely unlike her to shut him out, especially now, but he'd had to hope that's all there was to it.

"You didn't try to call her this morning?" John asked.

"No, because...there's more," Will said, and related the early morning's episode with the sheriff. "When Randy compares my prints on the cup to those I left on the body, he'll have all the evidence he needs to arrest me. I didn't kill Trey Hall. I'm telling you that under the seal of the confessional, but if I'm charged, I'm going to say I did it."

"Will, listen to me!" John threw back the grill. "You have done nothing wrong, and neither has your mother. You can't even for a second believe she's capable of murder—"

"I don't, but the police may."

"They'll have to prove it, and there's nothing to put her at the scene of the crime. She probably came upon the body same as you did, which was the reason she looked upset, so there's no need to confess to something you didn't do. If Randy comes for you, say nothing—not one word—until I get you a lawyer. Your actions were perfectly reasonable, and your failure to call the police understandable. You did what any son would do who found his father lying beside the road and was afraid his mother would be charged with the crime. Your mother had no reason to kill Trey. Remember she knew he was dying."

"But *I* didn't know until after I found the body," Will reminded him. "When Randy finds that out"—he shook his head hopelessly—"it will be one more nail to hammer into my coffin."

John massaged his forehead in thought. Will was right. An autopsy would reveal Trey's cancer. Randy would ask when Will had learned of Trey's terminal illness. While the time frame of that information would serve in Cathy's defense, it wouldn't in Will's.

His father could always lie for him, of course—a bad option. He'd sell his soul to protect his son, but as John well knew, lies beget lies that snared and entangled when the truth had the chance of setting you free.

"And by the same token," Will said, "I didn't know Trey wasn't my father until after he was dead. I've been thinking that if that information gets out, won't it make my motive to kill him look even worse if I go to trial? I killed a man out of vengeance for being a lousy father when he wasn't my father at all?"

"W-w-w-ell, I—," John stammered, rendered at a loss by Will's astute reasoning. If he and Cathy announced the truth of Will's paternity, they'd be adding weight to the murder charge. He didn't dare lay claim to his rightful son publicly, at least not yet.

"Randy is not going to find that out," John said. "We're going to keep that information under our hats. Somebody killed Trey. It wasn't you, and it wasn't your mother. I repeat, Will, under no circumstances are you to admit to a murder you didn't do. We have to keep the faith that the killer will be discovered." He pointed to his neck and tried to grin. "I don't wear this collar for nothing."

"I hope it carries a lot of weight with the man upstairs," Will said, but his eyes betrayed his doubt.

When Will had gone, John went to his office and telephoned a fellow Jesuit and graduate of Loyola University who was practicing criminal law in Lubbock. After he related the details of his concern, the attorney said that yes, Will's arrest was probably imminent and to let him know when he was taken into custody. He would leave immediately for Kersey.

John wandered back into the nave of the church and sat down in the same spot he'd occupied all those afternoons ago following the one that had changed his life forever. He'd not filled the seat since. Today he went to it automatically, the site where he'd poured out his greatest anguish and fear. Here in this eighteen-inch expanse he'd found peace. Here he'd found the answer he was seeking for his life. With the same desperate hope for deliverance, he knelt on the prayer bench and pressed his clenched hands to his forehead, but he could not pray past his horrible memories of Pelican Bay Prison or the mental image of his son confined in such a hell.

If Will was charged, Cathy would admit to the crime. John had no doubt of that. She would sacrifice herself rather than allow her innocent son to be found guilty of murder. The motive she'd give would be simple: She'd hated TD Hall. She'd never reveal her real motive for wanting him dead for fear of exposing Father John Caldwell, and Will had pointed out a reason she could not use his paternity as cause to kill him. It was doubtful the police would buy her confession in light of the evidence against Will, but it would certainly raise the possibility in the county that she was the killer.

For the first time in his ministry, John found he could not sincerely pray, *Thou will be done.* He wanted *his* will done, and that was to see the real killer found and his son and Cathy exonerated. God's will was always right but not always just.

John returned home to hear from Betty that Trey's lawyer, Lawrence Statton, would be flying in from California the next morning and had requested a meeting with her and Lou that afternoon. "Now what do you suppose that's all about?" she asked.

Guilt, he could have answered. Trey had left them a sop in his will. "We'll have to wait to find out," he replied.

"He asked if you'd help him make funeral arrangements. Trey's to be buried beside his aunt," Betty said. "He also said that Trey had requested you officiate at his burial." She handed him a notepaper. "He's staying at the Holiday Inn on I-Forty. Got the last room. That's the number where you can reach him."

John took the slip of paper and studied it. What could he say over the grave of a man who even in his death continued to devastate his family?

Chapter Sixty-Two

The bishop of the Amarillo diocese had advised
John to say and do nothing concerning his admissions until he had time to consider his counsel. His
preliminary opinion was that John's act had been
committed before he took his vows and therefore
did not fall under the Church's purview to determine the course he should take.

As a result, Saturday evening John had resumed
his place as presiding priest at the celebration of the
mass at St. Matthew's when Sheriff Randy Wallace
filed a complaint with the county magistrate formally charging John Will Benson with the murder
of Trey Don Hall. He presented as probable cause
fingerprints from a Styrofoam cup the accused
willingly gave him at his residence that matched

the fingerprints taken from the scene of the crime. Warrants were issued for Will's arrest and a search of his property and vehicle for further evidence linking him to the crime.

The sheriff and his two deputies found him feeding his horses at sunset, Silva at his heels. After reading Will his rights and allowing him to call his mother and Father John, Randy left him to finish his duties while a deputy stood guard and he and Mike searched the house and Wrangler. The only gun found was a .22 rifle in the house, but the Jeep's glove compartment yielded a receipt for gas purchased in the vicinity where Trey Don Hall's body was found and on the date and time that corresponded with his murder.

"We're going to have to impound your Wrangler, Will," Randy said. "We'll need to compare your tire treads with a mold that we took at the scene of the crime."

"My keys are hanging inside the door," Will said.

"And your dog can come with us, if you like. Either Father John or your mother can pick him up at the department and take him home."

"What about your allergies?" Will asked.

"Oh, that was a temporary thing."

Chapter Sixty-Three

By Monday, Will Benson had been charged, arraigned, and released on bail. On Tuesday, Randy Wallace finally returned Deke's calls. His protégé had rightfully guessed that his mentor still had a bee up his butt about some crime Trey Don Hall may have committed when he was seventeen. What difference did it make now? The boy was dead.

Deke could appreciate that Randy had his hands full. A media frenzy had ensued when the Department of Public Safety in Amarillo disclosed full forensic and pathology reports to the public that included the shockingly ironic information that Trey Don Hall was dying from a brain tumor when he was shot and killed. This sensational news was followed by Cathy Benson, mother of the accused, also confessing to the murder of the former NFL football star. As proof, she produced a sweater with the victim's blood on its sleeve and maintained she had wiped out the tire tracks of her Lexus with a hand whisk broom kept in her car for sweeping the grave sites of family members. Her son had come along after her departure from the scene of the crime and parked in exactly the same spot opposite the victim's BMW, leaving discernible tread marks. What other reason would explain why that section of the shoulder was pristine when the rest of the area was too heavily scored for the police to take clear impressions? To corroborate her story, a farmer driving a tractor had reported seeing the top of a white car "going a mite fast" down the road about sundown. She'd thrown the murder weapon away and denied knowledge of the victim's inoperable brain tumor prior to the shooting. Against the irrefutable body of evidence against Will Benson, the district attorney had brushed off her confession as a mother's desperate attempt to save her son from prosecution.

Deke took Randy's call feeling disconcerted. His reason for bugging Randy was now a moot point that would remain undisclosed to the current sheriff. Randy could return the evidence bag dated November 4, 1985, to its proper place, and

the monogrammed water glass bearing the logo of
the Jesuit Order would remain in Deke's possession
until he decided what to do with it. Father John
Caldwell would not be investigated as an accomplice in the death of Donny Harbison.

Yesterday, Lou Harbison had shown up unexpectedly, looking as if years had dropped from his
face. He explained that he had brought Deke something he and Betty thought he ought to see. Deke
had taken him into his study.

"What is it, Lou?"

"Read it and see for yourself," Lou said, and
handed him a letter. "Trey Hall's lawyer gave it to
us. Trey wrote it when he learned he was dying.
He instructed Mr. Statton—that's the name of the
lawyer, awfully nice fella—to get it to Betty and
me upon his death."

Deke had read while Lou was speaking, his neck
hairs lifting. The letter, dated months ago, was a
confession from Trey Don Hall to Lou and Betty
Harbison that he was responsible for their son's
death on November 4, 1985. He explained the reason he was on the premises, described the fight,
and admitted hanging Donny's body in the barn
to simulate a death by autoerotic asphyxia. He was
writing the letter to assure them their son had died
bravely and was innocent of the impression Trey

had deliberately created to throw off an investigation. He asked them to forgive him.

Nowhere in the letter was John Caldwell's participation in the incident mentioned.

Feeling as if the air had been whacked from his lungs, Deke had coughed and handed the letter back. "That's it then. You and Betty can rest easier now that you know the truth."

"You always did think Donny's death wasn't what it seemed, didn't you, Sheriff? Betty and I have been grateful to you for that, and this proves you were right."

"For your sakes, I wish the case could have been solved earlier."

Lou had ducked his head sheepishly. "Oh, well, we all know why it wasn't, don't we, Sheriff, and of course we want to keep this letter a secret only you and Betty and I know about. For obvious reasons, Father John is never to know that we ... misled the Church about the cause of our boy's death, and ... I suspect it would mean trouble for you, too."

"Don't worry, Lou. This will stay between us. Trey didn't give any indication to you and Betty of the contents of the letter while he was with you?"

"Nothing but his mention of the rolling pin he refers to in it. Betty says he asked her if she'd gotten a new one. She wondered how he could have

646

known it was missing from all those years ago. She said she spoke to you about it."

"Yes, she did."

"She also said you'd asked her if Trey could have known we'd be out of town that day. That leads us to believe you knew he was involved in Donny's death. How was that? And why now?"

"It doesn't matter, Lou. You know the truth, and that's all that counts."

"That's a fact, thank the loving God. Too bad somebody had to go and kill him. We can't believe it was Cathy or Will. If whoever did it had only waited a while, he'd have died anyway."

Deke had pondered what he should do with the rest of his suspicions. Nothing, he decided. The Harbisons had their peace; Trey, his justice—of a sort. Father John could continue his good works and settle up with God in the afterlife, and Lou and Betty would not be denied their second son. John Caldwell had not escaped punishment for his part in the accident. Father John had suffered and would continue to suffer, if he knew anything about the man. Deke wasn't entirely easy about it, but he could live with it.

Nonetheless, he had a few things to say to Randy that the sheriff ought to hear. He put the receiver to his ear. "Will didn't do it, and his mother didn't, either," he said by way of greeting.

"Good morning to you, too, Deke, and I hope to God you're right," Randy said, "but what are you going by other than that crystal gut of yours?"

Deke picked up a press photo of the crime scene from other news clippings of the murder spread on his desk. "The Jeep tracks. They're parallel to the BMW parked on the opposite shoulder. Trey's body was found slightly to the rear of his vehicle as if—like you speculated—he was walking toward someone who had stopped behind him. If Will or Cathy had shot him, Trey's body would have fallen closer to the middle of his car. It's a small point, but an important one."

Dismayed silence greeted Deke's conjecture.

"One other small thing," Deke said. "It's a logical assumption that neither Trey nor the other driver recognized each other until they were fender to fender. In that situation, how would it be possible for them to come to fast, parallel stops? One would have to backtrack or stop farther up the road."

Randy let out a weary sigh. "Jesus, Deke."

"It's no proof of the Bensons' innocence, but you can't refute the location of the Jeep's tire tracks. I believe Cathy came on the scene first, found the body, parked on the opposite shoulder, got out, and felt Trey's neck for a pulse. That accounts for the blood on her sleeve. Will comes along later, suspects the worst, but takes a minute to grieve for his father and leaves his DNA and fingerprints."

"And his mother throws her rifle away so we can't prove it wasn't the murder weapon when she takes the blame for her son," Randy finished for him. "Holy cow, Deke, if neither one of them killed him, who the hell did?"

"I wish I could answer that. You're going to have to keep digging. Trey's lawyer is in town. The Harbisons can tell you where he's staying. Maybe he can give you some ideas. By the way, you can replace the evidence bag you've probably still got in your trunk. It's inconsequential now."

"I was thinking you'd come to that conclusion."

He had barely hung up when the phone rang again. He let Paula answer it and tilted his chair back to rake his memory for names of anyone in the county with motive to kill Trey after twenty-two years. The caliber of the rifle suggested some-one local. The question always went back to who knew Trey was staying at Harbison House.

Paula appeared in the doorway, pressing the portable receiver of the kitchen phone against her thigh. "This is your week for unexpected visitors. You'll never guess who's on the line asking to come talk to you."

Why did his wife, Deke wondered a little

irritably—after almost forty-four years of marriage—make him guess the name of the person calling when he couldn't possibly have a clue of who was on the other end of the line?

"Your aunt Maude from North Dakota," he said shortly.

"Aunt Maude died three Easters ago, and it was *South* Dakota," she said. "It's Father John."

"What?"

"I thought that would get your boxers in a twist," Paula said.

Deke snatched up the receiver on his desk. "John?"

"Good morning, Deke. I imagine this call is somewhat of a surprise."

Deke heard a click as Paula replaced the kitchen phone. "It is somewhat," he said, and waited, his breath held. He'd been wondering if they'd get back to that tense moment between them Friday night at mass when he'd snitched the glass. Every instinct in him had shouted that John had somehow sensed why he was there.

"I wonder if I could come see you today?" John asked. "I can leave now and be there in an hour. I'm convinced Cathy and Will are innocent, and I was hoping you and I could go over details the police may have overlooked, kick other possibilities around. Sheriff Wallace seems to think the case is sewed up."

"I share both your doubts and belief. How about if I meet you in Kersey? I have an appointment with Trey's lawyer this afternoon to sign some paperwork for Mabel's house."

"It would be better if I meet you at your home, Sheriff, in case the news media get wind of something in the air. Some of them are camped outside Harbison House, and it's important I see you as soon as possible."

"Come on then. I'll be waiting."

Well, well, Deke thought, as he hung up the phone. *"Come into my parlor,"* said the spider to the fly.

Chapter Sixty-Four

You look a little...wasted," Deke pronounced in a tone of surprise when he opened the door to him.

"It shows, huh?" John said. It didn't take much for him to shed pounds he could ill afford to lose. His last attempt at eating a meal had been Friday night, when he'd done little justice to Cathy's lasagna and cheesecake, and he'd hardly slept since. He knew he looked drawn and weary in his black suit, a man of the cloth who'd lost his faith.

"You look like you've missed a couple nights' sleep, not to mention a meal or two."

"You're an observant man, Deke Tyson. Hello, Paula."

Paula had come up behind Deke, and her expression, too, widened slightly. John recalled they'd met last at a christening in May at St. Matthew's when the world had been sunny and bright and this blight on the land unforeseen. She rebuked her husband with a swipe of her kitchen towel. "Don't mind Mister Blunt here, but I bet you could use a good helping of my daughter's fabulous chicken casserole I've made for lunch."

"Paula, babe, I don't think John's here to eat lunch."

"Well, then, how about a glass of my good sun tea?" she asked, quick understanding of the seriousness of the occasion in the look she shot each man.

"That would be nice," John said.

They settled in Deke's overstuffed study. "Thanks for seeing me at such short notice," John said, alert to anything in Deke's manner that would explain his unexpected appearance at mass Friday night.

"Things pretty tough in Kersey, Father?"

"Very. Cathy has closed the café indefinitely and Will has to report to a preliminary hearing in the morning. Swarms of reporters are in town. Odell Wolfe laid into one with his whip, and the reporter is pressing charges. Odell is sixty-five years old, for goodness' sakes."

"I thought Odell had retired Ol' Bull."

"He did, but it's back in action—or was until

Randy confiscated it. What's so disappointing and sickening is the general attitude of the county." John did not hide his disgust. "People understand Cathy's and Will's grievances against Trey, but they have no problem believing that one or the other killed him."

"That doesn't surprise me. People rarely surprise me anymore—sometimes, but not often," Deke said.

John heard a world of meaning in that statement and it seemed directed at him, but before he could interpret it Paula entered and placed a tray with a pitcher of iced tea and glasses on Deke's desk. "Enjoy, boys," she said, and patted John's shoulder encouragingly before she left the room.

"You've got a good one there, Deke," John said, taking a glass.

"The best. What's on your mind?"

There it was again, John thought—the clipped, almost unfriendly tone he'd first picked up on during their earlier telephone conversation. His ear had not mistaken it. He would get to the source of it later. He indicated the news articles. "It's good to see you're following the case."

"Such as it is."

"Exactly. This case has not been properly investigated, despite the evidence collected against Will."

"That's what I told Randy a little while ago when

I spoke with him. The evidence appears damning, but it's not clear-cut proof."

John released his breath and relaxed a little as he crossed his legs and sipped the tea. He had known to come to Deke. Deke would get to the bottom of this. He hoped to convince him to conduct his own investigation. "I've arranged a good lawyer for Will. Any idea who may have done this?"

"Not a one. The question always goes back to who knew Trey was staying at Harbison House."

"That's what has Randy hung up. He believes the only people with a motive to kill Trey who knew where to find him were Cathy and Will, but suppose somebody spotted Trey in town Friday and followed him there, then later drove out to shoot him?"

Deke grunted agreement. "Sounds possible. Bobby Tucker mentioned seeing Trey in town about noon, and he told me that my darling daughter had made no secret that I was buying Mabel Church's house and meeting with Trey. When I questioned her about it, she said she couldn't remember where all she'd spread the news, and of course, her husband knew of the sale and our meeting, but I didn't mention to them or Paula or anybody else that Trey was bunking with you."

"Well, then, considering there were others

in town who knew of your meeting with Trey, shouldn't Randy and his deputies be trying to track them down for information that could lead to something?"

"It's what I would do."

John uncrossed his legs and leaned forward. "Deke, we all know that Trey was bound to have had enemies. Who's to say that somebody from out of the county didn't kill him? Someone in San Diego or Santa Fe or wherever he hung out that he told where he was headed and that person followed him here to kill him? Shouldn't the sheriff's department be canvassing the area for anyone who saw a stranger in town and motels for someone who rented a room for a day or so—just long enough to get the job done?"

"It's worth a shot," Deke said.

"And...I know this is grasping at straws, Sheriff," John said, hardly heartened by Deke's lack of enthusiasm, "but...what if there was a hit on Trey?"

He detected an amused twist of Deke's lips. "A paid assassin using a .30-30 rifle, Father?"

"I thought of that. I think it would be pretty clever to use a country bumpkin's weapon for the hit. Make the police think somebody in the county did it."

Deke gave him a wry look over his tea glass. "Well, it's been my experience, not firsthand, mind you, that hit men are not particularly interested in laying blame for a killing as long as they get away with it themselves."

Right, John thought, feeling foolish. He put up his hands to concede the absurdity of his suggestion. "Okay, so maybe that's a little far-fetched, but there have to be other rocks Randy and his deputies have failed to look under." Disappointed, he stared at the unforthcoming Deke. *But where and who and why?* The questions had hammered him like stones for almost four days, and he was defenseless against them. He'd come to Deke for answers, but he suspected even the canny and resourceful Deke Tyson would have no more success in finding them than Randy and his bunch. The murderer would forever elude the authorities. His son would be convicted of a crime he did not commit and a cloud of suspicion would hang over his mother the rest of her life.

He fell back in his chair, suddenly drained of energy, faith, and hope. His mind was numb from despair. He looked at Deke helplessly. "Do you have any ideas at all, Sheriff?"

"I'll look around, make inquiries. Like I said, I'm meeting with Trey's lawyer this afternoon. I'll question him about Trey's associates—those who might have had it in for him."

"His lawyer knew where Trey was staying?"

"But his lawyer knew he was dying, John."

Deke had heard the lift of hope in his voice, read his mind. Ashamed, John said, "Right. Scratch the lawyer as a suspect. As a man of the cloth, I hate thinking this way, but I'm frantic to save an innocent boy from going to prison and his mother from disgrace."

"Understood." Deke sipped his tea.

There was that short tone again, dismissive, not at all like Deke, who'd always held him in special affection and respect. He'd come in hope of a warm hand but been given a cold shoulder. Something was wrong. "Why were you at mass Friday night, Sheriff?" The question slipped out before he meant to ask it, but John had the eerie feeling, almost as if it had been delivered on angel's wings or the devil's fork, that Deke's appearance at St. Matthew's the night of the murder had some connection with Trey's death.

Deke got busy arranging the news clippings into a neat pile. "It doesn't matter now."

"*Everything* matters now," John said. "What's bothering you? Something is. I can tell."

"It has nothing to do with the case."

"Let me be the judge of that."

Deke paused in his assembling and addressed him with a stern eye. "Believe me, you don't want to be the judge of that."

John stood up. He'd known Deke a long time and he respected no man more, but he would not leave here without being told what was going on behind that hard stare. He put his hands on the desk and leaned down into Deke's face. "If it pertains to me or Trey or Will or Cathy, I need to know, Sheriff."

"You'll be sorry you asked, Father, and I'll be sorrier I answered. I wouldn't answer at all, if I wasn't sure what I have to say will never leave this room."

John plunked down again. "Tell me," he said.

Deke pushed his chair away from his desk, extended his legs, and locked his hands over his paunch. "All right. This may be my only opportunity to get the assurance I need to salve my old policeman's conscience."

"What kind of assurance?"

"The assurance of your innocence. Now be quiet and I'll tell you what I know and what I've conjectured since I discovered a stuffed bobcat in Mabel's attic on Friday after Trey left the house. It had a front paw missing—the same paw I found under the picnic table in the Harbisons' backyard on

November 4, 1985, when I investigated the hanging death of their son."

John's mouth had frozen open. His staring eyes had locked in their sockets. He felt like a man paralyzed who could feel every pain. A deep-throated clock struck the hour of eleven somewhere in the house. To his ears, the tones sounded like drum beats knelling his walk to the gallows.

Deke continued. "The limb is in an evidence bag in the Kersey County Sheriff's Department along with the extension cord used for the noose and some porno magazines found around the feet of Donny Harbison's suspended body. All the items I collected from that time, including my notes and interviews, are in it as well—preserved for the day evidence would surface to prove Donny didn't die from autoerotic asphyxia."

Deke's glare held no mercy and did not invite dispute, even if John had been capable of offering it. So he had not escaped the shadows after all. Trey's death had not delivered him.

"When I found that leg, and with a little unwitting help from Melissa," Deke went on, "I started putting two and two together. I took a football trophy of Trey's to the forensics lab in Amarillo to compare to the prints on the cord and magazines. They matched. There was only one set unidentified, but again, after some investigating, I had an idea who they belonged to."

"Mine," John said.

"If you're missing a water glass from the altar, I'm guilty. I pilfered it Friday night after mass to take to the forensics lab."

"And...the prints on the glass matched those on the cord?"

Deke shrugged. "Don't know. I never got that far by the time Trey was murdered. I still have the glass. You want to tell me what happened that November afternoon? What you say here stays here. That's a promise."

John had ceased to listen. Light had begun to dawn over the darkness of his despair, and as his brain began to grasp the gift Deke had handed him it burst forth full and glowing, transfixing him, blinding him, filling him with a happiness so great he could have kissed Deke's feet. God had not forsaken him. Once again, when his faith had faltered, God had lifted him up. He had given him a way to save his son.

Deke was saying, his tone now gently urging, "You can tell me, John. I'm thinking it all had to be that rapscallion Trey's crazy idea to go out to the Harbisons' that day and you went along to keep him out of trouble. I'm sure the autoerotic asphyxia idea was his, too, but what's bothered me about the case—about you, a Catholic—was the agony you let the Harbisons suffer all these years believing their boy died in such a shameful way."

John uttered a sound of jubilation and got to his feet. He threw back his shoulders and buttoned his clerical coat, a man with a weight no longer on his back. Deke rocked back at the sudden change in him.

"That's soon to be rectified, Sheriff, and the autoerotic asphyxia idea was mine, not Trey's, precisely for the reason that I was a Catholic. I'm going to tell Betty and Lou the whole truth of that afternoon when I get back to Kersey."

Deke stood hastily, nearly upsetting his tea glass. "No, that won't be necessary. The Harbisons already know the truth—or at least part of it. I can't tell you how I know, but I do. You've got to trust me on that."

"Oh, I trust you, Sheriff—completely. That's why I know you'll do your duty and take me in for killing Trey."

"*What?*"

"I killed Trey to keep him from implicating me when he confessed to the Harbisons how Donny really died." His voice came strong and confident. His strength had returned. "Trey was dying and didn't want our sin upon his conscience. He was going to tell the Harbisons everything when Lou brought the kids back from mass. I couldn't let that happen. The people's faith in me—in the Church—would be destroyed. I would lose everything I cherished—the Harbisons' affection, my parish, my ministry..."

Deke tore from around his desk. "Think what you're saying, John. Remember you're talking to a retired officer of the law. Why are you telling me this?"

"I can't let Will Benson go to prison. I can't let my son take the blame for something I did."

Deke's jaw dropped. *"Your son!"*

"Will Benson is Cathy's and my son."

Deke rolled back on his feet. *"What!"*

"That was another truth Trey came home to reveal. Trey was sterile and had been since he was sixteen from a bad case of the mumps. He kept the secret from Cathy and me and let us believe for twenty-two years that Will was his. She and I... had a moment during a time when Trey had broken up with her. So you see, I had plenty of motive to kill TD Hall."

Deke gasped, "I don't believe you."

"You don't have to. All that matters is that the jury does. Now, if Paula wouldn't mind, I'd like you to go with me to turn myself in to Randy. You don't have to bring along the water glass. I'll be glad to give you a sample of my fingerprints. And Deke, none of this will reflect against you. You had no proof in 1985 that Trey and I were guilty of the death of Donny Harbison."

Deke rushed to stand between John and the door. He put up his hands. "I can't let you do this. You were at mass when Trey was killed. You have an alibi."

"Not fifteen minutes before. Father Philip can attest that I was late for mass."

"But you didn't kill him," Deke moaned.

"My confession and that evidence bag will prove I did."

Chapter Sixty-Five

Members of the news media were still camped out in the parking lot of the Kersey County Sheriff's Department when John and Deke arrived in their vehicles. Scenting new fodder for their news stories at the appearance of the county's well-known priest and its former sheriff, the men had barely slammed their doors before microphones were stuck before their faces. John and Deke brushed them aside and made for the double glass doors, the reporters trailing in the wake of their "No comments."

Randy listened to John's confession with his mouth open in dumbstruck awe. The box containing the taped bag of Deke's articles of evidence from 1985 was on his desk, not yet returned to the storage locker. Only he and Deke were in the office. His other two deputies had gone to lunch.

"It's all in there, right, Deke?" John said, pointing to the clearly marked box.

Deke made a face and nodded.

Randy began to thaw from his frozen position. He squeezed his eyes shut and held up his hands like a man surrendering but expecting to be shot. "Let me get this straight. *You* are now confessing to shooting Trey Hall, Father John."

"That's right. You have all the evidence you need to arrest me. I had motive and opportunity. Will Benson is innocent."

"Your son."

"My son."

Randy pursed his lips. "Where's the rifle?"

Deke drew to listening attention. He'd been hoping for that question.

"What?"

"The rifle. The murder weapon. Where is it?"

"I...threw it away."

"Where?"

"Somewhere on the prairie."

"You possessed a .30-30 rifle, Father? What for?"

John looked perplexed. Deke and Randy exchanged glances.

"Tell you what," Randy said, getting up as if he

needed more breathing space. He hitched his gun belt to a more comfortable position. "I'll have to drive to Amarillo to get your fingerprints analyzed, then back." He set the paper sack containing the monogrammed glass in the evidence box. Deke had brought the glass along to avoid the embarrassment of John having to be fingerprinted in the sheriff's office. "Then if your prints bear out your story of being involved with the Harbison kid's death, I won't be able to get the paperwork done and a request for an arrest warrant until after lunch tomorrow. Mavis Barton gets her hair and nails done on Wednesday morning, and God help me if I disturb Her Majesty, the magistrate. You go on home, Father, until I can make heads or tails of this mess with the DA. Meanwhile, I imagine you and the Harbisons have something to discuss."

Deke drew Randy aside as John stepped into the hall. "About your chat with the DA, Sheriff," he said, lowering his voice, "I'd appreciate your keeping that part of John's confession between you and him until it's absolutely necessary to make it public."

"Believe me, I will. I'm sick to my gut about it. John may have had a humdinger of a motive, but if he killed TD Hall may worms eat my ass. A double-wide could pass through his story. However, I want you to look at something Trey wrote just before he died and left on John's desk." He unlocked a drawer and removed a plastic evidence bag containing an open note. Deke read the brief message. "For the kids. I'm leaving, Tiger. I've reconsidered and have decided not to go through with it. I'm trusting you to keep your silence as you always have. Spare me that blight on my name. I'd appreciate your prayers. Love to the end, Trey."

"Good God," Deke said.

"That note bears out John's statement, and with the evidence you collected and if his fingerprints are a match to those on the cord..." Randy looked in pain. "Even with two other suspects confessing to the crime..."

"John could be the one to hang," Deke said.

"Pray he gets a good lawyer."

Before leaving the building and to escape the cameras and microphones, Deke asked John to meet him farther up the road before John left for Harbison House and Deke for his appointment with Lawrence Statton.

When the black-suited figure got out of his Silverado, Deke couldn't resist comparing the man to the teenager who used to climb out of his old pickup in his letter-jacket days when his future had stretched before him like a plush red carpet. But for that afternoon in November and Trey Don Hall gumming up the works, would he be wearing the black and white of a Jesuit priest today or a Super Bowl ring? No matter. Whichever course he would have chosen, John Caldwell would still be walking on that red carpet.

"John, I have to tell you something," Deke said when they met between their vehicles. John's dread and pain from what he was about to do once he arrived at Harbison House were as clear as his own face in Paula's gleaming pans. "I swore I wouldn't, but I'm forced to for the sakes of Lou and Betty Harbison. When Trey learned he was dying, he wrote a letter that he instructed his lawyer to give them after his death. In it, he confessed to the accident and took full blame for Donny's death. Your name was not mentioned. Lawrence Statton brought it to them, and Lou drove to Amarillo yesterday to show it to me as proof I was right to question Donny's death."

John looked surprised. "Trey wrote them a letter? Well, then, that explains why Betty and Lou seem to be happier lately, despite what's happened. Donny's picture used to be partially hidden. Now it's on a shelf over the sink where Betty can look at it."

Deke took a step closer to John and squinted at him with the hope he could bore through his obstinate skull to a more reasonable mind. "They won't show you that letter because they are afraid you'll think less of them for concealing the circumstances of Donny's death from the Church. Let them have their peace as long as possible. It may be that—somehow, someway—they may never have to know of your part in it. Even if they were to guess Trey had an accomplice, they'll never suspect it was you."

"I don't see how my confession can be avoided."

"You're a priest, John. Have a little faith."

"I'm guilty, Sheriff."

"And I'm a monkey's uncle. Think over my advice. Hold off telling them as long as you can."

An hour later, Lawrence Statton capped the fountain pen with which he had signed the final papers on behalf of Trey D. Hall's estate giving Deke legal possession of Mabel Church's house. He was a small man dressed in a navy-blue pin-striped suit, his silk tie precisely knotted within the pointed collar of his crisp white shirt. It was an unseasonably warm day, and they were sitting in a picnic area along Highway 40, batting away flies and finishing cups of coffee Deke had picked up at Whataburger, but the attorney looked as fresh and dapper as if he had spent the last hour in the cooling room of a florist shop.

"Well, that's it, Mr. Tyson," he said. "I trust you and Mrs. Tyson will be very happy in the house."

"We'd have been happier if Trey hadn't met his death this way."

"I can certainly understand that," the attorney said. "I would have been happier putting Trey away with at least a little more fanfare, but I'm thankful his good friend, John Caldwell, has agreed to officiate at his burial. Trey thought the world of him. He seems like such a good man."

"He is a good man. When is Trey to be buried?"

"This afternoon."

Deke drew up in surprise. "Trey's to be buried this afternoon?"

"Yes. At six. Very private, very secret. I'm determined to keep the information from the media. The medical examiner's office in Lubbock was kind enough not to inform the press that his body has been released. It was sent to Jamison's Funeral Home last night. If I can just get Trey buried with the least possible fuss..." He whipped out an immaculate white handkerchief to clean his glasses and fixed Deke with a myopic gaze. "Do you suppose you might like to stay for the burial? Trey respected you. He didn't many people. He was most happy that you bought his aunt's house."

"At six, you say?" Deke glanced at his watch. It

was four o'clock. He had plenty of time to go to a florist and be back in time for the burial. "Sure I'll come," he said.

They shook hands and parted, Deke to order a funeral arrangement at Martha's Flowers in Kersey. "Red carnations," he said to the owner since he thought Trey would have liked the color red. "A big wreath of them."

"We're all out," Martha said.

"All out? I thought red carnations were a staple in a florist shop."

"Not when one customer comes in and buys all you have."

"Oh, I see. How about white ones then?"

Deke was early at the grave site. Lawrence Statton had not arrived. Typical of June evenings before dusk in the Panhandle, the constant wind had begun to subside along with the heat. There would be a pretty sunset. That was good. Deke carried the wreath of white carnations to an open grave beside Mabel Church's resting place. *Trey Don Hall* had been crudely written in cursive across the bar of a wooden cross that would serve as a marker until a tombstone could be erected in its place.

Deke took a seat on a stone bench. Across the cemetery the tempered wind rustled the floral tokens left to the dead in urns by loved ones or placed against tombstones. Most were artificial. A few were real, left to wilt and decompose in the sun. A distance away, he saw two graves side by side heaped with tributes of flowers still fresh. *Ah, there were his red carnations.*

He stared at the mounds reflectively for a moment, then got up and slowly walked toward them. An old familiar sensation thrummed in his brain. Even before he reached the ornately carved stones, he was fairly certain whose names were inscribed on them, who had bought the dozens of red carnations, and why. The card tucked among the blossoms convinced him. "Now, my darlings, rest in peace."

Deke let out a bereaved howl. *Fool! Fool! Fool!* How could he have been so blind not to have seen the obvious right in front of him?

Like a deranged man, he raced to his car, grabbed his cellular, and punched in Melissa's number. *Let her be home. Let her be home.*

She was. "Daddy?" she said in a voice that seemed perpetually filled with surprise when addressing her father these days.

"Melissa, I have something very important to ask you, and a lot depends on your answer. I want you to think back to the summer after your senior year in high school and tell me if my guess is correct."

A long pause. "Daddy, Mother and I are worried about you."

"*Melissa!*"

Deke stated his question.

"There were rumors to that effect among us kids," his daughter answered, "but out of respect for her parents, we kept our speculations to ourselves. They were hurting enough, and everybody else seemed to have bought the story. Would Trey have had anything to do with her? Not on your life. He despised the girl."

Oh, me, Deke thought, recalling the only line from literature he remembered from his high school English class. "Oh, what a tangled web we weave when first we practice to deceive."

Chapter Sixty-Six

The hearse was arriving, followed by Lawrence Statton's car, and Deke saw John's Silverado turning into the cemetery gate. He felt himself trembling when he went to meet the lawyer. "Mr. Statton, I'm terribly sorry, but some important business has come up that requires my immediate attention. I won't be able to stay for the burial."

Lawrence glanced around his shoulder at the white carnations. "Thank you for the wreath, at least. That was very kind of you."

"I have your number. I will call you later with news you'll want to hear."

"I won't allow my curiosity to delay you, but I'll look forward to hearing from you later. We could all use some good news."

Deke opened John's truck door almost before the Silverado rolled to a stop. "Did you tell them?"

"Tonight," John said, looking startled. "I decided to wait until tonight."

"Thank God." Deke blew out a noisy breath. "Well, don't say a word to them until you hear from me. I mean it, Father. You've got to trust me. Where can I reach you?"

"I'll be at Cathy's with Will until after dinner. We want to be together as a family before..."

"Stay put there. I'll need to speak with all of you."

"Deke, what's going on?"

"Can't say now. I'll tell you then. Don't move a muscle until you hear from me."

Ten minutes later, Deke pulled into the driveway of the house belonging to the murderer of Trey Don Hall. Behind one of the doors of the three-car garage, he was certain he'd find his wife's last white Lexus, the car the farmer saw from the seat of his tractor speeding away from the murder scene. The killer had gone expecting to shoot Trey at Harbison House and perhaps turn the gun on himself, but he had passed the object of his vengeance on the road. Recognizing the face behind the wheel, Trey would have pulled over immediately.

Deke felt a moment's pity for Trey in those final seconds of his life, the hurt and puzzlement he must have felt to see the gun raised against him by the idol of his youth. He withdrew a Colt Python from the glove compartment and slipped it inside his belt behind his back.

The door was a few minutes opening to the sound of the bell. Deke was surprised at the change in the man standing in the doorway. He was cleanly shaven and dressed in fine casual attire. He smelled of a recent shower and expensive cologne. "Hello, Coach," Deke said.

"Deke!" Ron Turner bellowed pleasantly. "How nice to see you again. You're just in time. Come in! Come in!"

"In time for what?" Deke said, stepping inside.

"I've just finished typing a letter, and you're the very man to deliver it. Come on back. Want some coffee?"

"A cup would be great, Coach, but isn't coffee somewhat of a departure for you?"

Ron threw him a smile over his shoulder. "Yeah, but sometimes a change is necessary."

There had been other changes since Friday, Deke noticed as he glanced around the kitchen and breakfast room. They looked freshly cleaned and put to rights, and sack after sack of beer and liquor bottles were stacked neatly beside the back door.

"Those are going out to the rubbish for pickup

tomorrow," Ron said, following Deke's glance. "Help yourself to coffee. I just need to slip my letter into an envelope. I won't be a minute."

He was back shortly, licking the flap of the envelope. "You mind delivering it for me?"

Deke studied him. Ron stared back, cool as mint except for a barely perceptible film of sweat on his upper lip. "Who's the letter to?" Deke asked quietly.

"Randy Wallace."

"Ah," Deke said, taking the letter. "It was about your daughter, wasn't it?"

"It was about Trey's *betrayal*!"

Ron's face suffused with emotion so violent, Deke thought a pinprick would have started a hemorrhage. *He's mad*, he thought. Alcohol and grief and blind belief in his own interpretation of events had destroyed his brain. "What do you mean?"

"I mean that I trusted Trey with Tara. I trusted him not to take advantage of her . . . weakness—out of respect to me, if not to her—and the son of a bitch got her pregnant."

"Pregnant? Oh, Ron . . ."

"I didn't find out until Tara was a month along that she and Trey had met secretly after he dumped Cathy for a couple of weeks after graduation," Ron said.

"And she told you he was the father."

"Yes!" Ron's eyes snapped.

"And it was an abortion she died from, not a ruptured appendix."

"A *botched* abortion. We had her only a month afterwards before the infection got her. We told the ruptured appendix story to protect my wife from town gossip. Not that it made much difference." Ron's mouth twisted. "The loss of our daughter was too much for her. Flora had congestive heart failure, but she died from heartbreak. As far as I'm concerned, Trey killed them both."

"You felt nothing for the boy when you pulled the trigger, Ron?"

"Nothing. Zilch. He knocked up my daughter and left her just like he did Cathy Benson."

Sadness for the dismal waste of a good—a great—man gone wrong filled Deke from his boot tops up. He needed a moment. He was taller than Ron and looked beyond his head to a black streak of mold that had begun a descent down the once bright kitchen wall. Finally, he drew in a breath and addressed Ron directly to his face. "Trey was sterile, Coach—from the mumps at sixteen. He couldn't possibly have gotten Tara pregnant."

Ron Turner jerked his head back as if to avoid a blow. "The hell you say. He fathered Cathy's child."

"No, Ron. One of the reasons Trey came back

was to confess to Cathy before he died that he was not Will's father."

Ron gawked, his eyes rheumy prisms of disbelief. Deke could guess the trail of his thoughts. He was remembering the time when Trey fell sick during spring training his sophomore year. The whole town had held its breath waiting for the diagnosis of the ailment that had felled its promising quarterback. Mumps, the health report came back, and the population had expelled its breath. The local paper had carried the story of the head coach's visit to his player's sickbed and his admiration for a boy who had borne his pain and put off going to the doctor rather than disappoint his team and coaches. Deke could see realization of his terrible mistake dawn in Ron's stare, but any compassion he might have felt was snuffed by imagining the look in Trey's eyes when his old coach pulled the trigger.

"Then, who—?" Ron whispered.

"Not for me to say."

Ron crumpled against the countertop like a collapsed puppet. A sickly gray overcame the fiery red of his face. "John Caldwell," he said, dazed. "Will Benson has to be John's son...God have mercy. What have I done?"

"How'd you know where to find Trey?" Deke asked.

Ron pulled himself away from the counter and walked stiffly toward the fireplace in the sitting room to take down the picture of his wife and daughter from the mantle. Staring at it, he said, "Tony Willis told me. He ran into Trey at the high school. He'd stopped by for old times' sake. He thought a reunion with my one and only All-State quarterback would perk me up. He suggested that I drive out to Harbison House and surprise him." Ron replaced the photograph. "How'd you figure it out?"

"I saw the red carnations at the cemetery on the graves of your wife and daughter and read the attached card. Then it started coming together. Melissa filled in the rest." Anger at the tragic senselessness of it all sharpened his tone and forced him to say, "You killed a dying and innocent man, Coach. According to Melissa, Trey would never have touched Tara—out of his devotion and respect for you."

Ron shut his lids tightly and weaved a second. "She knew how much I cared for him. . . . Oh, God. Oh, Trey . . . Trey, forgive me, forgive me. . . ."

After a moment, Ron opened his eyes. "You know, Deke, you always were one hell of a policeman. Too bad you're still not on the force. Tell you what. Give me a minute, and you can take me in. Randy Wallace certainly doesn't deserve the honor. He was ready to hang Will and any fool would know he's too decent to kill anybody. I regret with all my heart the hell I've put that boy and his mother through. They were like family to me. You'll let them know how sorry I am and that I wouldn't have let Will take the rap? I just needed time to sober up."

"You can tell them yourself, Ron."

"Right," he said. "Well, let me go take a leak and get a blazer. I want to look good for the papers. Turn that coffeemaker off, will you?"

He was gone for less than a minute when Deke heard the shot. For the second time that day, he called himself a fool, worse than a fool, when he gazed at the envelope in his hand. He'd been an idiot not to have guessed what Ron had in mind.

WITH SILVA BESIDE HER, Cathy sat on the porch stoop of her son's rented ranch house and recalled that this was the second time she'd experienced this moment. The first happened twenty-two years ago when she'd waited on her grandmother's front porch for John Caldwell to drop by before he headed for Loyola University. She'd been three months pregnant then, Trey was two weeks gone, and the anticipation of seeing John's battered pickup draw before the house for the last time had felt like a knife blade imbedded in her chest. Then, like now, she'd held out faint hope that John would marry her, be the father of her child. Now, like then, her dream was not to be. It was the second time she had lost him to God.

She'd thought they'd been given their lives back the night Deke Tyson brought them news that Ron Turner had written a letter confessing to the murder of Trey Don Hall and then killed himself. She and John and Will had gathered for one last evening together before their son was to be formally charged with murder the next morning. But John had come to say that *he* had confessed to the killing and would be arrested in Will's place. He had presented Randy a far more compelling motive than Will's and the evidence to back it up. In great shock, Will had listened to his father explain the proof that was sure to convict him.

"But, Dad, you were a kid back then, and you didn't kill Trey!"

"Neither did you."

"You're not going in my place. I won't let you. You're too *old*!"

"And you're too young. You're my son."

"And you're my father!"

They'd held each other, everybody crying, when into the wailing had come Deke's ring of the doorbell, followed a short while later by Lawrence Statton arriving with his briefcase.

The next day, better news, again delivered by Deke. He'd asked Randy what he planned to do with the bag containing the incriminating evidence against John Caldwell.

Randy's brow had puckered. "What evidence? You mean this?" He'd handed the marked box containing the pouch to Deke. "How about tossing this into the trash when you get back to Amarillo and giving Father John back his drinking glass?"

Even with the storm clouds rolled away, they had all known their lives would never be the same. The town had once again shown its fickle colors in rushing to judgment against her and Will. Morgan Petroleum had granted Will's request for a transfer. The café was still closed, with Bebe and Odell on paid vacation leave. And John . . .

Cathy sighed. She'd assumed that with his reputation intact, his achievements unmarred, a son publicly acknowledged and accepted as his, John would continue his work in the parish he loved. She should have known better. He would continue to live out his penance.

"I can't stay, Cathy," he'd said. "I can no longer accept from the Harbisons the love and devotion I don't deserve. I can't continue living a lie in their presence. They'll be all right now without me. They'll have Father Philip. He'll take my position at Harbison House, and no doubt in time Lou and Betty will come to dote on him as they have on me."

While they had waited to hear in what light the Church would view his long-ago transgression, she'd secretly and shamelessly hoped that the upheaval in his life and his love for her and their son would sway John to leave the priesthood and marry her. Trey had willed her his condominium in California. Its sale would give them the money to start over somewhere else.

The bishop of the diocese delivered his verdict. The Church would take no action against John for the deed perpetrated before entering the Order of the Jesuits, but it would grant his request to be relieved of his duties as pastor of St. Matthew's and director of Harbison House.

"Let's take a drive, Cathy," he'd invited her the day he heard. "I'll pick you up."

That was a week ago. It was a drive down memory lane. They passed by her grandmother's house, now the home of a couple with two young children. The porch swing was still there, and a dog lay stretched out in the front yard, keeping watch over a toddler on a tricycle. Cathy's eyes had grown moist.

Next, they swung by John's old house. The owner had attempted to renovate it, but halfheartedly. It still retained an uncared-for look, but yellow roses climbed the trellis of his mother's gazebo in back. The appearance of Kersey Elementary School and the surrounding playground was virtually unchanged since she and the boys had pushed open its heavy, storm-fitted doors. It had remained a cheerless-looking place, the grass around it hard packed, unfriendly to tender young elbows and knees.

Finally they had turned toward the high school. Neither had said much, but the cab of the truck was filled with their thoughts and feelings, their good-byes. John parked in the space where Old Red had spent much of its life, next to the spot that had been home to Trey's Mustang. Summer school had begun. Voices from the ball field drifted to them as they got out in the June sun and mild wind. Like in the old days, they leaned against warm vehicle metal and folded their arms.

"We had some good times, Cathy."

"Yes, we did."

"He loved us, you know."

"I know."

"Do you forgive him?"

"In time."

They spoke profile to profile. John did not turn

his head to her when he asked, "When did you fall in love with me, Cathy?"

She should have been shocked that he knew, but she was beyond shock. She had kept her attention diverted as well, watching a scrap of paper pirouette in the gentle wind as if twirling to a song. *Jack's in love with someone who loves my brother Jim, and he's in love with someone not in love with him.*

Such was life.

"I don't believe there was an exact moment," she said. "One day, years ago, the feeling was just there. How long have you known?"

"For some time. One day the knowledge was just there."

"It wasn't by default. I want you to know that."

"I've always known that."

The heat of the metal was soothing to their backs. The day was crystal clear. After a while, John said, "I'm leaving, Cathy. I've asked to be reassigned to teach at Loyola."

She looked off across the road to where the prairie began. The wildflowers were dying. Didn't they always? But they'd bloom again in spring. "When?" she asked.

"In a week's time."

"Why so soon? Classes don't start until fall, do they?"

"They want me for the summer session."

"Oh."

He unlocked his arms and took her hand. "What are you going to do?"

In that instant, she made up her mind. "Turn the café over to Bebe, and use money from the sale of Trey's condo to go to medical school."

She felt his surprise but his lack of it, too. "Trey would like that."

"At fifty, I'll probably be the oldest doctor on record to graduate."

He squeezed her hand encouragingly. "And the finest one, too."

They would share holidays and vacations, summer breaks, outings, and Sunday evening telephone calls. Distance would not separate them. They were family. She could live with that.

She heard a rumble at the gate far down the road. Silva shot out from under her hand as Will's Wrangler came into view. Father and son sat in the front. Will had been helping his dad pack. The Silverado had been turned in to the parish, and in a little while Will would be driving John to New Orleans. Lunch was waiting, their last meal together for a while. Cathy stood to greet them and lifted her hand to shield her eyes from the sting of the sun.

Emma's Hot-Water Corn Bread

Pour 2 cups of yellow cornmeal into a good-sized mixing bowl.

Sprinkle the top with salt.

Pour *boiling* water over the mixture and stir with a wooden spoon until it resembles soft mush.

Drop by tablespoons into hot oil. Fry until brown and crispy. Turn over and cook the other side until brown and crispy.

Drain on paper towels and serve with molasses or honey.

Enjoy.

Acknowledgments

Embarking on the idea for this novel meant entering territory I had never been before or ever thought to enter. A Protestant, I knew nothing about the Catholic Order of the Jesuits. An armchair reader in the room my husband and I share while he watches football games on Sunday afternoons, all I knew about the sport was that the teams wear differently colored uniforms. Yet somehow I felt the urge to write about a priest and a quarterback and a girl who serves up hamburgers, and so my journey into the unknown began. I will be forever grateful to those who shed light on my way and left me with an understanding of and respect for worlds I would never have known. Without their input, I could not have accomplished my tale. Any errors in details and information rest at my feet alone. I am in debt to the following:

Michael S. Bourg, executive director for advancement, Jesuits of the New Orleans Province. Mike, our time with you in New Orleans and later in San Antonio at Our Lady of Guadalupe and points beyond... magical.

Father Martin (Marty) Elsner, SJ, who long ago and far away counseled the difference between a Hollywood ending and the real deal.

Reverend Richard A. Houlahan, OMI, Chaplaincy Services Administrator of the Federal Bureau of Prisons (U.S. Department of Justice), retired. Father Richard, this is what you get for being charming.

Paul Jette, Jr., defensive coordinator and secondary coach for the Miami Hurricanes, 1985. Paul told me when I expressed my gratitude, "I didn't do anything but answer the right questions you researched," to which I thought, *Bull. In your explanations, you suited me up and sent me out to the field.*

Christopher Palmer, offensive coordinator for the Tennessee Titans, quarterbacks coach to the likes of Drew Bledsoe, Tony Romo, Eli Manning, and Mark Brunell, and wearer of a Super Bowl ring earned as quarterbacks coach for the New York Giants in 2007. Chris, there are no words to express my gratitude (or room to list all of your accomplishments).

Along the way, too, there were those whose simple professional courtesy and assistance meant so much to the novel. Thank you, Mary Jo Sarkis and Regina M. Morales. And, in step with me always, my husband, Arthur Richard III, in whom I have two kings, and Janice Thomson, my friend for all seasons.

And, of course, as always, my enduring appreciation for the cast of three whose roles in my writing life make me feel God has kissed me between the eyes. They are, incomparably, my treasured agent, David McCormick; my intrepid editor, Deb Futter, editor-in-chief of Grand Central Publishing; and her lovely assistant, Dianne Choie.

And, finally, I am grateful to my late brother for the recollection I have of his high school quarterback year. From time to time, it cast a glimmer of light upon the trail. Semper Fi, Leiland.